The fires of Revolution heat!

PRAISE FOR *BLAZING PASSION*

"The nonstop action will leave readers both breathless and satiated."

—*Romantic Times*

"I thoroughly enjoyed this very exciting and stimulating romance . . . [it] will leave your heart racing a little faster."

—*Rendezvous*

PRAISE FOR *FRONTIER FIRE*

"*Frontier Fire* paints a colorful picture of life in the colonies and is rich in historical details. Ms. Cummings shows great promise . . ."

—*Romantic Times*

"Rich, evocative, clever, lusty, *Frontier Fire* is an exciting debut from a bright and talented new author."

—*Patricia Gaffney,*
Golden Heart Award-Winning Author

PLAYING WITH PASSION'S FIRE

From across the dark room, David rushed the little thief and tackled him. But as David struggled to finally straddle the wriggling body, he heard the thief giggle—in a *woman's* voice!

"By the look in your eyes," said Savannah through her giggles, "I already wagered with myself that you wanted to get me in a compromising position." She turned her head and ran her lips against David's wrist. "But don't you think things like this are best carried out in privacy, my lord?"

From the mocking lilt of her voice, David knew she was goading him. But she had severely underestimated the surge of feelings that now coursed through him.

"Privacy or no privacy," David muttered, "things like this are best carried out to the end."

"No! Wait, David! Remember who I am."

"The minx who's made my life a living hell?"

Her responding laughter was as clear and as calling as a dinner bell, and it beckoned to something deep inside him. Yes, he wanted to hear that soft, tinkling laugh again—after she had become replete with his loving. . . .

DISCOVER DEANA JAMES!

CAPTIVE ANGEL (2524, $4.50/$5.50)
Abandoned, penniless, and suddenly responsible for the biggest tobacco plantation in Colleton County, distraught Caroline Gillard had no time to dissolve into tears. By day the willowy redhead labored to exhaustion beside her slaves . . . but each night left her restless with longing for her wayward husband. She'd make the sea captain regret his betrayal until he begged her to take him back!

MASQUE OF SAPPHIRE (2885, $4.50/$5.50)
Judith Talbot-Harrow left England with a heavy heart. She was going to America to join a father she despised and a sister she distrusted. She was certainly in no mood to put up with the insulting actions of the arrogant Yankee privateer who boarded her ship, ransacked her things, then "apologized" with an indecent, brazen kiss! She vowed that someday he'd pay dearly for the liberties he had taken and the desires he had awakened.

SPEAK ONLY LOVE (3439, $4.95/$5.95)
Long ago, the shock of her mother's death had robbed Vivian Marleigh of the power of speech. Now she was being forced to marry a bitter man with brandy on his breath. But she could not say what was in her heart. It was up to the viscount to spark the fires that would melt her icy reserve.

WILD TEXAS HEART (3205, $4.95/$5.95)
Fan Breckenridge was terrified when the stranger found her near-naked and shivering beneath the Texas stars. Unable to remember who she was or what had happened, all she had in the world was the deed to a patch of land that might yield oil . . . and the fierce loving of this wildcatter who called himself Irons.

Available wherever paperbacks are sold, or order direct from the Publisher. Send cover price plus 50¢ per copy for mailing and handling to Zebra Books, Dept. 3812, 475 Park Avenue South, New York, N.Y. 10016. Residents of New York and Tennessee must include sales tax. DO NOT SEND CASH. For a free Zebra/Pinnacle catalog please write to the above address.

BARBARA CUMMINGS
Rebel Wildfire

ZEBRA BOOKS
KENSINGTON PUBLISHING CORP.

*To Alice Alfonsi Kane, my editor, my friend.
She helped me pull this one through tragedies
no team should have to endure. She is the consummate
editor, a gracious woman, and a true professional.
Every writer should be so lucky.*

ZEBRA BOOKS

are published by

Kensington Publishing Corp.
475 Park Avenue South
New York, NY 10016

Copyright © 1992 by Barbara Cummings

All rights reserved. No part of this book may be reproduced in any form or by any means without the prior written consent of the Publisher, excepting brief quotes used in reviews.

If you purchased this book without a cover you should be aware that this book is stolen property. It was reported as "unsold and destroyed" to the Publisher and neither the Author nor the Publisher has received any payment for this "stripped book."

First printing: July, 1992

Printed in the United States of America

Chapter One

Friday, December 11, 1772

The streets of Savannah, Georgia Colony were clamoring with the sounds of the upcoming Christmas season. Vendors of all kinds hawked their wares, waving silks and linens and foodstuffs in David Montgomery's face. He shrugged his way through them to a crowd that was gathering round the town pillory—one of the last in the colonies, so he'd been told.

Two pirates, captured three days before, were still in the stocks. David was pleased to note that neither looked as fierce as they had when the revenue cutter crew had brought them in. Brown head and blond drooped, lifeless and smirched with bird droppings. Beards hung dispiritedly, caked with spittle. Bodies sagged like empty sacks of flour. And skin was blotched black from the mud and offal of the town pigs.

"Fight's gone out of 'em," Lawrence Fenton said to David.

"Yes, poor slugs."

David saw satisfaction in the murky brown depths of Lawrence's eyes. Yet, he still felt that inexplicable wariness about the man. It was as if Lawrence were waiting—quietly, expectantly, and with a great deal of amusement—for David to make a mistake. Any kind of mistake that would underscore his youth and inexperience.

Not unusual, that, David supposed.

His grandfather, Richard Montgomery, the sixth Marquess of Lorton, had hired Lawrence Fenton to oversee Lorton Crown Traders, an enterprise equal to Hudson Bay Company. And Fenton had performed his duties with skill and loyalty. But Fenton was forty-two, thirteen years older than David's twenty-nine. For the past nine years, Fenton had had the running of the mercantile business all to himself. Then, only six months ago, David had arrived to take over the entire operation. Hell, it was only natural for Fenton to keep an eagle eye on his new master, to be sure nine years of his hard work wasn't ruined by an upstart—one who had gotten his post as director of one of King George's most important commissions only because he was his grandfather's heir.

So, although everything in this land was totally foreign to him, especially the hidden feelings of the people, David was determined not to make any mistakes. His future, the future of Lorton Crown Traders, and perhaps the future of Georgia and the Carolina Colonies depended on him. It was a damnable burden, but one he'd learned early was his and his alone.

"How much longer before the poor devils are brought to trial?" David asked.

"Three days," Fenton said.

"Three days? On only bread and water, they won't last that long."

A man next to David spat on the ground. "Bound for ta King's hangin' noose ennyway. Which would you call ta better way ta die, guv'ner?"

Just then—before David could answer that there was no *better* way to die—two scarlet-coated militiamen, one tall and one short, shouldered their way through the crowd and stopped at the stocks. The tall one stood at attention, with bayonet fixed. The short one dropped the bucket he'd carried and, stooping, scooped out a full ladle and poured its contents over the head of each man. Then he gave them as much cool water to drink as they could swallow.

A collective sigh went up from the men and women gathered to watch the mid-afternoon ritual. The people strained forward, as if, David thought, they would offer more than a simple dipper of water. As if they would offer succor, sanctuary, safety.

David blinked. He'd had this feeling before and it was inexplicable. Those around him were good English men and women. A full hundred years later than most who had come to this new land they called America, they or their fathers before them had accepted the call to colonize Georgia Colony. When they had signed on, they'd known it was the only way to help King George keep a buffer between Spanish Florida and the English Carolina Colonies. They knew their importance in the King's scheme and seemed to do their jobs willingly enough.

The Spanish garrisons in Florida had been abandoned as soon as the British garrisons in Georgia had been fully manned. Why, then, David wondered, did that sigh and that slight shifting of myriad bodies worry him so much?

It was one more mystery to add to the growing list he kept in his mind. Such as, why—except for those worked by the Salzburger Germans—were the silk plantations failing? What was it about this land that was inhospitable to the ever-toiling insects? Or why were Lorton Crown Traders' revenues down for the second month—and with Christmas just around the corner, the time of year when even the poorest of the poor spent precious coppers for gifts to exchange? He had four ships on the open seas, bringing finished clothing, trinkets, and accoutrements—furniture, kitchenwares, whiskey, and tools—into the settlement. Another two took silk, rice, cotton, wine, herbs, lumber, and maize back to London. What he exported was easily sold in Manchester or London. But what he brought back to Savannah . . . Hah! Like as not, half of it would find their masters were eight-legged spiders and six-legged mites instead of two-legged settlers.

The worry crouched in the back of his mind as he watched the tall militiaman nail up another reward poster onto the central public notice board. The man with the water bucket waited quietly until his cohort was finished, then they nodded at each other and clicked their heels. The one with the rifle hoisted it in front of his chest, and they both double-stepped back toward the barracks.

A grumbling, then a roar of protest went up from the crowd as they read the latest bulletin, and David's unease increased.

"Who is this Robert Sears listed here on the poster?" he asked Fenton.

"Only the best captain on the trade route."

"A pirate, the best captain?"

"No pirate!" a voice behind David said. "Rhode Island privateer, he be."

"Pirate, according to that broadside," David argued.

A tailor, hearing David's words, turned and sneered. "If Rob Sears is a pirate, then I'm gentry." He cackled. "Much as I'd like to, guv'ner, I can't claim that distinction. But neither can Rob Sears be called pirate. And I'll fight any man here what says so."

He looked around for someone to take his challenge but none did. In fact, to David's horror, a dirty ham of a hand darted out and ripped the wanted poster from the wooden board. Before he knew it, the paper was ground into the dirt of the streets by dozens of shoes and boots as the crowd began to disperse.

When only the two of them were left, David turned to Fenton, intending to ask what his assistant supplied.

"That's what many of your new neighbors think of King George's edicts," Fenton said.

His voice once again seemed to David to hold a note of warning—and speculation.

So, Fenton wondered where David's loyalties lay, did he? Why? Was he a spy for David's grandfather? In his reports to the marquess, did Fenton also include a detailed record of all David said and did? Or was Fenton an agent for David's young brother, Drew, who wanted nothing less than to see David make a mess of potage of this assignment so their grandfather would turn it over to him? Turn it over to Drew, who *knew* the colonials needed a heavy hand. Drew, who *knew* the competition could be eliminated by the right words whispered in the right ears, so Lorton Crown Traders would hold an absolute monopoly.

David sighed with weariness and frustration. No matter what he said or felt, he was uneasily aware that the King's agents—or worse, his grandfather's—were everywhere. Yet, David didn't believe his views were all that different from most of his friends and family in England.

"That's what *some* of our neighbors think of King George's edicts, yes, Fenton. But not all. *These* are not gentry. And it is the gentry who run things in this colony, as in all the others."

With that, David took abrupt leave of his manager and headed for the stables where he kept his horse and carriage. As usual, they were ready for him. Sunshine, his sister Arabella's gelding, pranced and whickered, awaiting the call to gallop, but was easily brought under control by a young stablehand. David climbed up into the sparkling black phaeton, flipped a ha'-penny to the boy, and clucked to the overeager horse. Thanks to Sunshine's exuberance, it took them only ten minutes to arrive at Honesty Dunn's School for Young Ladies. He pulled the phaeton around to the side entrance of the finishing school he'd chosen for his fifteen-year-old sister because of its teachers. They were the best faculty in the colony, especially the drawing, dramatics, and poetry teacher, Savannah Stewart, and the French instructor, Elizabeth Leduc. Arabella would learn as much from them as she would have, had she remained in England.

He quieted Sunshine, bracing himself for the explosion of chattering and giggling girls who always burst through the door and surrounded him when he came to collect Bella. But the quiet reminded him that the girls had already left with their families for their large plantations built far inland. Christmas in the colonies, it seemed, was house party time, though the women-that-be here in Georgia didn't call it "the little season" as did their counterparts in London. He chuckled. She was so looking forward to her first little season in Savannah, that if Lorton House wasn't finished this week as the builders had promised, David had no doubt but that Arabella would play Salome to his John the Baptist.

Absentmindedly and instinctively, he fingered his neck, to feel for its vital spots, to be certain they were in good working order. Headcheese was tasty, as long as it wasn't *his* head that was carved and served on squares of toasted bread. But after all those dramatic lessons Arabella had received from Savannah Stewart, he could definitely see his sister as the seductive Salome. *Off with his head! Off with his head!*

. . . No, that was Herodias, the mother. Her daughter, Salome, was more subtle, more seductive. Not Arabella at all.

But most definitely like Savannah Stewart.

Ah, yes. Savannah. When they'd met that first day he'd brought Bella to the school, she'd been hard to overlook, harder still to forget. Petite, hair so dark brown it was almost black, blue eyes. Blue? Too mundane a word for orbs whose fiery gold and green sparks softened their cobalt depths, turning them into a female's imitation of the quiet surface of Scottish ponds. Turquoise would more aptly describe them. Yes, turquoise.

"Sir? Does you want anything, sir?"

David shook his head, hopped down, and handed the reins to Honesty Dunn's colored house servant. "Is

Miss Arabella ready, Tom?"

"Her boxes and trunk is jest inside the door, sir. But Miss Arabella, she not here."

"Not here? Where, pray, is she?"

"Miss Stewart, she say they's goin' to a weddin' at Miz Leduc's, sir. You can pick her up there, I s'pose."

David chuckled and shook his head, then followed Tom inside to help load Arabella's belongings into the wagon. Weddings! What was there about women and weddings? Even at fifteen his sister became aflutter just at the mention of the word. Trust her to follow behind anyone who offered to take her along to observe the festivities.

Although . . . the observation wouldn't have been the only inducement. It was the woman Savannah, herself, who would have made the difference. She'd made an impression on Arabella. So much so that David realized he knew almost everything about her — or at least everything Bella thought important.

Imagine, David, Miss Stewart's waist is smaller than Felicity Rogers's, and Felicity is eight years old!

Tiny, Savannah's waist might be. But the rest of her anatomy was no child's. Her curves declared her a woman above all else. And why not? According to Bella, Savannah was twenty-two. Twenty-two. Hmm . . . Why had the inestimable Miss Stewart not been the principal player in one of those confounded weddings Bella and her friends chattered on about? By rights, had Miss Stewart been in England, she'd have been married and pushing ahead of her some lucky man's heirs. Yet here she was, a spinster schoolteacher, the part usually taken by some pug-ugly hag who couldn't have gotten a husband if she tried. Perhaps it was her other profession that was her undoing. Her . . . what had Arabella called it?

Did you know Miss Stewart is a celebrated author, David? She's been published! Not once, but six times! All her books are the rage in London and the biggest cities here in the colonies! Why, she's the Stewart who did all those wonderful watercolors in that book you so liked. Remember? A Colonial Farmer's Sketchbook Describing the Terrifying and Wondrous Natural Life of the Carolinas and the New Colony of Georgia. *And she was only my age when she did them. Imagine!*

Yes, that must be it. Miss Stewart was too busy traipsing around the lower colonies, sketching flora and fauna, to give heed to her future position as some worthy plantation owner's wife. But that would change . . . perhaps was already changing if she were so engrossed in weddings. Why, even he might consider offering . . . No, that was foolish. She was the daughter of Phillip Stewart, the former overseer on his grandfather's estate. According to grandfather—whose rules were more law than King George's—one did not marry the children of the servants, regardless of the position they'd achieved in the colonies.

He could picture his grandfather, sitting in his favorite overstuffed chair, puffing on his long-stemmed pipe, a wreath of smoke around his bald head, one leg negligently crossed over the other, as he gravely intoned, "One must respect the proprieties, my boy, even in that wild country. If we Montgomerys don't, who will?"

Respect the proprieties. His grandfather had taught him well that *that* was his most important mission. "To civilize the uncivilized" was the way his grandfather had often put it, as if British Georgians were wild Indians. So, David sighed, one did not even consider a liaison—no matter how innocent—with the daughter of former servants.

But the thought was stimulating. Especially when he remembered those freckles.

We counted Miss Stewart's freckles today, David. Well, not all of them, of course, because she says there's more covered by her frock; but those we could see . . . Imagine it, David . . . there were twenty-seven of them across the bridge of her nose.

Ah, yes. Freckles. Twenty-seven on the bridge of her nose. But how many, and where, under her frock? He could picture them, spicing up the tantalizing curves Miss Stewart's simple dresses concealed.

Dear God, yes, very stimulating. Too stimulating for tight lambskin breeches.

David blanked out the interesting portrait of Miss Stewart he'd conjured in his mind and concentrated on his horsemanship. Soon, he drew up at one of the newer additions to Savannah's growing residential section. The house was one of those that had been plopped down in the middle of Oglethorpe's set-aside five-acre garden plots behind the main settlement. It was spanking new and fashionable, but not as large as the plantation houses much farther inland, surrounding the former Lorton silk-worming acres. There David and Arabella had decided to construct their own house as a refuge from the constant heat and humidity of the land bordering the Savannah River.

The Leducs, David saw, had put to good use Elizabeth's modest dowry and her husband's much more substantial inheritance from his merchant Newport father. Although still built mainly of white painted wood like those in most of the settlement, also in evidence in its trim and the portico out front was the new masonry material they used here in Savannah. Tabby, they called it. A curious blend of lime, crushed shells, and sand, it gave the appearance of dun-colored brick. Yet, when the sun hit it, it sparkled like hundreds of thousands of tiny diamonds.

Bella had insisted they incorporate tabby into the house in Lorton Woods. But by agreeing to her demand he'd bought himself enormous delays, since there weren't many artisans who knew the art of compressing the mixture.

He'd have to ask the Leducs whom they had used, for he liked the way the tabby set off their home, from foundation to roof friezes. David admired the simplicity of the square front facade and centered doorway; the stone of the end chimneys; the short, curved, crushed shell drive that seemed to beckon the caller into the cool, tall oak-shaded interior.

The Leduc home was well constructed and much larger than that of the earliest structures. Gad, looking at what had evolved, David couldn't even begin to imagine how the first settlers had managed to survive in the squared-off plan of Oglethorpe's! Gentry, merchant, or indentured servants, they had moved into one-story houses only sixteen by twenty-two feet. For an entire family! No wonder they had quickly moved inland as they prospered and built houses such as these.

Now most of the first structures that fronted the river and harbor housed shops and storage facilities. Lorton Crown Traders took up seven of the small former quarters.

When he alighted, David steadied Sunshine, expecting a servant to take the reins. When none came, he dropped a large iron standing weight onto the ground to keep horse and phaeton from bolting. Whistling to himself, he took the steps two at a time, anxious to be on his way. He raised the acorn-embossed brass knocker, banged it twice, and waited. Other than the twitter of birds in the overhanging oaks, not a sound emerged from the house.

He banged the door knocker again, then shouted, "Haloo! Haloo!"

Finally, after a few moments, he heard a rustling sound that got louder as it slowly approached the door. The glass-topped oak panel swung open to frame a wizened woman, her head wrapped in printed dimity in place of the usual mobcap.

Tilting her head and squinting almost colorless eyes, she peered up at him. "Aye? Who be you?"

"It's David Montgomery. I've come to collect my sister Arabella."

"Huh," the woman snorted. "Collectin' no one this time o' day. Ever' man, woman, an' chile be at the weddin'."

"But I thought the wedding was here."

"Here? Aye. Supposed to be. But Cap'n Sears, the groom, be runnin' for 'is life from the King's men. They all be down to the harbor. Mayhap on 'is boat by now. Ye bes' try there."

Without further explanation, she slammed the door in his face. No amount of knocking would bring her back.

Wedding. Harbor. Cap'n Sears.

Sears? Sears! Good God!

David bolted for the phaeton, picking up the long whip and snapped it in the air. Sunshine whickered, rose on his hind legs, took two long strides, and was brought up short. The horse pawed the ground, neighing loudly as David cursed and hauled in the standing weight. He flipped the switch at Sunshine, and as the horse quickly reached a gallop, David strained over his haunches, urging him on, remembering that huge hand ripping the wanted poster off the board.

Robert Sears, Pirate. His sister was attending a wedding on board a pirate ship and the groom had a price on his head!

Sunshine was in a froth by the time David reached Lorton Crown Traders' dock. Luckily, their small sloop, *Dragon*, was in port, awaiting orders to traverse the coast with goods for various merchants who took David's wares. The crew wouldn't half like the orders they were about to get; but David didn't give a damn. They'd give chase or they'd walk the plank!

Christ! He sounded like a parody of a pirate and shook like a schoolboy. And he, twenty-nine years old! But it was Arabella who was in danger, not himself. If it had been only himself, he'd probably swim out to the damned wedding and to hell with the revenuers' bullets that pinged behind.

Deliberately, he calmed himself, to be able to give orders as he'd been taught, with an authoritative manner befitting his station as his grandfather's heir. But it was no good. He wasn't his grandfather. He couldn't cock an eyebrow, posture his foot in front of his body, crook his elbow—altogether putting on the kind of gentleman's haughty attitude his grandfather expected of him.

Instead, he scrambled down from the phaeton, leaped aboard the sloop, and barked, "Hoist the mainsail! Get under way. Fast you go, Captain Wilholm."

Swifter than he would have responded for the marquess, James Wilholm barked back, "Aye, sir." He snapped a hand in the air and the crew jumped to their tasks, hoisting the mainsail almost as quickly as David breathed. James turned to David. "Well away, sir. But where are we bound?"

"Damnation! After that pirate, Robert Sears. My sister is aboard his ship."

James sucked in his breath. "Three revenue cutters went out after the man. There might be guns blazing. And we have naught but small fore and aft cannon."

"I don't care if we have naught but cutlasses! Did you not hear me? Arabella's aboard the pirate's vessel! Get after them, man."

"Aye, sir. But where? That's a great sea out there. He could be halfway to Guadeloupe by now."

David frowned. Great sea, it was. But Arabella had been at school that morning; he'd stopped to remind her to have her bags packed. And they'd been ready when he went to pick her up. So, she couldn't have left much before ten. Eleven at the most. It was now three o'clock. They'd have had only four or five hours head start. And with the revenuers after them, Robert Sears, as good a captain as he might be, could not make a beeline for the broad sea. It was too dangerous, would expose his crew too openly. No, Sears would have to dodge among the islands, keeping scant leagues ahead of the cutters until nightfall.

"Do you know Robert Sears?" he asked James Wilholm.

"Aye. Good captain."

"Do you know his ship?"

"*The Patriot*, aye."

"Did you see it today?"

"Left the harbor at seven, heading for safe anchor north of Tybee, I imagine."

"And that's the last time you saw him?"

"Aye. But I did see the crew of that rascal Jack Saunders in town." James's eyes widened and he nearly choked. "Ah, m'lord . . . now that I think on it, I saw your sister, Miss Arabella. And that teacher of hers, the artsy one."

"When?"

"Noon. They arrived at the next dock in a hired carriage, their arms overflowing with fabric . . . or maybe it was a dress."

"Skip the descriptions. Where did they go?"

"Several boats rowed out to a large ship . . . Saunders's ship. The boats carried almost two dozen others, including women and children . . . and a preacher, I think."

David clutched James's neckcloth and almost shook him. "Where did Saunders go?"

"Toward Tybee Island."

James pointed to the horizon, and David made out the salt marshes and hilly land where pirates held sway. It was only lately that the governor, James Wright, had suggested it be "cleaned out" and a British fortification erected.

A garrison now camped on the southernmost tip. But the rest of the island was still pirates' domain. Which was why, though Sears was wanted, he and Jack Saunders, another pirate, would head for Tybee, and damn the garrison.

David pictured the islands that protected Savannah and the southern Georgia coast. Tybee, then south to Ogeechee, then Hope, then Midway, then a half dozen more until St. Simons, and more beyond that. And north? More than the others. Sears could round Tybee, then dodge in and out of scores of safe harbors and put out to sea *anywhere!*

"Damnation."

"M'lord?"

"Where, Captain Wilholm? Where would they be?"

James Wilholm hardly got the words "I don't know" out of his mouth before the boom of cannon echoed across the waves.

David's head jerked up. "There! Damnation. There!"

"Aye, sir."

It took them almost an hour to traverse upriver and ferret out the ships engaged in battle; and when they did, all they saw was smoke—from guns, from fire.

"I can't go in there, m'lord!" Wilholm said. "We risk the whole crew *and* the ship."

"Damn the ship! My sister's in that unholy hell."

Suddenly, the guns quieted. The eeriness of the new calm was skin-crawling, and for the first time in his life David was truly terrified. What would they find inside the choking grey mist?

"God in heaven, let her be safe," he pleaded.

As they entered the night of day, David's eyes watered from the sulfur that hung heavy in the salt-laden air. His throat constricted, not from the smoke but from his first glimpse of what must have once been a mast. It bobbed over each wave, its thicker end sinking slowly. From it hung six men, feebly grasping the tattered stays on which only a section of a Union Jack lay sodden.

"Get those men on board," he ordered.

"Aye, sir."

David's eyes fought to see through the yellow-grey air and the green-black sea. A shadow ship, at first fleeting but moment by moment becoming more substantial, bore down on them. As he helped to haul the half-drowned men over the taffrail and onto *Dragon*'s deck, all the while he concentrated, trying to discern the ensign the shadow ship flew.

Black-hulled ship with white waterline. One red pennant with an anchor. But another . . . white overlaid with black skull and crossbones.

Pirates!

"Do you recognize her, Mr. Wilholm?"

"Aye, sir. One-eyed Jack Saunders good and truly, sir."

"Then why is he, too, hauling in British seamen?"

"Impressment, if they be willing. Or, he'll drop them off at the nearest safe harbor, with a few provisions. Saunders is one of the more compassionate of his ilk."

"And what about Robert Sears?"

"If he's called pirate now, it's new, sir. Yesterday he was a licensed privateer."

"How do we signal this Saunders so he won't fire on us?"

"If we take down the Union Jack . . ."

David had never run with anything but his country's flag flying high and proud on the mainsail. But his sister was more important than his standing as a loyal Englishman. "Take her down," he ordered.

Within moments of the standard being lowered, Jack Saunders—it couldn't be anyone else, with that powerful, huge body, the colorful costume he had on, and the crossed cutlasses at his waist—hailed them.

"Do ye 'ave room fer women an' children, guv'ner?" he bellowed above the screams of men. "Ken ye take ta lot back ter Savanny?"

"Aye," David shouted back.

Saunders tested the wind with a wet finger. "We'll board ter leeward. Sail close an' me crew'll 'eave ower ta grapplin' 'ooks."

"I'll get the boarding plank ready," David offered.

"Aye," Saunders said. "An' guide ropes."

David knew he wasn't expected to help ready the ropes, which would be strung from ship to ship as a brace for the passengers to hold as they crossed over the plank. But he was too nervous to sit and watch while those not involved did all the work, so he pitched in with the others. As soon as the hulls of the two ships were lined up and close enough, seven long spiked grappling hooks whizzed through the air and crashed onto *Dragon*'s deck. David rushed forward with the rest of Wilholm's crew to secure the dangerous four-pronged hooks. Saunders's crew heaved, moving *Dragon* through the water until it was almost dead against the black hull.

"Should we drop anchor?" James Wilholm asked David.

David looked across, into the one blue eye of Jack Saunders. With the grappling hooks stuck fast to the sides of *Dragon*, they were at risk. However, up-anchor, they could still cut the ropes and maneuver under sail. *But* . . . if the pirate was using the women and chil-

22

dren as a ruse to take over *Dragon,* then by ordering the smaller ship to drop anchor, David would render it totally defenseless. Should the pirate revert to form, *Dragon* and its crew would be easy pickings.

Saunders stood there, short, wide, and menacing. His teeth glinted as he drew his mouth open in a broad smile. He crossed his arms against his chest, as if to say, "Welladay, guv'ner, wha' be yer decision?"

David gritted his teeth. "Drop anchor."

Chapter Two

After the boarding plank was affixed between *Dragon* and the pirate ship, David carried across the guide lines. A soot-coated member of Saunders's crew accepted the ropes and tossed one to a waiting compatriot. They wound the ends round a stay and secured them tightly with square knots.

As David watched, a hairy hand clamped over his shoulder. He turned to look into the twinkling blue eye and the black patch that had given the pirate his name.

"So," One-eyed Jack said, "yer took ta gamble. Yer 'ave courage, lad!"

"Foolhardiness, some would call it."

"Oh, aye." Jack laughed long and loud, and his belly shook with each guffaw. "Fool'ardy, aye!" He gave a signal to a mate, who disappeared down a hold. "I do na lie, guv'ner. We 'ave women an' children aboard, an' they be needin' an escort back to Savanny. I'll no be botherin' yer wee boat. This time." He laughed again and peered closely at David. "Yer be Montgom'ry?" At David's indrawn breath and surprised expression, he laid his finger aside his nose and bobbed his head. "Need ta know ta diff'rence atween friends an' enemies, guv'ner. Else we be li'ble ter get ahr 'eads blowed off." He drew David over to the scuttlebutt, dug out a carved bone pipe, tamped it with tobacco, and lit it. "Me guests be 'ere shortly," he said. "They be locked in me cabins, wi' cargo crates stowed round em 'gainst cannon shot. Take some wee time ta move ta crates."

While One-eyed Jack smoked, David noted the pirate's crew. They were efficient, knowing what to do and doing it without tripping over each other. With more speed and efficiency than David had ever seen, sails were trimmed, repaired, and made ready again. A quarter dozen boys and one man moved among bleeding and moaning men on the decks, bringing salves and water to tend them. Another quarter dozen sturdy men worked with a surgeon on the worst cases.

David caught the flash of red and gold and turned to Saunders, aghast. "You patch up British crewmen, too?"

"Aye. Those we don' kill, we does. 'Tis good seamanship. Each cap'n patches what 'e ken. Ta British make prisners o' us iffen we survive. We make pirates o' them iffen they survive. Evens out."

"Yes, I suppose it does."

The logic of it amazed David. He'd always assumed pirates were bloodthirsty and would run a sword through a man as easily as most men breathed. But here was one of the most notorious of the colonies' breed, without blood lust of any kind.

Preconceived notions. He'd come to the colonies with hundreds of them. This one, at least, he decided, was best dropped into Davy Jones's locker.

Suddenly, children—boys and girls, towheaded and brown-curled—scampered noisily on deck, closely followed by the adults. David searched for Arabella and found her with her arm around Savannah Stewart's waist, giggling.

Bella's skirts were stained with pitch, her hem as tattered as a street urchin's. She'd lost her mobcap and her blond curls hung limp, having escaped their pins. But once she saw David, her grey eyes widened and she gave a whoop of delight, then bounded closer, to stand beside him.

"Oh, David, it was so exciting! Imagine! First a wonderful wedding. Emily—that's the bride—wore the most delightful peach dress, all lace and broidery. And Robert—that's the groom—gave her a delicately wrought topaz and gold brooch, which she pinned right here!" Bella pointed between her breasts. "They stood with the preacher on the quarterdeck, and we all stood beneath them to hear the words of the service. And when it was over, they went back to Robert's cabin and we stayed here on One-eyed Jack's ship, and he brought out rum and cakes and sassafras tea. And we had a jolly time." She frowned. "Then some really vicious curs boarded Jack's and Robert's ships. And their leader, an old man with a horrible scar, came and took Emily away at gunpoint. And the British gunboat roared down on us before One-eyed Jack or Robert could go after Emily. And Jack put us in his cabins, with lots of boxes around us and a dozen armed guards to protect us. And the guns boomed over our heads. Over and over they boomed. And we all crouched down and waited for it to stop. And it did. And now you're here. Imagine!"

Exciting. Wonderful. Delightful. Jolly. Vicious curs. Scars. Cannons. Armed guards. Oh, yes, David could well imagine it. The danger. The danger!

And all because of that sloe-eyed little wench who stood next to Bella. Her hands were nonchalantly clasped behind her back, straining her bodice to set off the only pair of breasts that had him tongue-tied at the mere thought of speaking to her. And as if she could read his thoughts, a wicked lopsided grin spread slowly across her absolutely amazingly beautiful face, causing a dimple to indent her cheek, right below her sparkling seafoam eyes.

And no penitent expression. None whatsoever.

"Miss Stewart," he said, glaring in what he hoped was a stern brotherly, if not fatherly, way, "what explanation do you have for putting my sister's life in danger?"

"Explanation? Really, Mr. Montgomery, you cannot expect me to foresee every slight contingency!"

"Slight? Pirates and cannon shot and vicious curs? *Slight?* What, pray tell, would be major to you?"

Savannah wanted to laugh aloud at the posturing of David Montgomery. He looked like a terrier pup trying to imitate a bulldog. And he looked mighty embarrassed at doing it. His was a far different nature, if those powerful black eyes were any indication. They sparked with more than the cold of flint. She was sure she could see a warmth he fought very hard to hold back. A warmth that was more a mirror of his soul than any lordly posturing could ever hide.

She supposed he postured because of his grandfather. Bella had told her much about the old gent who, kicking and screaming about the injustice and humiliation of the King's order, had reluctantly gone "into trade" but, when shown how much profit he could make, had embraced it with alacrity. This David Montgomery, his heir, didn't look the type to wear his grandfather's stripes. He was in this dither because he had so much responsibility. Keeping Lorton Crown Traders afloat was hard enough. But for a brother not yet thirty years old to try to take the place of parents? He looked choked by the weight.

She wanted to tell him to relax, to take his role more easily than he was. She wanted to tell him she understood the pressures. But she knew she didn't really understand. She'd always had around her the love and comfort of dozens of Stewarts—sisters, brothers, cousins, aunts, uncles, grandparents, as well as her own mother and father. Why, it would be . . . it would be like moving to England with only an elderly retainer *and* having to provide food, shelter, schooling, guidance, and protection for her younger sister Purity or her younger brother Stephen. She knew it would overwhelm her as much as it must at times overwhelm David Montgomery—like now.

Yet she couldn't give in to his censure. He was not much older than she. And the Stewarts' Scots pride was one of the only things she had to sustain her when she came up against her "better." Damn the social standings in this, King George's most royal of colonies!

Besides, what had she truly done wrong that she wouldn't do again?

"I wasn't taking any chances with your sister that I wouldn't have taken with my own, Lord Montgomery," she said. "I'm here, too. And, as you can see, we did come out of it in one piece."

When a wounded man screamed out, David glared; Savannah winced. With that one sound, her explanation was rendered totally inadequate. "Well," she said grimly, "I suppose your invitation to join you and Bella for the Christmas holidays is withdrawn. I don't blame you, and I really do understand."

She hugged Bella to her and kissed her softly on the cheek, whispering so the future marquess wouldn't hear. "Don't worry, Bella. Stephen will bring the you-know-what to Lorton House in plenty of time."

Nodding her head to David, Savannah curtsied and said, "May you have a wonderful first Christmas in our lovely city, my lord."

As she glided away to help Jack Saunders's surgeon, Bella clutched David's arm. "How could you, David! I especially wanted her to be our first guest at Lorton House. I think you're being absolutely and positively vile."

"Bella, if you use one more featherbrained adverb or adjective, my teeth will be ground to nubbins."

He threw a glance at the friendly way Savannah worked with pirates and British seamen, treating everyone as equals, with a sunny smile and quiet words. But when he turned once again to his sister, the pout on her young, round face nearly undid him. He had all he could do not to laugh, hug her to him, and give in to her wiles.

"And don't look at me like that, Bella. It was Miss Stewart who *assumed* she wasn't welcome at Lorton House. She didn't give me the chance to get one word in to correct her impression."

"Well, correct it now, David. Please."

"I shall speak to Miss Stewart tomorrow, Bella. Right now, I'm taking you home for a good hot bath and a change of clothes. Then, I'm taking a quick trip out to Lorton House to see if the carpenters are finished so we can move in, in comfort. Wait here while I round up our other passengers so Captain Wilholm can get them back to Savannah harbor."

"May Savannah come with us, too, David?"

"Yes, Miss Stewart may come, too."

He sought out Jack Saunders, who introduced him to the wedding party. Counted among the celebrants were two competitors of David's, both wealthy merchants; the Leducs, with all their children; and Jonathan Hobbs, a duke, though he'd renounced his title and sold his lands. What kind of country was this, that dukes consorted with pirates and thought little of it, making merry while waiting with lovely wives and large families to be ferried back to land?

David knew he had much to learn about the colonies. How much was too quickly being revealed. How different it was from his existence as the heir to a marquess was not going to amuse his grandfather. Nor his brother, Drew, who had wanted this post more than David had. Wanted the responsibility. Wanted to assert his position, to lord it over the colonials, to fill his and the family coffers with colonial taxes and gold and silver specie. But David had assured his grandfather that Lorton Crown Traders was safe in his hands.

And he'd also assured him that Bella was safe, too. No, his grandfather would *not* be amused at the day's near disaster. Richard Montgomery would expect David to—how did the pirates put it?—lower the boom on the one responsible for Bella's being in the fray.

David gritted his teeth as he helped One-eyed Jack's men begin to lead the most boisterous of the children back to *Dragon*. Gingerly, one by one, women and children crossed over the boarding plank. Savannah, he noticed, kept her distance from him, mingling with the restless young children left behind. Some quickly gathered around her, raptly listening to her soft voice tell a story about a girl with a red hood and a wolf with sharp teeth.

And the better to eat *you* with, he thought. Sharp teeth? None sharper than those of the Montgomerys, he decided.

As his grandfather would expect of him, David supposed, he would have to put together sharp words to go along with his sharp teeth. And they'd have to be delivered to Savannah and her headmistress the first thing in the morning.

Right now, however, he had more important things to do than demand Savannah Stewart's removal from the faculty at Honesty Dunn's School for Young Ladies. But come morning, he intended to do exactly that.

He was busy phrasing the speech he intended to give on the morrow about responsibility and irresponsibility, when he heard the short, high-pitched screech of a child, a loud splash, and the eerie silence that descended as those who had heard searched the waters for . . .

"There!" a seaman pointed out.

"It's Samuel!" a woman's voice screamed. "He can't swim! Oh, Lord, help him!"

A blond head bobbed, then went under the water

. . . water that was being churned up by two ships whose great hulls crested the waves and created hellish turmoil in an already choppy sea. Within a heartbeat, the towhead bobbed back up and a small, horror-stricken face turned round. His pleading eyes gazed full on David just as a piece of broken mast slammed into the back of the boy's head.

Without a thought, David jumped feet first into the midst of a bedlam of flotsam, which had accumulated from the battle. Two splashes next to him told David others had joined the rescue effort.

But the boy was not where he'd last been seen. The snap of the wood against his small head must have knocked him out and he'd gone under.

"Find him! Find him!" the woman pleaded.

"Montgom'ry!" Saunders, the giant pirate, yelled.

David turned to see One-eyed Jack pointing to a spot near his right. "Here?" he yelled back.

" 'Bout an arm's span ta yer right." When David swam to the spot, Jack yelled, "Aye! Dive, man!"

The murkiness of the water surprised David. Wood floated above him. But the kicking and flaying arms of himself and the other two rescuers had created a maelstrom below the surface the likes of which he'd never seen. Bits and pieces of blasted hulls and masts, shreds of cloth, and red streams that could only be blood from those who had been wounded made the water almost as black and as dangerous as night.

A shape dove down next to David, kicking up more debris and mud, and a string of curses flashed through his mind. It was now so dark that he had lost sight and bearings. There was naught he could do. He would have to find the boy from feel. And he'd have to keep his head about him, as well as keep the air in his lungs, or they'd both be food for the fish.

David kicked down, using his arms to part the water and to feel for the boy's small form. His eyes strained to see the white of the boy's shirt or the red of his waistcoat and breeches. Thank God they weren't green or indigo. With red, he had a chance. With red . . .

Red! Ah, God . . . Not some spiny lobster or crab, it was a good swatch of red he saw! There . . . there!

One more kick and he had hold of an arm. A real arm. A small arm, no bulkier than a walking stick, but soft, pliant.

He tugged but the boy didn't move. What the hell?

He was almost out of air. Another tug, and David knew the boy was stuck on something. He would have to drop the arm and get back to the surface for more air.

Ah, God! If he, a man in his prime, had no air, then the boy's small lungs were surely out of their own supply. If David went up to the surface, the lad was truly drowned.

He tugged again and was about to abandon hope, when a dark form floated past him, diving deeper. With two of them, maybe . . .

He tugged once more, then wrapped his arm around the boy's middle and gave a heave. Twice more, and then suddenly the boy jerked free. And David knew whoever the sailor had been who had braved the deep water, he'd managed to untangle the boy from whatever had held him prisoner.

Losing no time, David stroked for the surface, cresting it just as his lungs took a mighty spasm of air. He swallowed a great mouthful of foul seawater but didn't lose his prize.

Holding the boy up above the waves, David kicked closer to Saunders's ship, until he came within reach of a grappling hook on a rope. He attached it to the boy's breeches, making sure it held fast. When he let go, he watched with trepidation as the boy was hauled aboard.

"Will he be all right?" he called out.

"Ole Bones be workin' on 'im, now," Saunders said. "Should be jest fine. Git up 'ere, man! Need ta git under way afore ta rev'nuers spy us out!"

Instead of a grappling hook, this time a strong rope came down. It had dozens of knots up its length for purchase. David grasped hold, only to find himself sharing the rope with another pair of hands, which came from over his shoulder. The hands were draped with seaweed and long, thin vicious-looking blades of grass.

Ah! His helper in the boy's rescue.

"You did well," he said. "Never could have gotten the lad up without your help."

David reached behind him, to offer the rope to the man who had dared the deep, and his hand brushed against a form that was not that of an ordinary seaman. His fingers explored mounds that hardened at his touch.

Breasts! Soft, full, ripe breasts. And their peaks were hard against his palm.

David kept one hand grasping the rope and kicked until he'd turned around.

Savannah Stewart smiled, then looked down into the water. "You can move your hand now, my lord.

Unless, of course, you've found some anomaly?"

David cursed and snatched his hand away. "No anomaly, Miss Stewart."

No, not one. Everything he'd discovered was wonderful, in fact. Far too wonderful. Christ! That one touch, that simple exploration, and he'd become aroused. Still treading water, he backed up and away from the boarding rope.

"Women and children first, Miss Stewart. And since the child has already gone up . . ."

Savannah bit her lower lip. David Montgomery looked positively furious, and she had had enough experience with men—brothers, fathers, uncles, and grandfathers, not to mention a few who had courted her—to know what might have occasioned that response. Yes, *that* response. That telltale male response to touching a female figure.

Well, well, well. So Arabella's steely-eyed glacier of a brother sometimes heated up. For some reason, that thought was infinitely pleasing to Savannah.

Not so pleasing was the picture of herself being hauled onto the ship by that knotted rope. She was dripping wet and her clothes would cling to her, leaving nothing to the imagination. Then, once she got to the top, she'd have to bend herself in two to get over that taffrail. Bent in two, with her posterior . . .

Bloody hell! With David Montgomery able to see . . . well, everything he hadn't yet touched. It was a bit humiliating.

But it was also—if her artist's imagination was right—a bit enticing. She wondered if he'd be more— or less—uncomfortable than he was now. She'd bet on the former. And she'd never lost a bet yet.

Savannah stifled a giggle. It served the future Marquess of Lorton right, for his supercilious attitude before the accident. Served him right to be very uncomfortable for a little bit longer.

She grasped the rope and looped it under her arms. When David made a move to help her tie it, she warned him off with a shake of her head and made a double loop to hold the rope fast. Grasping it with both hands, she held tight as her arms were raised, and she was hauled out of the water and up the side of the ship.

As she'd guessed, her once lovely blue satin dress and delicately embroidered, finely woven underskirts were plastered to her body, outlining every hill and valley. She swung in the air and once chanced to look down. Such joy! David's gaze was fastened on her progress. He might say he'd done it so he'd be able to help if she lost hold of the rope. Or he might say he'd done it so he'd know when his turn came to be hauled aloft. But from the consternation on his face as his eyes flicked from one shadowed area of her body to the other, Savannah knew better. And, oh, how she hugged to herself the pleasure that came from David's inability to stop himself from his careful, absorbed search.

So, she deliberately exaggerated the final few inches of her ascent by wiggling suggestively. And she managed to hang motionless for a few moments, so the unladylike way her posterior protruded when she heaved herself over the taffrail was quite evident down below.

When she quite literally plopped onto the deck of Jack Saunders's ship, there was a great smile on her face.

Which was a mistake. Six seamen thought her smile an invitation. Each pretended she might need help untying the knots that hung so near her breasts. And each got a resounding slap on a wrist or a cheek. Jack laughed heartily and took the rope when she was finished. He swung it out over the rail and ordered that it be lowered once more. Then he hunkered down next to Savannah and drew a smelly blanket across her shoulders.

"Not 'cause yer cold, lass. But 'cause I need ta cover yer up or I be losin' good hands ta tha lash fer they's impudence." He picked out pieces of wood and lengths of seagrass from her hair. "Ya done good, lass."

"Had to do something. The British lord might be a good swimmer, but he doesn't know beans from biscuits about the treachery of our seagrass patches."

"The British lord does now," David gasped out. "And he's much obliged to the American girl for her help."

"And he wants her to be his houseguest for the Christmas holidays, doesn't he?" Arabella asked, glaring at her brother. "After all, the American *lady* might have been drowned down there! She helped save you, too! An invitation to Lorton House for the Christmas holidays is the least the Montgomerys can do to show their gratitude."

David wasn't sure it *was* the least they could do. He was dreadfully afraid that if Savannah Stewart was a guest in his home, he'd have far too many of her unwanted intrusions. Saved his life, indeed! He would have been all right. . . .

But one look at that figure huddled under the crude, dirty blanket and one glance at those big seafoam-blue eyes, and he was lost. Damn this country, anyway!

There were no rules of etiquette. Here, young ladies jumped into the deep to rescue a young boy, and everyone thought it just another of life's little happenings.

In England, she would have been ostracized for such an act. Hell, in England, no woman he knew would have jumped in, and the boy would have drowned. But there next to Jack's Ole Bones was the boy . . . Stephen, no, Samuel . . . circled by his family and friends, looking almost as he must have before his slip overboard.

And there *she* was. A waif, indeed! A vixen. A sloe-eyed wench. A woman. Beauty and grace and courage. God, what was he going to do?

He extended his invitation, then made a mental note to have his tailor make his breeches and trousers a little looser. When she was in his house, he wanted to be able to sit down once in a while.

Chapter Three

There were no future mishaps getting the wedding party from Jack Saunders's ship to *Dragon*. Arabella and David bid good-bye to each couple and their children, and invited them to their Christmas open house at Lorton House.

"We thank you for the invitation," Lyle Leduc said. "But without knowing what happened to Robert and Emily, this is no time for festivities for us."

"When you have word, will you send it to us?"

"Of course, my lord." Lyle bowed to Bella. "May your first Christmas in America be all you desire, Lady Arabella."

Bella curtsied and smiled. "And may you have good news about Emily and Robert."

As the gentlemen helped their ladies and children into waiting carriages, David had a word with Captain Wilholm.

"Your men were a credit to you and Lorton Crown Traders, Captain."

"Thank you, my lord."

David dug into his pocket. "Would an extra forty

shillings be enough to get you all a good Christmas dinner and a few personal extras?"

"More than enough, sir. And you are more than generous."

Once she and David were safely ensconced in the phaeton, Arabella teased, "Well, well, well! A Montgomery being 'more than generous'! What will Grandfather and Drew say?"

"They'll probably say I'm not fit to carry on the Montgomery name."

"And if you're not, then who is?"

Bella sniffed. She pursed her lips haughtily and glared at nothing in particular. Her furiously indignant expression so mimicked the one the "inestimable" Miss Stewart had had when David had chastised her that he almost laughed aloud.

"The way Grandfather . . . and Drew . . . push us around . . . And you let them get away with it, David. Drew, the younger of you two! Honestly! Attitudes and actions like that would not happen in American families."

David gave his sister a look that was a mixture of pride and astonishment. "Your tongue prattles on *here*, sister, dear, thousands of miles from their hearing. But back in London . . ."

"Kent. Grandfather and Drew would be in Kent now, for the holidays."

"Don't change the subject, Bella. It's particularly unnerving and most exasperating from a lady of your standing. I suppose it's one more thing you've learned from Miss Stewart. That woman is bolder than a courtesan."

"She is far from a courtesan, David! She's a lady."

"She's the daughter of Grandfather's former overseer, or have you forgotten?"

"David! That sounds more like Drew than you. You must be working too hard and worrying too much. If you weren't, you'd know that here, in America, it's not title or family that makes a woman a lady. It's demeanor. And Savannah has the best disposition.... Why, she's the most gracious, thoughtful gentlewoman in the colony. If she seems a little rough on the outside, it's because you haven't gotten to know her. On the inside, where it counts, she keeps ... well, I can only describe them as treasures. Yes, that's it...." She bobbed her head for emphasis. "Inside, she keeps treasures, just waiting for someone very lucky to take them out and polish them up. Oh, David, she shines now! But with someone special, she would gleam!"

"I wish she had gleamed underwater. I could have used a beacon. And what was she doing, jumping into the deep like that? A gentlewoman, indeed! A slip of a woman, trying to show *me* what to do!"

Bella stared at her brother, pleased and nonplussed. "Well," she pointed out, "she *did* show you, didn't she? The treacherous seagrass—which we don't have in England ... or, at least, not that kind—remember?"

"You don't have to remind me!" He shook his head and muttered, "Rubbing it in ... another Savannah Stewart trait. Damn that woman!"

"I do not understand your attitude, David. Savannah pleases everyone who knows her ... except *you*. What is it about her that rattles you so? Why don't you like her?"

"I don't see anything to like."

And that, thought David, was a damnable lie. He saw too much . . . had touched too much . . . even physically felt too much . . . way too much. . . .

Ah, hell . . . He more than liked Savannah Stewart. And if there were only himself to consider . . .

"She may have helped rescue Samuel," he conceded, "but by her actions you were in danger, Bella. I don't like that. I don't like that at all."

Bella gasped, in quick understanding of the deliberate tone to her brother's harsh words. "Surely you will not make trouble for Savannah just because she took me to that wedding, will you, David?"

"Why should you think I was going to make trouble for Miss Stewart?"

"Because I know you, David. I've heard that worried tone before . . . thinking you have to step in to protect me from every sinister shadow. Really, David, you take your responsibility for me far too seriously. I am fifteen, you know. And our mother was married at sixteen. So, I'm practically all grown up."

Although he'd been angry and upset only a few moments before, the absurdity of Bella's comparison, together with the thought of his sister as a bride, plucked waggishly at David's humorous side. He laughed heartily and with one hand hugged her to him. "Grown up, is it? God help the young men when you decide it's time to marry, Bella. And God help the one you choose for husband. You'll rule his home, his life, and his pocketbook with illogical logic and beguiling guile."

"But of course, David. That's what women are supposed to do."

A quick flash of seafoam eyes and dimpled cheeks

blotted out the sun for a moment. David sighed. "God forbid!"

There was no need for Bella to keep David from making trouble for Savannah with Honesty Dunn. The older woman—who had devoted her life to becoming one of the southern colonies' "great ladies" by developing a school for the daughters of gentry—discovered the full extent of the escapade directly from her art instructor that evening.

Before Savannah was half finished with her recitation, Honesty hiked up her tartan-patterned satin skirt and rustled pell-mell into her drawing room. Her red curls (from the telltale orange-red marks on her collar, Savannah was sure she hennaed them) bounced against her broad shoulders. Her mobcap bobbed along with the curls, and when she whirled to face Savannah, it was tilted at a rakish angle over Honesty's right ear.

Ruffles and lace at throat, bosom, wrist, waist, and hem. Never had they looked so incongruous. True, Honesty Dunn usually wore simple, unadorned frocks while the school was in session. But once the last girl left, she all but dove into a collection of silks and satins so lavishly trimmed with expensive lace and deep gathered ruffles that she rivaled every woman on the pages of the Paris fashion gazettes Honesty seemed to devour whole. But what might have graced the tiny, fashionably thin Marie Louise only made the square, strong Honesty look like a misshapen child playing "dress up."

Still, Savannah liked the woman. She was kind and generous to her staff. She refused to buy slaves but hired indentured servants to do the work for the students. Best of all, she supported the foundling home and often ignored payments from families whose fortunes had temporarily taken a downswing. In all the world, Savannah didn't want to do anything that would hurt so good a soul.

Which didn't mean, however, that Savannah didn't see Honesty's faults. As an artist, she saw them all too clearly. The worst was Miss Dunn's penchant for the dramatic.

Savannah had grown up in a household of . . . well, they could only be described as "strange" women. Scotswomen, vociferous and headstrong. Their burrs had fascinated her, and as a child, she had quickly learned how to mimic each odd sound. She had also learned that these fearless women — her mother and grandmother, most of all — wanted Savannah raised as a "lady," like the ones they had served in England. But being born and bred as a lady was one thing; being trained for the lady position by servants was quite another.

Savannah had retreated yet given them what they wanted. She had read every play of Shakespeare — *The Taming of the Shrew* a dozen times. She'd read Sir Walter Scott. She'd read Margaret of Navarre's "Heptameron" tales. She'd read Spenser, Fletcher, Beaumont, Middleton, and *The Tatler* and *Examiner*. And since childhood, she had taken every part of every lady in every play, poem, or news article.

So Savannah knew the difference between the real, the good, and the awful. She had decided never to be awful. Subtlety was the key. Being subtle meant being believable. And, if her family, friends, and colleagues could be trusted, she had succeeded in being believable, even when she had the hardest role to play — as with David Montgomery.

Not so, Honesty Dunn.

Savannah was convinced Honesty wouldn't recognize subtlety if it came up and introduced itself a dozen times. She'd probably mispronounce its name!

No, subtlety was not Honesty's hallmark. She overplayed the "great southern gentlewoman" role, her curled little finger when drinking tea looking less like an example of good manners and more like she had palsy. She overplayed the "educated headmistress" role, often making far too many mistakes in grammar and misquoting almost everyone, including Matthew, Mark, Luke, and John. And she was now overplaying the part of the overworked, overwrought lady.

Savannah pursed her lips to hold back a chuckle when Honesty picked up a crystal bottle labeled "Aromatic Spirits of Ammonia." Savannah had once had occasion to use it on one of the students. There was so faint an aroma from the bottle that she decided Honesty had substituted rock sugar crystals for the more potent ammonia ones.

Dramatically wafting the bottle under her nose every few seconds, Honesty her words punctuated with sniffs that had Savannah fighting hard to keep from laughing — or crying. At this point, she wasn't sure which was more appropriate.

Savannah waited as the tall woman sank onto an upholstered settle she imperiously referred to as a "fainting couch." Honesty brought the back of her hand up to her forehead . . . and Savannah's first thought was that her upper arm and hand looked too solid for a schoolteacher. It wasn't hard to imagine her hand clutched tightly around a hammer, ready to swing down to an anvil.

Savannah could almost feel the force of the swing, see the arc, hear the clang . . . coming right down on her tiny, vulnerable neck. Trouble she neither needed nor wanted; but she was sure it was coming! And come, it did.

Honesty wafted the bottle. "Savannah . . . Oh, Savannah, my dear . . ." *Sniff. Gasp.* "David Montgomery is the grandson and heir of a sixth generation marquess."

As if Savannah needed to be reminded! The unspoken implication was there: a sixth generation marquess for whom your father once worked as overseer.

Savannah straightened her spine, fighting her automatic reaction — to fling her resignation in Honesty's face and flounce out of the room. But she held back. Though the woman would deny it to all and sundry, Honesty needed her.

In fact, Honesty needed Savannah far more than Savannah needed the headmistress. The latest Savannah Stewart monograph and book of watercolors was selling so well in major American cities, as well as in London and Paris and other places where people were interested in the colonies, that she was told there was a copy on every drawing room table in the best of houses.

So Savannah held her tongue. Her heart was filled with conflicting emotions. It was best to take this one step at a time.

Honesty looked at Savannah out of the corner of her eye. Like Savannah, she gave no indication of her true feelings, except to wail, "I don't have any other royals in this school! Our enrollment nearly doubled as soon as Lady Arabella became my student." *Sniff. Gasp.* "What if . . . oh, God, Savannah . . . what if he takes her away from us?"

Honesty's white lace handkerchief fanned her face, and her great round brown eyes blinked fiercely with unshed tears. "It will be my ruin if the other parents and guardians find out what happened today!"

"They *will* find out, Miss Dunn. You can't keep secrets like this in our small city, where everyone knows everyone, their great-grandmothers, their grandmothers, their cousins, and their unborn children."

"Then you must *do* something!" *Sniff. Gasp.* "You must apologize profusely . . . and penitently . . . and genuinely. You must. You simply must!"

With that, Honesty sank back on the fainting couch, shut her eyes, and shooed Savannah out of the drawing room.

As she walked to the bakery to pick up a loaf cake for her family's dessert that night, Savannah seethed at the order she'd been given. After all, she had tried to apologize to David Montgomery before they'd rescued young Lawrence Leduc's friend, Samuel. But David Montgomery had been impossible! His actions in the water . . . well, really!

Well . . . really . . .

Savannah was in a quandary. Despite the silly, dramatic antics, her headmistress, a woman she liked, was truly frightened. Could anyone blame her? Honesty, herself, had been left at the door of a foundling home in Baltimore. It had taken forty years for her to rise from scullery maid to schoolmistress. It was common knowledge in the young colony that Miss Dunn continuously financed her school from overextended loans. Having a Montgomery as a student had saved her from debtor's prison.

Savannah sighed. Should David pull Bella out . . .

Damnation! Savannah couldn't let a royal cut down one of Georgia colony's own, no matter how irritating he was!

Bloody hell!

She had to admit that she *might* have made matters worse with her teasing.

Much worse. For him, for her, for Honesty Dunn.

Of course, matters had appeared to quiet a little when Bella had persuaded David to include Savannah once more in his house party. After that, the two adversaries had almost been civil to each other.

Civil, yes. But not quiet.

Her nerves were raw from the static in the air whenever she was near him. And judging from the reaction of David's body, so were his.

Good Lord! From David's point of view, had she acted the strumpet?

With that horrific thought, Savannah stopped suddenly in the middle of the shopping crowd. A broom seller got his feet and arms tangled in his wares in a vain attempt to avoid colliding with her. The spectacle of him brushing her down, dropping two brooms and brushes for each one he picked up, and getting himself more flustered and tangled than he'd been before, soon drew a crowd, which hooted and laughed at the antics.

Savannah glared at the assembly and snapped to the skinny young man, "Stand still! I'll hand you your wares."

It took several minutes, but she soon had each long stick shoved into his two hip carriers and each short stick jammed into the leather strap that encircled his waist and held the carriers in place.

With a jaunty bow and a "Myrrh, I have none, pretty miss. Accept, please, in honor of our Lord's birth," the young man offered her a small hearth broom as if it were a bunch of the most delicate roses. Though she was awash with anger and guilt feelings, his gesture was so gallant and so ingenuous that Savannah couldn't help but smile and accept his Christmas gift in the same manner in which it had been given.

She dropped him a curtsy and gaily said, "Thank you, gentle lad. Happy Christmas."

"And to you and yours."

It was too late for the bakery now, she decided, so Savannah hailed a passing carriage, giving the driver directions to Glassleigh Hall, the Stewart estate outside the city. As they passed the small houses and gardens of the earliest inhabitants, Savannah pushed the thought of herself as a strumpet to the back of her mind. She wasn't one, of course; but if by not slapping him when he touched her, David had thought she was . . .

It was not a pleasant thought; so she would not, could not, dwell on it. But something else nagged at her about her second—or was it third?—confrontation with David Montgomery—the one on the deck of One-eyed Jack's ship.

Although they had come to an uneasy truce and she'd accepted his invitation, she had *not* apologized for bringing Bella into a dangerous situation. She had made excuses.

That was totally unlike her. In a family famous for the artistic talents and temperaments of its members, she was the one known to follow her heart but to keep her head.

As she had done with Honesty Dunn.

Yet, she had let things carry her away today. First, the hurried wedding preparations. Then, acceding to Bella's pleas to be included in the wedding party. Then, when she'd discovered it was to be held on a pirate ship, had she put her foot down and dragged Bella away to safety? No. She had been swept right along with the excitement, right into the jaws of death. That she and Bella had survived was a miracle. That she had gotten Bella into the predicament was inexcusable.

Yet, when confronted by David Montgomery, she had tried to excuse it. And had failed. Lord Montgomery had a perfect right to be angry. He had a perfect right to seethe. He even had a perfect right to demand her removal from the school's faculty or to remove Arabella from Savannah's sphere of influence.

If she were in his place, she would probably do both.

Regardless of his invitation . . . regardless of his body's reaction to her . . . would he do either? Both?

If he did demand her resignation, what would she do? Or, if he did remove Arabella, what would happen to poor, good Honesty Dunn?

David Montgomery's invitation to his first Christmas fete at Lorton House had more import now than it had had several days ago.

Chapter Four

David was astounded at what Arabella had accomplished. She had turned Lorton House into Shakespeare's Ring—the abode of the Fairies. He half expected to turn around and catch a glimpse of Peaseblossom; Cobweb; the Puck, Robin Goodfellow; or Titania, herself, queen of the fairies.

On the floor in the spacious entrance hall, tucked into corners away from drafts, were dozens of candles in silver and glass holders, or simply jammed onto nails protruding from rounds of unstripped wood. They cast varying patterns of light and shadow on unfinished pine paneling and bare whitewashed walls. A mingled scent of bayberry, attar of roses, and a pure Christmassy ginger-spice wafted from the candles and from great bowls of dried flowers, herbs, and spices, a mixture that Bella insisted be called potpourri. Boughs of long-needled pine were wound around and between the spindles of the curved oak staircase, tied in place with a rainbow of colors that turned out to be the entire contents of Bella's ribbon collection.

In the large parlor to the right and the keeping room

to the left were more candles and potpourri. But here Bella had made certain the lighted candles would not be in the way of their female guests' skirts. She had had every servant and day laborer whom David could coerce into working on both sides of Christmas sawing, planing, and banging together rough plank tables and circular side tables. David surmised that Bella had bought out every yard of muslin or lawn fabric in Savannah. And while the men were working on the tables, she'd had their wives cutting the yard goods to fit and their daughters raveling the edges of the makeshift tablecloths to give the illusion of deep fringes.

But the circular tables were her greatest triumph. She had covered them with her old taffeta and satin skirts, held in place with large tacks. The lace and ruffles had been left to add fullness and a sense of style. Atop, she'd spread either beggar's lace or woolen shawls and more pine boughs, in the center of which was a glass-topped candle holder.

Next to each round table were two or three chairs that blended in color or pattern with Bella's skirts. Yet, not one grouping of chairs matched any other! A steady stream of carriages had brought them to Lorton Woods—borrowed finery from the homes of Bella's schoolmates. Each contribution came only after she'd sincerely promised that naught would happen to them and that they would be returned promptly after the last guest had departed.

Of course, that meant each family who had contributed chairs had also, of necessity, been invited to at least one night of festivities. It would have been ungentlemanly and shown willful ingratitude not to have done so.

Thus, the original list of twelve house guests who were to occupy the upstairs bedrooms had swelled to over fifty. Thank God the additional merrymakers would merely attend one of the functions, then take their leave.

How Bella had managed to calm down Dora, the cook, David didn't want to know. Bella *had* managed it, however, because she assured David they had enough food to feed the entire city if need arose. He didn't doubt it. Last time he looked, six whole hams had been hanging from the rafters in the smokehouse, seven geese trussed and soaking in rum and molasses water, and two barrels of fish steaming Indian-style in a pit behind the kitchen under a layer of seaweed and hot rocks.

A child a week ago, Arabella had overnight become a woman who could supervise an entire household of servants, settle disputes, plan meals and musicales, and turn an empty shell of a house into a delightful home.

But it still made David cringe when he remembered how livid Bella had been when she had first seen the dimensions and contents of these rooms five days previously.

The drive from town stretched her nerves, until she was fairly jumping with anxiety. David had deliberately gone the long way round, so she would get the full measure of the magnificence of the grounds: tall spreading oaks, thick juniper groves, and the crushed shell meandering drive that led to the brick and tabby three-and-a-half-story house. He'd instructed his houseman, Falconer, to have fires laid in the six fireplaces, and as they rounded the final bend, the smoke from the chimneys was a welcome sight.

Not so the interior. Bella had taken one look and very nearly bitten her brother's head off.

With her arms outstretched as if she were measuring the space around her, Arabella had whirled in a circle in the parlor, fury turning her grey eyes so black it had David chewing on his bottom lip.

"I can't believe this! Are the parlor and keeping room really so large, or do they merely seem that way because there is naught a stick of furniture in them?"

"What do you call the armoire and side chairs?"

"Oh, David! We can hardly call two rooms fully furnished if there is only an armoire in one and six chairs in the other!" She stood contemplating the empty spaces, which even two brightly colored Turkey-work carpets didn't do much to make hospitable. "Is there no possibility the ship will be here before our guests?"

"None."

David frowned, too. Almost nine months ago he had requested the furniture they needed. One cargo had supplied enough for the master bedroom and Bella's bedroom. But a long missive from Drew had bemoaned the shortage of good pine and maple, which he assured David they must have for the tables, chairs, settles, sofas, and armoires.

. . . And all because your colonial rebels refuse to ship it to their monarch's needs! Of course, we will try our best to accommodate you, brother. But perhaps you should impress on your colonial underlings that their attitude must effect an immediate change or they will be facing the wrath of the finest naval force and militia in the world!

Try explaining taxes that King George had imposed on a colonial freeman's own goods? Drew must be out of his mind.

So, another letter had crossed the Atlantic, this time requesting some of the furniture from David's own townhouse in London. But Drew had demurred, explaining:

> *. . . Because I must be in London to carry out this end of our mercantile venture, I have taken residence in Kentlands. Naturally, you are still master here. But surely you of all people should understand I cannot be impoverished at this time, when I am actively seeking a wife.*

Actively seeking a wife? Drew, the eternal bachelor? The wencher? The gamesman? That he had taken residence in Kentlands was not surprising. But that he considered the furniture his to keep from its rightful owner was astonishing!

As the younger grandson, Drew had always been jealous of David's status as heir to the title and holdings. Getting his hands on at least part of his older brother's patrimony must be more important to him than David had imagined.

David could have pressed his rightful ownership, he supposed. But it seemed best to let Drew enjoy his largesse while he could.

So, David had sent a letter to his grandfather, outlining the things he and Bella needed for Lorton House. The letter should have brought a full cargo hold on the next ship, and in time for their Christmas fete, since there was enough furniture in the storage rooms at Kent to fill up the rooms in six houses. Instead, the letter had brought naught but a long diatribe from the elderly man, which ended with:

> . . . *Lorton Crown Traders is in Georgia to sell furniture to the barbarians there, to fill our coffers and the King's. How would it look if I took up King George's precious cargo space to supply you with more than you need? Make do, man. Make do!*

Make do! When David needed to make an impression, he would look an impoverished fool. Between Christmas and the New Year, he expected as houseguests three of his most tenacious competitors—George Peale from Baltimore, Benjamin Clough from Williamsburg, and Mason Aldrich from New Haven. Each was bringing his wife. Peale would also bring with him a niece and nephew, who were "artistic," he reported; Clough, a daughter five years older than Bella; and Aldrich, two sons—Lawrence, who was already a minister, and Richard, who was reading for the law.

David could relax about the bedrooms and dining room. He had "made do" by purchasing from his own inventory a large maple trestle table with matching side chairs. The bedsteads, chests, chairs, and linens upstairs had come from several auctions given by families who were moving back to England or farther north, away from the insects and diseases, to climes more reminiscent of the ones they'd left in England. But Bella was right about the rooms downstairs. David could hardly expect to entertain his guests if they had naught but a carpet to sit on!

Bella had taken one more look around the rooms, then peeked into the adjoining dining room—also empty. "Well, then," she said as imperiously as his grandfather, "we've naught to do but to make do. You leave everything to me, David. It won't be Lorton House in Kent, but it will be as festive and as comfortable as I can make it."

Now, while the other women napped from their long journey, David held out his hand to Lavinia Clough to escort her into the parlor. He wasn't sure how she'd respond to the "making do"; but he was proud when she gave a startled gasp and laughed delightedly at the magic Bella had wrought.

She circled the room, touching the fabrics, smelling the aromas wafting from the potpourri and a punch bowl full of spiced ale, then walked up to a grouping of three candle sconces—which David had never seen until that moment. Another of Bella's miracles, he supposed. Lavinia reached up to touch the sparkling surfaces.

"Quillwork sconces! I haven't seen the likes of these in years . . . not since I visited the Fairfaxes in Virginia. Sally said the collection came from the imagination and skills of two generations of Fairfaxes. Each sconce was made by a young woman to grace the walls of her marriage chamber. Those were lovely. And their history made them precious to Sally. But these are finer . . . so imaginative . . . so . . . artistic. Who did them? I'd like to purchase some for my daughter's dowry chest."

"I have no idea where—"

From over his right shoulder, David heard an unmistakable giggle.

57

"Those were made by my friend Savannah Stewart, who is a fine artist," Bella said.

The raised brow and mischievous smile she directed at her brother as she came to take Lavinia's other hand held a message David was too bemused to try to figure out. She turned her back to her brother, effectively shutting him out of this "female" talk. But he heard every word she said, as he once again was regaled with Bella's valuations of the wonderful Miss Stewart. Bah! Was he never to get any peace and quiet? Was the woman always to be haunting him—even here in his own home, where he should know what was happening every minute but obviously didn't.

"The figures, as you see," Bella said to Lavinia, "are cleverly fashioned from tabby masonry of the same kind that festoons the front of Lorton House. And the embellishments are a combination of rocks, nut cases, seashells, broken ornaments, and jewelry. Over everything, Savannah applied a rainbow of paints. And over the paint, a liberal coating of mica, to shimmer in the candlelight."

"One of the ones Sally Fairfax lit for me had figures of wax," Lavinia said.

"Oh, no!"

"Oh, yes."

"They melted?"

"All over the beautiful maple chest of drawers beneath it."

"A shame."

"Absolutely." Lavinia looked longingly at the three sconces.

Bella patted Lavinia's hand. "Don't worry. I'm sure if you asked her, Savannah would be delighted either to make some for you or to show you how."

"When can I talk to her about it?"

"She's to attend some of this week's festivities. I will introduce you and explain." Bella reached up and straightened a candle on the one on top. "This one she calls 'The Serpent Strikes.' "

"The Garden of Eden."

"Yes. And the two below are from Shakespeare. 'Kate Triumphs,' and 'Capulets Lament.' "

A second or two passed before Lavinia gave a startled "Oh! Oh, but she's not saying . . ."

"Oh, but she is. . . ."

"I'd like to hear more."

"Come with me, Mistress Clough. I'll tell you all about Savannah Stewart."

David could also tell Lavinia a thing or two about Savannah Stewart. But he was positive they wouldn't be the same thing or two that Bella was whispering in the plump grey-haired woman's ear.

At something Bella said, Lavinia turned to give David a searching look, and her chocolate-brown eyes widened and her hand covered her mouth to smother giggles. David cursed inwardly and went to fetch Mason, George, and Benjamin for a hand of Foxes and Hounds.

What had the women meant? *Oh, but she's not saying . . . Oh, but she is. . . .* Cryptic! Women were cryptic, meaning what they didn't say and saying what they didn't mean.

As he lost the second round to Mason Aldrich and saw his money pouch poorer by ten guineas, David glared at the two women, who were now busily engaged in two identical needlework frames.

Those confounded quillwork sconces really did shimmer in the candlelight! But he couldn't for the life of him see anything more than . . . hell . . . naught but sconces.

Pay attention, man, he scolded himself. Whatever Lavinia saw there, if he studied it long enough later on, he would see, too. But Foxes and Hounds came first. What he needed in order to get the puzzle out of his mind were gentlemanly games, with unchangeable rules and conversation filled with talk of shipping schedules and tide tables and the going rate for tobacco.

What he did not need was to hear George Peale curse the influx of Georgians into his city.

"Baltimore needs skilled craftsmen, not more farmers and laborers who have no money to buy land and end up in potter's field, the poorhouse, or on the road further north."

"We've had our fill of them, too," Mason Aldrich said. He stuffed his cigar in his mouth and scooped up the next round, adding six guineas to his pile of winnings. "Why can't you keep your hired help in Georgia?" he asked David.

While Lavinia and Bella passed the men tankards full of spiced ale, David dealt the next hand. "I didn't know they were leaving," he said.

"Of course they're leaving, David," Bella said. "Savannah told me the city is losing more than fifty people a week and they aren't half being replenished by newcomers."

"Exactly!" Mason crowned David's fox with a hound. "They see war coming. And the latest horror in Newport this summer when those blasted idiots set fire to a revenue cutter only whets the blood of the rebels."

George had two hounds to cover Mason's two foxes. He slapped them down and dropped another fox in the middle of the table. "Georgia will soon be the only truly royal colony left, the way things are going." He scowled as David scooped up six foxes with six hounds, wiping out the other players. "Probably why you're not making more progress, my boy," he said to David. "A royal trading company is the last thing these colonies want . . . and the absolutely last thing they'll support."

As David counted up his guineas and found he was three up for nine hands, he mused, "But there must be some who are loyal to King George who will trade with Lorton Crown Traders. After all, we hold a royal commission."

"Aye," Benjamin Clough said. "But ye must needs seek them out, laddie. Ye can't do it this far from the fray."

"What do you suggest?"

"Make a circuit of the port cities. Specialize in goods the merchants can't get except through you. With yer connections in Parliament, ye could get a monopoly on one kind of staple foodstuff like rock sugar or a building material like glass."

Mason harrumphed. "Here, here, Clough! We're all of us competitors. Why give the newcomer the upper hand?"

"Because," Benjamin sighed, "when war comes — and make no doubt, t'will come — Lavinia and I will be in Scotland."

"You're selling out?"

"Aye. There's serious talk of moving Virginia's House of Burgesses and the courts to a more central location. If those who are pushing for the move succeed, Williamsburg is finished as a center of trade and culture. I don't want to be here when that happens. And I don't want to be here when one American takes up arms against another, or against his brothers in British uniforms. I'm getting too old. I belong in Scotland, where my father was born, where I spent my school years, where I met and married my wife." He rose and took the paltry two guineas he had left. "My enterprise is for sale, laddie. If ye want to talk about taking it over, I'll be available at five on the morrow. But for tonight, sleep well, my friends."

But David couldn't sleep well. He tossed and turned in the new feather bed, reviewing every syllable that had been spoken over the gaming table.

Benjamin Clough had been brutally honest. War. He believed there would be war. And if Savannah was right, and their city was losing fifty men, women, and children every week, Lorton Crown Traders would be harder pressed to find buyers for its goods within the confines of Georgia Colony.

Benjamin's assessment was troubling. But if it be half correct, David had no choice but to make the circuit *and* to persuade his grandfather to take over Clough's enterprise. It had a sterling reputation. It had always been loyal to the Crown. It had always dealt honestly with the colonial settlers. Not to buy it would be foolish.

He must get the information he'd learned to his grandfather. Immediately. Captain Wilholm could carry it to England with the outgoing tide. But first, he'd have to pen the letter carefully, to make absolutely certain that Grandfather knew this was the best course for Lorton Crown Traders. And to make damned sure the old man didn't get wind of Benjamin's assertion that war was coming. David knew what his grandfather would do then.

. . . Dump the merchandise in the hold of all the ships. Don't even sell it to those traitors! And come home on the next tide.

But David didn't want to go home. He didn't want to leave things unfinished. . . .

He blinked away an unbidden and unwanted apparition, and swore.

Of course he didn't want to go home!

And for no other reason than that he had a commission from the King and had to try to fulfill it until there was no chance it could succeed.

David tossed aside the lightweight wool homespun blanket he favored for his night covering and slipped his feet into the wool slippers awaiting him at the side of his bed. He parted the heavy embroidered linen night curtains and groped for his robe.

Damn, it was cold!

Willy, the colored servant who always slept in David's room, came awake immediately. "Sir?"

"The fire has gone out, Willy. Lay another. And light it. Don't go back to sleep until it's blazing hard."

"Yes, sir."

"And don't forget to put the fire grate back."

"No, sir. I won't forget." He wouldn't. The last time he had forgotten, he'd damned near burned down the house David had rented while waiting for Lorton House to be completed.

David stopped to light a candle, then decided to wait until he got to the office wing built off the parlor. He'd padded the halls enough. And there was plenty of light from a full moon.

One thing could be said for a half-empty house: You weren't likely to trip over furniture in the dark.

As David made his way past the guest bedrooms, the only sound he heard was a raspy snore. Lavinia or Benjamin?

The house had sounds of its own. Settling sounds that a new house made as heat from the fireplaces caused the wood to shrink. A crackling here, as a beam dried out. A creak there, in the stair treads. A groan below, as masonry that didn't shrink rubbed against wood that did.

But clicks and shuffles, grunts and a startled "Ouch!"?

David followed the sound. Silhouetted against a window in the parlor was a cloaked and hooded figure standing on one of Bella's precious borrowed chairs. The man had his arms stretched above his head and he was wrestling with the curved arms of the ceiling candle holder.

The damned fool was stealing the only twelve-candle, two-tiered chandelier in the city!

"Oh, no, you don't!"

David rushed the thief and tackled him at his knees. The chair toppled and the full weight of the thief smashed into David's left shoulder. An elbow gouged his eye and a foot jabbed painfully into his midsection.

The thief was a wriggling, spitting mass of fury, but

David managed to flip him onto the carpet and straddle him.

Now what? He had no rope to tie the bugger. But Willy was still awake. As he opened his mouth to call out, the thief giggled.

"By the look in your eyes these past six months, I wagered with myself that you wanted to get me in a compromising position. But don't you think this is a little dangerous, my lord?" Savannah Stewart asked. "With all your guests upstairs, anyone could walk in on us." She turned her head and ran her lips against David's wrist. "Privacy. Things like this are best carried out in privacy."

From the mocking lilt of her voice, David knew she was teasing him, goading him. Though he was the stronger and had her in his power, she still thought herself the victor, in charge of the situation. It had been that way from the first with her and him. But this time she had underestimated her weakness and severely underestimated the surge of feelings that coursed through David—all because of the way the softness of her body molded itself around the hardness of his.

"Privacy or no privacy," David muttered, "things like this are best carried out to the end."

"No! Wait, David! Remember who I am."

"The minx who's made my life a living hell?"

Her laughter was as clear and as calling as a dinner bell, and it beckoned to something so deeply rooted in David that he was befuddled by the reaction he had. He wanted to hear that soft, tinkling laugh again. Wanted to hear it after she had become replete with his loving.

Jesus! When had it happened? When had the living hell turned into a burning need?

Oblivious to his confusion, Savannah blithely blathered on. "That, too. But I was thinking more along the lines of your grandfather's overseer's daughter."

David ground his teeth together, trying to get control of the torrents coursing through his body. "There are too many twists and turns to that relationship to remember it all. I'll just remember that you broke into my house and were stealing my chandelier."

"Bella let me into your house. And I wasn't stealing anything. I was merely hanging what passes for mistletoe in this colony."

"Did you hang it?"

"You toppled me from my chair. How could I hang it all?"

"Don't be evasive, Savannah. It doesn't suit you. Is there some above us?"

Reluctantly, she croaked, "Yes."

"Good. I don't need an excuse—since you are obviously my prisoner—but if anyone does come in . . . or ask . . . your nocturnal mistletoe hanging will be perfect as an explanation for what is about to happen."

He tightened his grip on her wrists, gave her a long, assessing look, then lowered his head to capture her mouth. A gasp of surprise escaped her, but her lips didn't clamp shut.

A small victory, that; but he'd take what he could get.

When David nibbled on the corners of her mouth, Savannah thought she would go mad. She was crazy, allowing this liberty! But she would be crazier if it stopped.

"I wish I could see your eyes," David murmured. "They have all the colors of the sea. Beautiful, the way they curve up at the corners."

His kisses fired a path up her cheek to her eyelids and she sighed with pleasure, then gasped in astonishment as his tongue flicked out to wet the corners.

"You always smell good," he whispered. "Like roses or lilacs."

"Distilled by my aunt."

Oh, Lord! What was he doing now? His lips behind her ear . . . The sensations . . . Ah! That felt so good!

"Your skin not only smells sweet, it tastes sweet."

"There's not enough mistletoe for all this!"

He laughed. "One berry and one leaf would be more than I needed after the past months."

"What bothers you most about me—my honesty or my influence over Bella?"

"The way your earlobe beckons."

He licked her left lobe and she thought she saw fireflies flickering against the solid dark walls. Lord, why had she teased him? For this? For the way her body melted when he gently sucked the traitorous beckoning earlobe? Or for the way fire fled up into the roots of her hair when his tongue outlined the ridges in her ear?

It was hard to breathe. Harder, yet, to gasp, "Enough, David. Please."

He pressed his head into the crook that her head made with her shoulder, then licked at the cords of her neck. She gasped and her lower limbs jerked open.

When his weight settled between them, he asked, "Enough? Are you sure?"

She nodded, but even she knew it was a feeble movement.

"Perhaps I should give you a little more punishment for what you've done the past year and this night?"

Yes, David thought, more punishment was definitely in order. But he wasn't sure who was getting the worst of it. His loins were taut and near to the point of enormous tremors. His blood throbbed through every vein and sinew. His manhood reached to the heavens and ached with a fierceness never before felt.

So who was punishing whom?

And was this a punishment at all?

God, her body was luscious! Small-boned, delicate, yet round and soft and warm.

Fairy land. They were in fairy land. A midwinter night's dream brought on by a fiery Tempest. In the morrow life would intrude. But tonight he had to know this woman . . . had to teach her how much she affected him.

It would make him vulnerable, but what did that matter? He was vulnerable, anyway. Vulnerable and prisoned.

But regardless of the fact that she had bewitched him, he owed her the chance to get out from under . . . him, as well as the situation.

"Name your punishment, Savannah. Should I let you up and you will never know what it might have been like, or should I continue?"

Chapter Five

She stared up at him, at the shadows and planes that the moonlight chiseled in his face, and imagined his black eyes softened to a midnight-blue. That was the color they would be, she believed, had he not so much weight on his shoulders.

Broad shoulders. Muscular arms. Tight flanks. Long, sinewy legs. Light brown hair always clean and tied in a queue at the nape of his neck. Slashing brows. Piercing gaze made fearsome from too many scowls. Straight, aquiline nose. A man's mouth, not full from overindulgence and dissipation, but wide and strong, with tiny lines at the corners. Laugh lines, they should have been — and probably had begun that way — but now they turned down more than up.

A face and body growing out of youth into true manhood. A face of pride. A countenance of courage. A body for work . . . and for pleasure.

"You hesitate," David whispered. "Perhaps you need a demonstration. . . ."

His strong left hand imprisoned her two wrists above her head. She tried to draw inward the arc of her chest, but the natural bend caused her backbone to arch and her breasts to become more defined in the faint light.

He hesitated, staring at the vista, and groaned, "Lord, have mercy."

"My Lord Montgomery, have mercy," Savannah croaked.

"You have but to say naught, Miss Stewart."

Her tongue pressed against her lower teeth and her mouth opened to get the syllable out. But as a cloud moved across the moon and a full beam of light showed her the agony and ecstasy on his face, she drew in her breath at the beauty she saw there.

"Say naught, Savannah!"

It was almost a plea . . . it *was* a plea. But she could no more say it than she could stop the fingers of his right hand from combing through her hair. Could no more say it than she could stop the path of that hand as it stroked her cheek. Was reluctant to say it when his fingers brushed back her hair, traced the slope of her forehead, moved over her eyelids, down her nose into the small indentation above her mouth, then outlined her lips before discovering the curve of her chin, the hollow beneath the hill of her cheeks.

"Twenty-seven freckles. And more hidden, Bella says."

Because she knew *where* they were hidden, Savannah gulped. And his fingers were again at her throat, tracing the small mound where her voice box was . . . the cords in her neck . . . the V of her collarbone. His full hand fanned out over her shoulder and back again to her throat.

Once more, she gulped.

"You're sculpting me," she whispered. "The way an artist learns his subject."

"Are you my subject, Miss Stewart?"

"No, my lord." Not yet.

Once again, he asked, "Are you sure? I could be the world's best sculptor, given the right subject. And I think, Miss Stewart, that you are the perfect subject. Shall we see?"

Dear God! The heat in her lower body was excruciating . . . and delicious. Oh, how she wanted to throw her arms around him and pull him down to her. To kiss him would be bliss.

Like the day of the pirate wedding, ever since they had first met, they had thrust and parried with each other, fencing around an attraction that was so dangerous it had gotten them to this point, to this room, to this languid exploration of feelings. And she, who usually kept her head in every situation, had lost the art of reason.

She preferred the art David was making . . . even though it might be her undoing.

"David!"

"Say that again."

"David?"

"No. Say it the way you just did. I want to hear that need calling to me. I want to hear *you*, Savannah. All of you. Just as I want to know you, all of you."

"Is that possible?"

"God, I hope so!"

Savannah held her breath when David pushed aside her cloak and tugged at the ribbons holding her bodice together. Traitors that they were, they came apart easily. Almost as easily as she was coming apart.

"Ever since Bella told me there were more freckles under your clothes than those on your nose and cheeks, I've fantasized about where they lay."

He pushed aside the gingham, then began working on the blouse underbodice.

It was torture. Delicious, delectable torture.

She wiggled, trying to free her hands to help him; but he tightened his hold. Then the last of the ribbons were free and his hand stilled.

"How many, I wonder? And where?"

Slowly, as if he'd imagined doing this a hundred times and had it timed to perfection, he folded back her blouse a scarce inch. "It's too dark in here. . . ." David frowned, then looked up at the windows that had no draperies. He shifted himself so the moonbeam illuminated the mounds of her breast. "Better . . . beautiful."

Another inch. Another. And Savannah couldn't breathe.

His fingers brushed the softness at the swell of her breast and he chuckled. "Freckle dust. Fairy dust. Fairy kisses."

Her body obeyed a law of its own, and her breasts swelled as his hand and lips brushed back and forth across the pied flesh, which until now had seemed unattractive. Fairy dust? Is that what he truly saw? What he felt? She would never again be able to look at her speckled body and see anything less than a golden sheen, which had been left there by fairies for David to discover.

What kind of man was this, to compromise her on his Turkey-work carpet in his new parlor . . . and to make her want it?

Suddenly, he dropped her wrists, surged to his knees, and held out his hand. "Come with me to my bedroom, Savannah. Come and show me every kiss the fairies left. Come and let me kiss you as they did. Let me love you tonight."

David cursed the streaming light of a mid-morning sun.

Cursed, with a string of obscenities that would have melted the glaciers on the highest mountains.

Let me love you tonight. Tonight!

What an ass he was. With that one word he had turned from lover into Lord of the Manor, expecting her to be subject to his whims. With that one word he had smashed Savannah Stewart's precious and hard-won self-esteem.

He fingered his left cheek, where her nails had raked across and drawn blood.

"Damn you!" she had cried. "And damn me for not saying naught, for forgetting who you are and who I am. There weren't complications enough for you? Well, now there are a thousand more!"

When she ran out of the room and through the front door, he hadn't run after her. With a clarity that made him cringe, he had heard what he hadn't said yet had meant: that he believed what they were doing was only fit for one night; that as the daughter of one of his grandfather's servants, he would not allow her to expect more from him.

He was a hundred asses. A thousand fools.

Tempests, midwinter night's dream and fairies. And he hadn't even been drunk!

He stumbled through his morning ablutions. Shaving over that torn skin was such agony that he almost considered avoiding it altogether. But they were to have a musicale that night—New Year's Eve—and every member of the community had been invited. Plum pudding and syllabub were on the menu, and he had orders from Bella to look his best. But when Willy dabbed sassafras root salve on his cheek, the sting was so bad that David nearly swatted him.

He apologized immediately, of course. It wasn't the lad's fault.

Damn this haughty Montgomery hide! To do that to a woman like Savannah was unconscionable.

His grandfather's lessons ran long and deep. Perhaps it was good that he was away from the damnable heritage of the Marquess of Lorton—to see his grandfather's and Drew's faults, to try to mitigate them in himself.

Strange, before coming to Savannah—the city and the woman—he had never questioned Grandfather's rules and regulations about preserving the heritage that was his.

. . . *Other people have faults, David. Never the Montgomerys.*

. . . *Other people must needs have laws to guide them, David. Never the Montgomerys.*

. . . *Other people petition the Montgomerys, David. To hunt. To fish. To farm. Why, even to fornicate! The Montgomerys take what they want and the King applauds them.*

And from all David had seen growing up, it was true. Except, of course, for the gentlest of the Montgomerys—his father.

Carlton Montgomery hadn't started out with faults.

He had been a little like Grandfather: strong, prideful, with a demeanor that made him appear omnipotent to his own children. But he had been gentle, too. And loving. He had loved his wife with a passion that Richard Montgomery called "unseemly." And he had loved his children. Played with them instead of shrugging them off onto the servants. Instructed them himself. Invaded the nursery so often they'd had seventeen nursemaids and fourteen tutors!

Then Jean, David's mother, had died suddenly from a riding accident. Pregnant, she had demurred when Carlton insisted she accompany him and their houseguests on their annual spring hunt. Then, when he teased and cajoled, she had given in. A hare had shied, spooking Jean's horse. Before the doctor could arrive, Jean had hemorrhaged the child out of her womb and the life out of her body.

For Carlton, alcohol dimmed the way his wife died. But it couldn't erase the guilt he felt. Still, he sought oblivion from the terrors of that golden-haired woman looking at him and whispering, "Good-bye, my love."

When alcohol wasn't enough, Carlton laced his whiskey with laudanum, opium, herbal mushrooms. His addiction gripped him in tentacles neither his children's love nor his father's bullying could loosen. A man of sensitivity, he slid downhill with such speed that David feared every time his father stirred his drink, touched a tankard to his mouth, and drained the contents.

And his fears had been well-founded.

One day, during a four-week alcohol- and opium-induced stupor, Carlton Montgomery had beaten his valet for a small infraction. The man's spine was shattered.

There was no petition sworn out, of course. Who would dare bring charges against the only son of Richard Montgomery, the Marquess of Lorton?

As magistrate of the district, Richard Montgomery swept his son's misdeed out of sight by pensioning the valet's family and establishing a small annuity for three tiny children. And the valet? He ended up in an invalid's bed for five years before he died at thirty-one.

But the marquess exacted his own form of punishment on his miscreant son—his heir, who could no longer be trusted to tie his own shoes. A black-bordered notice appeared in the *Times* and the *Lorton Beacon*. All of society in London and the shire read the obituary for Carlton Montgomery, clucking at the irony that he, too, like his wife, had died in a hunting accident on his estate, and that the line of succession to the title now led through David Montgomery, Carlton's eldest son.

In fact, today David's father was safely ensconced in a comfortable, well-guarded room in an otherwise uninhabited wing of Lorton Manor. His alcoholism and addiction had turned to violent tremors and hallucinations. He didn't know what day it was, didn't recognize his children, didn't know he was alive.

And it was that heritage that had sent Savannah Stewart running out of the house into the night.

"Damn it to hell!"

"David?" Arabella banged on his door. "David, open this door. I want to talk to you."

"It's not locked."

Bella looked fetching. She wore a soft linen dress of

dove-grey, which was slightly darker than her eyes, making them appear deeper, more mysterious. There was long lace at the cuffs of her blouse and a triple layer of tucks at the hem of her full skirt. An embroidered stomacher, with pale yellow ribbons that tightly tied her midriff—and David was not sure he approved of this—accented Bella's firm, young breasts, pushing them up until they looked more . . . more 'fleshy' than they were. Her blond hair was piled in elaborate curls on her head. Tiny yellow ribbons that matched those on her stomacher held the curls in place.

"Which one of our houseguests should I warn?"

"I don't know what you're talking about."

"Bella, if that isn't a husband trap you have on, then I don't know anything about women."

Bella reached up and touched the scar on David's cheek. Her scathing look was more telling than if she had said, *You don't know a thing about women.*

What she did say was, "She's gone, you know."

"I know."

Bella stamped her foot. "No, you don't! I mean she's *gone!* Left the city. Left Glassleigh. Packed her trunks, took her painting supplies and her younger brother, Stephen, and headed north!"

A deep ache began in the pit of his stomach. Accompanying it was pain so acute he could hardly breathe.

"What are you going to do about it, David?"

"What can I do?"

"Go after her!"

"Go where? Do you know where she's gone, Bella?"

Bella shook her head. A tear slipped over her eyelid. "When I woke up this morning and found she hadn't slept in her bed . . ."

Arabella's eyes flicked to David's bed, and the question lay unasked. David sighed. "No, Bella. She did not sleep here last night. She left just before midnight."

"The slamming door?"

"Yes. And before you hate me altogether, I did not take advantage of her." *Much.* "I did, however, insult her. And for that I am sorry. But I don't know how I can do what you want me to do. Unless her family gave you her destination . . ."

"No one at Glassleigh would tell me where she's gone. They are very angry with you, David."

"Yes, if she told them that I insulted her and her family, I suppose they are."

"I don't think she told them. They said that she was crying as she packed her trunks. When pressed, she said that she couldn't bear to be near you when she knew there was no way you would be able to look on her with true affection. They said she thought it best to go away and forget you. I think their anger is more directed at losing Savannah's closeness than it is at anything you might have done or said."

Stunned, David looked at himself in the mirror. He didn't like what he saw. "She didn't tell them. She protected me. Why?"

"Will you never understand these Americans, David? Those who have shaken off the dirt of England and risen to the heights of society in this new land have as much pride in themselves and in their accomplishments as a family who has seventeen generations of titles behind it. And perhaps they have better reason to be proud. We only inherit what others have worked to achieve before us. These Americans work for it themselves. And Savannah worked harder than any other woman I know.

"She is a far better person than I, David. If I had her power—and make no mistakes, brother, her power is much more than yours—had you insulted me, I would have whispered the right words into the right ears and your enterprise would have crumbled before your eyes."

"Power? Savannah?"

"Yes, David. You didn't know it because you've been so blinded by the fact that her father was Grandfather's servant, but if, as you say, you truly did insult her, then you insulted one of the leading families in these colonies. The Stewarts have published over a dozen books and more than forty newspaper articles. They are known far and wide for their monographs and paintings, especially their nature studies and portraits. Savannah is the best of them. She does the finest work, is welcome in the highest level of society. Political leaders, doctors, ministers, magistrates, even a royal governor have asked for her hand in marriage. And for some reason I cannot fathom, she favors you."

Bella shook her head and took his hand. "Come, brother. Let me show you what you've thrown away."

Late breakfast smells—ham, eggs, creamed fish, and brown bread—welcomed them when they descended the stairs. Their guests were gathered in the dining room, where David heard the clink of serving pieces against china.

But Bella walked right past the open door and into the parlor. She pushed her brother forward, almost to the exact spot where he had lain with Savannah the night before.

For several seconds he could not speak. When he did

find his voice, he whispered, "Dear God!"

In front of him, centered on the far wall, where there was the most room—and where anyone who entered Lorton House would be sure to see them—were two portraits. Because the ceilings were so high, they were almost life-sized.

Bella's portrait showed his sister as she would be in a few years: Her beauty was the bloom of a full-blossomed rose, with a touch of creamy pink to her cheeks. Her eyes sparkled with the mischief he knew she'd never lose. Her mouth smiled with a secret she always seemed to hold. That it was the secret of life, and of womanhood, he had no doubt as he stared, mesmerized, at the miracle Savannah had produced.

This was his sister.

This, too, was his mother.

What talent. What beauty.

But he frowned when he looked at the portrait hanging to Bella's left. There was something wrong there. This David Montgomery's eyes were the blue of a dark, stormy sky. The true color of his eyes, they were; yet David knew everyone else thought them black. Only Savannah had seen beyond or behind his facade and painted them as they really were. Had she also painted the other parts of him as he really was? My God, had she stripped him naked, then, as she had done with Bella, clothed him with what he could become?

His head sat on square, strong, broad shoulders. His chin was held high . . . but not in haughtiness or pride. In challenge . . . yes, that was it. Savannah had painted him standing tall, with his hand on the smooth, round surface of a globe. Challenging the world. But his finger did not touch the outline of England. Instead, Savannah had placed it on the middle shores of North America.

What was she saying? That his challenge lay there?

He cursed inwardly. Wondering and not being able to ask the only one who had the answers . . , all because he had caused her to flee into the night, to escape the horrors of being *used*.

Ass!

He looked up at the man Savannah thought he could become. Lord, what kind of vision did she have?

Above that determined Montgomery chin was the faint upturned shadow of a smile—as if bubbling laughter lay behind and merely waited for the right moment to burst out and envelop the viewer.

This was Savannah Stewart's David Montgomery.

This, too, was his father as he had once been before the demons of hell took hold of him.

The mother and the daughter, one person.

The father and the son, one person.

If Savannah truly had the gift of seeing beneath the surface, into the future, she had given Arabella a joyous life, a wondrous journey.

But David Montgomery's future . . .

Was he, too, to know the demons of hell? Was he to be firmly linked with the horror his father had suffered? Was he to succumb to the role his grandfather had seared into David's soul? Was there no hope, no escape, except in the madness his father had fallen heir to?

He cried, "No!" Groping for a chair, David sank onto a damask-upholstered pillow on one of their borrowed seats. "No. Ah, God . . . no."

Chapter Six

"My friend has a touch of grey in his hair, Miss Stewart."

Savannah looked up into the sparkling blue eyes of Thomas Jefferson, who frowned at the portrait she was doing of his friend, the famed Virginia politician and business leader, George Wythe. Savannah finished the brush stroke, which added a mahogany sheen to George's hair, and said, "But our esteemed host insists that he be shown in his prime, sir."

"He *is* in his prime. And he has grey hair. I was led to believe that you sought the truth in your portraits, Miss Stewart."

"I do, Mister Jefferson."

"Yet, it does not truly reflect George as he is."

"Perhaps there is more truth in this kind of portrait than in those which copy a form in every detail. I prefer to take the measure of the man, sir. And the measure of George Wythe is impressive."

Jefferson bowed and smiled. "I agree. But a few grey hairs also add wisdom, which he has in abundance."

"I will tell him you said so," Savannah declared.

"No need," a booming voice crackled the air. "Thomas, are you now an art critic?"

"Only of my friends and mentors, George. Of which, you top the list."

George contemplated the almost-finished portrait. "And you think grey hairs add wisdom?"

"Ask Miss Stewart."

"Savannah?"

Savannah sighed. She had locked horns with George over this very issue, and almost from the time she stepped out of her carriage in Williamsburg and ascended the brick stairs to a miniature of the Wythes' frontier plantation house. "As I have tried to explain previously, a touch of grey would, indeed, be exactly right, sir. Please let me, as the artist, make the final decisions."

"Well said, Miss Stewart!" Jefferson proclaimed. "A little like the way you run your enterprises, isn't it, George? What do you always say? 'Until you become the expert, stay out of the way.'"

"Branded with my own words! Thomas, how could you?" He smiled and nodded to Savannah. "All right, Miss Stewart. You win, thanks to this rascal. I bow to your skill and Thomas's art of persuasion. The artist makes the final decision."

The two friends left her to her work, which was now, finally, satisfying to her. Working quickly, she mixed a soft grey color from white, the mahogany she had used previously, and a touch of blue-green, then added it to the temples of George Wythe's hairline. A few strokes at the crown. Some faint ones in his eyebrows. Then she got up, walked across the room, and viewed the painting from a distance and from several angles.

Yes, absolutely satisfying.

A rustle of silk warned Savannah that her studio was once again being invaded. She sighed. Perhaps four hours of painting was enough for one day.

As she dipped her brushes in turpentine to loosen the oil paints she had carefully mixed that morning, a slender woman whisked her way into the room. She ignored Savannah and frowned at the still-unfinished portrait.

"What is taking you so long, Miss Stewart? I have been waiting three days for you to begin to work on my portrait."

Three days was six weeks too short, Savannah decided.

Though Lady Ann Skipwith's husband was a friend of George Wythe and Thomas Jefferson, his wife had the tongue and arrogance of a shrew; Savannah didn't know how anyone in the household put up with her flares of temper and bad manners.

As hired help, Savannah wasn't due many courtesies from Lady Ann. According to Lady Ann.

But, then, no one in the house got much more than Savannah did.

Why, Savannah wondered, were some women with the same background and from the same family—like Lady Ann's sister, Jean—so amiable, while another was an uncommon harridan?

Yet it was Lady Ann who wanted a Stewart portrait, and wouldn't settle for the miniatures Savannah was doing for the other members and guests of the Wythe household.

Sixteen adults and nine children were in residence at that time, when the House of Burgesses was in session. All were there to take one side or the other in the debates concerning the "great troubles," as Benjamin Franklin called the resistance to the never-ending tariffs and taxes. And Savannah had witnessed Wythe, Jefferson, Patrick Henry, and James Madison meeting nights to compose a proposal for the next session, which would have Virginia join with Massachusetts and other colonies to oppose the new taxes — with force, if necessary.

From all she'd seen and heard, the world was changing, and Savannah had to put up with a willful woman whose only concern was her new pair of high-heeled red evening slippers with buckles of brilliants.

"You could sketch me now," Lady Ann said. "Then we could begin the sittings on the morrow."

"Your husband has not yet supplied your canvas, Lady Ann."

If poppies could instantaneously change from pink to red, as Lady Ann's cheeks had just done, they'd be glorious flowers, Savannah decided. But with those white specks of fury mottling her chin and forehead, Lady Ann looked more like a daylily. And about as common.

"You wait right here," Lady Ann said imperiously. "I will have the correct canvas in a few moments."

"I will wait here until the brushes are clean. After that, you may find me in the dining room, having the lunch I missed because I was working."

George Wythe's was a large, beautifully proportioned house, with thick brick walls, spacious rooms, several wings, individual work houses and offices, and a springhouse and freestanding kitchen. Its size and sturdiness usually served to separate even the most feuding of family members. But it could not muffle the shrieks of Lady Ann when she confronted her husband, Sir Peyton Skipwith, a wealthy planter from Mecklenberg County.

The result: Sir Peyton immediately sent his servant to Ridgewell's stores. A half hour later, Lady Ann swooped into the dining room with a small brown-skinned servant behind her. The poor lad struggled to keep upright a canvas that could cover the north end of Christ Church.

Savannah swallowed the last of her cold venison and pork pasty and gasped, "My God! It's twice as big as anything I've ever done!"

"It will just fit the new ballroom at my plantation house. Life-sized, of course."

Savannah rose to give the boy a hand. They stood the canvas next to Lady Ann. It towered two feet over her head and was at least three feet wider than Ann.

"Are you planning to stretch and gain weight?" Savannah asked.

"Don't be impertinent! I'm paying what you asked . . . and it's a fortune at that."

Triple it, and it wouldn't be enough.

But Savannah had agreed—long before she had come to know Lady Ann's temper—to do the portrait

. . . and at a fair price. She had no choice but to get on with it.

"Change into the dress and shawl and shoes you want to have in the portrait. Have your maidservant fix your hair. Come down to the studio in one hour and we will begin."

"It takes me longer than that to put on my morning dress!"

"It's three o'clock, Lady Ann. If it takes you more than an hour, we will have to postpone it until the morrow."

"Very well, then. On the morrow. Eleven o'clock."

"Ten o'clock, Lady Ann. I do not intend to miss lunch again."

"Neither do I, Miss Stewart. We'll have it served in your studio."

"That won't do."

"I beg your pardon? Are you questioning my edicts?"

"Why, I wouldn't think of doing such a thing. But I must warn you. . . . Some of the paints are poisonous, my lady. If you wish to chance them tainting your food, who am I to question?"

"All right! Ten o'clock. We will break for lunch at the noon hour, then work from two until four."

Agony.

If anyone were to commission her again, Savannah decided she'd give them an extensive interview, accompanied by a week in their home. Only then would she make up her mind whether to accept the commission or not.

From the first moment, Lady Ann complained

about the position Savannah wished her to assume. Savannah suggested she sit for the portrait. But Ann wanted the full force of her presence to grace the wall at her home. Sitting would diminish it, she believed. So, stand she would!

Yet, after five minutes, she moaned and groaned that her feet were killing her. Gritting her teeth and smiling when she wanted to scream, Savannah suggested Ann wear simple slippers. But Ann showed such a burst of haughty pique that Savannah decided she could grow a thousand bunions for all she cared.

After an hour, Lady Ann dropped to the floor in a faint. And why not? Her bodice was laced so tightly, she probably hadn't had a real breath of air since her maidservant had struggled to get her into that willowy form. When Ann was revived by liberal applications of smelling salts—these didn't have rock candy in them—she refused to pose for more than fifteen minutes at a time and demanded a half-hour nap between sessions.

Fine. Wonderful. Savannah used the escape from the "Lady's" tongue to finish George Wythe's portrait. In a few days, it would be dry enough to frame and hang.

George had hinted that all the females in the house were planning some "diversion" to christen the new portrait and put it in a place of honor in the drawing room. What diversion it could be was a secret. Savannah had but to enter a room where the women were gathered and the conversation halted immediately. Soon, groups trooped over to the inn and gathered on the green, whispering, whispering, always whispering.

Then one day Savannah's good velvet gown disappeared from the peg in her wardrobe and no one in the house would admit to seeing it.

Harridans. Conspiracies. Mysteries. Her days were filled with them.

She would have lost her mind while painting the preliminaries of Lady Ann's portrait. But she was saved when, because of her reputation for the clarity of speech she had used in her books, she had been singled out by three publishers to write short articles and sketch some of the debates in the House of Burgesses. Now, she could take time at night to finish the painting and only rarely had to see or talk to the good Lady Ann.

During the day she occupied her time with painting miniatures of children and wives of the merchants, magistrates and councilors, and sitting in a corner of the House of Burgesses, watching the debates, penning the members' speeches during various heated exchanges, then quickly working up a charcoal sketch of the assembly.

Already six of her articles and sketches had been published in various newspapers. For some reason, she favored those men loyal to the King and Parliament. Their speeches were either short and vociferous or long and windy, so she could condense them and still get the essence of the point. And they were easier to sketch quickly because they postured more than their adversaries.

Also, there was something amusing about the confrontation between bewigged planters and royal commissioners and the more sedate merchants and "gentleman farmers." Her interest was piqued more than she thought it would be and she listened carefully to the full, long days of speeches.

The Tories, as those loyal to George III liked to be called, were hot-tempered. The Rebels, especially that tall planter from the shores of the Potomac in northern Virginia, were quieter, more likely to debate the issues with logic and—oh, wouldn't Thomas Paine love this!—common sense.

She didn't know if she agreed with everything these young men said, but she liked the way they said what they did.

And liking them, she had to be very careful not to focus in on just the Rebel leaders' ideas and portrayals. Both sides in this important issue deserved equal treatment.

She thought she had achieved it until her latest article and accompanying illustration brought a missive from the Royal Governor.

"My word, Miss Stewart," Lady Ann trilled, "you are honored!"

"I'm not sure it's an honor, my lady. It's a summons. I'm to appear in his office tomorrow at precisely eight o'clock to discuss my articles."

"Oh, dear! Well . . . I did warn you that you should avoid occasions which put your femininity in a bad light. You are, after all, the only woman allowed in the chamber. Hardly something a real lady would do!"

As she flounced out of the room, Savannah stuck

out her tongue at the ramrod-stiff back. If this were any indication of a real lady, Savannah would forever choose to be "hired help."

She blushed when a deep, throaty chuckle sounded from behind her.

"Oh, no," she groaned. "You saw that?"

"I did, indeed. It is fortunate for you, Miss Stewart, that there isn't another artist sitting in the corner to catch that lovely tongue wagging at the back of one of King George's loyal subjects."

Turning, Savannah saw the handsome face of her favorite Virginian. A grin split his features and brightened her day.

"Mister Henry! How nice to see you! Or is it?"

Patrick Henry took Savannah's hand, bowed over it, and brought it to his lips. "Now, Miss Stewart . . . you can hardly blame me for your royal summons. I was only one of a clear majority who approved your access to the chamber."

"You were one of three who plied the other members with spiced ale and sweetmeats until four o'clock in the morning! Until they were so drunk and their heads pounded abominably the next day. Fie, sir! They didn't know what they were being asked to approve."

"Caught, by God! And by one of the loveliest women in Williamsburg."

"With paint-besmirched apron and turpentine for fragrance, there is not much to admire in this woman."

Patrick sat and contemplated Savannah's face until he had her so confused and flummoxed that she dropped her head and stared into her lap.

"Don't do that."

"Ah, then some man *has* admired you in much the same way. I wondered."

"Sir, remember the problems and trepidations which plague your lady wife, Sarah. It is not seemly for a man who is not free to . . . to do what you are doing."

"Not seemly, no. But human."

"Ah, yes. Sometimes our humanity gets the better of us."

"God, I hope not! I hope it *gives* the better of us."

"You are, sir, more eloquent than I."

"Nay, Miss Stewart. You have eloquence in writing and in your drawing. You beggar me and most of my colleagues." He picked up the sketch she was finishing with quill and ink and studied it silently. "Why did you center Mister Washington? He usually sits to the side."

"He did yesterday, too. But there is something about him . . . his height . . . his quiet demeanor . . . his lack of ambition . . . It's hard to put into words. All I know is that I feel he belongs in the middle, even though he rarely engages himself in the debates."

"If only he would . . ."

"He carries the decisive votes, doesn't he?"

Patrick sighed. "I fear he does."

"And you're not sure which way he'll fall?"

"He is a man who has been rejected and failed many times in his young life. I'm not sure he would take another chance. . . ."

"But you need him?"

"Yes." Patrick gave a short laugh and swiped his hand over his neatly groomed hair. "We are not so strong that we don't need *every* important man in Virginia."

"Are you so sure you are right, Mister Henry?"

"Call me Patrick."

"I think not, sir. There might be talk."

"There is always talk, Savannah. Especially when a young politician admires a beautiful young woman."

Savannah sat quietly, exchanging glances that were long missives, knowing all she needed to about what would happen if she encouraged Patrick by even a blush.

Carefully, using every acting skill her background had prepared her for, she sought the center of Mr. Henry's spirit and quietly asked, "Do you, then, take chances with your cause?"

He took in a breath and let it out slowly. The minutes ticked by before he broke his intense gaze. "Ah . . . and you said you were not eloquent with words! Fie, *Miss* Stewart! You debate better than most of the Burgesses!" Patrick touched her hand once, his fingers lingering to feather across the knuckles. Then he snatched them back and picked up the sketch. "Damn! If it had been four years ago . . ."

"We would have been worlds apart, Mister Henry."

His knuckles were white as he gripped the sketch and studied it closely. "Thomas Fairfax was the major speaker yesterday."

"Yes."

"There is a great difference between how you've depicted him and how you've depicted Mister Washington."

"But of course! Mister Fairfax always dresses in the height of fashion. Great yards of lace at throat and wrists. Heavily embroidered waistcoats. Gold or silver braid. Huge buckles on his shoes. Two watch fobs, sir! Two! Does not one watch tell the correct time? Or can it be that one is set for London time and one for our time?"

Patrick threw back his head and laughed. "He is a fop, you think?"

"Oh, no, sir! He is a hereditary baron, a loyalist! And he believes his station in life demands that he always . . . always reflect his King and the standards of the British nation. I think he is a good representation of that kind of gentleman. I think, too, that he is a good man."

"Yes, he is a good man. Many of the loyalists are good men." He stabbed his finger at the figure of George Washington. "And he is also a good man."

"But poorer than Fairfax?"

"My God, no! At least, not here in Virginia. One third of his estate borders on the Fairfax holdings. He and Fairfax are best friends. Sally Fairfax is a frequent visitor and a great admirer of all George has done with his plantation. No, Miss Stewart, George Washington is not the impoverished next-door neighbor who needs the Fairfax's largesse. I think, given the circumstances, that George could probably buy up all of Fairfax's American holdings and still have enough to support his plantation."

"Then why does he dress so simply?"

"He is a simple man."

"With simple needs?"

"Exactly."

"Are his needs simpler than yours?"

Patrick assessed Savannah. "What does that speculative tone mean, Miss Stewart? What are you suggesting?"

"That artists, sir, are trained to see what other people miss. And what you and your followers have missed is that Mister Fairfax mirrors his beliefs. And Mister Washington, his. Lace and ruffles are naught but embellishments, Mister Henry. They flaunt riches in the face of the common man. They will not win advocates to the Royal cause. And they place their wearers outside the stream of the majority of Americans."

She picked up her quill, dipped it into the ink, and sketched in the elaborate wig of a good friend of the Royal Governor. "Wigs, Mister Henry, are another affectation. Mister Washington doesn't wear one. You don't wear one. Mister Jefferson seems to have lost his, since he always borrows one from Mr. Wythe when they have an audience with the governor." A stroke of the quill added another fillip and curl. "Was it Mister Shakespeare that said . . . yes, in Polonius's speech to his son, Laertes . . . 'Clothes doth make the man.' American or British. Of course, Shakespeare put those words in the mouth of a foolish old man; but that's exactly the point. Men like Mister Fairfax believe their fashions show that they are one step closer to God. Mister Shakespeare would have it that naught but what a man *does*, not what he wears, makes the man. But try telling that to the ordinary freeman. He sees the velvets and silks, knows that until recently he could not by law wear them. Hence, there is a relationship between clothes and law which is, to him, inedible."

"Good Lord! I do believe you have seen something which has eluded us enlightened legislators." He kissed the crown of Savannah's head. "I thank you, Miss Stewart."

"You are welcome, Mister Henry. But don't do that again. I will not be compromised by you or by anyone."

"I stand corrected. And I promise . . . only handshakes from now on."

Savannah dipped the quill back into the ink and began putting a border on the sketch. It was a simple border, but she couldn't help putting a few flourishes at the corners.

Patrick laughed. "Embellishments, Miss Stewart?"

"If I don't do it, the publishers will have climbing vines or wood nymphs. Or worse, a border as thick and as black as an obituary notice."

"Perhaps a star or two . . . right there?" Patrick offered.

"Pah! Everyone thinks he's an artist!"

Savannah added the last of the border strokes, a simple crosshatch design that resembled a picture frame, and wiped off her pen. "Finished."

"I like it."

"Good. Let's hope Randolph Wilson likes this and the article that goes with it. They're for his edition tomorrow."

Patrick escorted her out of the studio and down to the parlor, where Wythe and Jefferson were in whispered conversation. They broke off when Savannah and Patrick came in together.

Savannah sighed. "First the women, now the men. I'm beginning to feel like a pariah. I'll leave you gentlemen to your discussion."

"No," George Wythe said. "Stay, Savannah."

He looked embarrassed and Savannah said with a laugh, "It seems I'm the general topic of conversation around here lately. What sin have I committed now?"

"Good heavens, it's not that!"

"What George means," Jefferson said, "is that we have a favor to ask of you."

"If I can do you a favor, gentlemen, I would do it gladly."

"We would like you to tell us what the governor has to say to you." George stood and paced. "There! I know it isn't gentlemanly to ask you to repeat a private conversation; but since that accursed Boston Tea Party . . . well, we are getting desperate, my dear."

Savannah looked at the anxious faces in front of her. "You are asking much, sirs. Perhaps the governor will ask me to keep our conversation private. Whose wishes do I respect? And how do I reconcile my final decision?"

"That is for you to determine, Savannah," Thomas Jefferson said. He came and took Savannah's hands in his. "I like you, Miss Stewart. I admire your intelligence, your indomitable spirit, your fairness, your ability to hold your tongue. . . ."

Patrick snorted, and Savannah remembered with

97

chagrin that wagging tongue at Lady Ann's back. She glared at him but he refused to stop grinning.

Thomas looked confused, until Savannah said, "Pay no attention to Mister Henry. Methinks he sees things that are not there."

"Hah!" Thomas laughed. "Methinks he likes to make mischief—even when he should be more sobersided." His warning to Patrick finished, he continued, "Miss Stewart, you have heard the debates concerning what we in Virginia should do to support the brave men in Boston. You know that we will be offering a bill to form the first Virginia Committee of Correspondence. We need to know what the governor will do about it. If he tells you anything . . . any hint at all . . . we would be most obliged to know what that might be."

"I repeat, it is an awkward position I will be in on the morrow."

George Wythe sighed. "We know that, my dear. And we are very sorry that we have to ask it of you. But the times are making many of us do what we would never have thought of doing ten years ago. I pray to God that what we have asked of you and what you decide to do will not come back to haunt any of us later."

Chapter Seven

"A portrait, my lord?"

"Only a miniature, Miss Stewart. Well . . . really, *two* miniatures."

John Murray, the Earl of Dunsmore and the Royal Governor, straightened the lace at his cuffs, stood, and pulled down on his vest. Savannah almost sighed, but held her tongue and smiled sweetly. Pulling down his vest could not hide the paunch that strained at his buttons. Why did men—and women— think tighter clothes disguised the plumpness of their aging bodies? Soft folds of material, with enough room to breathe and not encase the flesh like a sausage, were far preferable. They actually made the person appear more youthful because they didn't constrict breath or movement.

But it wasn't fashionable. And for most of the inhabitants in this capital city, fashion was all.

"Will this commission be for your wife?"

The governor coughed and patted his mouth with

his lace handkerchief. "Shall we say . . . for a *special friend*, Miss Stewart?"

"Oh! Oh, my!"

"Good Lord, Miss Stewart! There are hundreds of your precious ovals hanging from ribbons or sitting on deal tables. Surely one more would not be amiss. Or by mentioning my special friend, am I asking too much?"

He wiped his sweating brow but the perspiration still poured, and Savannah knew he did not like to make the request. His *special friend* must be a very special woman, indeed!

"No, you are not asking too much. But I will, of necessity, have to have access to the lady. I can hardly sketch and paint her without seeing her."

"That will be arranged. Of course, you may have to give up some of your time in the chamber."

"Sir, now you do ask too much. Would it not be better for me to simply lunch with the lady? It would not take long for me to sketch her. I could paint the miniatures in private and deliver them to you myself."

The Earl of Dunsmore looked confused. "Ah, no . . . you misunderstand. One miniature is for her, of me. One is for me, of her."

Savannah removed her small sketchbook from her skirt pocket, where she always kept it in case she saw a particularly entrancing scene and wished to make a quick rendition of it. "If you wish, I could do yours now. It will take but five minutes."

"Well . . . yes, of course." He struck a pose by the fireplace but it seemed not to suit, because he rounded his desk and stood behind it.

"I do not sketch the whole person for these miniatures, sir. Simply sit, and I'll get your face and shoulders."

"Ah, yes, of course."

As she plied rock-hard charcoal to paper, Savannah remembered her mission for George Wythe. She could so easily compromise herself that she hesitated. But there was something that nagged at her, an attitude of the governor that was too familiar.

An ache so deep struck her with such force that she had to suck in her breath to make it go away. The familiar attitude of the Montgomerys. The attitude of David.

Let me love you tonight . . .

Special friends.

Lace and ribbons. Satins and silks. Royal commissions. Royal governors. Royal pains in the neck.

She was hired help and could know secrets of the highest authority in this colony, secrets that no one else dared to whisper.

She was safe, because hired help never forgot their place.

But, thank God, in America, she and her family had no *Place* — and every place.

Servants of Richard Montgomery, they had been sent by him and King George to establish the silk farms the gentry wanted so much, for the fabric they favored. The Stewarts had marked out a large plantation for the Marquess, planted mulberry trees, coddled the silkworm cases, built crude huts for their families and sturdier outbuildings, warehouses, and harvesting shacks, then waited patiently and expectantly to harvest the crop of long, delicate, yet durable strands of silk. Every Stewart worked the farm, toiling until sweat poured from the men's bodies and they were bitten by unfamiliar insects, causing welts to pockmark their skin. The women—Savannah's mother and grandmother and aunts—readied spindles, grubbed out gardens, foraged for game and fish, wild fruits and nuts. They spun linen and salted meats to last the winter. They petitioned for chickens and rabbits and hogs, which never came. They begged for clothing, which—when it did come—was too expensive for their paltry allowance. They birthed babies, traded with Indians for scarce medicinals, yet still saw their children die while they waited to spin the precious silk onto spindles. Silk, which would then be sent back to England to be woven and manufactured into shawls, draperies, dresses, and other gentry niceties—things the Stewarts would never put on their backs because they would never be paid enough to afford them.

For ten years this family of hers had struggled, sometimes going hungry because their annual allowance from King and marquess was not enough to sustain the silk-growing process *and* fill the bellies of the large Stewart clan.

For ten years they were defeated by inhospitable climate, unproductive soil, and the fact that someone had neglected to realize that it took mulberry trees more than seven years to produce a crop. Meanwhile, having nothing to eat, the silkworms died. And in place of the chickens, which they needed more, silkworm cases arrived by the score. And the struggle began again, because of the tenacious stupidity of the British royalty, who would wrest from a land what it could not give.

Through it all, the only things the Stewarts sent back to England of any worth were letters and hundreds of watercolor and pen and ink sketches, each in its own way describing their new home and the lands to the north. Luckily, a good friend showed them to a struggling publisher, Sean Lanning. He compiled the sketches into a book he titled *A Colonial Farmer's Sketchbook Describing the Terrifying and Wondrous Natural Life of the Carolinas and the New Colony of Georgia.*

When it was brought out it was a hit at court, where everyone was hungry for news about and pictures of the wilderness they believed the colonies to be. Sean Lanning clamored for more sketches and more travel tidbits.

And the Stewarts obliged them. Why not? Their offhand notes and art put pence in their pockets! For years the whole clan journeyed through the wilderness of the southern American colonies, using their pens, paints, and printed words to detail the ordinary and extraordinary life they found around them—human, bird, animal, or plant.

Savannah remembered the anger of Richard Montgomery at the failure of the silk farm, and his fury at the audacity the Stewarts had shown by supporting themselves—he called it flaunting themselves—without his permission or largesse.

Though she could not have been more than five, Savannah recalled the letter from the marquess that had sent tremors of anger through the house. She remembered being dragged out of her bed one morning by a red-coated guard and pushed to the ground. Her father had picked her up, dusted her off, and carried her at the front of the procession when the Stewarts proudly walked away from the Montgomery lands. Lorton House now stood where the Stewarts had once buried fourteen children from marsh fever.

Months ago, she had fled from Lorton House.

Her father and her family had walked proudly.

The failure of the silk farm was not their failure. Nurtured by necessity, they had used their wits and their talents to forge a new identity for themselves. Former Montgomery overseers had become the first American family dynasty to be based on art and literature. For the Stewarts, it was poesy, paint, or perish.

They triumphed.

Within a week, they purchased the land on which Glassleigh now stood. And by 1770, a Stewart monograph or travel book sat on deal tables in most taverns in the colonies and in England, beside Shakespeare and the Bible. Stewart sketches or paintings hung in the keeping rooms or parlors of every notable family from Savannah to Boston. Miniatures, like the one she was now sketching, graced the necks of Abigail Adams, Sally Fairfax, and Mary Custis, or sat at an honored place beside the bed or on the fireplace mantel in the homes of Jefferson, Rolfe, Mason, and the Carrolls of Carrollton.

So much for *Place!* So much for hired help!

Without making a commitment to the cause, she had made her decision.

Or, it had been made for her . . . years ago, when that redcoat had torn her from her bed.

She smiled sweetly at the governor and sketched the outline of his wig. "Perhaps I should make several of these, my lord? For your wife, your daughters?"

"Harrumph. Yes . . . well, good thought, Miss Stewart. Yes, several. Ah, seven I think will do."

"Seven it is, then, sire." She added fluffy lines to simulate the lace cascading from his neck. "Do not scowl, sire. Your face is too strong for aught but a smile."

"If I scowl, it is because of these damnable debates. New bills to usurp the authority of the Crown. Committees of Correspondence? Bah! I'll show these traitors what happens when they sport with their King. . . . I could dissolve the whole stinking fish barrel of them in a trice, and where would they be then? Corresponding with air, with shadows!"

"There is much unrest, I fear. The women in Williamsburg have been nervous of late."

"What do women know of politics?" He studied her carefully. "What do *you* know of politics, Miss Stewart? You are much on the floor of the House, so you must have picked up the innuendos of the place."

"I, sire? I am but a describer of scenes. I am too busy taking accurate notes. And I have to sketch so quickly that I have not the time to pay attention to what the words mean." Savannah looked up and smiled, knowing she had given her best to the governor, who puffed out his chest and for the first time creased his cheeks with uplifted mouth. "Besides, sire," she said, "it is up to you, your councilors, and your good burgesses to work for the benefit of all, including us women."

"So true. So true, my dear." He sighed. "How I wish all goodwives saw it as you do."

So that was why he had a special friend. The governor's wife had brains in that curled and beribboned head of hers! She probably plied him with questions, as Mistress Wythe did George. But Savannah could not see this man sitting patiently holding his wife's hand the way George Wythe did. Nor could she see him getting any pleasure from explaining the conditions in the chambers to a woman.

No, he probably went right from chambers to his special friend, had a "pleasant" evening, returned to a cold supper, then went to bed in a separate room from his wife. The Royal Governor's Palace was aptly named. The manor was so huge that intrigues would be as easily managed there as at the King's palaces in England.

Savannah put a final stroke to indicate John Murray's smile, then announced, "Finished." She closed the sketchbook and pocketed it. "At least this step is. When shall I meet your special friend, sire?"

"Nine on the morrow. I want it completed before my ball, Miss Stewart."

"Ball, my lord?"

"Have you not heard? On the morrow, two weeks." He held out his hand and escorted her to the door. "You will be my honored guest. I will send my coach for you."

"But it's merely a few paces from George Wythe's house! I could easily walk, as I did this day."

"Nonsense. You will have fancy dress and high-heeled slippers. You do not wish to turn that pretty ankle of yours, do you?"

High-heeled slippers? What a laugh. She was hired help, wasn't she? Hardly Lady Ann's league. Savannah still preferred boots and sturdy leather shoes, and she intended not to deviate from comfort.

That afternoon, she slipped a note to George Wythe, warning him that the House of Burgesses was in danger. For the next week, she and the others waited for the governor's move. It came immediately upon the passage of the bill to institute a provisional Committee of Correspondence. The governor dissolved the legislature and appointed a council of his own. The members refused to disperse, meeting instead at the venerable and popular gathering place for all Williamsburg residents: The Raleigh Tavern.

Still, everyone—Rebel and Tory alike—readied themselves for the grand ball the following Friday evening.

The capital filled with guests, until every home and inn was overflowing. Members of other Committees of Correspondence came to meet with those who had sided with them in their cause. Tory sympathizers—merchants, politicians, military leaders, and gentlemen planters—came to offer support to the royal governor. Carriages and coaches and phaetons crowded the small streets. Shops were so busy that they made enough money that week to last the whole next year. Tailors and dressmakers ran from house to house, taking in and letting out ball gowns, vests, and waistcoats. Every cook had helpers, every helper had sore arms and aching backs. Soon, there were no more ducks to dress, no more crabs to steam, no more hogs to slaughter.

Savannah loved the excitement. She relished the crowd scenes, making some of her most important large watercolor paintings right there on the spot. Like the shopkeepers, her money bag filled quickly; she sent some specie home to help her family with her younger brother and sister's school bills.

And she finished up the portrait of the governor's special friend.

Abigail Drummond was an actress in one of the British touring companies that came to Williamsburg before going on to the other major southern cities. As she told it, Abigail had taken one look at the lavish surroundings, seen the gleam in the eye of John, the Earl of Dunsmore, and decided the harsh life of the touring company wasn't for her.

To keep up appearances — and to keep tongues from wagging about where she got her spending money — she had returned to her old trade in Wales: midwifery. And she had prospered enough at midwifery that she soon wasn't dependent solely on John's allowance for her favors.

She was an attractive woman, hardened by her years before the footcandles but still able to turn a man's head when she walked by. Whatever time of day, whenever Savannah saw her, Abigail's blond hair was always carefully coiffed; her wigs, high and elaborate; her silk, satin, or lace gowns, never soiled; her slippers, delicate or fancily embroidered. She had four Negro slaves and a shiny mustard-colored phaeton, with a matched pair of coal-black geldings. Her face was delicate, with a widow's peak at the crown and a dimpled chin at the bottom. Flawless skin, big green eyes, and carefully applied salves and rouges added intrigue and mystery where there might have been more beauty with simplicity.

During the first sitting, she refused to discuss anything but the unrest and the tension she felt she was under, and Savannah wondered if the governor had requested that Abigail draw her out to see if she actually knew little about politics or was pretending.

Savannah wasn't to be drawn out, though. She preferred, she said, "to sketch in leisurely fashion, without tensions to mar my model's beauty."

But Abigail prattled on about meeting Peggy Shippen—Lieutenant Benedict Arnold's sweetheart—and Sally Fairfax—wife of the Sixth Baron of Cameron, who had maternal estates next to that scalawag, George Washington—and how she had been called on to attend births from Baltimore to Charleston.

"In fact," Abigail said, "I've almost decided to flee this madhouse of Williamsburg. It is getting so shabby of late, you know. And there is talk of moving the capital further inland. That would not suit me. I wish to live as I do, with enough slaves to tend to my needs. I cannot do that in a town controlled by these damnable rebels. I must be in company with the gentry." She patted her hair and smiled—briefly. "I have royal blood in my veins, you know. That is why I fit in so well with the British agents. So, when Williamsburg crumbles—or before—I will find another situation and set up my practice there."

"Midwifery?" Savannah asked sweetly, though she wished she could taint the syllable with malice.

"Of course! What else?"

What else, indeed!

Ah, Savannah thought later, she, too, was tired of Williamsburg. She had seen enough to know she didn't like the subterfuges and playacting of its residents. Perhaps, after all, she should find another "situation."

After the Royal Governor's Ball, of course. But before that great day, Savannah wakened to hear giggles and muffled noises outside the door to the guest room, which also housed her studio. The giggles subsided, along with a furtive shuffling down the hall, then burst out into great laughter, which floated up from the great staircase. The deep contralto of George Wythe's second wife, Elizabeth, was counterbalanced by the high opera of Lady Ann.

Now, why would two women who had absolutely nothing in common be sharing laughter? And what did it have to do with Savannah?

That it did, she had no doubt, since it had begun at her own door. Hmmm. Savannah slipped out of the high four-poster, pulled on a quilted robe, and padded across the room. She pulled open the door, looked up the corridor and down, but saw no one lingering. She was about to close it again, when her toe brushed up against something that rustled. She looked down. A sheet had been spread on the floor and there, laid out neatly from neckline to hem, was the most beautiful ball gown Savannah had ever seen.

It was blue-green in color. Not cobalt or grass-green, but turquoise, like the gemstone; more green than blue. No! In spots it was more blue than green. Watered, that was what it was called, she thought. Dash it! For an artist, she was having too much difficulty describing the stupid, wonderfully marvelous thing.

Savannah picked it up and carried it carefully to the large standing mirror, held it up, and examined it. The color matched her eyes, as if it had been painted on! Someone had taken great pains . . .

"Do you like it?" Ann Skipwith asked.

Savannah looked up to find seven of the females in the house crowded just inside the door. She smiled, then laughed; and they joined her.

"How did you ever—?"

Elizabeth Wythe snapped her fingers and a maid brought in Savannah's good velvet dress, the one that had disappeared weeks ago. "I hope you don't mind. We copied the size from this dress. We all wanted you to have something new for George's entertainment tonight."

"What entertainment?" Savannah sought out one pair of sparkling eyes after the other, but none gave any indication of what was being planned. "Secrets! How do seven women manage to keep so many secrets?"

Lady Ann shook her finger at Savannah. "Seven women and their husbands, children, servants . . ."

"And lovers!" her sister Jean supplied.

Ann's body stiffened and she bit her lip. Her eyes locked with Savannah's, and for the first time Savannah had some notion about what terrors drove this lady. Ann's eyes dropped quickly in embarrassment and Savannah whirled about, giving Ann time to once again paste on her rock-hard facade.

Obviously, Jean didn't notice, because she blithely sang on, "A whole household . . . and you had no hint?"

"None," Savannah admitted.

She held the sleeves of the gown out and whirled round once more, loving the way the skirt swirled, imagining what it would be like to curtsy so it puddled on the floor, or dipped and swayed in the minuet so it made that delightful *swish, swish* sound.

"Thank you. All of you. The gown is truly beautiful."

"The gown is *you*, dear," Elizabeth Wythe said.

If it was, then she was fit to be presented at court.

What the women had given her was the latest fashion—or as close to it as the dressmakers of Williamsburg could get.

At the top, three layers of tiny, fine Valenciennes bobbin lace lay under a creamy white satin trim on the neckline, which started off square, then dipped into a double curve resembling the top of a valentine heart. A chain of crystal drops and turquoise brilliants hung over the lace. Here and there, the chain was caught up in loops by delicate rosettes of seed pearls, each rosette centered by an irregularly shaped single turquoise. The rest of the gown was plain. The sleeves were puffed at the top and belled out at the elbow. Gathers at the sides and in the back gave fullness to the skirt, but it dropped down in front in a straight piece that allowed the eye to travel up without pause to the fabulous neckline. Even the stomacher had been craftily sewn to blend into, instead of overpower, the richness of the specially dyed silk.

Silk.

She was to wear silk instead of spin it.

"When is this entertainment to be given?" she asked.

Seven voices, one very faint, chorused, "Tonight!"

The houseman had opened and closed the front door so often that Savannah was sure everyone in Williamsburg had filed into the house. Sitting alone in her room — where Elizabeth had ordered her to remain until she was called down — was damnable. She felt lonely. Music wafted up to her and she found her feet tapping to the fiddles, harpsichord, and George Wythe's new pianoforte.

Thus, she didn't hear the tap on her door until it became a loud knock. She rushed to open it and was surprised to find Lady Ann on the other side, a small traveling case in one hand.

"May I come in?" Ann asked.

Savannah was so surprised Ann hadn't merely barged in that she stood there for a moment. "Oh! Oh, of course. Please, do."

Once inside, Ann assessed Savannah from head to toe. "I thought so." She poked her head out the door and waved in her maid. "Really, Savannah, you must get a maidservant. You simply do not know how to fix your hair properly. Although—" She walked all around Savannah and stopped in front, cocking her head to one side. "Although, I must say, the simple upswept style does suit you. Perhaps only a few tiny whorls at her ears, Clara."

"Yes, my lady."

Clara bore down on Savannah with a piece of iron, which looked positively lethal with its glowing ends.

Savannah backed up.

Ann took Savannah by the shoulders, turned her around, and pushed until she had Savannah settled to her satisfaction on a slipper chair. "Do not move. The iron is hot."

Savannah believed her. She could feel the iron's breath. Dragon's breath. And her hair was to be its victim! As Clara picked the first few strands out of her carefully piled coiffure, Savannah closed her eyes.

Clara tugged. Savannah cried, "Ouch!"

"Pain for beauty, Savannah. That's the curse of being women."

"The curse of being women? It's the curse women do to themselves!"

"But of course. How else can we catch . . . and keep . . . a man?"

"Sometimes," Savannah said softly, "the man might not be worth the pain."

"The man is always worth the pain, Savannah. Always." Ann Skipwith touched a finger to Savannah's chin. "Open your eyes, dear." She tilted Savannah's head to the right, up, down, and back again. Smiling, she said, "Yes, Clara. Exactly right for that dress." She waved her maid away.

When the door closed, Lady Ann drew up the matching slipper chair and popped open her traveling case. From it she took a small tapestry box, which she placed in Savannah's lap.

"A special gift, for being so patient when I was—" Ann gulped, "when I was abominable."

"No."

"Yes." Her eyes glistened with unshed tears. "There are reasons. . . ."

"Lady Ann, you don't have to tell me."

"I shan't tell you, Savannah. I shall never tell anyone." A small tremor began at her waist and continued up her spine, until she held her head high to stop it. She closed Savannah's hands over the box. "But I want you to have this. I chose it as soon as the embroiderer finished the rosettes. Please, open and accept it."

When open, the box revealed an exquisite pair of seed pearl and turquoise earrings. They were shaped like the rosettes on the dress but were a quarter their size.

"Your ears have been pierced to wear them?"

"Yes," Savannah said. "Oh, Lady Ann . . ."

"That's not all. . . ."

Ann dug into the traveling case and brought out a delicate fan. It was the exact match to the silk dress. Ann snapped it open to reveal a tracery of white and silver threads, which had been embroidered across the fullest part of the fan into a chain of roses and leaves. And at the bottom of the fan was a braided loop meant to wear over the wrist. From it hung a fall of crystal and turquoise drops.

"I've never seen you with a fan, but this is such a special occasion, I took the liberty. . . . I'm afraid I always take liberties. . . . Never mind . . . I merely thought you wouldn't mind having one for the evening. Flirting with it is complicated, and I really don't have time to teach you."

Ann's hands once more dipped into the traveling case. This time, they emerged with a pair of creamy white low-heeled silk slippers. Tiny crystal beads had been sewn in loops to simulate, but not entirely match, the chain at the neckline of the gown. "I could not see you in higher heels, dear. Your feet are not used to them. But these should not pinch or tire your arch."

Savannah opened her mouth, but no words came. There were no words that would adequately express her feelings.

Lady Ann patted Savannah's hands. "That's all right, Savannah. I surprised myself, too!"

She was gone in a swish of satin.

Savannah sat for some moments, overwhelmed by the generosity of a woman who had been so rude, so often. And it wasn't because of the glance the two had exchanged when Jean had made that stupid remark. It was obvious Ann had been planning this . . . these gifts . . . from the beginning, when the others had gotten together to have the gown made. Weeks, and never a softly spoken word. In that glance and the few words they had just exchanged, Savannah knew she had seen only the surface of a very complicated woman.

Lady Ann's pain sliced through to her core.

How could she, an artist, have been so blind?

She prided herself on seeing beneath any disguise

or facade. But she had not divined even a hint of Lady Ann's distress—a husband who took lovers, most probably.

Savannah sighed, then ran her fingers over the softness of the slippers. She hesitated only a moment before kicking off the black shoes she had on. Even if the slippers didn't fit, because of Ann she'd wear them until her feet bled.

But the slippers fit perfectly. Their softness on the outside was repeated in a puffy, silk-covered layer of down on the inside. The heels felt awkward. Luckily, because she wasn't expected in the drawing room until later, she could take time to adjust to the height without looking the fool.

When she was satisfied and felt comfortable in her new slippers, Savannah sat down at the dressing table and hooked the earrings in her ears. She raised the fan and flicked it a few times, mimicking the gestures she'd observed over the years. She felt awkward but had to admit the fan looked graceful and completed the effect of the gown and jewels.

She stared at herself in a small three-sided mirror that sat on the table. Astonishing what a few curls, a fan, and one set of earrings could do.

Yet, not so astonishing.

Her family had been admonishing her for years to know her correct place in the scheme of things. When she had fled Lorton House that night, her mother had helped her pack her belongings. No recriminations came from any Stewarts' lips. Only quick hugs and kisses and one loving missive from her father.

Niver forget who ye be, goirl! Some may think ye less than they, but ye be a Stewart. From yer survival, we took hope. From yer talent, we survived. In all these colonies, ye be the only female artist. Ye be the only female author. Savannah Stewart, named for the city in which ye be borned, ye be the heart and soul of Georgia Colony. Take pride in it, goirl. There be no many men who ken claim a smidg'n's worth of yer distinction, regardless their titles.

For short periods, she had forgotten.
But the Savannah Stewart who looked back at her from the many-sided mirror would not forget. Not now. Not ever.

Chapter Eight

Finally, the summons to go belowstairs came. George Wythe, himself, escorted Savannah into the crowded drawing room. The women's gowns and men's frock coats were a wash of colors too garish for rainbows, too brilliant for sunsets. So many white wigs bobbing together sent a fine spray of talc into the air, so the aisle that opened up for her looked as if it were wreathed in mist and fog.

And at the end . . . on the wall . . . above the mantel . . . nearly dwarfing the enormous fireplace . . . between two new brass and crystal candle sconces . . . were her portraits of George and Elizabeth, in matching gilded mahogany frames four inches wide. The candlelight played over their features, bringing out the depth and pleasantness of their personalities. They were the best things she had ever done, and the way George had displayed them was an unspoken tribute to her talent—one she wasn't sure she deserved.

"Oh, my! Did I really do that?"

"You really did," George said. "Thank you, my dear. They are all, and more, than I or my good wife dreamed." He turned Savannah around in a semicircle, until she faced the assembly. "My friends, I present the best portraitist in the colonies. Miss Savannah Stewart."

Praises for her work rang in Savannah's ears. The women were effusive, each—if they hadn't already been one of her subjects—requesting, *pleading* to be her next patron. So much adulation and so many choices! Savannah did naught but nod her head and agree to check her schedule, before she was pulled into another circle of men or women. Sally Fairfax won her over with her sweet smile and gentle manner as she explained that she would only be in Williamsburg another week.

"In that case, Sally," Savannah whispered behind her fan, "I will certainly attend you before all others. But *please* do not whisper a word of this. . . ."

Sally laughed. "Say no more, Savannah. It will be our secret."

"Secrets! I've had enough to last me a lifetime!"

"I fear we have not heard the last of them."

"I fear you are right."

Minuets and line reels were the order of the evening, and Savannah lacked no partner. After the seventh dance, she begged off the next gentleman and took to the dining room, where a long table had been set to groaning with bite-sized delicacies. She sampled strong, salty ham, which was cooled by the sweetness of pineapple. Liver, onion, and potato pasties were flaky and hot, glacéed pheasant, cold. Grapes of every color were her favorite and she sampled them all. She accepted a cool silver cup of spiced cider laced with white wine and wandered out onto the back verandah, then farther still, into the candlelit boxwood maze, where she sought a secluded corner far from the noise and bustle of the party.

Savannah was the guest of honor, surrounded by people who liked and admired her; yet she felt a white-hot stab of loneliness that took every ounce of strength to endure.

She missed her family . . . her city . . . Glassleigh . . .

David.

How was that possible? How had it happened so quickly?

He had stolen her heart, made it beat with more life than it was possible to contain, then broken it into a million pieces—and all in less time than most people took to break in a new pair of shoes.

The leaves rustled to Savannah's left and a series of exasperated sighs turned quiet solitude into an invasion.

"Darn, I never could figure out this thing! Savannah, are you out here? George said he thought you might be coming this way."

At least the army was someone with whom she could relax and laugh. "Yes, Sally. Just take two more right-hand turns and you will find me."

More rustling, then an "Oh! Darn! When will George have his paving stones replaced by good, flat grass? These aren't meant for ladies' slippers."

Savannah laughed. "George intended that this be a trysting place. The ladies are supposed to be carried in men's arms through this, you know."

"Trust George." Sally's green skirts preceded the lovely lady. "I've brought my cousin to meet you. I thought you could do her portrait while she's here. Well, she's not actually *my* cousin, but Thomas's distant relative."

"Who has already had her portrait painted by the inestimable Miss Stewart."

Savannah's head jerked up. "Bella!"

The girl rushed forward and hugged Savannah. "How I have missed you!"

"Well, really, Bella," Sally said, "you could have told me you already knew Savannah."

"And spoil the surprise?"

Sally took one look at the delighted sparkle in Bella's and Savannah's eyes, and she laughed gently. "Surprises *are* such fun, aren't they? And, I will leave you two to have your reunion."

She swished round the corner and along through the maze, tripping and muttering oaths as the paving stones gave her more trouble. The two friends giggled, before sitting down on the bench.

"What are you doing here?" Savannah asked.

"I'm on my way to New Haven, to attend Miss Tysdale's Academy. To be, as Grandfather put it, *polished* before my entrance at court."

Oh, no! Poor Honesty. She had finally lost her royal, but—thank goodness—not because of Savannah. "You travel alone?"

"Not exactly," Bella said, and her eyes sparkled. "I travel with the Mason Aldriches, and their sons, Lawrence and Richard."

"Ah, the way you say his name should have your brother breathing fire."

Bella shook her curls and smoothed down her skirt. "I don't have any idea what you mean," she said, her eyes downcast.

That wicked grin of hers belied her actions. Savannah laughed. "Richard, of course. But does the young man know you have him in your sights and ready to be poached?"

"Savannah! Honestly . . ."

"Honestly?"

"Well . . . Oh, posh, Savannah! Can you truly tell from my voice?"

"Absolutely."

"Huh! David must be as observant as a stone. He hasn't suspected a thing."

"No wonder he allowed you to accompany the Aldriches. Had he known, he would have locked the door to Lorton House and thrown away the key."

"There's never been a lock to Lorton House, Savannah. I think David has always hoped you'd come back." Bella frowned. "Why *did* you leave? David would never say."

"Perhaps because he didn't understand that what was there wasn't enough."

"Now *I* don't understand."

"Never mind, Bella. The evening's too wonderful for regrets." She pulled her friend up and tugged her toward the corner of the maze.

Bella shook her head. "Thank you, Savannah; but I think I'll sit here a while."

Because of the gleam in her downcast eyes and the heightened color in her cheeks, Savannah could guess why the young girl wanted to be "alone."

"When I see this wonderful Richard Aldrich on the path and he's confused, how shall I recognize him to tell him the way?"

123

"Fie, Savannah! Can you see right through to a person's soul with those magic artist's eyes?" Bella smiled with that secret smile most young girls have when they're in love. "Blond hair, grey eyes. Embroidered waistcoat and grey breeches."

"Huh! You never were much for details, Bella. Tall? Short? Fat? Lean?"

Bella shut her eyes, then popped them open again. Obviously, Savannah decided, she had this Richard Aldrich's impression stamped on her brain. Her estimation was confirmed when Bella catalogued the rest of her beau's characteristics.

"Thick, arched brows. Deep eye sockets make him look fearsome, but he's really very sweet. Straight nose. Firm mouth — and don't ask me how I know that! Square chin. As tall as David. Lean and muscular."

Savannah waved to Bella and rounded the corner of the maze. Only a few yards beyond and two turns later, she saw the young man of Bella's dreams, and he had definitely become confused by the myriad of twists and turns. She gave him the proper directions and watched to be sure he made the right move.

Amazing what young women found in their first beaus! He was a perfectly ordinary young man when compared to David Montgomery. His face was as Bella had described it. But it was softer than David's, with that telltale roundness of a man only a year or two past his twentieth birthday. Tall, yes. But not as tall as David. Lean, yes. But muscular? Now, *David* had a frame that filled his shirt and coats and breeches. His muscles were so delineated, she could still remember the way they'd expanded and contracted when he walked. And that day of the pirate wedding . . . when he got out of the water and his clothes molded around his form! There was no doubt *he'd* not been indolent. Only someone who used his body could be so well-defined.

Why, this Richard Aldrich! . . . Nothing like David. Nothing.

From the elegant way he was dressed and the modulated tone he'd used, she couldn't see Richard Aldrich braving a new world the way David had had to do, with nothing more than his wits to get him through. Richard, like Bella, was used to the support of his family, and would use it to make a life of comfort for himself, if not of luxury.

She couldn't picture Richard jumping into an unfamiliar roiling sea to rescue a child he had never met and was never likely to see again. She couldn't imagine him bathed in moonlight, a sheen of passion on his face, his hands hunting out hidden freckles, and when they were found . . .

"Bathed in moonlight . . . sheen of passion . . . hidden freckles . . . Damn!"

Tears stung her eyes, and she rounded the next corner to take her away from the entrance, not closer to it. What was wrong with her? Why had seeing Bella and Richard shaken her so much?

Bella's association to David.

David.

Her nemesis. Her magnet. The one man above all the others who made her feel like a woman . . . and act like one. There was no explanation for it. For how it happened or for why it happened. She had been drawn to him from the beginning, as if there were something fated about their coming together. Overseer's daughter and Lord of the Manor. Shakespeare would have made a comedy of it. Instead, it felt more like a tragedy.

From the first day they met, she had baited him . . . over and over and over again. Gongs had gone off in her head, telling her she was pushing him too far, but still she'd rushed right on. Teasing him. Laughing at him. Being self-righteous . . .

. . . Like the day when he brought Bella to Honesty Dunn's school for the first time.

His fawn-colored lightweight wool frock coat was cut simply, with only a touch of a brown soutache trim on the false buttonholes and collarless neck. But his brocade waistcoat was all the fashion, rich with gold and silver threads on a deep chocolate ground. The two top buttons were fastened, the next six left open to show the pristine ruffles of his white lawn shirt, and the last two again buttoned. His fawn-colored wool breeches had brocade buttons below the knee. He wore clocked stockings, with the long arrow-shaped trim from bottom of sole almost to the knee, which denoted the clocking, cleverly embroidered on instead of woven in. Round-toed brown leather shoes with a delicately wrought gold, not brass, buckle completed the outfit.

Ah, if she had not known it before, by his dress he proclaimed himself right off the boat from England — and in a first-class passenger cabin at that.

Honesty Dunn preened, then introduced her teachers one by one. Each bowed or curtsied for the Marquess of Lorton and their new pupil, Lady Arabella Montgomery.

Savannah, however, merely pursed her lips, raised one eyebrow, and held out her hand.

David looked at her, glanced down at her hand, took one step backward, dropped his walking stick, bent to pick it up, and his head—actually, his gritted teeth—collided with her outstretched hand.

"In the colonies, it is customary to shake the hand extended to you, not bite it," Savannah said, deliberately masking the admonishment with a broad smile.

Honesty gasped. The other teachers stifled giggles behind their hands, the maids, behind upraised apron hems.

David Montgomery had the good grace to flush. Not from anger—Savannah could tell that by his sudden blink of confusion and astonishment—but from embarrassment.

She could have stopped there but had gone on, refusing, from the first and all the way to the last, to acknowledge his title and the deference he had expected when he'd walked in the door. Instead, she tucked her arm in David's and tugged him toward the stairs.

"Let me show you and your sister the classrooms and sleeping quarters, Mr. Montgomery. We think they're the best in the colonies."

Giving David his due, he didn't lose stride, but he didn't take her hand, either. He simply let her lead him and Arabella—and the whole damned contingent of teachers—through the succession of classrooms, listened to her chatter, and made no more than polite, noncommittal grunts or *Ah, yes. Of course. That does seem important. Yes, the light does make the room cheery.*

Only when she finished *la grande tour* and they were

descending the back staircase—alone—did he finally voice what must have been niggling at him all along.

"You know my family name, Miss Stewart?"

"Why, of course, David . . . I may call you David, mayn't I? After all, we *are* intimately acquainted, so to speak. I mean, my father was well known by your grandfather, and my grandfather before him. Sixty years, I believe, our families have been connected. So, of course, that makes us old . . . well, acquaintances, doesn't it? So, you may call me Savannah and I'll call you David. Much simpler. And friendlier, no?"

"Savannah? But that's the name—"

"Of the city. Yes! My mother wished to leave the old problems behind, to tie us firmly to this new land. I was the first child born in America. So, she rooted me in my native soil. And the sound of it! Say it, David. Savannah. Go ahead, say it."

"Savannah."

"Yes! Musical, isn't it?"

David—at last—broke into a smile, and Savannah was completely delighted with the effect her charade had on him.

He tasted the name on his tongue. "Savannah . . . Hmm . . . Savannah. Yes, very musical. But I don't recall my grandfather ever mentioning a Savannah. . . . Uh . . . what's the rest of your appellation? Your family name?"

"Why, Stewart, of course!"

She laughed then. Laughed, and fled through the back door with a wave of her hand. Laughed all the way to the carriage stand at the corner. Laughed getting into a hired carriage. Laughed till the tears coursed down her cheeks. Then she stopped laughing with a hiccup, a painful lump in her throat, and a fire that coursed through her body and left her limp and aching.

David, of course, made the connection between his grandfather's Stewart overseer and Savannah Stewart, as she knew he would. But she didn't let down her guard. She could not. The pain of knowing the Montgomerys thought her less than their tailor made her burn with a fierce desire to best David. To tease him. To flaunt herself in his face until he was forced to deal with her as an equal.

She befriended his sister and used her position as teacher to befuddle a man who held more power over her than he knew.

Oh, not political power, nor even social power. Though she — and probably he — had thought it that, at first. No, David's power was that of a man who held the key to a woman's heart in his hand and hadn't yet recognized it.

Fool, her, she thought she could taunt David without giving any part of herself to him. But it wasn't that simple. And it certainly wasn't that easy.

Because David Montgomery was *not* Richard Montgomery.

Because David Montgomery had intelligence, and he soon learned how to conduct himself so he gave no offense to his customers or competitors.

Because David Montgomery had humor, was personable, did not treat her as a servant, smiled often, laughed joyously, loved his sister and wasn't embarrassed to show it.

Because, all in all, David Montgomery was a good man. Handsome and rich, yes. But when were those two attributes something from which to flee? A Montgomery, yes, damn it! But could he have refused to be born into the family? What, was he going to question the angels who sent him? How? No, he had to live with his background, just as she had had to live with hers.

Because — and this was the worst part — David Montgomery was the first man who intrigued Savannah enough to hold her interest for more than a month. She found herself fighting a spirit that yanked her closer to him. And that devil spirit — that spirit inside herself — placed her in his company, when she should have run like the devil himself to avoid David.

Placed her in his company. Yes, at first it was to taunt and flirt and rub in the fact of her paternity, her *acquaintanceship* with his family. But later, all those weeks and months later, it was something else, something intangible, something live.

And because he was who he was — Richard Montgomery's grandson — she couldn't afford to let him know that he had that kind of hold over her. So she increased her teasing, using her acting abilities to show amusement at his actions, with an underlying contempt implicit in them. In short, with David — and only with David — she became what she most hated in anyone else: a supercilious snob.

And by her actions, she'd succeeded in flummoxing him. That, she was sure of. All because she refused to be what he expected her to be — the cowed daughter of his grandfather's overseer, the girl who had been thrown out into the street.

She had demanded he take her as equal. And had thought she'd succeeded . . . until that word. That abominable word.

Tonight.

"David," she whispered, and surprised herself at the desolation in her voice. "David, I made so many mistakes. I'm sorry. Ah, God! I made you think me a . . . a strumpet!"

Suddenly, a hand closed round her shoulder and a head of burnished brown hair bent to bring its owner's lips to the cord in her neck. She jolted and almost jumped up, but the hand held her firm.

"I never thought you a strumpet, Savannah. Never."

He stood behind her and his hands gently brushed back and forth across the skin of her back, shoulders, and neck. There was no one else in the maze. No one to see her arch her head back and look into David's eyes, seeking what she found: passion that swiftly brought her back to the drawing room in Lorton House and the way he had made her feel *before* those thoughtless words had been said. Regrets that seared his soul. Pain, the twin to hers.

His gaze never wavered. "I've missed you. God, how I've missed you! I've looked for you for months. I wanted to tell you . . . so many things. Savannah, forgive me. I was a fool. I'm sorry."

As he said the words that she'd longed to hear but never thought he'd say, his voice broke. Yet he wasn't embarrassed by it. That show of emotion touched her where nothing else might have.

There was too much joy in her heart, it seemed, because it grew and grew, then spread in hot waves through her veins. And she dared not let him see it.

"If your grandfather heard you now, he'd choke."

"I don't care."

"Good." She put her hand on his and smiled at him. "I always felt you were a better man than any pompous old Marquess of Lorton."

"No, just a young pompous Marquess-of-Lorton-in-waiting."

She took his hand, got up from the bench, and asked, "Shall we stroll?"

David tucked Savannah's arm in the crook of his elbow and smiled happily to himself. She had made it so easy! No name-calling, no anger, no smugness. She was, after all, the victor in this war they'd been having.

Or was she?

If they were at truce, wasn't he also victor?

Or was there any victor?

Suddenly, he stopped short and drew in his breath. "My God! That's what she meant. . . ."

"David? What is what *who* meant?"

"The quillwork sconces." He laughed long and heartily. "You minx! You put them there, right there in my drawing room—*my* drawing room, by God!—and they said . . . they meant . . ."

For the first time that evening, Savannah snapped open the beautiful fan Ann Skipwith had given her and covered her grinning mouth. "Oh, dear. Are you very angry?"

Chapter Nine

David's eyes traversed the length of her body and he smiled in satisfaction. Her gown was beautiful, but only because *she* was beautiful. The jewels, the fan, the slippers . . . everything was what it was because of Savannah, not the other way around. But did she know it? He'd wager not. There had never been anything of the coquette in her. He could not, however, let her know exactly what he thought of her. Better she should be on the defensive. Hell, she had put him there often enough.

"Just how angry I am depends on one thing, Savannah. . . ."

Oh, the warning in his voice! And his eyes! . . .

Her cheeks heated, becoming as hot and as telltale as the burning embers against a ground of midnight-blue, she decided. Warily, because she'd seen that expression before—on the night he'd made his damnable proposition—she peeked up at him over the edge of her fan. *"One* thing? My lord, if 'tis only one thing, then you cannot be too angry."

David's mouth gaped. Good Lord, she was teasing

him, actually playing the coquette! And she was no good at it. She was not like the women at court, nor like those here in Williamsburg, whose fluttering eyelashes and tittering laugh set his teeth to grinding. No, Savannah was too real for this sort of thing. Too appealing without the subterfuges. Too beautiful to need a bejeweled fan.

But minx she was. And he'd have his revenge, his delight . . . *if* she didn't bite his lip in the process.

He pushed the fan down and his eyes fastened on her lips. They trembled slightly, as did her chin. But this time, he knew, it wasn't from laughter bubbling beneath.

"Do I make you nervous, Savannah?"

"Fie, my lord! Of course not!" *Oh, you will pay for that lie, my girl.* "But this one *little* thing on which your anger depends? . . ."

"Did I say *little?* Hmmm . . . no, I don't recall ever saying *little*. Because, of course, it isn't little at all."

His finger came up to trace the outline of those kissable lips. When Savannah jumped and a tiny, almost inaudible moan escaped the soft flesh he fingered, David smiled. "My anger can be cooled, Savannah."

"Methinks, my lord, that your anger is not in tune with the other parts of you."

He laughed, throwing back his head and feeling for the first time since he could remember the sweet, wonderful *freedom* laughter was. And she gave him that. This woman. This minx.

His nemesis.

"Put me in tune, Savannah. Put every part of my body in tune." His head lowered slowly, his eyes never losing sight of the target. "No, don't back up, Savannah."

"My lord . . ."

"Shh . . . This has been waiting too long."

Too long for what?

Savannah was in a quandary. Should she allow this? Should she shove and flee? But if she shoved and fled, what would she miss? What would she feel if she allowed it?

She was no prissy miss, but rather a woman who had postponed the knowing of a man. Postponed it well beyond the age of most of her friends, all of her sisters and cousins. Postponed it because there had been no man who tugged at her heart enough . . . until David had stepped into the foyer of Honesty Dunn's school and chipped away at the antagonism she held for the Montgomerys.

So, what choice was there?

Breathlessly, she waited while the hand whose fingers were slowly caressing her cheek went to the back of her head, the other to her waist. He tugged, and the step backward Savannah was about to take before his words stopped her only threw her off balance, and she teetered into him. She watched with wide eyes as his mouth descended. Her eyes widened more when his lips brushed slowly back and forth across hers. Back and forth. Back and forth. Feather light. So soft. So very soft.

"So . . ."

He spoke against her lips and the warmth of his breath seemed to seep into her every pore. She was mesmerized and didn't know if she should like it or fear it.

"So . . . you think my home a battleground, heh?"

Back and forth, more feathers, more heat.

"Not your *home*."

"Ah!"

His tongue licked at the curve of her upper lip and she could hardly breathe. When she did, it came in one great *whoosh*, which made him smile and flick his tongue across the slight opening she'd allowed.

"The battle, then, begins and ends with me?"

"Us."

"And who is the serpent? Who Kate? Who the Capulet?"

"The play has not run its course yet. I do not know."

"Ah, Savannah . . . that's the first lie you've ever told me."

He fingered an errant curl at the nape of her neck and tugged to bring her head back, causing her breasts to arch up invitingly. Too invitingly. "My lord . . ." she protested.

He pretended not to hear that plaint in her voice, preferring to feast his eyes on the charms exposed by the delicate lace of her neckline. "Perhaps I was wrong. Perhaps it will take *two* things to assuage my anger. Two delectable . . ."

His mouth left her lips and traced a molten hot path down her throat, lingering long enough to moisten the cords in her neck, before continuing an unendurably wonderful journey to the flesh exposed by her gown.

Savannah was lost. Lost! And she didn't care if she ever found her way back.

What was softer than feathers? A zephyr? Sable? Whatever it was, *that* made its home at her breasts. She gasped at the first touch, then moaned when delicious torment built a raging fever in her blood; when softer than feathers created a roaring echo in her head. The fever, the echo, a need so great she sobbed, "David!" *I surrender.*

Oh, Lord, his body was taut as iron, rock-hard. Yet, at the touch of her hands on his shoulder, his muscles rippled, quivered. Perhaps, she thought, her surrender was too precipitate. Who was overpowering whom?

Power. The power of his kiss. The power of his touch. The power of midnight and faint candlelight and soft background music. The power of seduction.

Torment and power could be sweet; she wanted to show him how much. So, framing his face with her hands, she brought his lips back to the first place they'd touched. But they were beyond feathers, sables, or zephyrs. She knew it the moment their lips came together. Hers opened for him. His covered hers greedily. And she wound her arms around him, arched her body into his, and kissed him.

It was more than she imagined . . . and everyone said her imagination was a tangible thing.

With tiny lapping touches, his tongue coaxed her to open her mouth. As he had traced the outside of her lips, he learned the interior. Tongues touched, danced. Breaths mingled, sighed. Hands explored, trembled. Bodies molded, shivered.

"David," she finally managed to whisper, "where has your anger gone?"

"Anger? What anger? It was never there."

She reared her head back and fixed him with an accusative stare.

"Well, all right, it was *often* there. But not now."

"Good." She leaned her head on his shoulder and wound her arms around him. "I like you, David."

"You make it sound as if it surprises the hell out of you."

"It does." She giggled. "I shouldn't, you know. You were abominable to me."

"And you weren't abominable to me?"

She snuggled against him. "Oh, I was. I was. But I didn't want to explode all your notions immediately. After all, you *are* your grandfather's heir. As such, would you really expect anything else from a Stewart?"

"Could we please leave my grandfather out of this and get back to what we were doing a few minutes ago?"

"Ah, but what we were doing a few minutes ago will not suffice now, will it? It will escalate . . . deliciously . . . and this is neither the time nor the place to continue where we left off."

"I can't think of a better time. And certainly George Wythe has provided the perfect secluded place."

"David, I will not couple with you on the dewy ground in a watered silk gown!"

He plucked at the ties of her stomacher. "Your gown would pose no problems."

"No," she said, "I don't suppose it would." She batted his hands away and retied the stomacher. "I am the guest of honor at this fete. We will not couple here. Not now."

"When?"

"And where?"

"Savannah, are you laughing at me?"

"Perish the thought!" She moved back into his arms and snuggled her head in the crook of his neck. "There will be a time and place for us, David."

David grunted. "With all the inns filled to overflowing, a grand ball in preparation, and war talk on every corner, I'll have to be very creative to find any time or place."

She tucked her arm in his and tugged him away from the shadowy bower, onto the lantern-lit path that led back to the house. "Create, David. Create every minute of every day."

But five days passed and the grand ball arrived before David found time or place. Savannah got caught up in the excitement permeating the people of Williamsburg; but David was never far from her mind.

The square was bustling with servants running pell-mell from one end to the other. Though the residents had tried to anticipate every contingency, at the last minute harnesses broke, whips cracked, slippers pinched the toes and must needs be stretched, wigs lost their bounce and only responded to liberal applications of the wigmaker's curling iron and hot glue, rose water lost its scent and more had to be fetched from the apothecary's.

Finally, however, everything was ready and the night arrived.

Savannah declined riding with George Wythe and his family, requesting instead the governor's coach, to arrive fully an hour after the festivities began.

Taking her paint box, portable easel, and a sturdy stool, she sought out a good vantage point as colorful carriages began to circle the square. Most were closed, since the ladies wanted their gowns, wigs, or hairstyles to be seen in the glow of candlelight, where they could be appreciated for what they were—the badge of their husband's standing in the community. But some had braved the elements in open carriages. These, too, however, kept their seamstress's, hairdresser's, and maidservant's creations in hiding, by covering them in fur-lined cloaks with deep, full hoods.

Naturally, no one wanted to be first to arrive. It would spoil the effect. And, of course, the first to arrive was not the best quality, since gentry sailed in later than the time of arrival.

Savannah thought the social rules silliness taken to the limits of absurdity. But these past months she'd come to realize how much social standing meant to these people. It was one of the only things they had to distinguish them from what one of John Murray's councilors called "the common, the very common, lot of the mob called Americans."

Clothes doth make the man.

This night, for certain.

But if there were to be war and the Americans won, would this be the last of the gentry? If it were, she had to capture it—them—for posterity. A title for the sketch she meant to do came to mind: *The Last Carriage Rides Round Williamsburg Square*. How ironic that she was to make the parade in John Murray's royal coach. But not yet. She had much to do yet.

Savannah found the perfect spot to set up her equipment—behind a tall privet hedge that angled enough to give her a good perspective of the square, yet hid her from those in the procession. She had only sketched three scenes, however, when a large black coach stopped at the corner, blocking her view. She frowned up at the driver, and found herself staring at a tall and muscular man's frame—with his head hooded like a hangman's and a gun in his hand pointed straight at her middle. She opened her mouth to scream, but a rough hand clamped itself over her mouth and another rough hand reached round to pluck her up from her stool. She struggled. Kicking mightily, she upset her drawing paper and charcoal, knocked over her easel, and sent her paints and sketch pad end over end into the privet hedge.

Damn! She had chosen her vantage point well. Too well. She was concealed from view, the better to see than be seen. Now, with the coach for cover, her abductor had easy pickings, without fear that he'd be seen.

But she would not give up without a fight. Her fingers scratched at the hand at her waist and Savannah knew a moment of satisfaction at feeling the skin give way.

It didn't stop her abductor from hustling her quickly to the waiting coach and tossing her unceremoniously into the dark interior, however. She landed atop three pairs of boots. As the door to the coach slammed shut and the horses started up with a loud "Ho!," she looked up at the men who had taken her prisoner. And gasped.

David escorted Arabella into the large drawing room of the royal governor's mansion. He left her with the Aldriches and made another circuit of the house. Where the hell was Savannah? He knew John Murray, the governor, had sent his coach for her. To be fashionably late was *de rigueur;* but this was ridiculous.

When he didn't find her on his second search, he ordered his cloak from the colored houseman, threw it over his shoulders, and bolted for the Wythe house. He arrived in the square just as a covered coach rounded the far corner, sending up a spray of dirt and crushed stones as the hooded coachman whipped the horses into a gallop.

And perfectly framed in the side window of the coach was Savannah's profile.

Savannah? "Savannah!"

A hooded coachman? Judas!

He "borrowed" the nearest horse, swept onto its back, and tucked himself over the strong neck as he urged the animal into a teeth-jarring bolt after the coach.

It didn't go far. Only seven blocks away, the coach stopped at a large brick and board home. It waited only long enough to discharge four men and Savannah, then took off in another cloud of dust.

Four men, one stationed at the door with crossed arms, two sabers, and two firearms. And he without any weapon at all!

But Savannah was there, brought by a hooded coachman, hustled into the house by her captors! There was naught for it. He had to find a way to get her out of there.

David tied the horse to the nearest tethering ring and streaked through a nearby meadow. He skirted the side yard of the house where Savannah was. He admonished himself: Keep to the shadows. Avoid open space. Bolt from tree to tree, hedge to hedge. Reach the windows on the far side *without being seen!*

It took so long, David worried that anything could be happening in the house. Anything! But gradually he managed to attain his goal, creeping along the side of the house until he was able to discern noises. He moved along the side until voices, low and rumbling, penetrated the heavily curtained windows. Moving cautiously but always toward the sound, he strained to hear what was being said. More importantly, he tried to find an entrance and something inside that he could use as a weapon to protect Savannah.

He discovered his "something" inside the window closest to the street, a window that gave access to a hall. Rifles on the wall. A powder horn. Horse whips. Cutlasses.

Swearing beneath his breath because there was only one of him, David tried easing up the window. It didn't budge. He heaved. Nothing. Every curse he'd ever heard or used flew through his thoughts. But he didn't give up. There was an entrance. He just had to find it.

Before he did, however, a side door opened, and he ducked behind a hedge as two of the men came out to join the one who had been stationed in front.

"Will she cooperate?" the guard asked the newcomers.

"Cooperate? She's in there now. Cooperating better than any Polly Pitcher."

David froze. He'd heard the name in every tavern or inn in the colonies. Polly Pitcher. The common name for a whore because a pitcher was always upended. And they likened Savannah to this image? What the hell was going on here?

As he was about to jump the three men—weapons or no weapons—Savannah swept through the door, her arm tucked into that of the man who had been left with her in the house. David stared. Something was different about Savannah, something . . .

She had a different dress on!

She'd gone into the house in a plain pale blue muslin frock. Now, she was attired in a rich, creamy velvet gown with deep chocolate-brown lace at the low-cut bodice. And instead of her old mobcap, she wore her thick, wavy dark hair tied back and a matching lace-trimmed pinner cap perched jauntily on her head.

"You will be circumspect, my dear?"

Savannah smiled up at the tall man at her side. "Of course. No one will find out, I promise."

"If they do . . . well, I needn't tell you the outcome."

"No," Savannah said quietly, "you needn't." She shivered but reached up to pat his cheek. "Don't frown so. It was my decision. My risk."

David heard the clop-clop of horses' hooves and kept himself well hidden as a dun-colored carriage bearing the royal governor's crest pulled up in front of the house. The tall, auburn-haired gentleman took Savannah's hand and made a courtly bow over it. He kissed her fingers. "My dear," he said, "we will meet again. I hope under as pleasant circumstances as this night."

"Sir, every minute with you is always pleasant."

The four men handed her into the coach and waited until it pulled away. The short, bespectacled man assessed the tall man. "Satisfactory, Patrick?"

"More than satisfactory, Ben. Much more."

The men went back into the house and closed the door. And David stared off into the distance at the back of the receding royal coach.

Chapter Ten

The ball was in full swing when Savannah arrived at the governor's mansion. There was more ostentatious satin, silk, tulle, and velvet — on both men and women — than she'd seen in her whole life. But Williamsburg was rumored to be the most sumptuous of the colonial capitals. Next to Newport, of course, which had so much French influence and, therefore, up-to-the-minute French fashions.

What was she thinking about? Fashion! After what had happened to her tonight . . . well, it was surprising she could think about aught but manacles and freezing dungeons. She giggled. If the gentry could hear her thoughts, what would they think?

That she was a Rebel sympathizer, naturally.

Naturally.

That she was not to be trusted, surely.

Surely.

That she had been changed? No, they probably wouldn't think that. She looked no different; and she would act no different. But she felt different. She had made a commitment, given her word, and she would not compromise it.

Though she felt silly doing what she had been asked.

When she poked her head into the drawing room, however, she amended her thoughts. She was not silly. But there in front of her were the silliest group of women! Pannier hoops brought their hips out to enormous, unnatural curves, as if they had two tables attached to their waists. Why, they could hardly maneuver themselves through the crowd.

And their wigs! When one bent over a sumptuous board of tasty treats, she almost lost the infernal contraption. It was elaborate, standing at least a foot high, and it was a cascade of whorls and curls and ribbons and jewels.

Oh, no! The height—Savannah was certain it was truly *fashionable*—wasn't equal to its weight, and just a nod sent it askew. Bending over like that . . .

Oh, dear! The lady caught it just as the pins gave way. Had she not, it would have toppled into the macaroni and cheese pudding.

Savannah had missed the opportunity to sketch the full carriage promenade. But here . . . here was her chance to capture the full pomposity of life in Tory country.

If only she had a sketch pad and charcoal . . .

Perhaps, in the study . . .

She elbowed her way past several suitors, who offered to lead her in a dance. But she shook her head or gave her regrets, promising to come back when she could. Once in the hall, she had the devil of a time dodging through the line of dancers that had spilled out of the crowded ballroom for a sedate minuet.

As she retrieved paper and searched in vain for charcoal, she felt as sedate as a popinjay.

The nerve of Patrick and that grandfatherly man . . . no, hardly that. More *dangerous,* more sinister than anyone's grandfather. Mister Benjamin Franklin of Philadelphia, indeed! Whisking her away like that. Scaring the skin off her.

Why, if anyone had seen . . .

She shuddered at the thought and nearly fell to the floor as her legs caught up with her fear.

She was a spy now. A spy. Good God.

Savannah stumbled toward the fireplace, groped for the arm of a highly polished Windsor chair, and plopped into it. She stared into the dancing flames and tried to understand what had happened, what her life was going to be like now.

Naturally, Patrick and that rascal Ben had waited for the cover of darkness and the confusion of the promenade before making their move. But to snatch her right off the street! And then to make that damnable proposition.

Of course, after the way the British government had closed off the port of Boston, following what was now being called the Tea Party, and thrown up garrisons and lookout posts around almost every major port in the other colonies, Patrick and Ben truly did not have anyone else. Savannah realized and agreed with them that the name Savannah Stewart—and her talents—were well known in colonial social circles; that she could go and come as she pleased; that she was welcome in Tory and Rebel homes alike; that she had a singular position because she overheard much of what was said among the household—wherever she was.

And, of course, she had her published illustrations and articles.

Publication was the key to Ben's and Patrick's whole plan. As long as she could stay published in a variety of newspapers and broadsides, she could get valuable information about Tory activities to the Rebels, without anyone else being the wiser. She could do it whatever way she chose, but she alone could do it.

And that was the conundrum.

How was she going to do it?

How was she going to transform herself from artist and writer to spy?

Patrick—the rake—had suggested she make up an alphabet code and secrete messages within the text of her articles. But such a code would have to be simple enough to remember, yet complicated enough to withstand scrutiny and avoid detection. And Patrick had warned that it would probably have to be changed monthly, so no one could break the code and discover the hidden message. And since she would be traveling all over the coast, staying only as long as it took to complete her commissions, she wouldn't be in one place, with access to friends who could get messages to Patrick or Ben or whoever needed the information. Which meant she would have to trust the mails to deliver a new code to Patrick or his allies.

But there was no such thing as private correspondence in the colonies. Mail was opened by anyone who wanted to know anything. There wasn't one letter from her family that hadn't had its original seal broken and new wax seals affixed. Her mother's last missive had had *five* blobs of various colored wax, indicating it had been opened four times—and God knew how often it had been passed from hand to hand, how many eyes had seen what was in it.

So, she couldn't rely on the mails. Thus, she couldn't use a letter code.

But she had to fix on something within the next forty-eight hours. Patrick was leaving for Philadelphia then and he wanted to take her decision, along with her method of transmitting the messages, to the men who were gathering to discuss the dangerous days that had just passed and those they feared were coming.

"A . . . b . . . c . . . x . . . y . . . z," she mumbled. "No, not letters."

What then? What?

"You should wear velvet more often, Savannah."

David's softly spoken words in her left ear and his hot breath tickling her earlobe startled her, and she dropped the miniature she had been fingering as she thought. It shattered on the bricks of the hearth, sending pieces of glass everywhere.

She dropped to her knees and began gathering the shards in her hands. "David, why must you always pop up and scare the wits out of me?"

"I cleared my throat four times, each time louder than the one before. But you acted as if you were in another world. Where were your thoughts, my dear?"

"On a problem I have. One I can't quite grasp . . ."

As Savannah picked up another piece of glass, the firelight flashed off it and drew her gaze. Light and shadow danced among the broken shards, creating a pattern that resembled lace. Lace. Patterns. Shapes.

Her eye looked closer, harder. Flickering firelight. Light and shadow. Shadow and light.

Shapes. Patterns.

Patterns. Borders?

"I've got it!"

She dropped the glass and surged to her feet. Looking into David's frowning face, she laughed. "Don't be so dour, David! All's well." She threw her arms around him. "All's wonderful!" She linked her arm through his and felt a momentary tightness of his muscle, almost an involuntary jerk backward; but Savannah was so filled with the solution to her problem that she thought nothing of it. "Dance with me, David. For the first time in my life, I want to dance the night away."

"Are you sure you wish *me* for a partner, Miss Stewart? Wouldn't a tall, red-haired man be more to your liking?"

Savannah felt the heat rise to her cheeks. She peeked at David from under her eyelashes. "You saw me?"

"You went into that house in one dress and came out in another. And I thought you were in trouble, hooded coach driver and all! But I was mistaken. You trifle with me. You dally with others. Just what kind of woman are you, Savannah? Or don't I have to ask?"

This man . . . this damnable man! How could he be so appealing one moment and so arrogant and disrespectful the next?

No matter what the circumstances had looked like, David should have known she wouldn't compromise herself. He should have known . . . He should have!

She expected more from him, wanted more from him, needed more from him. She was getting dangerously close to falling in love with him. All right, she had already crossed that line. She was in love with him.

No. Not with him. Not with a man who could think

the worst of her. She was in love with what she as an artist instinctively knew he could be, should be, must be. She wanted David to shake off the shackles of his birth and join the human race, not the Montgomery clan. To be loving, loyal, trusting. In short, all the things the other Montgomerys held in disdain, she wanted for David. Yet every time she thought he had made that giant leap, he reverted to the stripes he had been born with. How sad. How *maddening*. She was a fool to put up with it any longer.

"You are the only man in this world who treated me like a strumpet. Now you accuse me of playing the strumpet. And I let you get away with it not once but twice!" She whirled, shook out her skirts, and glared at David. "You shall not have the chance to do it again, my lord! Not ever." With a swish, she swept from the room, remembering her father's admonition to *"Keep head high, goirl. Always. And niver firget who ye be."*

She would never forget.

She was Savannah Stewart. Georgian. Artist. Daughter. Friend. Confidante. If wife and mother were not on her list, she at least had something no other woman in the colony had. She was a spy. A spy . . . It had a thrilling ring to it. Thrilling and dangerous and a little romantic.

Romance? Pah! She was through with that part of her life. David's mistrust had burned it out of her.

As she rounded the corner to go back to the ballroom, Savannah heard soft voices in the small pantry to her left. She popped her head in.

Romance. Intrigue. Lore. There was too much of it in this world. She had not wanted to see Lady Ann's husband speaking softly to her sister as he framed her face with his hands. Had not wanted to see their heads bent closely together. Had not wanted to see that starry-eyed expression in Jean's eyes nor the corresponding doleful one in Peyton's.

She popped her head back out and took two steps away from the frightful encounter, only to be brought up short by the voice of the one woman who should not be there at this time.

"There you are, Savannah."

"Lady Ann." Savannah turned, grasped her friend's elbow, and tugged her toward the dining room. "How nice to see you. Have you had any of Governor Murray's delicious lobster salad? And I heard his cook got the recipe for macaroni and cheese pudding from Thomas Jefferson. From the smell of it, it must be delicious."

Lady Ann shook her head and held Savannah back. "It is. I'm filled to my gills with it." She fanned her face and dropped into a small slipper chair upholstered in green and white brocade. "Don't rush off."

Her fan fluttered faster than a hummingbird's wing, almost as fast as Savannah's heart was racing. She had to get Lady Ann out of the hall before disaster struck.

But Lady Ann was not to be moved.

"I must take a breather, Savannah. I've been dancing for hours. And you . . . where have you been? Everyone has been looking for you."

"I stopped to sketch the festivities and . . ."

Lady Ann stiffened and her eyes grew round as her husband and her sister sailed out of the pantry, Peyton's arm firmly fixed round Jean's waist.

"Oh, God!" Ann Skipwith rose with the grace of a lady-in-waiting; but her face mirrored grief beyond description. "No. Dear God, no!"

Before Savannah, Peyton, or Jean could utter a word, Ann fled down the hall and out the front door.

"Go after her," Jean urged Peyton. "Don't let her think . . ."

Peyton took a halfhearted step forward, but Savannah held up her hand and said, "I'll go, Sir Peyton. You make formal regrets to the governor for us both."

It hadn't gone at all the way David thought it should have. Why, Savannah had been indignant, instead of apologetic or self-abasing, the way she ought. As if she had nothing to hide. As if *he* had made the blunder and not she. As if she were innocent . . .

As innocent as that night in Lorton Woods? As innocent as the sweet kiss under the moonlight last week? As innocent as his own sister?

This damn woman flummoxed him!

He thought he'd had it all postured out. Colonial wenches, colonial whims. Why not? It was what his friends always speculated. Why was Savannah less than what he expected? Or more? How had she once again coolly stripped him of his chance to knock the pins from under her and shown him up for a fool? Hell, why had he given her half the chance? Why hadn't he simply upended her and had her, the way his brother would have done, or his grandfather in his day? Why was she so different?

Or was it as she had said last week in the moonlight, that he was shedding the Montgomery skin . . . and perhaps the Montgomery curse?

Would that it were so.

But if it were, why this anger when he thought of her in some other man's arms? Why this desolation?

She was, after all, only a woman.

He ground his teeth together—he'd been doing that too much lately . . . since she had come into his life—and heard a commotion in the hall. Going to investigate, he found Sir Peyton Skipwith, one of the few Virginians with whom he did business, standing stupidly with his mouth agape, staring out the open front door.

"We did nothing wrong," Peyton said. "She misunderstood. Misunderstood . . ."

"There is nothing you can do now," a lovely girl said, and patted his arm. "Ann has been more melancholy than usual lately. I don't know why . . ."

"She's . . . well, she's with child," Peyton said miserably. "You remember the last confinement. High-strung, she was then. But this . . ." He caught sight of David in the doorway and screwed his face into a half-hearted smile. "Was merely extracting a cinder from Jean's eye. Ann didn't wait for explanations. Know it looks damned suspicious. But simple, really." He pulled down on his waistcoat and shrugged. "There it is. Can't remove the impression, can I? Have to try, though. Must follow her, Jean. Sorry."

"Of course you must." She snatched a long cape off one of the overflowing pegs in the hall and helped him on with it. "Savannah will calm her down and then you can explain. Don't be sad, Peyton. All will be well."

In a pig's eye, David thought. If Peyton was as bumbling in his explanation to his wife as he had been the past two minutes, the poor fool would be sleeping in the barn for a year.

Nothing for it but to go along with him and help . . . if help would be accepted.

David smiled at the lovely young woman named Jean and shrugged into his outer frock coat. He caught up to Peyton in the middle of the square. The man was bending to pick up a red satin slipper with bright red brilliants on buckle and heel.

"She'll catch her death, hobbling about without shoes," he said. Absentmindedly, he turned as David came alongside. Peyton held up the high-heeled shoe as if it were a trophy. "Sent to Paris for it. And now the heel's bent." He knocked it with his finger and it flopped back and forth, in rhythm with his head. "Broken. Everything is broken." Peyton tucked the useless slipper into his coat pocket and trudged across the rest of the square with his head bent low and his brows drawn together.

"You may have misconstrued it all, Lady Ann. Truly."

"Ah, Savannah. I always knew he had liaisons. All men do. But with my sister!"

"Which is exactly why it can't be true."

"But the servants . . . they've been talking. . . . I've simply refused to credit it . . . until now."

"But there could be an innocent explanation. Why, I, myself have been misunderstood . . . and tonight, too!"

"By someone you love, Savannah? Someone you should be able to trust but has disappointed you more than once?"

"Yes. Someone like that exactly. He thinks me a Polly Pitcher."

155

Ann's gasp was more disbelief than surprise. "Lore, Savannah, the man needs a keeper! You, a Polly Pitcher!"

"Ridiculous, I know. But so is the notion that your own sister could be playing loose with your husband. You are right to discredit that notion, because it cannot be true."

A discreet tap on the library door—the room Ann and Savannah had chosen to escape the servants' prying eyes and ears because it was right inside the front door and relatively deserted—preceded Peyton Skipwith's entreaty to be allowed to speak to his wife.

"Speak to him, Ann. You need to get this straightened out."

"I'll speak to him. But unless he can convince me altogether, I will reserve my affections."

"Oh, Ann! Unbend. There is no gain in being rigid without cause."

"And if there is cause?"

"Then sock him in the eye, refuse him his conjugal rights, and spend every damned copper he earns."

Ann's eyes glinted with expectation and humor. "Oh, Savannah! You are refreshing. And, I suspect, very, very wise." She crossed to an upholstered settle bench, seated herself, tucked her unshod feet under her skirts, and smoothed out the fullness. She held her head high and crossed her hands on her lap. "Send Peyton in, Savannah."

Savannah confronted Peyton in the hall, pushing him away so Ann couldn't hear her whispered warning. "It's a lion's den in there, my lord. And unless you are truly a Daniel, with spotless soul, you won't survive it."

Peyton sighed and straightened his shoulders, but they quickly sloped forward in defeat as he shuffled into the library and his fate.

Savannah shook her head in dismay. Perhaps, after all, there really was something in the servants' talk. Mayhap Sir Peyton had not broken his vows with his sister-in-law; but the inclination seemed to be there in his eyes. Savannah only hoped Ann would not see it or, if she did, would survive the knowing.

Hurrying down the hall to the main drawing room, Savannah did not see David until he stepped out of the shadows and into her path. As she had seen Ann do, she raised her head imperiously, stared him straight in the eyes, and quietly demanded, "Let me pass, my lord."

"I will let you pass after you have heard me out, miss."

Savannah turned on her heel and fled. She had gained the front stairs when she heard David's "Damnation." She had heard him out before. Once more and she'd scream, or gouge his eyes out. Beautiful midnight-blue eyes, with naught but haughtiness and scorn in them. She couldn't allow them to sear her with condemnation again. He might as well cut out her heart.

She slammed her bedroom-studio door behind her and locked it securely. Then she paced the floor to the tap-tap-tap of his knock. "Go away, my lord. I will neither see you nor talk to you."

"Will you not even allow me the privilege of apologizing to you?"

"Your apologies are worth naught, my lord. Go away."

"You are being headstrong, lass."

"That is my curse and my salvation. Go away."

"I was wrong, damnit!"

"Yes, you were. Go away."

"I misunderstood the situation . . . whatever it was. What was it, Savannah? The tall red-haired man . . . was he a friend of your family?"

"What kind of apology is that, my lord? Go away."

"All right. All right. I won't ask questions. Just let me in and we'll get this straightened out."

"I am a Stewart. You are a Montgomery. It could be no straighter than that. Go away, David, before you begin to question your destiny."

"Too late, Savannah. I questioned it and decided to walk away from it."

"Good for you. Now go away and find someone else to pester. Someone who cares."

"You care, Savannah. You're just too damned stubborn to admit it."

"I might have cared, David." She sighed and all the pain she had suffered at his hands came out in that sigh. "I might have cared . . . I wanted to . . . but you . . . you . . . Ah, God, just go away!"

Chapter Eleven

David was ensconced in a soft, richly upholstered wing-back chair next to the fire, perusing the latest issue of a Boston newspaper, when Peyton Skipwith shambled in and took up the seat opposite him. Peyton reached for a Canton ware tobacco container on the table next to him and a long-stemmed clay pipe from a rack on the wall. He tamped tobacco into the small bowl of the pipe, lit it, and dragged on the fragrant mixture until he had a steady stream of smoke wreathing his head.

"Did you ever wonder why the Lord . . . with all his wisdom . . . afflicted us with wives?"

The question would have been funny yesterday, but after what had happened upstairs, David was of the same mind. "Mayhap He has a sense of humor."

Peyton thought it over, then shook his head. "No," he said seriously, "I think it was to chastise us. To keep us tethered. To let us know we cannot enjoy *anything*. Not even fantasies."

That was a slip, David decided. Peyton had remonstrated at the governor's mansion; but he had protested too much. There might not have been anything going on in the closet. If he were assailed with fantasies, however, then Peyton wished for more than merely cleaning out cinders from his sister-in-law's eye. And his getting caught had reminded him too forcefully of his less-than-honest feelings. His wife's reaction now stuck in his craw, nibbling on his conscience until he blamed her, the victim of his wayward thoughts, instead of himself, who had thought them.

But pointing that out to Peyton was something David couldn't do. Not after creating almost the same situation with Savannah as Lord Skipwith had with his wife, Ann. But there was one thing that David still knew to be true.

"Women bring much joy," he said, remembering the closeness he and Savannah had had in the garden the week before, the closeness and fun they had shared in the drawing room at Lorton Woods. The image of her burned into his mind, invaded his heart, leaving him bereft because of this, his latest stupidity.

Peyton sucked in on the pipe, held it out, and examined it closely. David wondered if the man had examined his own conscience that closely.

"The right woman, mayhap, will bring joy," Peyton agreed. "But the wrong one . . . Think thrice before tethering yourself, your lordship. Choose a humble woman who smiles often, speaks softly, listens intently, and has only one thing on her mind: your happiness. A woman who thinks for herself and will not be led in all things is a woman who will chastise you every minute of every day for eternity. Avoid such a woman. Run from her as if running from the plague."

A loud snort of amusement made David and Peyton turn their heads toward the door. David felt white-hot rage when the short bearlike man and the tall redhead entered ahead of George Wythe.

"Run from her as if running from the plague! Are you of sound mind, sir?" The bear pulled up a Windsor chair and sat comfortably, with his feet pointing to the fire. His blue eyes twinkled as he looked into the flames and intoned, half seriously, "Women who think for themselves are jewels, sir! Jewels. They generally have sound and healthy constitutions, produce vigorous offspring, are active in the business of the family, are specially good housewives, and are very careful of their husband's interests."

"And contentious as hounds from hell," Peyton mumbled.

"But, of course! 'Tis their nature. And 'tis but a trifle, you know. A trifle, when a man becomes used to it. A mere habit. An exercise which is well meant and ought to be well taken." He accepted a tankard of ale from George Wythe and quaffed it to the bottom. "Marriage. Now, marriage is the best and most natural state of man, for it unites the man with the woman into a complete human being. Separately, she wants the force of his body and the strength of his reason; he, her softness, sensibility, and acute discernment. Together, they are more likely to succeed in this world."

"But succeed at what?" Peyton asked. "And is it equal to our misery?"

The bear fixed Peyton with a gnawing stare. "Is your wife young and lovely?"

"Yes, damnit!"

"And you chose her for her loveliness?"

"Of course!"

"There you made your first mistake."

"And last," Peyton mumbled.

"Ah, no, sir. Your first of many for the rest of your life. And why? Because handsome women do not study to be good. And the opposite of their sex—the ugly woman—is better than good. The ugly woman learns to do for you a thousand services great and small, and is the most tender and useful of friends when you are sick. She is amiable, prudent, discreet, and very grateful for any small pleasantry from you. So, you should have sought out an ugly woman if you wished harmony in your home. But since you didn't, you will have contention now and forever. Get used to it, man. Get used to it."

Peyton groaned, threw his pipe into the fire, and stalked from the room. The bear clucked his tongue and shook his head. He looked over his wire-rimmed spectacles at David. "Don't tell me you, too, have woman trouble?"

"Are you a soothsayer, sir?"

"Dear me, no. Merely a scientist and publisher. Benjamin Franklin of Philadelphia, sir. And my friend, the rascal, Patrick Henry."

David was so stunned at learning the identity of the two men who had spirited Savannah away that he lost his speech while he shook the hands proffered him. When it finally came, he was thoroughly confused. "Benjamin Franklin? The electricity genius?

The publisher of the *Philadelphia Gazette* and *Poor Richard's Almanac?*"

"Guilty."

"And Patrick Henry, a representative in the Virginia House of Burgesses?"

"Until his royal pain in the neck disbanded the group." Patrick took the seat vacated by Peyton and stretched full out. "Sorry, George," he said to their host. "I know John Murray is a friend of yours, but he's a damned loony if he thinks he can stop what's coming merely by closing us down."

George Wythe drew another Windsor chair over to the fire and set it next to Ben. "He's no loony, Patrick. Never has been. He's loyal to King and Crown, and if disbanding a group of men he thinks speak seditious acts will show his loyalty, then he'll disband them."

"Spyglass vision," Ben said. "Looking neither right nor left, he's bound for perdition. What's so awful is that he and his ilk want to take us all with them."

"Not if we can help it," Patrick said. "Not if this evening's plan succeeds."

George leaned over and put a hand on Patrick's wrist. "Friend . . . David, here, is new to the Americas. He's unused to the favorite pastime of us colonials — complaining of everything royal. He looks confused as hell. Or, as the heir to the Marquess of Lorton, have you interested yourself in the affairs of the colonies, my lord Montgomery?"

From the way it had been phrased and the tone George had used, David knew the exchange was both a warning to Patrick to hold his tongue in the face of a marquess's heir and an attempt to find out where

David's loyalties lay. The only problem was, David couldn't care where his loyalties lay. He only cared that Savannah was somehow mixed up with these two men and that quite possibly she was part of this evening's *plans* Patrick Henry had spoken about. And if she were part of those plans, then she was dab in the middle of more intrigue than he had ever encountered at court.

"I haven't formed any alliances, sir," David said. He chose his words carefully. If Savannah were involved, he needed to know and had to be able to help her if she got into trouble. "Although, sir, I have been astounded at the arrogance and stupidity of many of my friends. They don't seem to grasp the colonial view of things. They expect to make a profit from the sweat of colonial brows, and they expect the colonials to keep their mouths shut and let the Parliament rule with impunity. Yet the British gentry, in Parliament and out, know little or nothing about this land and its people. Worst of all, they don't *want* to know anything about it . . . or you."

"Methinks," Patrick said, "they will know a great deal about us very soon."

"And not much of it to their liking, I'd hazard a guess," David said.

Patrick cocked his left brow at David. "Sounds to me as if you *had* formed an alliance, sir."

"Perhaps I have, at that."

Patrick and Ben exchanged glances, then Ben turned to George with raised brows. George shrugged and looked at Patrick with a gesture of his hands that said *I leave it up to you*. "Are you willing to take up the cause, then?"

"Mister Henry, I must be honest with you. My grandfather is a full-titled marquess and opposed to anything which smacks of treason. Pointedly taking up the cause, I'm afraid, would be impossible for me. I am, however, willing to keep an open mind. Especially when it concerns Savannah Stewart."

"Lord help us!" Franklin laughed in such a manner that his eyes crinkled and his thick body bounced, until David thought he'd jounce himself right off his polished seat onto the floor.

"A pretty face," Franklin chortled. "A pretty face and more than pleasing figure. Either should have alerted me, my friends. *La belle dame* has reverted to her sex's worst trait. She has not been discreet."

David bristled. The offense to Savannah struck him more than he'd anticipated, regardless of the hearty glee that had occasioned it. No doubt was left in his mind. Savannah Stewart meant more to him than a pretty face and more than pleasing figure.

"I beg to differ, Mister Franklin," David countered. "Miss Stewart has been discretion herself. But you, I'm afraid, have not." When Patrick Henry and George Wythe sat forward angrily and expectantly, David felt intense satisfaction. "I saw her with you this evening. In fact, before I saw her with you, I saw her in your carriage with a hooded driver. My goodness, Mister Franklin! A hooded driver in these days . . . far too suspicious and melodramatic, don't you think? Of course, I followed her. She is, you see, very important to me."

Ben's eyes twinkled even brighter than before and he rubbed his hands together. "And does the lady know of your interest?"

"Knows of it, but spurns it at the moment. But I'm persistent, sir. 'Tis the mark of the Montgomerys. Sometimes our curse."

Ben eyed David's body in such a clinical way that it made the younger man squirm.

"Now, now. Don't be embarrassed, lad. I merely wished to ascertain your strength. From your muscular build and lean length, you seem a strong and agile young man. Are you a good horseman? Can you run swiftly? And are you proficient in sword, cutlass, and pistols?"

"Aye to all three. As are all good British gentry, sir."

"Hmm . . ."

Ben tapped the nail of his index finger against his teeth as he thought for a few moments. The endless ticking of a hall clock was the only sound save the crackling fire. It made David more nervous and expectant than a cat in a barn full of swallows.

"Patrick, we might be able to allay your fears by getting this gentleman to assist us." He glared at David. "*If* the lady does not reject you completely, that is."

"I'm not sure if she does or doesn't. But does it matter, sir? Isn't it more important that I don't reject her? That, in fact, I wish to protect and care for her? That *is* what you have in mind, isn't it?"

"A quick-witted man, Patrick! Mayhap he needn't be a principal player. In fact, now I think on it, it may work better if he were what he is. . . ."

Twenty minutes later, and David knew exactly what the colonial burgesses had in mind.

Savannah would hate it.

If she found out, that was.

But David had given his word that she wouldn't find out. And in giving his word, he had taken another step closer to alliance with the Stewart clan. If his grandfather—and Drew—ever found out, he would surely lose his inheritance. Mayhap, even his head.

"I have a wonderful new commission for you, Savannah."

The summons to attend Abigail Drummond, the governor's special friend, had come just as Savannah had put the small oval frames on her latest miniatures. Abigail had looked each over carefully before sending her maidservant to fetch her money box. Though the governor had paid for the miniature he'd ordered, Abigail had ordered five more for herself. She counted out the correct silver specie and handed it to Savannah, along with her grand announcement. Savannah was about to refuse any other commissions, since she didn't want to remain in Williamsburg much longer. But the rest of Abigail's pronouncement had her sitting up straight to listen.

"Peggy Shippen, a dear friend of mine whose sister has called me in on each of her confinements, saw the portraits you did of Mister Wythe. Naturally, I told Peggy how talented you were in miniature making. She wants one for her latest beau . . . a Colonel Benedict Arnold, I think she said. But she had to leave for her home in Philadelphia and wondered if you would be willing to travel there. By the time you arrive, I'm sure she'll have many more women awaiting your talents, Savannah. And if you're worried about finances, I could take you with me."

"You're leaving Williamsburg, Miss Drummond?"

"Friday, a week. I crave the excitement of a city like Philadelphia, where I may take my rightful place in society. After all, I am known by the very best of people and welcome in their homes. But here, there are too many whispers about me. And in the new capital! Well, I don't like cows and sheep and bales of hay. They make me sneeze."

"I am not sure I can finish all my commissions by Friday, a week, Miss Drummond. But I'd be most grateful for an introduction to Miss Shippen. I, too, must be moving on."

Abigail went to her escritoire and drew out a fragile piece of parchment, on which she penned a few lines. She folded it and handed it to Savannah. "Miss Shippen's address in Philadelphia. I'm told her father entertains only the best of the best at his table. No riffraff like that gruesome Patrick Henry. The man of the people! Pah! He dresses like the lowest of farmhands. The people can have him."

Savannah held her tongue, which was her first lesson in spying, she decided. Her second came only a few hours later, when she proposed to her publisher, Randolph Wilson, that she become a roving reporter for him and his newspaper editor friends.

"Of course, I wouldn't take sides, Mr. Wilson. It would merely be a travel column . . . illustrated, of course. I would start in Philadelphia, where the Continental Congress is being held."

Randolph Wilson thought over the possibilities a moment, then dropped into his scarred desk chair and took up quill and paper. "Franklin in Philadelphia. Parkinson in Boston. Walters in New Haven. Linnington in Newport. And they are only the beginning . . . the publishers I can get to right away." He smiled up at Savannah, and his dark brown eyes gleamed with excitement and surprise. "Yes. Yes! A travel column in these times would be a wonderful contribution. . . ."

"With illustrations, don't forget."

"Of course, of course. I'll just pen a note to each of them. Come back in a week and I'll have the first answers."

"But I had hoped to begin right away. In Philadelphia. For you."

"Of course. Of course. You can do that. And now I recollect, I did see Mister Franklin in the square. I will approach him here and get a commission for you from him immediately. Then, as the others come in, I'll merely send you their acceptance and you can add them to your mailing list. Of course, they will probably not want a reprint of something you've already sent another publisher. You will have to work up a different illustration and travel article for each of them. Will that suit?"

"Perfectly."

But taking leave of George Wythe and his family was not as easy as simply packing her trunks and booking passage on the first coach to Philadelphia. Elizabeth Wythe insisted on a round of farewell suppers, which included Sally and Thomas Fairfax, Martha Wayles and Thomas Jefferson, Sarah and Patrick Henry, and Thomas Jefferson's good friend, Richard Henry Lee, who had been elected along with the other men to the Committees of Correspondence. Savannah and Elizabeth examined every recipe book in the capital to insure wonderful food at each gathering. And everything went off with naught but small problems, until the last night of Savannah's stay. Accompanying Elizabeth's guests, the Aldriches of New Haven, were two other visitors. While Arabella was welcome, her brother, David Montgomery, was so irritating that he had Savannah biting her tongue often enough to not enjoy her supper.

And worst of all the things that could have happened: David was seated right across from Savannah!

Her enemy watched her as intently as a bullfrog watched a nearby fly. His gaze said as much. If she made a false move, she would be David's supper.

Then it was that Savannah couldn't keep her peas on her knife. Twice, they rolled off into the neckline of her dress, the same watered turquoise silk she had worn the night of George Wythe's portrait unveiling. And she would not . . . she absolutely would *not* reach inside to retrieve the sneaky little devils. Especially not with David's eyes glued to her every move. And that spark of merriment! It flummoxed her so much she slammed the knife down and picked up her spoon.

How infuriating! She'd not had to use the utensil since her childhood. The knife had been perfectly all right at each of the other suppers. Now . . . now . . . That man. That awful man! And his smile. Oh, yes. His smile. Ghostly. Haughty. Proud. A pox on him! He was laughing at her. Laughing. And noting every move she made with the stupid old spoon.

She tossed that, too, beside her plate and picked

up the two-tined fork that Elizabeth had positioned above each dinner plate. Knives and spoons had been good enough before. But this new contraption was gaining acceptance. Savannah speared some stranded peas and raised them to her mouth. Why, how easy. They stayed on the sharp tines without a bit of trouble, and she closed her mouth over them with just a touch of *That shows you, Lord David!*

David grinned. "Amazing what the proper utensils will do, isn't it, Miss Stewart?"

"Yes."

"But I'd be delighted," he whispered across the table, "to retrieve those peas which you lost in the shadows of your dress. Only say the word. . . ."

Savannah choked.

Bella, who had been seated one place to Savannah's left and had been listening to every word, reached behind Richard Aldrich and thumped Savannah on the back. She glared at her brother. "David! Where are your manners?"

"I didn't know he had any," Savannah gulped out.

"Somehow, you bring out the worst in me," David explained. "Why is that, do you suppose?"

"Probably because you don't have any best!"

Pointedly, she turned to engage in conversation with the man on her right. Jason Taliaferro, an elderly cousin of Elizabeth's, stared from David to Savannah, to Bella, to Richard Aldrich. His mouth worked over a piece of lamb and he ruminated like a cow. Though Savannah tried to draw out his opinions of the upcoming Continental Congress, the only thing he did was to chew faster, as if a word to her would somehow ruin his supper.

"He's deaf, you know," David said. "But he followed the path of every one of those peas which now reside somewhere amongst your lacy and embroidered undergarment. And by the look on his face, he enjoyed every inch they traveled."

"Enough, my lord!"

"Yes, David," Bella said. "Enough is enough. I have never known you to be so rude."

"You have never known me to be so desperate." David tucked his wayward napery into his neck and sighed dramatically. "Savannah, I am deeply sorry if I offended you. I did not think before I spoke. . . ."

"A general failing of yours, sir," Savannah snapped.

"Guilty as charged, ma'am. But a lady such as yourself, one with such beauty and graciousness, with such tact and tender feelings, cannot still hold a penitent man in so little regard. Faith, a lady such as you must needs help a penitent man such as me to make amends, or you doom his soul to eternal torment."

Savannah didn't know whether to lash out or laugh out. She had not heard such drivel since the Reverend Mr. Wilborne Mather—a direct descendant of that horrible Cotton Mather—had come to preach at their local church.

Eternal torment!

She suffered eternal torment merely looking at David. And if she were to forgive him . . . again . . . what would happen if he reverted to type as he had done twice? Could she risk it? Dare she? Especially now, when she had so much on her mind, so much to do to help Patrick and Benjamin?

To help Patrick and Benjamin! By God, she had not thought it out completely. And here, in front of her, with his powerful dark blue eyes searching for an answer, his broad shoulders leaning over his plate, awaiting something from her . . . Here, she had her perfect foil. A gentleman. A British heir to a title. A Tory. A merchant who carried King George's commission. Her foil. Her blind. Her calling card into the bowels of the aristocracy and perhaps the political arena, where she could learn what the Rebels needed to know.

David Montgomery, soon to be the sixth or seventh or one hundredth Marquess of Lorton, you are about to become my shield and my armor. . . .

Ah, she had much to learn about the spy business. But if it meant getting closer to David, there could possibly be some pleasant moments in it. There already had been, if she discounted his damnable attribute of seeing her as a strumpet. Good Lord, if he thought her less than ideal when she had done naught but tease him, what would he think if he knew her true intentions?

Savannah hung her head to hide the smile that had formed as she thought and planned. It wouldn't do to let David know that she was inclined to enjoy the role she was about to play. He might get it into his head that she was attracted to him.

Which, of course, she was. But she would make very certain he would not know it. Not now. Not ever. She knew her station in life precluded anything with him but the mildest of flirtations and the empty-headedness of romantic intrigue. So, she would step into the role, play it to the back row, and do her duty to her compatriots.

And if she broke David Montgomery's heart in the

process, good. He needed to be taken down from the pedestal on which his grandfather had put him.

When Savannah raised her head to pierce David with a friendly glance, she was perfectly composed. "My lord is silver-tongued. His argument shames me. I should have listened to your apology, David. That I did not is unforgivable."

"Yet, I forgive you, if you will forgive me."

She nodded once. "Perhaps we could start from the beginning?"

"I had hoped for nothing less." David smiled and reached over to take Savannah's hand. "Miss Stewart, may I claim the first dance?"

"Delighted, my lord."

David held Savannah's hand for a fraction of a moment longer than necessary. He squeezed it, then reluctantly let go.

Good, he thought. She didn't suspect a thing. And she was reacting with dispatch to his proposal. Which meant, as Patrick had suggested might happen, that she saw the wisdom in having him for a friend. Ordinarily, he would have been outraged to have anyone use him in the way Savannah was planning to do. But he had his own reasons for allowing her to do it. And if she knew them, she would probably hang him from the nearest tree.

And, damnit, he would deserve it.

"I hope your stomacher is tied tightly, Savannah," David teased forty minutes later. "Else you'll leave a trail of peas behind you as you bow to the music."

"Tied tightly and completely, David. And will always stay that way, sir."

Savannah smiled sweetly at him and he winked at her as he led her to the line forming in the drawing room. As they bobbed and turned in the stately minuet, David's hand held hers possessively but not so tightly that Savannah felt stifled.

"My lord, it is a shame this is our last night together."

"Not so, Miss Stewart. George tells me you will be in Philadelphia, just my destination. I'm sure we'll be seeing each other there."

"It's a big city, my lord."

"Not so big as London. And I will make it a point to seek you out."

Chapter Twelve

Philadelphia was everything Savannah had dreamed it might be, and more and less. Peggy Shippen guided her around the city, pointing out the homes of the most prominent families, all of them strongly aligned with the British government.

After two days of sightseeing, Savannah decided it was difficult for anyone in this city to profess himself as anything but a Tory. On the major thoroughfares, Redcoats predominated. Most carried muskets or rifles at the ready. All had highly polished swords in intricate scabbards at their waist. Almost every man was bewigged, every woman in the most elaborate of dresses. It looked as if they were heading to a ball. Yet, Savannah soon learned from Peggy that this was their ordinary street costume.

Ah, Polonius, you would have loved Philadelphia! Clothes doth proclaim more than the man. They proclaimed his politics.

And as a guest in the Shippen house, Savannah heard more politics than she had ever heard in Williamsburg—even while she had sat in the House of Burgesses.

One such conversation needed to be transmitted to Patrick Henry and Benjamin Franklin, so they could get it to the proper channels. But before leaving Williamsburg she had been so hurried she had not been able to tell them what she was going to use as her code.

A letter describing her ingenious method would not do. Even here the mails were opened by everyone. She thought of using a private pony rider; but how could she explain why a mere artist needed one? No . . . she had to take the chance of a personal meeting. But she didn't know how and she didn't know when. She only knew it had to be soon, because General Gage had stationed his own spies right inside the seven taverns and inns the delegates were using. Patrick, Ben, and Jefferson had to know who was loyal to the cause and who was suspect. She had gleaned a list of seven names thus far; but she knew there must needs be more. They had to be warned. Now.

The only way she could see to do it was to try to meet them quite by accident. Purposeful accident.

Savannah took to haunting the stores, with the excuse to Peggy that the blockades were making it almost impossible to buy the proper consistency of linseed oil and paint pigments that she needed to mix her special transparent colors. Too often, however, Peggy, who shopped for trinkets and bolt goods every day, would simply don her latest cloak and trot along behind Savannah. They would only get three houses down the thoroughfare before they were joined by several more Philadelphia belles, none of whom had anything better to do with their time than to visit at each others' houses and shop at the many merchant stores near the wharf.

It tickled and rankled Savannah that she was at the head of a procession of overdressed, giggling females, behind which came a long line of carriages. Empty, the carriages were, on the way to the stores. Full, on the way back.

But in the midst of this bizarre parade Savannah learned of the movement of British troops, because each of the girls had at least one beau in the military. Most waited breathlessly (but chattering like crickets) for Colonel Rogers or Lieutenant Battersea or Captain Brown of His Majesty's Fusiliers or Battery or Light Brigade.

Savannah's list of things to tell Patrick and Ben grew steadily. And she fumed, pacing her room each night as she was thwarted in her plans by bumbling and insipid *girls!*

On one such foray, she sidled over to the dyes and paint department, hiding herself behind a tower of hogsheads containing a pungent collection of salted meats and fish. Peggy's shrill laughter carried across the crowded store, and Savannah gritted her teeth. "If I hear one more forty-minute session about the merits of bobbin lace over loomed lace, I'll pull out my hair," she muttered.

"Oh, no, Savannah! That would be horrible."

Savannah turned and practically launched herself at Arabella. She hugged her dear friend until she thought the poor girl would expire from lack of breath.

"I've missed you, too," Bella laughed, after Savannah pushed herself away.

"But what are you doing in Philadelphia? I thought you were bound for New Haven?"

Bella pouted. "I was. Until David thought he detected too much interest on my part in Richard Aldrich. Isn't that ridiculous?"

"Observant, your brother. Doesn't want you to anticipate the preacher, that's all."

"Oh, Savannah!" Bella held her hands to her flaming cheeks. "It was hardly like that!" When Savannah pursed her lips and cocked her head, Bella hung hers in acquiescence and growled, "David says I have a face like an open book and he can read it as easily as his newspaper. You, too, I suppose."

"In that aspect, we are alike."

Just then, Peggy Shippen waved from the open door where she and her friends had gathered, urging Savannah to hurry her conversation.

"Drat!"

Bella looked around and caught sight of who had brought out Savannah's impatience. "Is that Peggy Shippen, the daughter of Magistrate Edward Shippen?"

"The same. I'm staying with her, painting her portrait and some miniatures of her friends."

"Do you think she'd come to supper? I've been prodding David to have a fete of some sort, but he's put me off. Now that you're here, I may just be able to coax him to open his money box a bit."

"I'd love to come. But you'll have to send Peggy a handwritten invitation. She's very aware of her position in society. Only the proprieties for our Miss Shippen."

"Sounds as if you don't like her much."

"She's not like you, Bella. She has mood swings which are truly frightening. But she's been very generous. Besides, I'm sure she'd be delighted to attend a supper at the home of the grandson and granddaughter of the Marquess of Lorton."

The night of Arabella's supper, Peggy insisted they use the sky-blue phaeton, even though the temperature had dropped below sixty degrees and was falling rapidly. She had a new sable-lined cloak and a towering white wig studded with diamonds and rubies, and she was bound that all of Philadelphia would see her. Savannah huddled in one corner, her thick wool cloak augmented by two wool shawls. But still her teeth chattered, like the sound the wind makes blowing through a field of empty, dead dry milkweed pods.

Acting like King George himself, Peggy bowed her head to right and left and waved to one and sundry. As if she knew them . . . which she didn't. As if they knew her . . . which would have amused them if Peggy wasn't known to snub most of them because of their rebel leanings.

For the first time, Savannah found herself the object of muttered oaths and shaking fists from citizens who were *her* people. Those were the people she wished she were with instead of these overdressed peacocks. The ones she could imagine herself getting into scrapes with; the kind of folk she had loved and taught and argued with and fought for all her life. Spying had sounded adventurous and dangerous. She hadn't realized it would also be terribly, terribly lonely.

Bella had shown great promise at Honesty Dunn's school. Tonight, she would have made her teachers proud. She was a gracious hostess, a perfect example of the first principle Honesty had drilled into her charges: that by being charming to everyone, a woman showed the softer side of God.

Indeed, to satisfy this, Bella had invited a good cross section of the city, including both Tory and Rebel, and firmly announced that there would be no talk of politics at table or while dancing—though she allotted a small room off David's office for the men to repair, smoke, and debate, provided they closed the door so the women didn't have to hear the shouts.

Among them was the entire contingent of Virginians and most of the prominent Rebel Philadelphians, including Patrick, Thomas Jefferson, and good old Ben.

Savannah couldn't have been happier. She finally had a chance to speak with her fellow insurrectionists. And she had a sample of her code tucked into her stomacher, ready to give to them at the first opportunity.

She might have done it, too, if David hadn't usurped her elbow from the first moment she came in the door and he handed her cloak to a maidservant.

After ten minutes of searching out Patrick and Ben

and trying to edge over to them but being unsuccessful because she couldn't get away from David, Savannah was as jumpy as a newborn kitten.

After forty, snapping like a turtle.

After an hour, ready to make those dark blue laughing eyes truly black.

"I do not need a shadow, David!"

"I need a dancing partner, Savannah."

"I'll introduce you to Peggy. She loves the titled nobility."

"I prefer a Georgian who thinks we royals are dirt under her feet."

"At least you're beginning to know your place."

"Oh, I definitely know my place, Miss Stewart. It's you who haven't recognized exactly where it is."

"In your bed, I suppose."

"Only if you want it to be, Savannah. What I had in mind was something a little more respectable . . . something unexpected by both you and your family."

"And yours?"

"Definitely mine." He grimaced. "God, yes. Definitely unexpected by mine."

She wanted to pursue it, ached to know if his meaning were what she thought . . . hoped . . . it might be. But there were too many people, too many conversations, too few opportunities for privacy, and not enough ways to distract David's attention so Savannah could complete her mission.

Another hour, and Savannah had had a surfeit of male attention. It would last her a whole lifetime. Well, perhaps not that long.

Surprisingly, David's attentions—and his presence—were not altogether unwanted. For the first time since that night at Lorton Woods, she noticed that his masculine scent was augmented by the subtlest of spices and cedar, probably from the chest in which his clothes had been stored. And the gentle pressure of his hand at her back, the warm breath at the nape of her neck, the sound of his buckskin breeches rubbing against his indigo-blue wool frock coat, the creak of his leather boots, the tiny click of his watch fob . . . each sound told her she was the sole object of a very handsome man's attentions and that she was protected, regardless of whether she wanted to be or not.

After five glasses of spiced cider, two of them hardened long enough to make them as powerful as a tumbler of rum, Savannah begged David to excuse her to "use the facilities."

"I'll show you where they are."

"David, for goodness sake, I can find them on my own!"

"Goodness has nothing to do with it. It's dark out there and very private. We could linger. . . ."

"Oh, bother! I hate to do this, but you leave me no choice. . . ."

She jammed her heel heavily on his booted foot and rushed for the side door leading to the brick alleyway and the back comfort house. As she passed a group of men lounging near the study door, she raised her eyebrows at Patrick and Ben and beckoned with one finger for them to follow her. She looked back to see David hopping up and down on one foot. The words he mouthed, she was sure, were not meant for a female's ears.

Served him right. She had a job to do and he was

in her way.

Abigail Drummond had watched David and Savannah all night. She had come to this damned supper party because it was the first one she had been invited to since she had arrived in Philadelphia. But things had not gone as she had planned. Rather than welcome her as a woman of the world, with important friends in high places, the women had shunned her. In the stores, she had heard them whisper about her, using such words as *pariah*, *strumpet*, and *courtesan*.

Yet there was Savannah Stewart, only an artist, with no family to speak of—certainly not the kind Abigail had, ones who were in direct lineage to several noble families. In fact, Abigail had heard that Savannah's family had been servants in England. Servants! And she was squired by the heir to a marquess.

America! It did not know how to treat women such as she, who could be most helpful in any enterprise. But in England . . .

How she longed for England. She would book passage tomorrow to return, if the damned inflation caused by this stupid uprising had not eaten into her cash reserves, draining them until she was forced to sell her beautiful mustard-gold phaeton and matched pair of grey geldings. Why, she had even had to sell her Negro slaves. But the money they'd brought had only lasted her three months. She was sure the slave master had cheated her. Although it was true they were unfit for much labor, since she had spoiled them by giving them far too much while they worked for her.

Had she not been so desperate, she might have gotten more for them in another part of the country. But here in the North, she must take what she could get, since there were so many abolitionists.

Rebels and abolitionists. This was not hospitable country anymore.

She must get to England, to a country where she could ply her arts and make her way in society, until she found herself a rich husband and settled down in royal splendor.

David Montgomery caught her eye the moment he and his sister entered the city. Heir to a fortune and title. Young enough to be unschooled, therefore perhaps willing to accept the attentions of a more "learned" woman, someone who could help him make his way in the world and wasn't afraid to use her femininity to get him where he deserved to go. Where *she* deserved to go.

But Savannah got to him first.

With what? She was not skilled in flirtation. She even looked annoyed that he was paying court to her. And at the first chance she got, she crooked her head to two of those awful Rebels! Abigail was shocked but astute enough to know that simpering little Savannah was probably about to have a liaison with someone with whom she ought not be seen. Abigail swiveled her head. No one, not even David Montgomery, seemed to have caught that suspicious exchange between Savannah and the tall redheaded man who dressed like a pauper. No one but herself.

Hmm . . . Perhaps it was time to ingratiate herself

with Peggy Shippen and her Tory father. And if Savannah got burned in the process . . . well, she shouldn't play in games in which she wasn't as adept as Abigail.

Quickly, before she lost the initiative, Abigail sought out Edward and Peggy Shippen.

"David, what *are* you doing, jumping around here like a chicken?"

"Bella, if I told you, you wouldn't believe it."

"Savannah?"

David assessed his sister. "When did you get so wise?" He hobbled over to the main staircase and plunked down on the first riser. "Damn, that smarts!"

Bella shook her finger at him. "Perhaps now you'll woo her the proper way." She sat next to David and hugged him. "You do love her, don't you?"

"Huh! I can't get close enough to find out."

Bella giggled. "There is not much you can't do, brother dear. You only have to put your mind to it, don't you know?"

"I've half a mind to hog-tie her and carry her off."

"Then do it."

"Bella!"

"Oh, David, you are entirely too prim and proper." She nodded her head for emphasis and pecked him on the cheek. "Yes, you are. If you are to succeed with someone like Savannah, you must become more like these Americans, David. Take what you want. Of course, don't mistreat her; but she seems to need a firm but gentle hand. And you . . . you sit back and tease the life out of her. It's annoying, you know. Especially when the lady craves more . . . uh . . . *adventurous* lovemaking."

Bella scooted away before David could shake some sense into her. That school of Honesty Dunn's! He should have brought a tutor from home. She had learned entirely too much there. Things far more masculine than were good for a lady.

Although . . .

He hoisted himself to his feet, wincing a little as his weight went down on what was sure to be a bruised instep, and headed outside to find Savannah. He rounded the corner in time to hear a dreadfully overdressed woman warning a portly gentleman, two lovely young women, and three British officers about the *Georgia lady who is involved with the Rebels*.

"I've been watching her closely, ever since she arrived here in Philadelphia. Knew her in Williamsburg, and she was much too embroiled in politics then. She even sneaked onto the floor of the House of Burgesses. Governor Murray was horror-stricken, I can tell you. It wouldn't surprise me if she was a spy."

"Oh, please, Miss Drummond . . ."

"Well, if you don't believe me," the lady said, "you can see for yourself. She's right outside with the worst of them . . . that farmer, Patrick Henry. If you hurry, you might catch her in some intrigue or other. After all, she is a guest in your house, and you do extend your hospitality and table to good British officers. No telling what she's heard and is at this moment passing on to her . . . well, dare I say it . . . her paramour?"

"Where there's smoke . . ." one of the officers said.

"Don't be silly. Savannah Stewart is as Tory as the rest of us."

"If that's so, then she has naught to worry her." The captain pulled at his lower lip. "It wouldn't hurt to find her and put the lie to these thoughts, however."

Christ! David nearly knocked down a half dozen of Bella's guests in his haste to get to the back gardens. The candle lanterns that his manservant, Willy, had set out lit the path to the comfort house, but shadows predominated in the rest of the small yard.

Some protector he was! He had to find her before those blundering fools. But how?

"The borders?"

"Yes, Patrick. The borders. You've seen my illustrations. You know the kind I mean."

Patrick slapped his forehead. "Of course!" He hugged Savannah. "Ingenious."

"Well . . ." She could feel herself blushing, even in the dark. "Well . . ."

She stepped back and stuck her hand into her stomacher to give him the first of the codes. She had hardly gotten a good hold of the edges of the sketch before she was enveloped in a great bear hug and she heard David's voice growl, "Get out of here. British officers coming."

"No . . . Patrick, wait!"

David whirled her around and crushed her to him. "Shut up, you fool. Some damned piece of skirt has denounced you as a spy."

"What?"

"I said, shut up."

He crushed his lips to hers to keep her quiet. But there was more to his emotions than simple worry. She was in danger. Savannah. *His* Savannah. And no one . . . *no one* was going to stop him from protecting her again.

A giant exquisite ache engulfed his body as his lips moved against hers. He breathed in her scent, loving the mixture she had chosen for herself. There was delicate lilac and a hint of rose water, combined with the delicious aroma of vanilla. Her lips were soft, moist, warm. And her mouth opened under his pressure. Opened and welcomed his tongue.

"Ah, God, Savannah!"

"Oh, David . . ."

"Over here . . . that's her . . . right there . . ."

As David tried ineffectually to conceal her from the searchers, he heard a rustling in Savannah's stomacher. His heart lodged in his throat and he remembered.

She had been trying to give Mister Henry something, had reached into her stomacher to extract . . . what?

Something dangerous, he'd vow. Something that might get her tossed into prison, if he knew his Savannah. And he knew her. God, he knew her. Not enough, of course. But he could remedy that *and* get her out of this. She might hate him later, but he'd have to chance it.

"Savannah . . ."

"Yes, David?"

"Don't scream. . . ." He yanked on her stomacher and the neckline above it. Yanked, until the silk gave way and tore down the front. Yanked, until her delicate breasts were exposed. He shoved the tattered stomacher into his vest, rustling papers and all, and covered her soft mounds with his palms. Once again he captured her lips, keeping her squirming head firmly in place with one hand as the other kneaded her breasts.

"There! I told you the farmer was her paramour. . . . Oh!"

"Farmer?" One of the women giggled. "But it seems this is our host, Mister Montgomery. Quite far from a farmer, he is."

David jerked his head up as if he hadn't heard them coming. "Good Lord!" He quickly slipped off his frock coat and draped it over Savannah. She would have bolted, but he held her right hand in his left and pulled her tight against him with his left arm. "Well, we weren't prepared to announce it yet; but you've caught us." He gave a quick laugh. Half fear, half promise, his gaze bore into Savannah's with an intensity he hoped she'd understand.

"We do beg your lordship's pardon," the portly man said. "My lord . . ."

"A little precipitate. But we had intended to announce our engagement soon. I hope you will be the first to congratulate me on my good fortune, Mr. . . . ?"

"Shippen, my lord. Edward Shippen. Magistrate in His Majesty's Assize. My daughter, Peggy, and her friends Theresa Broadbent and Hope Russell."

The girls bobbed a curtsy.

"Major Ford, at your service, my lord. And my junior officers, Lieutenants Gates and Gordon. We do apologize to the lady."

Peggy Shippen whispered to her father and he nodded. "To make up for this *unfortunate* happenstance, we would be honored if you would allow my mother and me to hostess an engagement party for you both. Imagine, a romance right under my nose and Savannah never said a word! Isn't it too wonderful?"

"Oh, no!" Savannah clutched David's coat about her and buried her head against his neck. "Damn you," she hissed in his ear. "Get us out of this."

"Savannah thanks you for your kindness," David said. "She is, of course, embarrassed. But we would be delighted to accept your kind offer. Now, if you will excuse us, I would like to get Savannah into the house so my sister can assist her in making repairs. . . . She will be staying here for the night."

He half dragged, half carried Savannah through the back gardens, warning, "You can yell your head off after the others have gone. But for now, if you don't want to lose your head, keep your mouth shut!"

Chapter Thirteen

"I'm going to kill him. I'm going to kill him."

"You'll do no such thing, Savannah. You and David are made for each other. If you'd both just stop for a minute and talk sweetly to each other instead of always arguing, you'd both see it."

"Bella, he . . . he . . ." Savannah groaned and buried her head in the soft down pillows on Bella's bed. "They must have seen . . . Oh, God!"

"Well, for heaven's sake, Savannah! It's not as if you have anything different from any other woman. Except for your freckles, of course. And I have always wondered. . . ."

Savannah raised her head and looked at Bella. "Are you serious? . . . You are!"

She stared at the young girl who was trying, delicately but definitely, to get a glimpse of what everyone else had already seen *and* those mysterious freckles the girls had always giggled about in Georgia. The thoughts that must be racing through that fertile imagination! Oh, God, it was too much. Suddenly, Savannah—like the girls she had once

GET 4 FREE BOOKS

Heartfire Romance

HEARTFIRE HOME SUBSCRIPTION SERVICE
P.O. BOX 5214
120 BRIGHTON ROAD
CLIFTON, NEW JERSEY 07015

AFFIX STAMP HERE

FREE BOOK CERTIFICATE

GET 4 FREE BOOKS

Heartfire Romance

Yes! I want to subscribe to Zebra's HEARTFIRE HOME SUBSCRIPTION SERVICE. Please send me my 4 FREE books. Then each month I'll receive the four newest Heartfire Romances as soon as they are published to preview Free for ten days. If I decide to keep them I'll pay the special discounted price of just $3.50 each; a total of $14.00. This is a savings of $3.00 off the regular publishers price. There are no shipping, handling or other hidden charges. There is no minimum number of books to buy and I may cancel this subscription at any time. In any case the 4 FREE Books are mine to keep regardless.

NAME _____

ADDRESS _____

CITY _____ STATE _____ ZIP _____

TELEPHONE _____

SIGNATURE _____

(If under 18 parent or guardian must sign)
Terms and prices subject to change.
Orders subject to acceptance.

HF 103

TO GET YOUR 4 FREE BOOKS MAIL THE COUPON BELOW.

ENJOY ALL THE PASSION AND ROMANCE OF...

Heartfire

ROMANCES from ZEBRA

After you have read HEARTFIRE ROMANCES, we're sure you'll agree that HEARTFIRE sets new standards of excellence for historical romantic fiction. Each Zebra HEARTFIRE novel is the ultimate blend of intimate romance and grand adventure and each takes place in the kinds of historical settings you want most...the American Revolution, the Old West, Civil War and more.

SUBSCRIBERS $AVE, $AVE, $AVE!!!

As a HEARTFIRE Home Subscriber, you'll save with your HEARTFIRE Subscription. You'll receive 4 brand new Heartfire Romances to preview Free for 10 days each month. If you decide to keep them you'll pay only $3.50 each; a total of $14.00 and you'll save $3.00 each month off the cover price.

Plus, we'll send you these novels as soon as they are published each month. There is never any shipping, handling or other hidden charges; home delivery is always FREE! And there is no obligation to buy even a single book. You may return any of the books within 10 days for full credit and you can cancel your subscription at any time. No questions asked.

Zebra's HEARTFIRE ROMANCES Are The Ultimate
In Historical Romantic Fiction.
Start Enjoying Romance As You Have Never Enjoyed It Before...
With 4 FREE Books From HEARTFIRE

Now you can get Heartfire Romances right at home and save

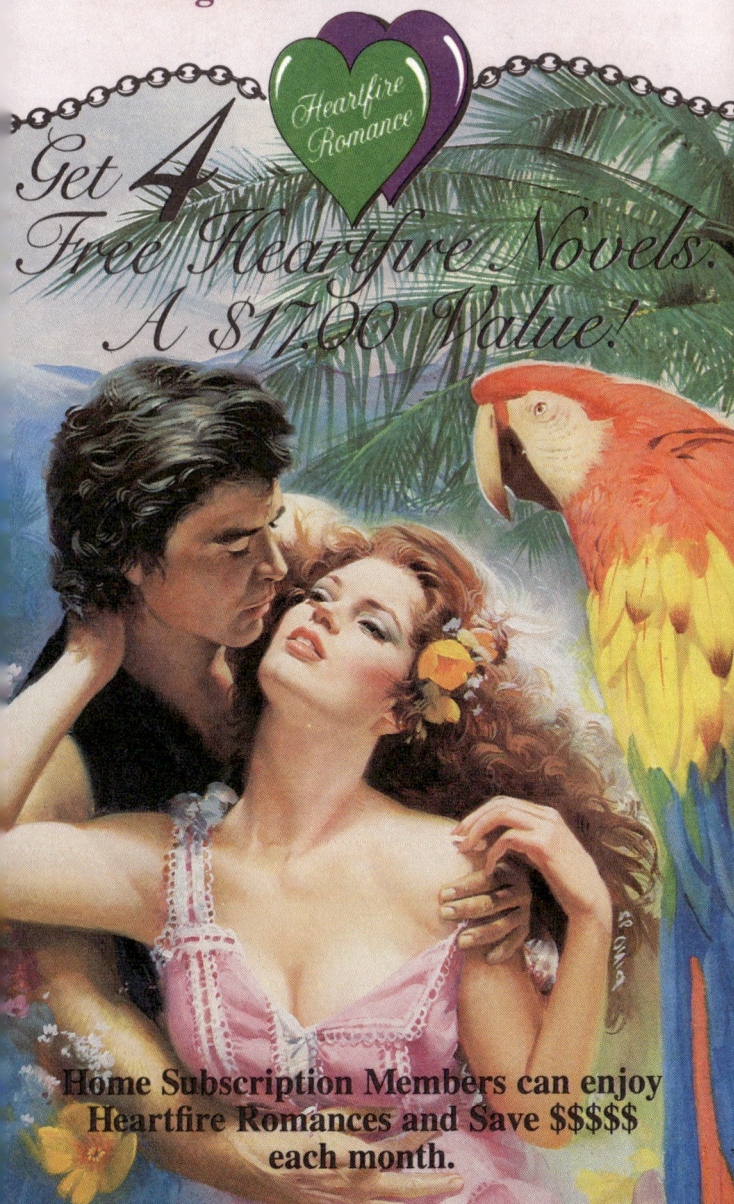

Heartfire Romance

Get 4 Free Heartfire Novels. A $17.00 Value!

Home Subscription Members can enjoy Heartfire Romances and Save $$$$$ each month.

taught—also began to giggle. She looked at Bella, held her hand over her mouth so David couldn't hear and have his own imaginative ideas, and broke into huge, refreshing gulps of laughter.

"Oh, God!" She clutched her stomach, as it hurt so much from suppressing the loudest laughs. "Oh, what a night!" Without caring that her "fairy-dusted" breasts—as David had called them—were exposed, she walked over to Bella's three-sided mirror and picked at her beautiful tattered silk. No matter how hard she tugged, she could not get the silk to cover her completely. "Can we fix it?"

"Lilah, my maidservant, can fix anything." Bella took a serviceable lemon-yellow linen robe out of the mahogany chest at the foot of her bed and tossed it on her upholstered slipper chair. "I'll help you get out of your gown and then I'll give it to Lilah. You put on the dressing robe." When Savannah was finally out of the gown, Bella held out her hand. "Give me the stomacher and the pieces that were torn."

"David has them."

"Huh! If he thinks he's keeping them as souvenirs, he's a cooked goose."

"Gander."

"Stuffed, trussed, and roasted!"

The two burst into another bout of laughter, which ended only when Bella went in search of her brother. She returned a few minutes later with the pieces of lacy cotton and watered silk.

"That man! He was going to keep them as souvenirs. Some of the pearl garlands are broken. I'll have Willy search the yard for them tomorrow. But the dress and undergarments ripped right down the seams, so Lilah shouldn't have any trouble putting the fabric back together. It will be as good as new. I promise."

"Thank you, Bella. If David hadn't lied about the engagement, I'd take great pleasure in knowing you were going to be my sister-in-law."

"That might happen yet, Savannah." At Savannah's cynical snort, she bobbed her head. "Yes, it might! Stranger things have happened."

"Not to us Stewarts, Bella. There's no way your grandfather will welcome that kind of liaison. The kind your guests saw in the garden, yes. But marriage? One whiff of the possibility, and he'll jerk David and you right back to good old England and the safety of your nobility. And I'll be left to salvage what remains of my reputation."

Yes, she decided, she was going to kill David. First chance she got.

In borrowed nightshift an hour later, Savannah climbed into the high four-poster bed, blew out the candle, and drew the bed curtains around her so she could keep in the warmth. Winter was fast upon them. Even multiple layers of quilts couldn't chase away all the drafts.

She snuggled down under the covers and closed her eyes, reliving and replaying the strange events of that night.

David had been so forceful, so much the kind of man she'd always known he might be. And his kiss! It had spread such warmth through her, Savannah had imagined herself as butter melting around an ear of maize. Languid. Her knees weak, her heart beating faster than a nor'east rain against the windowpanes.

After all the warnings her family had given . . . after hearing all the stories about the Montgomerys and their usual manipulation of events to suit their purposes . . . she was rapidly falling in love with the next marquess.

How droll.

How disastrous.

Because it couldn't work. What she had told Bella was exactly right. David's grandfather—the holder of the money box—would have apoplexy if he ever heard what had happened. And he was bound to hear. Lawrence Fenton had been a guest at the supper. Savannah wagered he was at this minute penning a missive. . . .

"Damn and blast!"

The letter for Patrick. It hadn't been in the folds of material Bella had brought back, since there was no rustle of parchment and Bella hadn't mentioned seeing it. Which meant only one thing. David still had it.

Well, not for long.

She absolutely could not risk his seeing its contents. He was still a Montgomery. Still the nobility. Still the agent of the King. Tory. There was no other word for it. He was a Tory and she was a Rebel spy. Regardless of the fact that he wanted to get her into his bed, he . . .

Into his bed . . .

Hmm . . .

She could strike up a bargain with him, a compromise of sorts. Other women did it. Peggy Shippen with her Benedict Arnold, for one. Yes, and that nasty Abigail Drummond and John Murray. Pah! They hadn't been engaged. Peggy and Benedict were, as were she and David. He had said so. Announced it to the world. Well, then, she had a perfect excuse to bargain with the devil, since among the Tory social set an open betrothal allowed liberties unknown to Savannah's family and friends in Georgia.

Savannah thought long and hard about the consequences if she did go to David. She also thought long and hard about the consequences if she didn't go and he read the letter for Patrick.

David might not betray her; but her effectiveness for the cause would be ruined. She might as well pack up her paints and canvases and head for home and a simple life in Georgia. She shivered. Savannah. The most Tory of cities. Four garrisons of British soldiers were already quartered in the best of homes, and there was an armada of ships in the harbor. She would hate it. Philadelphia was bad enough; but at least here there were two Rebels to every one Tory, so there was some semblance of pride. Back home, you were either openly Tory or toadied to them. Unless you packed up as her family had done and took to the road. Her father's last letter had underscored their haste in fulfilling the next publishing contract, though Savannah knew it wasn't due for another year. But worse than knowing that everyone was traveling from place to place to keep one step ahead of the British troops and magistrates was knowing that her father's home had been taken over by a British naval officer as his headquarters. No, she could not go back. Not until whatever was going to happen happened.

Which didn't bring her any closer to getting her letter back than she had been before.

But it did make her more determined to grit her teeth and go to David.

The hall was dark and shadows danced in front of her candle as she crept past Bella's bedroom door. She wished she could melt into the wall as the shadows did, melt and slither into David's room to retrieve the letter without having to face him. But she was human, with form and substance; and sometimes it got in the way!

The door handle clicked back so loudly, she cringed, hoping it didn't wake the entire household. Quickly, before she lost her nerve, she padded over to David's bed and held the candle aloft.

"Damn!"

He wasn't there.

David sent Willy on his way and closed the door. He tended the fire in the drawing rooms and the kitchen, adding several large logs to each to ensure continuous heat throughout the night. At first, the house was eerily quiet. But then he heard a footfall above his head. And another. Someone—Savannah, probably—pacing the floor? He listened intently. Those creaks as she crossed the floor, as she opened drawers and closed them, were not coming from the guest bedroom. They were in his own!

Well, well, well. He cleaned off his hands and smiled. The minx was going through his things. And he could just bet what she was looking for.

He removed his boots to muffle his own footsteps. He didn't want to alert her and give her time to slip back to her room. What would she be wearing? he wondered, as he carefully mounted the steps. Would her long dark hair be plaited or left loose? He hoped it was plaited. He wanted to run his fingers through the knobs, fluff out their thickness, feel the silk on his fingertips. Flashes of everything he wanted to do to her made him quicken his steps, until he was just outside the door. He stopped and listened. Whispered *damns* and *blasts* confirmed that she was still inside, still searching.

Cautiously, he eased open the door and stepped into the shadows. Her candle gave off a faint glow in which her figure was trapped. Yellow was a good color for her dark hair—plaited, as he'd hoped. And the linen was old enough to have lost its crispness. The robe was too small for Savannah, so it clung to her curves as it had never done to Bella's. Bare feet. She must be cold, since the fire hadn't yet been stoked and laid for the night.

As if she heard his thoughts, she shivered and hugged herself for a moment, before opening the last drawer in his chest of drawers.

"Whatever you're looking for, it isn't there," David said.

Savannah whirled and her foot banged into the open drawer. "Damnation!" She hopped on one foot. "Oh, that hurts!"

David crossed the room in two strides and picked her up. There was nowhere else to put her except the bed, so he plunked her down on the side and knelt down to finger her toes. Although she groaned, there didn't seem to be anything out of joint.

"Bruise, probably," he said. "Which should nicely match the bruises around your neck when I get finished throttling you." He sat back on his heels and looked into her defiant face. "Is this how you repay my hospitality, by stealing from me?"

"I am not a thief! I was merely searching for something which is mine."

"The only thing in this room which is yours is me."

Such outrageous words! But what a response her body gave to them. David's fingers kneaded her toes and Savannah felt a tingling begin. But it didn't stop there. It accelerated, moving up her ankle, her knee, her thigh, into the darkness, where heat so intense flashed upward and outward that she had to grip the bedclothes to keep from trembling.

Ah, God! There was no need for bargains. She would give herself willingly and damn the consequences. There would never be a future in their union; but she could have this night.

How ironic. He had offered her one night and she had scratched his face. Her hand reached out to touch the spot and found a slight indentation. Her breath caught as she brushed her fingers back and forth, up and down, remembering that night and the feelings he had awakened.

His eyes. His beautiful midnight-blue eyes were not hooded this night. He stared at her and she saw what she wanted to see: desire, perhaps even love. That it might only be lust didn't account. She wanted more. She would pretend there was more. She would take what she could get, because the ache that had begun with her first glimpse of him and had continued for two years had to be assuaged. And she knew of no other way to do it but to love him.

"David . . ."

"Shh . . . I know." His hands left her toes and framed her face. "Don't talk. Just let me show you . . ."

Tenderly, he splayed his fingers in her hair, tugging until the plait gave way and her hair tumbled freely over her shoulders. He finger-combed it, sending more tiny tremors through her body than she could count. His hands, his beautiful hands, arranged her hair over her shoulders, then continued down to the ends of the curls, skimming over her body like feathers.

She watched his eyes as he cupped her breasts. They clouded over and his mouth opened on a soft groan. His fingers kneaded, softly, so softly. She felt her breasts swell to fill his hands, felt the peaks pucker. Spasms shook her and she gasped, clutching his hands to her.

He was on his feet and leaning over her, pressing her down into the bed. His mouth covered hers. His lips were soft, coaxing; and she felt such joy that he didn't act the conqueror, though she knew he was.

The joy turned to awe when he peeled back her robe, eased down her borrowed nightshift, lowered his head, and took her right breast into his mouth.

The dark mysteries of the night were more beautiful than she could have imagined, especially since she was sharing them with David.

But a melancholy sweetness it was, because she

wanted this to go on forever and ever, into eternity, and knew it couldn't.

His mouth left her right breast, and with a slight shifting of her body, she offered him her left. "Ah," she said as his tongue wet her nipple and caused more powerful tremors. "Yes. Yes."

Somehow, even with a throbbing arousal, David managed to slip off Savannah's nightshift and robe. His eyes skimmed her body. Lush, glorious.

"You're beautiful, Savannah. So damned beautiful."

Her fingers clenched his shoulders, then thrust into his hair and she smiled. "So are you, David."

He believed it. Her turquoise eyes had darkened, and he could swear he saw the moon and stars in their depths. But more than that, he saw trust, confidence, truth—human traits he had never before seen in a woman's eyes. There was also passion, but that was nothing new. With Savannah, however, he was certain it lodged there for the first time.

And therein lay a deep problem.

He wanted her more than he had ever wanted another woman. He wanted to give her the best there was to give, but knew she would feel pain because she was still virginal. He could not ease it, though he wished he could. And knowing it would come, perhaps to ruin everything, he decided to give her so much pleasure beforehand that her mind might be clouded enough to withstand it.

So he took his time. He aroused her breasts until he thought he'd go mad or explode prematurely. He kissed her, tasted her, drank in her scent. He learned every hill and valley of her body, discovered that her freckles dusted not only her breasts but also her belly and thighs. He found a sensitive spot just in front of her ear that drew him back again and again, simply to hear her moan with pleasure.

And suddenly, he lost track of deliberately arousing her to overcome the pain.

Savannah took him away from himself, into a place she carved out for them. Whenever and wherever he touched, she responded with such wonder and delight that his heart expanded and nearly burst with pure joy. It beat harder and faster, pushing out his blood until there was a roaring thunder in his head and a throbbing pulse in every pore.

Society and royalty be damned! This woman, this American, was his. He loved her. Pure, simple . . . and more complicated than a spider's web. But he didn't care. They had *now*.

"David, is there more?"

"God, yes! Much more."

"Oh, good. Please show me."

Quickly, he pulled off his boots and unbuttoned his shirt. Savannah smiled and reached for the ties at his breeches. He slipped his shirt over his shoulders as she peeled down his breeches. As his hips were uncovered, her eyes got rounder and rounder. She gulped and looked up at him.

"We can't get to the 'more' until these breeches come all the way off," he teased.

"Are you sure?"

He covered her hands with his and helped her push them down the final few inches.

"Oh! I thought I knew all there was to know about anatomy. But . . . well, you *do* have larger feet than most other men, so this is possible, I suppose. But

". . . I've never seen . . . Oh, my . . ."

He moved her hand to it.

"Oh! S . . . s . . . soft. Hard, too. Aren't the good Lord's gifts wonderful?"

"Oh, my God, Savannah . . . you are the most delightful minx in all creation. And I almost lost all this. And you. With all my heart, I beg your pardon, Miss Stewart. And please, keep touching me like that."

"That's good?"

"That's very good." He reached for the delicate place covered by dark curls and caressed her.

"Oh! Oh, that's very good, too."

"I know."

He eased himself down beside her, rubbing his fingers back and forth until she gasped and shuddered. Her legs opened of their own accord and he rolled to kneel between them.

"Hold onto the bed covers, Savannah."

"Why?"

"Trust me."

"But I want to touch you."

"You will be touching me. But with a different part of you, a softer, warmer, moister part."

Savannah realized what he meant and smiled. She did as bid and clutched the bed sheets. David rocked himself into her, sliding in an inch or two, then out. It was wonderful, so wonderful! Deeper, he went. And deeper. And the rocking rhythm of their bodies lulled her. In and out. In and out. Deeper. Sleeker.

Her body ached for something more. . . .

"More, David. More."

"Yes, love. More. But gently. Very gently."

The beauty of it took her breath away. She couldn't breathe, couldn't think. She could only feel. And the feelings were like sparks. She pulsed all over, as if by entering her David had made himself part of every inch of her body. His soft hardness may have been there in that special place, but his essence was everywhere.

Suddenly, he sheathed himself much deeper and she felt a momentary pain. She gasped and tightened around him. He stopped for a few moments, then started again, and soon the pain was overshadowed by more pulses of heat, more sparks, more tingles.

She was climbing something, going somewhere . . . her body being carried by his higher and higher, through darkness and shadows, until her heart tore itself apart, a burst of white light exploded in her mind, and she cried out with the wonder and power of it.

"David! Oh, God!"

His body tensed. His legs trembled. She felt him take a great ragged breath and then thrust deeper inside her. And she was filled with him as he, too, exploded.

He sank down on her but the weight wasn't uncomfortable. In fact, she welcomed it. Wrapping her legs and arms around him, she snuggled into the crook of his neck and sighed. "So that's what it's all about. Why didn't anyone tell me?"

"No one can tell you, Savannah, love. It's something you have to experience."

"But not with any man, David. What just happened . . . the way I felt . . . that could only come from you."

David smiled and kissed the top of her head. "If you ever give me any more trouble, I'm going to remind you of those words, love."

"It won't be necessary. I'll remember."

David's arms crossed over her chest and his hands cupped her breasts. "Get some sleep."

"Mmm. I am."

She stretched her legs and wiggled until she could feel him against her back. It felt as if they were meant to lie like that, and it was a good feeling. Sleep settled easily and she tried to lose herself in it. But something niggled at the back of her mind . . . something she had left undone.

The letter!

Her eyes flashed open and she knew a moment of panic.

David chuckled. "I wondered when you'd remember what you had come in here for. Worry naught. I sent Willy to bring the letter to Mister Henry."

"Did you read it?"

"Not a line."

"Thank you."

"You're welcome."

"Aren't you going to ask me what was in it?"

"No. If you want to tell me, you will."

"I can't."

"I thought as much." He sighed and kissed her ear. "Go to sleep."

She settled herself against him again but sleep was a thousand miles away.

Who was this man who held her?

British agent. Heir to a title and fortune. Grandson of her family's enemy.

But his sending Patrick the letter without opening it . . . That didn't fit the man she had thought him to be; it did fit the man she wanted him to be. And she prayed God that he wasn't lying to her, would never lie to her. If he once did, dear God, she would be lost.

Chapter Fourteen

The crow of a rooster awakened Savannah and she struggled to remember where she was. It didn't take long. That sinewy arm with its dusting of light brown hairs, the legs that encased her own, the pressure of a hard chest against her back—unmistakable.

Remembering what they had shared, she smiled.

She supposed he could rightfully call her strumpet now. But she knew he wouldn't.

And she didn't feel like one. In fact, she felt glorious, magnificent. As did the pressure of David against her. Such magnificence should be captured on canvas; but she dared not broach it to him. She dared not *do* it. Men might paint or sculpt nudes; women, never. She would have to be content with creating an image of glory only in her mind and—she smothered a giggle—between the sheets.

The cock crowed again and she sighed. Servants would be walking the halls and she did not want to be caught in David's room. Reluctantly, she slipped out of bed and padded around to the other side, looking for her nightshift. David's clothes and hers were puddles of color on the floor, and her artist's eye became entranced with the contrast of texture, color, and light. For a moment she saw the tangle as representative of what they had done and thought that *this*, at least, could be put to canvas. But what would anyone make of it? Dashes of yellow, white, beige, blue, brown. That was not a painting. That was naught but her remembrances.

Savannah filed away the texture, light, and rhythm she had felt and seen, and slipped into Bella's nightshift and robe. She padded across the floor and cautiously tried to ease the catch back; but the click, which had made her nervous the night before, sounded worse this morning. She looked over her shoulder to be certain she hadn't roused David and found him on his side watching her, his arm bent in that manner that men had of pillowing their heads, his eyebrow raised in query.

He smiled, patted the bed next to him, and said, "Come back here, wench. We haven't finished."

"The servants . . . Bella . . ."

"The servants know we're betrothed and will breathe not a word, unless they wish to lose their station. Bella won't see the light of day until noon. We have several hours in which to indulge our every whim and discover what we missed last night."

"You mean there's more?"

"You'll never know unless you come back to bed."

She hesitated, but the smile on his face was so inviting, and the possibilities of there being something more, something better, brought a quick th-thump to her heart.

"That's it, Savannah . . . imagine what it could be.

Whatever you imagine, I will show you more than you ever dreamed."

"Oh!"

He threw back the sheets and quilts. She blushed to see how ready he was. "You anticipate . . ."

"I dream."

Her body responded with each step she took back to him. And the response had her almost as ready as he was.

"Take off your clothes," he coaxed hoarsely.

He tried to be so impassive, but the glint in his eyes and the way his voice had cracked told her it was not passivity he felt. He was, in fact, impatient, if the lengthening of his manhood could be credited.

Had that truly been inside her last night? The friction had been wonderful. But the realization made her blush.

"Your night clothing, Savannah. Please. I want to see your body revealed to me inch by inch."

"Slowly?"

His mouth opened and he blinked in surprise. "Yes . . . I think slowly would be tantalizing."

The robe slipped off easily, making another puddle on the floor. But the nightshift was harder. She couldn't take her eyes off David and the way his face changed as she pulled up the skirt to reveal her ankles, then calves, then knees. By the time the hem brushed against her thighs, he had swallowed three times. At the juncture, where he had found a home last night, his mouth opened and his tongue wet his lips. At her waist, his hand gripped the quilt. At her breasts, his arm trembled. And when she pulled the shift over her head and stood there enraptured by what she saw, his eyes clouded over and he groaned.

She moved ever so slowly toward him, watching the fire that she, too, was feeling smolder, then flare, in his eyes. When she got to the edge of the bed, she bent down to kiss him on the cheek. As she did, her breasts brushed against his arm and she slid them up and down, enjoying the tingle his hairs created.

Suddenly, he fell back, reached up to capture her breasts with his hands, and kneaded them. She climbed onto the mattress, holding his hands against her, loving the contrast between the darkness of his skin and the pink-tinged whiteness of hers.

His hands left her breasts and skimmed down to her hips. Effortlessly, he lifted her, kicked his legs between hers, and settled her so her legs were braced against the mattress, on either side of his hips.

He reached up and drew her head down. Kissing her, again and again. Slanting his mouth over hers. Nipping at her lips. Running his tongue over the ridges. Slipping it into her mouth. Dancing it against her own tongue.

His breath was ragged as he pulled her down until her breasts brushed against his chest hairs. Back and forth, he moved her body, building a friction that made her nipples tighten and pucker, increasing the tiny tingles into great pulses of electricity. She gasped each time her nipples brushed against his, delighted to find him as hard as she was.

He cupped her breasts and raised his head. Tenderly, he took each nipple into his mouth and sucked until she moaned from the delicious torment. From right breast to left, he kissed and sucked, as his hands slid down her body. One went over her hips, learning the contours of her derriere, then sought out the soft folds hidden beneath the springy curls. The other stroked a particularly tender spot until it hardened and throbbed, sending jolts through her body.

Against her thighs, she could feel his thighs quake, and she eased herself closer to him. As she did, she brushed against his arousal and he groaned.

"Ah, love. Savannah. Savannah."

"Like this?" she asked as she eased herself over him and onto him.

"Yes. Perfect."

It was perfect, David thought. Had he said he dreamed? Dreams were insubstantial when compared to Savannah, herself. She gave more than he had ever expected. She gave him her trust. He hoped he would never do anything that would make her regret having given it.

As she took him inside her, he felt as if he had vaulted to the sky. The sun wasn't as hot as the melting moistness of Savannah. The earth wasn't as glorious as her face in its full ecstasy. Thunder and lightning would never be as powerful as her heartbeat against his chest, her convulsive tremors surrounding his arousal.

"Oh, David . . . it *is* more than last night! So much more!"

Savannah cried out, and tears slipped over her lids and down her cheeks, to drip on his chest. He cradled her lovingly as her body exploded, sending ripples over himself. He kissed her as she cried, then allowed himself to climb with her into the mysteries of love. Again and again she convulsed, until she brought him over the brink and he poured himself into her, crying her name over and over, then whispering it as their bodies gradually subsided, their hearts slowed to beat in normal rhythm, their breaths mingled sweetly.

He tucked her head against his shoulder and kissed her nose. "Good morning, Miss Stewart. Did you enjoy your night's sleep?" He could feel her embarrassment as she wriggled her luscious body against his. He chuckled. "What? No caustic answer, Miss Stewart?"

"Fie! 'Tis not the sleeping part I enjoyed, my lord. 'Tis the waking up part."

He laughed and held her to him. "Thank you, Savannah."

Her head snapped up and she fixed him an incredulous stare. "You, thanking me? But . . . but you gave me such pleasure, you should not be thanking me."

"Ah, Savannah. Do you not know that when I give you pleasure, I am also receiving it? Perhaps I may even be receiving more pleasure, though I hope not."

"Not possible, my lord." She yawned and her eyes closed. "Not possible."

Chuckling, he allowed himself to drift into the slumber that had overtaken her body.

Two hours later, he awoke to a cold room and a fierce wind howling against the windowpane. In her sleep, Savannah's teeth chattered. He slipped out of bed, tucked all the quilts around her, and padded to the fireplace. Smoldering embers. Good. He threw wadded-up newspaper on them and fed pieces of apple twigs, until they caught and blazed. He added small branches, then topped them with large logs. Soon, a roaring conflagration warmed the room and he hunkered down to savor it.

Sweet apple-scented smoke drew Savannah from the erotic dream in which she and David had played prominent roles. She snuggled down into the soft mattress, peeking over the edges of the quilts to watch the firelight dance off David's skin. From her vantage point, he looked burnished, as if gold dust had settled on him.

Her golden man.

Well, hers for a time, at least. They were, after all, betrothed, even if in jest. And, now that she thought on it, that betrothal was, in the morning's light, something that would bolster her position in the community. She had been welcome into the homes of the best citizens. But she had always been held a bit apart, since she could not claim a heritage that matched the upper reaches of society.

With David as her fiancé, however, she was finally equal to the damned Tories. She would be treated as an already-married member of their set, and would be welcome in parlors and drawing rooms where she had heretofore been excluded. And because of that, she might be able to pick up information she had been unable to get without David's declaration.

"Good morrow, my lord," she called out. "Do you think we could have breakfast brought up to us?"

"Methinks breakfast is long since past, my lady." David rose and stretched. That spark in Savannah's eye had him chuckling all the way back to the bed. He leaned down and kissed her slowly and completely. "A hot bath, Miss Stewart? In front of a hot fire? Then midday meal and some ale mayhap?"

"Cider, please. With a spot of rum in it." She frowned as David went to ring for Willy. "I need my clothes."

David slipped into a dressing robe and nodded. He left her to drift off into daydreams of kisses and caresses. When he got back, Willy was right behind him. Savannah ducked under the covers until David said, "All's well, love. He's gone."

She peeked out to find David pouring a bucket of steaming water into a great iron tub, which took up almost the entire floor in front of the fireplace. A knock sounded and David opened the door to take in four more buckets. He poured the contents into the tub and sloshed the water around. Then he approached the bed, his hand extended in invitation.

"Your bath awaits, my lady."

She smiled with what she hoped was a demure expression and took his proffered hand. "Thank you, my lord." She giggled as they walked to the tub, in the same posture as if he were leading her into a minuet. "Methinks this is what sin is."

"Nay, my lady. We are betrothed. This is legal."

She stepped over the side and into the water, which was deliciously hot. Sinking down, she said, "David . . . I really wanted to talk to you about this betrothal. . . . I think, you know, that I will accept it — in the spirit in which it was given, of course."

"And what spirit was that, Savannah?"

"You were gallant, my lord. Gallant and very much the gentleman. But I cannot hold you forever to what you said, although I would like very much to hold you for a while. Thus, I offer to you the opportunity to back out of this arrangement at any time, should your future be compromised by it. But I hope you won't want to do so very soon, because I would be forever viewed as a woman not worthy to hold a man's interest."

David chortled. "You, not worthy to hold a man's interest? God forbid!" He knelt down, soaped a thick piece of wool with fragrant French milled soap, and swiped it across her cheek. "You are one of the most beautiful women I have ever known. The colors of the Stewart clan have been brought to the pinnacle of exquisiteness in you." As he listed her attributes, his hands and the soapy cloth gave punctuation to his words. "Hair so dark it is almost the color of a midnight sky. Eyes touched with the blue and green of the sea. Complexion of porcelain, with a pink tinge on cheeks and lips. And those lips! Delectably kissable. Long, slender legs. Lithe, generously curved figure. Breasts which taste of pure honey. Not hold my interest, Savannah? You hold it in the palm of your hand, in the whisper of your voice, in the spark of your eye."

"God, David! You flatter . . ."

"Nay. I speak the truth. I'm besotted with you, you minx! Have been almost from the first time you spoke my name with malice and challenged me to find out why." He washed her arms and hands, then kissed each palm. "My grandfather warned me about the Stewarts. But he does not know *you*. If he had, he would have forbid me to come to Georgia! For you are far too attractive. You are Venus and Circe and Eve, all rolled into a package I cannot resist."

"Well, in that case, my lord, won't you join your

Venus in her bath?"

The next twenty minutes were filled with merriment, as each tried to outdo the other in finding secret places that tingled from soapy caresses. Laughter was smothered so Bella wouldn't be piqued into trying to discover what the noise was about. The horseplay didn't end until a sharp knock on the door heralded Willy's return. David hopped out of the tub, slipping several times as he made his way to the door, leaving Savannah convulsed with laughter. He opened the door and held out his hand. When he turned around, he lifted a Turkey-work bag in the air.

"Your clothing, my lady."

Savannah held her hands to her flaming cheeks. "Peggy Shippen will know what we were doing!"

"Savannah, think. She will only *know* that you are planning to stay here for a while. She may guess what we have been doing—probably exactly what she and her betrothed have done already—but she cannot know for a certainty. I won't tell her."

"And you won't tell anyone else, will you?"

"No, you goose! What happens between a man and his beloved is too precious to be bandied about."

"I'm your beloved?"

"Oh, Savannah! When will you believe and trust me?"

When, indeed?

For the next three weeks, while she finished up the commissions she had accepted from the gentry of

Philadelphia, Savannah mulled over the changes that had taken place since she had been officially declared David Montgomery's wife-to-be.

True to her word, the romantically minded Peggy Shippen had given her a betrothal party, where David presented Savannah with a lovely turquoise and diamond brooch. Everyone, it seemed, joined the Shippen's admiration for David's choice.

Everyone, that is, except Abigail Drummond.

Too often in the days that followed the betrothal party, Savannah caught Abigail giving her sidelong glances filled with malice. She could not understand why Abigail felt as she did. There had been naught but kind, polite words between them until now. What had happened to change the woman?

As they snuggled one night, David postured that she might be jealous.

"Jealous? Why?"

"Because you have captured a rich, titled prize and she has to be content with illicit liaisons."

"Conceited, that's what you are, David Montgomery!"

"What? Do you not think me a prize?"

"A prize booby!"

"No, that's what I hold in my hand, love."

His caresses quickly and sensuously ended that discussion; but Savannah didn't forget what he had said. She watched Abigail and listened more closely to the gossip about her. From Peggy, she discovered David was right. Abigail had once again found a paramour among the titled class. This time it was a captain of Fusiliers. But according to other sources, there was also a captain in the Royal Navy, a magistrate, and an elderly merchant on whom Abigail showered her charms.

Poor Abigail.

Savannah had noticed when the phaeton, horses, and slaves had been sold. She also noticed the reduction in the number of Abigail's new ball gowns and day dresses. And the jewels that Abigail had always displayed . . . Savannah saw them in the window of a merchant who purchased family heirlooms for ready specie. Obviously, Abigail was in straightened circumstances and needed the support her many lovers provided. Equally obvious, Abigail was furious that Savannah, who was her equal in station, had not had to resort to such means to survive.

Savannah thanked God she had been blessed with the gift of artistry. Miniatures brought much needed specie. Portraits filled her family's coffers. And she had no need for fancy clothes or a matched set of horses or several slaves to do her bidding. Savannah could wash and cook and clean and sew. She walked where she wanted to go, unless David or Bella took her in their carriage. In fact, her largest expenses were her paints and canvases, and those she quickly turned into pictures, that brought in coppers and bank notes.

Though Abigail could have earned money by taking up her old profession of midwifery, she seemed to prefer to drive a wedge between herself and society by snapping up other people's menfolk and living off them. Someday, the ladies of Philadelphia warned, Abigail would choose the wrong man and find herself completely cut off from the community.

Savannah hoped not. Any woman who had to

make her way in the world deserved more than that.

Savannah never received an answer to her letter to Patrick. But she hadn't expected one. She had, however, continued to write her travel pieces, and within the borders of the illustrations, she included any inside information she could discover that she thought might help the Rebels.

Twice, she was able to give detailed descriptions of troop movements. Four times, she knew about a change in command before it was announced in the newspapers. And lately, she had heard rumors of counter groups being formed to head off the activities of the Sons of Liberty. She had also included that information in the borders of her illustrations.

Her travel column was mailed to seven newspapers, which carried it prominently on the front pages. She could only hope the code had been disseminated quickly enough to be useful. It was so frustrating to be working in the dark, with no information coming back to her.

But Patrick and Ben had warned her that once she started her work, they would not risk exposing her unless it were of the utmost importance. Thus, when Patrick approached her in Bristol's merchant stores and beckoned her to the back of the lumber department, a wash of excitement had her hands trembling.

"You have done very good work, Savannah. We've been able to use much of your information to plan some sneak attacks on British garrisons and map out strategies when the war comes. But . . ." He took her hands and held them. "Now don't be frightened, but we think the code has been compromised."

"Oh, God! Someone knows about me?"

"We don't think so. But to be sure, you will have to change it somehow."

"That's easy enough. But how do I get it to you?"

"There is to be a house party at Roger Morris's house in New York. Lieutenant Colonel Roger Morris was a loyal friend and comrade-in-arms of George Washington during the French and Indian War. Benjamin mentioned you to his wife, and she would be delighted to have you as her guest. You should be receiving your invitation within the week. Keep it. We'll all be there, as will many Tories, since Roger is known to keep his house completely neutral. You can even bring your fiancé. By the by . . . I must congratulate you. Nice touch, that . . ."

"What?"

"Pretending to accept a betrothal so you could ingratiate yourself with the Tories. Not many women would do the same. Shows your loyalty to the cause. We welcome it and wish you well."

"But that's not what happened!"

"Of course not!" He patted her hands and smiled. "It will be our secret, like all the others."

"No, truly . . ."

"Now, Savannah, you don't have to playact with me. I know you were in a bad spot and needed to have a good cover story. As David Montgomery's fiancé, you have the best cover story there is." He kissed her cheek. "See you in New York."

He left her standing behind a stack of oak boards, completely flummoxed by his attitude.

She had *not* accepted David's betrothal to give herself a good cover story. She had *not!*

She slumped against the solid wall of lumber. Yes, she had. Not the way Patrick meant, of course. But he was close to the mark. She had thought those things. They had become part of the reason she had accepted. And now, hearing them spoken for the first time, she knew how awful they were as a reason.

David deserved more than that.

But she wasn't sure how much more and whether she could give it.

Chapter Fifteen

"Oh dear!"

Savannah and Mary Philipse Morris peered out the drawing room window into the gathering twilight. There had already been six inches of snow on the ground when the house party started; but what they saw now was just too much!

Mary's Christmas Eve fete, to which she'd invited half the countryside and most of her husband Roger's army friends, had been well attended. When everyone arrived in their horse-drawn sleighs, there had been a new sprinkling of snow and the sky was clear. But as they enjoyed the afternoon musicale and a reading from the Book of Luke, the sprinkling had turned into a hard fall. The wind had begun to howl at three o'clock. And the sky had darkened ominously. But everyone—including David and Savannah—had been so engrossed in the festivities and the sumptuous noon meal that no one had left the comfort of the Morris fires. When the first departing family had attempted to make tracks for home, however, they were greeted at the front door with fully three feet of piled-up snow, with more coming down in great clumps. There was no way Mary's guests could leave now. Somehow, she would have to put them all up, including Savannah and David.

"Oh, dear!" Mary wrung her hands. "What am I to do? I must needs find room for thirty more guests than I counted on."

"Are there garret rooms?" Savannah asked.

"Of course. But they are hardly suitable. Very small. Very cramped. With the barest of furniture and no fireplaces. Only the servants use them."

"Come. You and I will find some way to house all these folk."

As Savannah and Mary climbed the central staircase in the large, comfortable house, Mary's lament began to become painful.

"A house party of twenty-six is not uncommon. But one of fifty-six! This is the worst thing that has ever happened. I have not enough beds. Nor enough quilts and blankets. And night clothing! Where will I get nightshifts and robes to suit? Some of the guests are short and fat, others, tall and thin. A hostess may be very good at what she does, but she cannot expect this kind of emergency!"

"No one expects you to provide them with night clothing. Food and mattresses are the most important consideration. Cloaks and outerwear can be used as blankets. And a servant can be sent to gather in the rugs and quilts from the sleighs."

Savannah surveyed each room in turn, judging how many people could sleep in each bed. There were fully nine bedrooms on the second floor, one of them the master suite and another the children's nursery, and four cramped servants' quarters in the garret. All the children would be very comfortable in the large, airy nursery. Of the seven bedrooms available for adult guests, most had a large four-poster bed in the center, which could easily accommodate three or four regular-sized bodies. And each of the beds had several feather mattresses piled on them. So they had room for twenty people. Which still left almost forty more guests for whom they had to make sleeping arrangements.

The attic rooms were, as Mary had predicted, not what most of those gathered downstairs would call comfortable. Small rope beds would only hold one, although another could be accommodated in the pullout trundle. And there were no mirrors, no nightstands, no Turkey carpets or hooked or braided rugs on the floor. What niggardly heat there was came from the fireplace wall. The bricks were warm but the heat hardly penetrated more than three feet.

"Move the beds right against the fireplace wall. That's the best we can do here. But in the guest rooms on the second floor, we'll simply put some of the mattresses on the floor," Savannah said.

Mary smiled for the first time in twenty minutes. The worry lines in her plump face eased out as she, too, saw the only possibility they had. "Of course! And all the unmarried women can sleep in one or two of the rooms, the unmarried men in another. Married couples can be given a choice. They can share bed and floor with other married couples, or they can repair to the attic quarters. But my betrothed guests . . . what will I do with them?"

"David and I won't mind a small room in the garret. We have warm clothing and several small quilts from the carriage. I'm sure when they realize what problems you have, Mary, dear, there will not be any grumblings."

But Savannah discovered how wrong she was as soon as Mary announced the decision to house all the unaccompanied men or bachelors in one room. Since the Boston Tea Party had only occurred eight days previously and the news of it had only been reported in the past two days, those who were loyal to King and Crown refused to share any kind of sleeping space with those who were sympathetic to the Rebel cause. And, since some of the guests preferred to remain neutral in the events that were shaping up to look like war, there was a third group of men who didn't want to be aligned with the other two.

"Oh, bother! All my plans for naught!"

David laughed at Savannah's fury. "There, there, sweetheart. Mary and Roger will sort it out, have no fear. Although, I wonder where they'll put a British agent such as I?"

"Upstairs, in a barren garret room with me. It's all arranged."

Though she tried to be, as the French said, *nonchalant* about it, David could hear the tentative tremor in her voice. And the delightful way she peeked at him from under those beautiful lush lashes to see what his reaction would be! It was very difficult not to laugh at her. But he reined in his merriment. She was not used to their status yet, and he had to tread carefully lest he frighten her and she take on that brittle shell she had once worn around him.

"Well, if you have arranged it, then I'm satisfied."

He smiled and tucked her arm through his, squeezing her hand possessively. "And make no mistake, my love, no room with you in it is barren."

Savannah allowed him to kiss her on the cheek, then fled to help Mary. It took them and Mary's servants almost two hours to sort out everyone's traveling cases, get them in the proper rooms, put down the mattresses, carry in any extra blankets and quilts and rugs from the sleighs buried in the snow, and pull down several fur pelts Roger had hanging in his hunting shed.

Because of her help, Mary gave a bearskin to Savannah. Its weight toppled her and she went to fetch David to carry it up to the garret room. When he got to the door of their sleeping quarters, he had to duck to enter because the lintel was so low.

"Women are shorter," Savannah pointed out.

"Hardier, too, obviously."

David surveyed their assigned room and Savannah cringed. Bed, scarred and battered oak chest, one candlestand, a Windsor chair with several back slats missing, one tiny window that creaked and rattled as the wind buffeted it, and floorboards so crooked they could see through to the room below.

"Not exactly Lorton Woods, is it, David?"

"Not exactly a hut in Lorton Woods," he admitted. He tossed the skin on the bed and tested the mattress. "Hard as nails. Good thing I have a nice, soft body to snuggle up to."

"It's awful!"

"It will do, love."

The dinner gong sounded, and they trudged down the two flights of stairs to join the others in the dining room. Astonishingly, Mary had managed to pull enough dishes and cutlery out of cupboards and chests so no guest would have to eat with his or her hands. A great turkey took up center place on the long lace-covered table. A ham sat next to it, with a bowl of rabbit stew next to that. Dishes of boiled potatoes, creamed maize, a mixture of that afternoon's squash and peas, and mashed carrots and turnips were scattered around the meats. One platter held delicately fried cornmeal cakes, another, slices of brown bread and raisin-studded sweet rolls. And in small crystal dishes resided samples of every sweet spread and pickle in Mary's larder.

Within twenty minutes, not a speck of food was left.

While the servants brought out several pumpkin, mince, apple, and custard pies, a syllabub, some vanilla pudding, and toasted pieces of bread spread with warm apple butter, Mary wrung her hands again. "What am I going to do for the next few days? I've used up all there is in the larder."

"Smoke house empty?" David asked.

Mary threw him a grateful smile. "Oh, dear! All this commotion has totally flummoxed me. We have smoked game and bacon . . . two more hams and a pheasant . . ."

She walked away, ticking off on her fingers everything she had tucked away in the smokehouse, cold cellar, and root cellar.

"The servants will be cooking all through the night."

"Which will keep the fires hot and our room warm."

"Pah! And I thought that was your duty, my lord."

"A pleasure, Miss Stewart. A pure pleasure."

One of Patrick Henry's children, William, tugged on Savannah's sleeve. "Father said you are an artist, Miss Stewart."

"That's right."

"Would you be good enough to do some sketches for the children?"

"Why, I'd be delighted!"

Savannah looked into the corner where Patrick stood. He raised his tankard of ale and winked at her. So . . . he had found a way for her to pass on her new code. How clever. And how like Patrick to do it out in the open, right under the noses of all these Tories, in the home of one of George Washington's comrade-in-arms during the French and Indian War. A place of neutrality. Pah! *Caesar had his Brutus; Charles I, his Cromwell; and George III . . . may profit by their example,* indeed! The man was too clever for his own good. But she could profit from his cleverness . . . and help the Rebel cause while playing with the children.

For the next two hours, while the other adults were gathered in the keeping room and drawing room, playing cards, taking turns at the pianoforte, or singing Christmas hymns, Savannah amused the children with exaggerated caricatures of them and their parents. She did both father and mother, so as not to arouse suspicion. She was at her best, making the children laugh with glee at each bug eye or bulbous nose. But she was deliberate. Every caricature must be like every other. Each a unique portrait, but none too terribly different from another. And each containing a delicate tracery of a border to resemble a frame.

However, in Patrick's funny portrait—and in those of other Rebel leaders who would pass on the code to whoever needed to know it—she made a special border, one they had seen before and therefore would be sure to study carefully.

When she was finished with each of the adults' portraits—including the ones that would not go to the Rebels—Savannah held them up so the children could see, waited for their laughter, then quickly rolled them up and tied them with fat lengths of wool yarn.

"Give these to your parents for Christmas," she instructed the children. When they squealed with excitement, she held her finger against her lips and cautioned, "Shh. This is our secret."

"But when can we give them to our parents?" William Henry asked.

"Not now. You must wait until just before bedtime. And then surprise them!"

As the children scattered to hide their special treats, Savannah cleaned up the parchment, charcoal, quills, and ink. She handed all of it to a harried servant and accepted a warm cup of tea from Penelope, one of the Morris cousins.

"You have a very delicate touch, Miss Stewart."

"Thank you. I love drawing and painting."

"Oh, I know. I've seen your work at several of my friends' houses. But I meant with the children."

"I like children. I miss my younger brothers and sisters."

"How long have you been away from home, Miss Stewart?"

"Almost a full year." She fingered a locket on a chain. "But I keep a piece of Georgia here next to my heart." She opened it to show Penelope the tiny faces of the Stewart clan.

"Lovely. I wonder if you have time to do a portrait of me?"

Savannah's heart was heavy with homesickness, but she nodded. "With the snow piling up outside, it looks as if we'll all be here for many days. I'm certain I could do a small portrait if there is a spare canvas in the house. I could even do it on wood."

Penelope clapped her hands and Savannah was reminded of Bella, who had been left behind in Philadelphia with Lawrence Fenton as chaperon. She had been sorry to bid Bella good-bye; but the exuberant miss had assured Savannah she would be content during the holidays because her special beau, Richard, was coming to town.

Immediately, Penelope hurried to have a whispered conversation with her cousin Roger. When she returned, she told Savannah that there was a collection of old paintings in a storage room. "Could you paint over one of them?"

"If they are in good condition, certainly."

"Follow me, then, and we'll see."

The storage room was tucked into the rafters over the drawing room, right behind the bedroom in which Warren Standish, a descendant of Miles Standish, had been staying. Although his family's traveling cases had been taken to other parts of the house, Warren was stretched out on the bed, snoring gently.

Penelope tiptoed across the room. "Shh. Papa said Mister Standish wasn't feeling well. We'll just take two lit candles in with us and close the connecting door."

Savannah had to duck to get into the chest-high opening to the storage room. Once inside, she combed through a scattering of cobwebs to the corner where the paintings were leaning against a large wooden barrel. She dusted off the first and found a delightful landscape; but the canvas was torn at two corners.

"We could cover the corners with a deeper frame."

"Which would make my portrait little more than a miniature. No, let's find one that's bigger."

Savannah found four paintings that were suitable. Each was dark and crusted with dirt. "They will have to be scrubbed with soap and water with oil mixed in it, then left to dry completely. The cleaning might damage one or more of them; but we should get at least one which we can use."

She and Penelope wrestled the paintings back toward the door to the bedroom. As they reached it, they heard angry voices on the other side. Curses, and the words *traitor* and *Rebel scum* made Savannah hesitate. But they couldn't stay in the storage room forever, so she shrugged and put her hand on the sliding handle. But Penelope stopped her.

"Papa thinks I'm a ninny," she whispered. "He never lets me listen to political talk. But if there is to be war, then Orrin Jones—I've been promised to him since we were children—will have to go and fight. I have a right to know what's going on, and this is my first—and mayhap my only—chance to hear it. So be still, Savannah."

Penelope plunked herself on the dirty floor and leaned her ear against the door.

Savannah's heart beat faster. She had become a spy for just these occasions and for just this reason—because she was trusted by her hosts and might be able to pick up information the Rebels needed to have. Well, there was naught for her to do but follow Penelope's example. The girl need not know it fit perfectly with Savannah's desires.

Quietly, Savannah leaned the paintings against the wall and blew out the candles. When Penelope gasped at the blackness enveloping them, Savannah whispered, "They might be able to see the light around the door frame."

"Oh, good thinking, Savannah."

The two women leaned their ears close to the door and listened. At first, Savannah could make out little except mutterings and an occasional oath. But by concentrating, she was able to pick out five voices. One she assumed was Warren Standish's. One, she knew to be Horst van Zett, a rich farmer from the Hudson Valley, rumored to have the largest collection of slaves in New York. The others must be neighbors of Roger Morris's; but she didn't recognize their voices.

"My Negroes can camp in the barn, for all I care," Horst announced. "Every cabin and storage shed will be readied to garrison British troops. And I suggest you do the same on your estates, gentlemen. If we don't hang with our King, we will certainly hang separately."

"And if the Rebels take the first round, they will see to it that your words are prophetic, Horst."

"They won't be able to take the first round in New York if you and everyone in this room agrees to stand with the troops. We'll have over a thousand of His Majesty's fighting men here soon. How can the ragamuffin Rebels expect to overpower the best fighting force in the world? It can't be done, I tell you. A week or two, that's all they'll fight once they see they're outnumbered. But we must act together, the way those damned curs did in Boston. If we don't, we'll lose our fortunes. Do you want that?"

"Horst makes a point," a gruff, deep voice said. "All my specie is buried in banks in England, as is most of yours, too. And if war comes, this paper currency which the colonies have issued for trade will be worthless. Where my money is, is my sentiments. I stand by the King."

"Then it's agreed. We'll house the regiments so they can use our estates as a base of operations," Horst said.

"For attacks against the fortifications on the Hudson?"

"Aye. And mayhap forays as far as Canada, where there are troops stationed, ready to join the fracas."

"Count me in."

"Aye. Me and mine, also."

Within a heartbeat, five rich and powerful men had pledged their lives, their honor, and their fortunes to the King. More, they had promised to band together in a secret society they called the Hudson Junta, named after the Tory band in Newport.

"Best get below to midnight supper," Horst cautioned. "Can't let Rebel scum discover what we're about. One word and they'll be after us like flies on molasses cookies."

The deep, gruff voice spoke up. "Best go down one at a time, Horst."

"Aye, Warren. Glad you're with us."

"My heritage is with the King, God help us."

"We won't need his help, Warren. We've money and power enough for this earth. And when the war is over, my friend, we'll have the lands of all the Rebels, too. You'll be a richer man than Miles Standish ever dreamed possible."

"I do not wish to be rich, Horst. I wish to be right."

Penelope was so overcome by what they'd heard she almost opened the door immediately. Savannah held her back. "I thought you didn't want anyone to know we were here!"

"But, Savannah," Penelope whispered, "we know their secret! Isn't it exciting!"

"It's dangerous, that's what it is."

"But that makes it all the more exciting!" She hugged Savannah. "Ooh, I can't wait to tell Orrin and my sisters. They'll be green with envy! Aren't secrets fun, Savannah?"

"These kinds of secrets must be just that . . . *secrets*. If the plans those men were hatching were to get out . . . and if they knew that you know . . . they would not like it, Penelope. They might even take out some kind of revenge on you, your parents, or your cousin."

"Oh!"

* * *

To be sure they were not seen coming out of Warren Standish's room, the girls waited in the dark for several minutes after they heard the last footfall. Cautiously, Savannah opened the door and peeked out at the bed. No one. And the room was empty.

By the fire that had been laid in the fireplace, Savannah noted the dirt and dust that clung to Penelope's dress and face. Before hurrying up to do the same, she urged her young friend to clean herself thoroughly before going belowstairs.

The garret room was so cold Savannah had to undress under a quilt. As she struggled to get her dress off, David opened the door.

"I wondered where you were." He gaped. "You look as if you've been burrowing in the pigsty."

"Burrowing in the storeroom, more like it." She had difficulty untying the fastenings on her dress and still keeping the quilt from falling to the floor. "Damnation! Don't just stand there laughing at me, David. Come help."

"Delighted."

But he didn't help her undress. Or, rather, he did. He just merely forgot to help her back into another dress. In fact, he slipped under the quilt with her and managed to thoroughly arouse her with only a gentle skimming of his hands.

"Well, sir, that's one way to get warm."

"I know a more delightful one."

"We'll miss midnight supper and the Bible reading."

"There will be another Bible reading on the morrow. And I'm not hungry . . . for food."

235

She forgot all about the secret she had to share with Patrick and the other Rebels. She forgot about everything except David and the wonderful things they did together under the quilt and bearskin.

Chapter Sixteen

The next morning Savannah awoke at her normal routine, getting up before dawn broke. She stretched and sought out the chamber pot under the bed. As she finished, she heard voices coming from below the garret room.

She wasn't used to snooping. But she had already been privy to one secret she had to get to the Rebels. If there were another . . .

Thank goodness for large cracks between the floorboards. By snuggling under the bearskin and lying on the floor, she could see right into the room below. She recognized James Otis, a Boston jurist and friend of Samuel and John Adams. She had met each man through an introduction by Ben Franklin in Philadelphia. Now, James was posturing about the recent Boston Tea Party and questioning the others.

"We, too, have to show our strength to the British! If we don't, they will not take us seriously."

"Seems to me they take us very seriously, indeed," a tall, white-haired man said. "There's talk of garrisons in the valley."

"Bother the garrisons! Otis is right. We must strike soon, or risk being overrun by the bloody Loyalists, those curs!"

Within moments, the men had agreed to mimic their compatriots in Boston, even going so far as to dress in Indian costumes and dump tea into New York harbor. They planned their attack for a few days hence, when the British would least expect it.

Savannah now had two secrets worth knowing. She climbed back into bed with David, wakening him simply by brushing her body against his.

"Ah, love . . . do that again," he urged, then demonstrated how aroused he was. She was happy to oblige.

They missed both Bible readings but were in time for a late breakfast of salt cod chowder, oatmeal gruel with rich thick cream and molasses, and hot fruit pies, with pots of coffee and tea and pitchers of buttermilk to wash it all down.

Savannah ate quickly and hurried back up to her room. She had to get everything she'd learned to Patrick, so she penned another caricature, including as much of the information in the border as she dared, with a note for him to seek her out to know the complete details. But when she descended the front stairs, she found Mary Morris waving good-bye to several of the houseguests.

"Are your guests leaving?"

"Yes, thank goodness! Twenty have cleared off their sleighs and set out for home." She reached into her pocket and gave Savannah a sealed letter. "Mister Henry wanted you to have this."

"He's gone?"

"Yes. He said he had urgent business in the city and wanted to thank you for your delightful portraits. They were lovely, Savannah. Everyone is talking about them. I imagine they will be displayed in every house in the area."

"Yes. Thank you. I suppose so."

Savannah hurried back to the lonely, cold garret room. She tore open the letter and skimmed it. It told her only that Patrick was delighted she had found a way to "please us all."

You will know that each of us found much delight in your artistry, Miss Stewart. May your success continue for years to come.

Damnation! He had left too soon, before she could tell him what she'd learned about Horst. Well, there was nothing for it but for her to pen a travel article and illustrate it, including the information. It would have to get to the papers quickly. Today. She only hoped there was someone left who could take her article to the printers. If there wasn't, she and David would have to do it themselves.

For the next two hours, Savannah holed herself up in a small study off the drawing room, explaining she had to get her work done. In her nervousness and anxiety, she made several mistakes in the code and had to make a complete new copy of the illustration. When she was finally finished, however, she had a good article, a better illustration, and all the information the Rebels needed was buried in the words and picture.

She folded it carefully, sealed it with a double wax seal, tucked it into the pocket of her apron, and sat back to take a breath. It was only then that she heard the insistent knocking on the door to the study.

"Come in!"

Penelope rushed in, stuck her head back out the door and looked both right and left, then popped back inside. She closed the door and leaned against it.

"Savannah, you will never guess what I've heard!"

"You look like the cat that ate the cream."

"Exactly! Another secret!" She plopped down in the chair next to Savannah, her brown eyes dancing with bright sparks of reddish fire. "I was in the music room, right next to Cousin Roger's office. Roger and some of his friends were in there. They didn't know the connecting door was slightly ajar. And when I heard what they were discussing, I didn't move or make a sound."

"You eavesdropped."

"Just as we did last night." She giggled. "Guess what I found out?"

"That Horst is planning to buy all the slaves in the colonies?"

"Oh, Savannah! No! That the Rebels are planning another version of the Boston Tea Party!"

Savannah's mouth dropped open. How many people had been up that early in the morning? And what other garret room—with gaping floorboards—looked down onto James Otis's bedroom? Obviously, at least one other.

But it was Roger who knew. Roger. George Washington's friend. There couldn't be anything to worry about.

"And is Roger going to join them?"

This time it was Penelope whose mouth dropped.

240

"Why would you think that? Of course, he isn't joining them. He's a Loyalist!"

"But . . . he's a friend of Washington's."

"Well, so is half the colony. But that doesn't make them all Rebels."

"I assumed . . ."

"These are not the days to assume anything, Savannah. My papa says we must be prepared for any and all surprises."

"Your papa is right."

Too right. If Roger Morris was a Loyalist and he knew about the Rebels' plans, then they could all be walking into a trap. She had to find out. She had to do something before good men became fodder for the fishes or ended up at the end of a rope.

"What's Roger going to do about the damn Rebels?"

"He's going to stop them, that's what! He's on his way right now to the nearest garrison to tell Lieutenant General Morgan about the planned raid. He'll alert the Army, Cousin Roger said. And they, in turn, will tell the Navy. When those stupid Rebels come down the harbor, the Navy will be ready and they'll capture them all! That should put a stop to any rebellion in New York."

It wouldn't put a stop to it; but it might set back the Cause for several months. From listening to Ben and Patrick and the debates in the House of Burgesses, timing was all important these days. If the leaders were arrested, the Rebels would be hard pressed to replace them quickly.

Now, she had more important information to pass on than that which was already in her next column.

It had taken her two hours to put that together. It would take her another two—or more—to put this latest warning in among the rest. And she couldn't risk doing it here in the study. If anyone saw her discard a perfectly good article to compose another one, she might come under suspicion. She had to get rid of Penelope and find someplace quiet, where no one would be able to spy her out.

The storage room! If anyone did discover her, she could simply lie and tell them she had been looking for another old painting.

She was saved the bother of lying to Penelope, when her mother came looking for her. As soon as Prudence shooed her daughter into the keeping room to help take charge of the younger children, Savannah fled up to the second floor and the safety of the storage room. Three hours later she emerged, a carefully worded and thrice illustrated article clutched in her hand.

Savannah climbed the stairs to the garret, once again to clean herself and change for the midday meal. But when she entered the room, she found a glowering David stomping back and forth, muttering under his breath.

He rushed up to her and gripped her arms. "Don't ever do that again!"

Guilt and shame washed through her. Did he know what she had done?

"Don't leave me without a word. Everyone was asking for you and I didn't know where you were. It made me look the fool."

"Oh, David!" *Thank goodness that was all.* "I had to pen my weekly column and do the illustrations." She held up the parchment. "It took me longer than usual because Penelope and the other children interrupted me. So I found a hidey-hole where no one could find me. If I hadn't, I would never have gotten it done. And I need the money."

He pulled her into his arms. "First, I'm so glad you're safe." He kissed her. "Second, if you give me a scare like that again, I'll put you over my knees and spank you."

"That could be interesting."

He kissed her again, longer and more erotically. "Minx," he breathed against her hair. "Third, you don't need the money. I'm willing to support you."

Savannah stiff-armed herself away from him. "I will not be kept like Abigail Drummond is kept! I make my own way in this world."

"I didn't mean to imply that you are anything like Abigail Drummond. I merely want to take care of you."

"You can."

"How?"

"Help me get this article to the newspaper office in the city."

"In this snow, that's a full day's ride there and another full day back."

"It's very important, David."

"All right. I'm expecting a packet of correspondence from my grandfather, anyway. Lawrence promised to forward it to me at the Merchant's Exchange in the city. I'll take your precious article to your publisher, then stop to pick up my packet."

"Thank you."

He bit on her earlobe. "You could thank me in

more than words, love. We'll be separated for two whole days."

She giggled. "I always wondered what it would be like to couple on a bearskin."

"With this cold, it would be better to couple *under* the bearskin."

They coupled under and on it.

Savannah was always surprised by the ardor David showed in his lovemaking. And she was astounded by the myriad ways he had of arousing her.

His nibbling kisses on her nose and ear were her favorites. No, she decided when he began another kind of exploration, the best were the tiny, wet sucking kisses he showered on her breasts and belly. After only five minutes of the delicious torture, she was moaning and clutching the bed sheets, fully aroused, hot and wet where their special joining place was.

Suddenly, David's stomach rumbled and he grinned up at her. "I'm hungry. Very, very hungry."

His head dipped back down to her breasts, then lowered to her belly. His tongue slid over her sensitive nipples, swirled inside her navel, lapped at her hipbones. At almost the same instant, her fingers curled into his thick, sun-kissed hair, and her legs fell open, awaiting his entrance.

But his sucking kisses didn't stop. His mouth and tongue continued downward, to bathe her thighs, her knees, her ankles and feet. He took her toes into his mouth one at a time.

She screamed and squirmed. "Dear God, that feels good!"

"Mmm," David murmured. "Mmm."

He retraced his path, lingering on her thighs,

which he kneaded and left wet from his tongue.

"Oh, David . . . please . . ." She opened her legs wider.

"Mmm."

He heeded her invitation, but not in the manner she expected. When she realized what he was doing, it felt so good it was too late to remonstrate. "Oh, God!"

"I love you, Savannah."

"Oh, God!"

"I love you."

He pleasured her in the most intimate of ways. He brought her to a blazing inferno of feelings that built like flames, climbing from the sweet torture of his tongue all the way up to the ends of her hair. She was all sensation, all feeling. And David was doing it to her. Asking nothing in return, he gave her everything. Only when she exploded did he raise his head and look at her. She stared down into his midnight-blue eyes and drank in his love. He smiled at her, then bent his head once more and began again.

This time, the ascent to the fires of heaven was quicker. And he seemed to know when she was almost to the summit. In one lithe motion, he moved over her, into her, and rocked with her.

Abandoning all resistance, she gave herself to him, crying his name at the end and promising, "I love you, David."

When it was over, he pulled her trembling body close to his and held her tenderly. "I have a gift for you."

"It was the most wonderful gift. . . ."

He reached down to his clothes and dug into his

pocket. Holding out a small velvet pouch, he smiled. "To go with the brooch. Happy Christmas."

Her fingers fumbled with the drawstring, which she shook to steady them. They snaked inside and she drew out a wad of cotton felt, which had been folded over several times. Carefully, she peeled back the folds and uncovered a golden ring, set with a tumbled turquoise stone surrounded by tiny clear chips that sparkled like . . . No! It couldn't be.

"Are they diamonds?"

"Mmm. I couldn't figure how to get the turquoise to spit fire the way your eyes do, so I had the jeweler mount the sparks on the outside. Do you like it?"

"It's perfect. I love it." She kissed him. "And you." That almost led to another round of lovemaking, but she only allowed him five minutes before she pushed him away. "I have a 'Happy Christmas' gift for you, too. Close your eyes."

"Why?"

"Close your eyes, I said."

"All right," he grumped. "But it better be as good as mine."

"Conceit. That's what I like about you, David. You don't hide your conceit."

"What's this about *like?* I thought you loved me."

"Love and like have very little to do with each other. The first is given by God. The second has much to do with respect; and for that, you have to earn it."

She took his hands in hers and placed her gift in them. "Open your eyes, love."

He looked down. A small silver watch fob with intricate carvings lay in his palms.

"I couldn't afford gold. But Mister Revere carved this to resemble the real thing."

"Whenever I look at the time, I'll be burning until the minutes pass and I can come home to you."

Savannah laughed delightedly. "No, silly. It's not a timepiece." She reached down and opened it.

"Oh, Savannah." David traced the miniature of him and Bella on the left, and the perfect rendering of Lorton Woods on the right.

"I wanted you to have a part of Georgia with you always."

"I am most grateful."

It was very difficult getting David to allow her out of bed. His hands, mouth, and loving words coaxed her into another lovemaking session. When they were once again replete, she managed to wriggle over the side of the small pallet and struggle into her fourth dress in the past two days. She didn't have another, so she scooped the other three into her arms to carry to the kitchen to be washed and brushed.

"Hurry, David. You'll need a good meal to hold you until you get to the city. I'll pack a bucket of cold meats and pasties for you. Do you want ale or rum?"

"Both. I'll be down in a few minutes."

Savannah pointed to her precious sealed parchment. "Don't forget my missive."

In the two days that passed, Savannah glanced often at the beautiful ring David had given her. It glowed in sunlight, shimmered in candlelight, sparkled in firelight. It was a constant reminder of all they'd shared and all they would continue to share.

Until he went back to England.

She was sure that was his destiny. She could not see him in America, as a Rebel. He was the heir to a title and huge estates in England, and she'd better not forget it. True, right now he was content with her and with the role he had in building his grandfather's merchant trade. But he was a Montgomery. Bella had often warned Savannah that to be a Montgomery meant David would have to sacrifice more than most men. He would be expected to marry well, produce an heir to take his place someday, and carry out his grandfather's wishes in all things. Savannah could not expect David to forswear his grandfather's demands. She was a Stewart and could not expect to be considered *suitable* enough to produce that all-important heir. David would have to bow to convention. To believe otherwise was to set herself up for a broken heart and spirit.

As if she had not already done so!

Loving David as she did, Savannah ached as she envisioned the day when he would take his leave of her. She hurt in every pore, thinking about the woman who would share his marriage bed, enjoy his beautiful lovemaking, bring his children into the world.

To hold back the terrors, she immersed herself in the portrait of Penelope. It went well. The girl was . . . what was that new word? Ah, yes . . . a chatterbox, but she was patient and held a pose for as long as Savannah bid. Her work went well and the portrait was complete except for a few details when David returned.

The entire household streamed to greet him when

they discovered he carried with him the latest issue of the *New York Gazette,* which contained her article on the Morris holiday house party. They stood in the hall and pored over the newspaper.

"Oh, Savannah," Mary gushed, "the illustrations are wonderful. Imagine, Roger, *three* of them! Not even the Vander Gelders got three illustrations when they ran the wedding announcement of their daughter."

All Savannah was interested in was whether the illustrations were crisp and clear. They were. The border and the code was easily discernible, if the right people were looking at the pictures.

David cleared his throat. "I know you're all excited about the article, but I feel I must warn you . . ."

Oh, God! Savannah felt a flush of danger mount her neck. What if someone knew . . .

"I met up with Captain Richardson, of the mounted Fusiliers. He was headed this way with a friend of his. I offered your hospitality for a night. If you mind, I'll be glad to head him off and take him to the nearest inn."

Roger harrumphed. "Of course we don't mind. The captain is welcome in our house. We found enough food to feed fifty-five. We can certainly entertain only two!"

"He mentioned they'd be in the area for a week or more. But I didn't promise them lodging for that long."

"Don't worry, my boy. The Morris home is known for its neutrality . . ."

And is that a lie, Savannah thought.

"We will be most gracious to your friend."

* * *

Captain Richardson arrived two hours after David, just in time for supper. His "friend" turned out to be Abigail Drummond, who swooped into the assemblage with an air of superiority that had Savannah gritting her teeth.

Abigail acknowledged Savannah with a stiff nod but lavished her bright smile on all the men in the house. Her hair was no longer blond but red; and Savannah wondered how many henna rinses she had used to achieve that daring color. Although, Savannah had to admit red hair did bring more color to Abigail's face. And it distracted the eye from the thickening of Abigail's waist. So did the low-cut necklines of the woman's gowns. Savannah could feel her own ribs aching merely with a glance at the extraordinary way Abigail's stomacher had been laced to push up her breasts until they almost spilled out of their lacy confinement.

Ah, but Savannah knew Abigail well enough to notice the tired lines around her eyes and mouth. It cost her dearly to put on the always-cheerful mask she wore, cost her more to become the courtesan of a man much lower on the social scale than Governor John Murray. Yet, Abigail faced it full on, never flinching. Savannah found much to admire in that kind of attitude. It bespoke courage, something none of the other women in the house would ever know.

So Savannah went out of her way to be nice to Abigail. And the woman was so surprised, she lost her composure. Her eyes filled with tears and she mumbled an excuse, fleeing up the stairs to the guest room she and the captain had been allotted.

* * *

Abigail fumed. How dare she! How dare Savannah Stewart point up the failings Abigail felt. Savannah's solicitude and the pity in her eyes had felt like a knife thrust between Abigail's ribs.

Pity! How dare she? How dare she!

Abigail kicked at the newspaper containing Savannah's article and illustrations. Why, she was naught but a common scrivener! Hardly in the class of Shakespeare or Cervantes. And she was even less important in art circles. Illustrations, bah! They would never equal the beauty of Michelangelo or Raphael. Why, they weren't even as good as that Rhode Islander with the same sounding name, Gilbert Stuart.

So Savannah pitied her, did she? Well, Abigail would show her! Someday she would be in a position to pity Savannah. Someday, when the British had beaten the senses out of these infernal Rebels, she would be some captain or general or magistrate or *noble's* wife, and mother to his children.

And Savannah? David Montgomery would leave her to take up his heritage. *She* would be at the bottom of the heap, scrabbling for a living.

And Abigail couldn't wait to see it happen.

Chapter Seventeen

"I understand it was at your Christmas fete that the plot to dump tea into New York harbor was uncovered," Captain Richardson said over port the next night.

"Aye. And it was damned good luck we *did* discover it, too."

David turned to stare at Roger Morris.

Roger laughed and winked at his two cousins, then beamed at David. "Did you truly think this was a neutral house, my lord?"

"Yes, I did. You said it often enough."

"Pah! Only lies to keep the riffraff from suspecting what is really going on. Of course I'm loyal to the King, just like you and your family are. Our good fortunes are bound hand and foot with that good man. These Rebels!" He said the word as if he had swallowed something bitter. "They are naught but scoundrels and thieves, who would steal the last copper from the pocket of the man to whom it belongs." He raised his glass to the assembled men in his office. "To the King, gentlemen."

Everyone, including David, raised his glass. "The King."

"And the Rebels are planning their escapade for two nights hence?" Captain Richardson asked.

"Aye. Got it from the mouth of the worst of the lot, James Otis."

"Our regiments and navy will be ready for them," the captain vowed. "I have been sent by the division commander, sirs. He wishes me to ask, would you and your cousins like to accompany us, Mister Morris? Your lordship? You will be privileged to see His Majesty's finest force in action."

"Delighted, sir! Delighted. Aye, David?"

David nodded. He wasn't sure he wanted to see His Majesty's finest force in action. After all, how valiant was it to send the *finest forces* against riffraff, scoundrels, and thieves?

Although a letter from his grandfather had been waiting for him in New York, it wasn't the one he had hoped for, the one that would give him his grandfather's permission—and money—to purchase the Clough stores and add to Lorton Crown Traders's inventory and purse. So a trip back to the city was inevitable, in any case. Besides, it was time he and Savannah took their leave of the Morris family. Already, Savannah was showing signs of restlessness. She had commissions to do several portraits in the city and in the environs of New Haven. He could not expect her to sit here in comfort and idleness, when her family needed the money she earned at her labors.

"Savannah and I will leave first thing on the morrow, sir. I have business to attend in the city."

"I'll send instructions where to meet us and when, my lord," Captain Richardson said. "Your agent . . . Lawrence Fenton . . . isn't that his name? . . ."

"Yes."

"If I cannot find you, I'll leave the letter with him."

Savannah was delighted to sleigh ride into the city. Though it was cold, she and David bundled under the bearskin Mary Morris insisted she take as a gift for her help with the emergency. When they got to their lodgings at the Walter Raleigh Inn, her feet were almost frozen and she dashed for the warmth of the fire.

On the morrow, she sought out the home of her next patron, Molly Worthington, and set a time for her first sitting. Molly insisted she meet a neighbor of hers, who had seen one of Savannah's miniatures and wanted a family portrait done for her tenth anniversary. Olivia Butler had a large brood and was pregnant with her eighth; but she was jolly and plump and obviously in love with her handsome husband, Robert, who was a lawyer. They agreed on a price and a day for the sketches to be done, and Savannah left with enough currency to purchase the paints and other supplies she needed.

The Worthingtons hosted an early dinner party that evening, which included most of the same people who had been at the Morrises' Christmas fete. She caught the excitement that emanated from the men and wondered about it. She wondered even more when the men didn't retire to Mister Worthington's study, but instead bundled themselves in their warm outer clothing and left the house, David included. Though she inquired of Molly, the only thing the lady knew was that they were all up to some *men's adventure*.

"If they aren't back by ten, his lordship has made arrangements for you to be called for by his steward, Miss Stewart."

"Lawrence Fenton?"

"Yes, I think that's the name."

Far more than a steward, Savannah thought. Though the Montgomerys had a way of relegating their employees to the lowest of ranks rather than the highest.

While Savannah joined in the needlework the women did beside the fire, she was too preoccupied to listen to the wild gossip that they exchanged. She wondered why David had not told her he was leaving her alone that evening. What could he be doing that he couldn't tell her? Certainly not whoring, as one of the ladies peevishly intimated. David didn't do such things. She was so bemused by David's lack of explanation that she stabbed her thumb twice, finally setting aside the needlework and picking up a well-thumbed copy of Shakespeare's sonnets.

Eight o'clock came and went. As did nine. And nine-thirty. By five minutes of ten, she had completely lost track of the women's conversation and heard only the clop-clop of passing horses, none of which stopped at the house until precisely ten.

Lawrence Fenton was apologetic and deferential. He kindly offered Savannah his hand to help her into the large coach David had hired for her convenience. He settled himself inside, across from her, closed the door, and drew down the curtains to keep out the drafts. He placed wool-wrapped warm bricks under her feet, then covered her knees with a warm tartan blanket.

"They've been waiting for three hours and nothing has happened."

"I beg your pardon," Savannah responded.

Lawrence snorted. "The tea party. It's a bust. No one has showed up."

Savannah's stomach did a complete flip. She had forgotten that this was the night originally planned for the New York version of the infamous Boston event. "And David is there?"

"Special invitation from the King's magistrate and the General. They hoped to catch the insurrectionists in the act."

Special invitation from the King's magistrate and general. Hoped to catch the insurrectionists. Special invitation.

David?

Lawrence dumped an oil-slicked paper packet in her lap. "Stopped at the office. His lordship is expecting those. Very important, they be."

Savannah's hand closed around the thick parcel. "I'll see that he gets them."

"Right away, now. First thing he gets to the inn."

She nodded and her eyes caught a royal seal affixed to David's mail. *Under Protection of His Majesty, King George III*. The only kind of seal that went from hand to hand unbroken. The only kind of seal that, if broken, brought a penalty of death to the one who had pried inside.

Once inside her rooms next to David's, she tossed

the packet on a deal table and paced the floor. David with the British to head off and arrest Rebels. David with a packet from the King. Their time together had been so wonderful, she had forgotten that he was a Montgomery, the heir to a marquess, second only to a duke in the royal lineage. Had she been coupling with a Tory loyalist? Was she in love with the wrong kind of man? Savannah groaned and paced some more, her eyes never straying from the infernal packet on the table.

When the clock in the hall bonged the eleventh hour, she gave it up and went to bed. David wasn't there when she awoke in the morning. She sniffed the pillow and knew he hadn't been there all night. She stuck her head into his own room and found the bed still made up.

She dressed, had fruit and coffee in the inn's keeping room, ordered a coach to be waiting at the door for her within ten minutes, and went back to pick up her drawing supplies. The missive from the King fairly shouted at her, and she didn't hesitate to stuff it into her Turkey-work bag, along with her parchment, charcoals, and quills.

When she got to the Worthingtons, it seemed as if all the demons of hell were bellowing from Josiah Worthington's office.

"Whatever in the world? . . ."

Molly sighed. "The houseboy said the men came in near dawn. Josiah has called for rum and ale three times and screamed every five minutes because the fire isn't hot. I'm about to serve them their breakfast. I'm afraid the sitting will be late."

"No matter." So the men were upset. Perhaps, after

all, she had done some good. . . . "May I join you for breakfast? The only thing I've had is a wormy apple and coffee."

"Of course, Savannah! You must get some good strong tea into you. And there's a solid breakfast waiting."

Savannah served herself from the sideboard and carried the plate of ham, kidneys, coddled eggs, and creamed salt beef to the table, taking a position right in the middle so she could hear and see everyone. Molly hovered at the sideboard until the men entered, then waved a maidservant over to take her place. She sat at the foot of the table and tucked into her own breakfast.

Savannah noted the worn, tired appearance of all the men. None had shaved. All had damp spots on their clothing and bright red noses. She wasn't surprised when a succession of sneezing accompanied the men to the table.

David sat next to her and smiled wanly.

"Bad night?" she asked.

"The worst."

Roger Morris cursed roundly and didn't even bother to apologize. "Those damned Rebels! Scoundrels to the core."

Molly looked puzzled. "What were you doing with Rebels?"

"Nothing! That's the point," Morris shouted. "We waited all night and no one showed up. All night! With temperatures cold enough to freeze brass balls."

"That's uncalled for," David said.

Morris looked perplexed. "Oh." He barely nodded at Savannah. "Beg pardon, Miss Stewart. Ladies' ears and all. But I'm damned why they didn't show up! I'm damned!"

"Perhaps they were warned off," David suggested.

"Warned off?" Morris looked round the table at each man. Eyes skittered over his stare and down to their plates. "Warned off? When we made our plans carefully and secretly? Warned off? If they were, then we've a traitor in our midst who is as insubstantial as a shadow!"

"It isn't the first time things have gone wrong," Warren Standish pointed out. "Though every piece of mail has been opened between here and New Hampshire, there have still been contingents of Rebels gathered together to storm garrisons, intercept shipments of specie, even give the guns to revenue cutters. Somehow information is getting through, and it isn't going the usual routes."

"The shadow, gentlemen. A rogue who delights in making us look ridiculous." Roger Morris banged his fist on the table. "I will not be made to look ridiculous by some scum who probably can't write his own name!"

"But if there was a traitor," David pointed out, "he must have been among your guests, sir. Their plans were discovered at your house party. And it was in your study that we learned about them and sent word to the authorities so they could be circumvented."

Warren agreed. "And there were so many Rebels there that weekend, you tripped over one every time you turned a corner."

"No," Morris insisted. "When we made our plans, every known Rebel had left. I saw them off myself. No, gentlemen, there is only one explanation. There is a man we are not aware of. A man who has infiltrated our ranks and has our trust. A man who flits around us, hears our conversations, ferrets out our plans, and turns traitor with his every breath." Morris dug out his purse and removed a large bundle of bank notes. "A bounty must be collected. And all of us must contribute our share. Two hundred pounds sterling, gentlemen. That will shake the rotten fruit from the tree. Two hundred pounds sterling, and we'll have the traitor's head on a pike. Who's for it?"

Each man, including David, added several bank notes to the pile. Morris counted them and grunted. "We'll need every man in the countryside to add his portion. And the King will have to kick in some, besides."

"Mister Morris," Savannah stammered, "won't you have people lying to get their hands on that money?"

Roger winked at her. "Not if we put restrictions on the reward. Bring me ink, quill, and paper." When it was placed in front of him, he penned the words he spoke:

"A reward of two hundred pounds sterling is offered and will be paid for information leading to the arrest and conviction of The Shadow, the man responsible for delivering Loyalist plans to Rebel traitors, for assisting in nefarious plots against His Royal Majesty, George III, His assigns, and armed forces. All those seeking this reward must present solid proof of the identity of The Shadow. Such proof will be studied and evaluated by the undersigned. The reward will only be paid when The Shadow is convicted and hanged.

"There," Morris said. "That should do it."

"That will do it *if* there is such a shadow," David muttered.

"Oh, there is," Morris affirmed. "I feel it in my bones." He folded the reward notice around the bank notes and tucked them into his frock coat pocket. "I'll have the notice printed and tacked in every public place. And we'll take out an announcement in newspapers from here to Georgia and New Hampshire. We'll get him, gentlemen. We have God and the King on our side."

If she were caught, she would hang. The only thing that comforted Savannah was the knowledge that the stupid Loyalists were searching for a man.

Thank goodness she had her commissions to occupy her or she'd go mad from fretting. The sitting that morning was harried because of the bustle within the Worthingtons' house, but she squared her shoulders and put her mind to getting the sketch exactly right. She smiled and gave encouraging grunts and ahs at the gossip Molly blithely conveyed, but Savannah didn't remember a word of it when she finally put the finishing touches to the sketch.

Molly gushed over it and had her maidservant pack the clothing that would be highlighted in the portrait. As Savannah accepted the bundle at the door, she remembered the oiled packet that she still hadn't given David.

Where was her head?

Firmly attached to her shoulders, thank goodness. At least, for now.

After settling herself in the coach, she ordered the driver to take her to David's New York stores. It was the first time she'd seen them and they surprised her because the name on the sign said Clough. But when she asked for David, he appeared from the back room and hustled her into his office.

She took the packet out of her pocket and handed it over with a sincere apology. "Lawrence said it was important, but when you didn't come back last night . . . and with all the excitement this morning, I completely forgot."

David kissed her as he tore open the paper. He drew out a short stack of letters and tore open the first. He read it quickly, scowled, then threw it aside. It landed on the floor. The second took up residence among a pile of papers with no order to them. At the third, he threw his arms around Savannah and kissed her with all the ardor she'd come to expect from him.

"Damn . . . and I spent the night with those pompous men, when I could have been enjoying your inestimable charms, Miss Stewart."

"I missed you, too." She nodded toward the letter in his hand. "What has you so animated?"

"Grandfather gives his permission—and his money, thank God—to take over Benjamin Clough's merchant stores. That will increase Lorton Crown Traders's outlets and, hopefully, help us turn a profit. Although with war on the horizon . . ."

"But won't the armies need refitting? And won't you be in a perfect position to do it?"

"Where were you six months ago when I was putting my case together for Grandfather?"

Savannah thought back to that time. "In Williamsburg. Trying to forget such an idiot as you ever existed."

"I'm glad you have a short memory."

Not that short.

"Wait here. I want to give Lawrence the good news."

Savannah heard David's shout from somewhere in the back of the large warehouse and Lawrence's answering laughter. She expected that David would be back in a short time, but when the minutes ticked by, she sighed and sat down behind his desk.

He was such an untidy man! Tossing his papers here and there, he was sure to lose something valuable. She reached for the letter that had fallen to the floor, and the heading caught her eye. She hesitated. Spying on Tories was one thing, but spying on David quite another. Yet, the heading screamed at her. And her eyes skimmed the parchment as she folded it.

Her hands stilled. The Royal Seal, once again. And a scrawled signature that she recognized from official announcements posted in local papers. *George, Rex.*

What was David doing with a missive from the King?

By order of His Majesty, King George III. To Whit: That David Kent Montgomery, the Viscount of Dwight and heir to Richard Kent Montgomery, the Sixth Marquess of Lorton, is hereby ordered by His Royal Majesty 1) to set up a Royal Trading Company to have jurisdiction in the entire colony of Georgia and parts west and south; 2) to barter and trade with all loyal interests of His Majesty, returning all specie to the

Royal Treasury, from which His Majesty will apportion a fair amount to the Sixth Marquess of Lorton; 3) in the extended interests of His Majesty, to act as agent provocateur *among the disenchanted subjects in the American colonies; 4) to ferret out enemies of the Crown; 5) to spy on rebel rabble; 6) to see that they are brought to justice; 7) to cooperate with all forces designated by His Majesty and do their bidding as needs be to ensure the continued success of His Majesty's interests in the American colonies.*

As she read, a wave of revulsion struck Savannah so hard, she had to hold her throat to keep the bile down.

David . . . her David. He was a viscount and he had never told her! Why? Was he carrying out his commission the same way she had been carrying out hers, by spying on the Americans, trying to get information that he could carry back to the Loyalists? Did he suspect Savannah? Was that why he had made that outlandish proposal?

She tried to think back to the time before David had announced their "betrothal." She had been with Patrick, trying to give him the code she'd devised. And David had torn it out of her stomacher. He had had it in his possession overnight. Yes, he had said he'd not read it. But soon after that, Patrick had warned her that the code was compromised.

Had David been so clever that he'd sent on the code after copying it, and then, after a few small successes that had not hurt the British forces very much, had he sent the code to the authorities before she *did* learn more than she should? Was he toying with her, keeping her close to him so he could discover what she knew before she could pass it on? Was he using physical union with her to ingratiate himself with all the Americans—Loyalists and Rebel sympathizers alike?

If it were true, she feared for her life, as well as the life of her country.

And, ironically, she feared for David's life. Should he be caught by Rebels whose lives had been cruelly shattered by Tory courts or British regulations, he would fare no better than she in British hands.

Dear God, I'm in love with a traitor to all I hold dear.

Chapter Eighteen

The days following her discovery, Savannah was able to fend off David's advances, pleading her monthly problem. Thankfully, it did come, and it kept her from putting the lie to all she told him. But even when she was once again able to take him into her bed and body, she felt such revulsion that she had to think up another excuse.

Added to her problem about David was the work she had to do for the Cause.

She knew from Molly Worthington's babble that the British were still keeping a careful watch over the harbor. But rumblings from Josiah's study alerted her to the fact that the lieutenant general who had been put in charge was certain the Americans had turned tail and run for good. And, because he needed to bolster fortifications in northern New York, he decided to take several contingents away from the harbor. They were to be moved in two days.

And her weekly article would appear on the day before their departure.

She had given her word. She had a duty to deliver the information she had gleaned.

David was not unaware of the change in Savannah. No longer did she drape herself over his shoulder as he read the newspaper or did his accounts. And while she claimed she was still "laid up" with her flux, he was too attuned to her schedule to believe it.

Mayhap he had been paying too much attention to his business. They were newly betrothed, after all, and should be enjoying a social life that would include introducing his future bride to people who would be important in their lives. And the theater was open, with a good comedy playing to enthusiastic audiences. What a ninny he was! Savannah must be feeling restless cooped up in these rooms in front of her easel all day and having to sit quietly by the fire while he worked all evening.

The next afternoon he left work early with a box under his arm. He entered his rooms and plopped the box down on the deal table, smiling when he heard an oath coming from Savannah's room. He opened the connecting door and watched her as she bent over the matching deal table to his. She had parchment, ink, and quills spread out on the surface. He recognized her scrawl on several sheets of parchment and knew she had finished her article for that week. Now, because of the concentration on her face, he judged that she was drawing the illustration to accompany it.

"What's this one about?" he asked, and picked up the article.

"The opening of *The Comedy of Errors*."

"You saw it?"

"Molly Worthington and Olivia Butler took me with them three nights ago, while you were busy with Lawrence."

"Was it good?"

She nodded and made a small scratch on the new illustration. "Damn!" She balled up the mistake and threw it at him. "Now see what you made me do? I'll have to start over."

"Sorry. I'll be still as a mouse, sitting here, reading."

He picked up her article and read quickly through the description of the theatergoers. She had a flare for this, an ability to capture the scene and present it in words so the reader would actually think he was there. David could almost hear the rustle of silk and satin, the whoosh of velvet. He could smell rosewater and pipe tobacco. He could feel the hard edge of the gilt seats and see the splash of color on the stage.

"Circle in a square . . . danger . . ."

David looked up. "Did you say something?"

"Me?" Savannah wrinkled her brow. "No. I don't think so."

David shrugged and went back to the article. He was in the middle of Savannah's critical analysis of the actors and the play, and he found himself smiling at her description of fashionable whorls and spirals in the pattern of the lady's skirts.

"Spiral . . . all clear."

This time David didn't ask. He had heard her plain as day. What had she said before? *Circle in a square, danger.* Now she said, *Spiral, all clear.*

He still held the article in front of him, but his eyes were not perusing the page. Instead, he watched Savannah as she painstakingly inked in the border of her illustration. Was there a circle in a square on that border? If there were, he would need a magnifying glass to see it. But he'd wager it was there. And he'd wager he'd find that spiral, if not in the border, then in some other part of the picture. *And* in the article itself!

Good Lord, what was she doing?

Savannah connected the final line and breathed a sigh of relief. She wiped her quill and her brow, then let herself relax into the chair.

"Finished?" David asked.

"For this week."

She waited for the ink to dry, not wanting to mar the design with any sand or salt because every line in it was important to the message it contained. She had to keep her illustrations simple, of course, because newspaper printing was not the same as book printing. The presses were worn, most of them clumsy contraptions that smeared the ink something dreadful! But she had chosen her publishers for their precision and artistry. Her New York publishers could etch her illustrations directly onto plates, as did the Massachusetts one. Others had to transfer the sketch to woodblocks, which they then fitted into the press. And others didn't have highly skilled artisans, so they couldn't include any illustrations at all. They could only use the borders around her article. Thus, she had to put the code in three places: the illustration, the border, and buried inside the text of the article itself.

While the ink was drying, Savannah examined her quills. Several were too squashed to be used again, so she discarded them along with her first false starts. Those quills that were still useful she sharpened with a small knife her father had given her many years ago, then put them in the drawer of the deal table.

She held her hands up to David and laughed. "I don't get this much paint on me when I'm at the easel! When is someone going to invent something which works as well as a quill but doesn't leak so much?" She crossed to the nightstand, poured water from the pitcher into the bowl, and scrubbed her hands with strong soap. "Why so quiet, David? And what are you doing here this early?"

"I brought you a gift."

"Where?" She toweled dry her hands. "I don't see anything."

David rose and crossed the room to his door.

"David . . ."

"What?"

"My article?"

He looked puzzled for a moment, then realized he still carried the sheaves of parchment. "Oh." He thrust them at her. "Here."

Savannah was astounded. David had never been so preoccupied before. Had something gone wrong at work? Had his grandfather made some trouble? Or was his conscience bothering him?

David returned and handed Savannah a large box. "Oh, my! It's heavy." She put it on the bed and tore at the paper. Inside was a deep blue embroidered wool cloak with a lining that reminded her of . . . "The bearskin?"

"Aye. I had it cut to fit. I thought you could wear it

to the theater tonight. But since you've already seen the play . . ."

So that was it! He had tried to surprise her, only to discover she had taken in the production without him. "But, David, there are other plays. Goldsmith's *The Good Natured Man* is at the Strand. And his *She Stoops to Conquer* is at the Lyceum."

"The latter seems appropriate to the occasion."

They arrived early enough to get good seats near the front of the house. Several men and women stopped to bid them welcome. And when the general audience discovered that Miss Savannah Stewart was among them, necks craned to catch a glimpse of the popular columnist and illustrator.

"It seems my betrothed is a celebrity."

"Hardly that," Savannah demurred.

"You will be when your next column appears tomorrow."

"I don't think so. If I stopped writing today, people wouldn't know my name next week."

"Then stop writing today! I'll send money to your family to keep your obligation to them."

"David . . . we've had this conversation before. It turned into an argument then. Don't spoil tonight. I'm going to continue my column. I have to."

Behind her, Abigail Drummond wondered *why* the charming Miss Stewart had to write her column when she could so easily be supported by the rich David Montgomery. She was, for all intents and purposes, already a member of his family. Why, then, did she not accede to his wishes? And why did he not demand she do so? He could. She was betrothed to him, so he had dominion over her. Yet, he chose not to use it.

Strange.

And worth looking into.

Mayhap there was something she could use to advance her own position. The good Miss Stewart wasn't the only American who could take her place among the sterling members of British society. Abigail smiled happily. Her escort that night was Philip Conroy, Baron of Trent and emissary of the King to his royal troops. Philip held the keys to the royal money box. It was to him that generals and admirals and lesser officers must needs apply for funds to pay and outfit their troops. A responsible job. And Philip was . . . well, he wasn't exactly generous, but he offered her a gift or two for her favors. She hadn't actually given him everything he asked for. Not yet. He would have to offer much more if he were to get what he wanted. Much more. As much as David Montgomery had given. This time, she would settle for nothing less.

And meanwhile, she would study Savannah and her attributes. That column. It occasioned the first anger she had seen from Montgomery. It must be important. It would appear on the morrow. Abigail decided she would read every line twice to see what made Montgomery so nervous.

"My goodness, Savannah," Molly blurted out when the young artist arrived the next day for Olivia Butler's first sitting. "You've made our season, my girl!" She waved the weekly newspaper in the air. "Olivia and I have been regaled with maidservants bringing us invitations to teas and dinner parties. And all because you mentioned our names in your latest article."

"And I won't be able to attend a one," Olivia lamented.

"Why not?"

"Her time is getting close, Savannah, and she'll be confined at her cousin's house . . . that rabble-monger James Otis. But I shall keep all the appointments and write chatty letters to Olivia so she won't feel totally left out. Though, I do not like to have my missives delivered to a Rebel sympathizer's house. Josiah will not be amused."

"Strange times, aren't they, Savannah, that families should be separated by political questions? My cousin James is a Rebel. We are Loyalists. But when it comes time to have my baby, I can always count on Mercy Otis and her wonderful midwife to see me through. So Rebel or not, I go there."

"When will you leave?"

"Tomorrow, week."

Savannah thought over what had to be done. She had used the present code long enough. To be safe, she had better change it. And with Patrick and Benjamin in Philadelphia with most of the other patriots, she had few contacts she could use to deliver a new version of the code to her friends. But James was in the city and would remain there until the New York tea party was successfully carried out. If she could get the new code to him . . .

"I have some miniatures for the Otises. Things I did while they were at the Morrises for Christmas. Would it trouble you too much to deliver them for me, Olivia?"

"No trouble at all."

Savannah spent three hours with Olivia and Molly, with a break for midday meal. Her afternoon was almost a repeat of the one the day before, only this time she had to labor hard to find another way to make simple shapes that corresponded to letters of the alphabet or entire words. She dared not use the same code she'd used before, so she made many false starts before she had a complete list for James Otis.

A quick hour of miniature painting followed, and then Savannah took a nap. She awoke to find David in the rocking chair by the fire, staring intently at her.

Dusk and the flickering fire had turned the usually bright room into a study of contrasts. Golden light. Dark grey shadows. And from time to time, as the light of the fire danced around the room, it looked as if the corner shadows were smoldering.

It also looked as if *David* were smoldering.

"Have I done something to displease you, David?"

"I hope not." He approached her and sat on the side of her bed, playing with the tendrils of hair that had escaped her mobcap. "I have to go back to Williamsburg."

"Why?"

"To finish the negotiations with Benjamin Clough. He is too old and tired to travel during the winter, and I want to have everything tied up quickly."

Hell, he *had* to have everything tied up quickly. In the letter from his grandfather, the marquess had demanded it, announcing that he would be sending an agent on the next tide to take the signed contracts back to England. He would brook no delay. Since Lorton Crown Traders had been steadily losing money, Richard Montgomery feared the King might take his largesse to another firm. By adding Clough's stores to Lorton's, sales were bound to increase.

"How long will you be gone?"

"Two weeks. Three at the most."

There was something in his tone that alerted her. "Don't worry so, David. I will be fine here."

"I don't want you here. I want you with me."

"I have my work . . ."

"Your damn articles."

"And my commissions. They are very lucrative."

"There would be commissions aplenty in Williamsburg."

"David, I can't go now."

"I know," he growled. He gripped her shoulders and shook her. "Damn, why can't you do as I bid?"

"Because then I wouldn't be me, David. I would be some empty-headed ornament who took your hand, curtsied whenever you came in the room, and said naught but 'Yes, my lord' or 'No, my lord.' You would soon find that very tiresome."

"But you would be safe."

"I am safe enough. If you will feel better, I'm sure I can lodge with Molly Worthington or Olivia Butler. No, not Olivia. She and her children are going to the Otises for her confinement. But the Worthingtons are a good family. They would be glad to have me."

"I'll ask Josiah."

"And if he agrees, will that take the frown off your handsome face?"

"Ah, Savannah . . . I'm not sure what will take the

frown off my face." *Or the fear from my heart*. He pushed a stray lock of her hair back from her face. "But I believe you—and only you—could put a smile there, at least for the next hour or two."

"Rogue!"

Though she had not reacted with anything but calm to David's announcement, the thought of his leaving left a burning ache in Savannah's breast. She loved him so much—despite the possibility that he might truly be an agent of the King—that even one day without him loomed as torture. Yet, there would come a time when the rest of her life on earth would stretch out, void of his presence. This trip to Williamsburg would show her how to stumble through the hours, how to survive without her very reason for breathing.

"David," she whispered brokenly, "I want to make love to you long into the night."

"Ah, Savannah! I've spent the past week waiting to hear those words."

David hesitated, wondering what he would gain—or lose—if he couldn't protect this woman from herself. She took so many risks, walking a path that no other woman would walk. She was courage and stubbornness, beauty and deceit, love and fear. And he wanted to hold her now, before he lost her completely.

So David pulled her into his arms, pushing away the wild thoughts of kidnapping Savannah and locking her in a dungeon until the troubles in America were ended. His mouth came down on hers and he tasted her sweetness, the essence he wanted to keep safe and knew he couldn't.

Savannah was stunned, not by the fierceness of David's kiss but because his hands were trembling as they skimmed over her breasts. Not only his hands, however. His arms and legs shook as well. It frightened her because there was no reason for it, except that he might be lying to her and the weight of it was killing him.

She pulled her head back and looked deeply into his eyes. No fear resided there, as he had implied. Nor anxiety, nor anger. Contempt? Was that what he felt for her?

No. She would not, could not, believe that. Not that. Yet, there was something different there in his penetrating gaze.

Lord, where had her instincts fled? She had never before had any trouble uncovering hidden traits. Yet now, when she needed to know most of all, she was flummoxed.

He didn't drop his gaze. He met her look quietly, though the unsteadiness of his breathing told her he was aroused beyond the norm. As was she!

She moaned and pulled his head down to the valley of her breasts. "Oh, David . . . I will miss you so."

Sweet misery! David's heart tore apart in agony. The rending left him with two minds. He had to leave. But his life was beneath him, in his arms. Damn! Oh, goddamn! He tore off his clothes in a frenzy that popped buttons and strained seams. As ferociously, he started to pull off her clothes. The apron gave him fits, until he finally tore it from its pins and threw it on the floor. Her stomacher came away in a quick tug on the ties, as did her skirts and bodice. His hands pushed down on the underbodice to free her luscious breasts, and he laved them uncontrollably.

His greed made her arch into him. "Oh, David, what are you doing?"

"Ravishing you."

He barely stopped before his hands plunged between her thighs, pushing them open to give him access to the prize he demanded. He knew he was crazed from fear and burning with need. He knew he was rough and somehow inconsiderate. But a part of him needed to conquer, just as he needed her to accept his hegemony. God, she'd led and he'd followed. She'd taught and he'd learned. She'd revealed and he'd transformed. But not enough. Never enough! If it had been, she would be coming with him, giving up this madness they were trapped inside.

He wanted to tear them out of it. Instead, he found himself bound more securely into it. If he could crawl inside her and make her feel enough, he could obliterate the pain of this mad reality.

But his need for her wouldn't slow him down enough to crawl. He thrust to the sweetness he needed, expecting it to calm him. Instead, it ignited an even more devouring urge to claim her, brand her, subject her to his will, and only his.

When he took her, Savannah was shocked by the wildness he provoked inside her. She dug her fingernails into his neck and ground her hips in silent supplication. She needed him. She needed to believe in him. And if this was all they had, all she could believe in, then it would have to be enough.

She wrapped her legs around his lean hips and encased him within herself, arching her hips higher to accept the throbbing length of him. She owned him now, if not forever, and reveled in the mounting excitement of their union. Higher and higher . . . hotter and hotter . . . she followed him to realms of bliss. She could not breathe, yet her heart raced with passion and her pulse accelerated to his rhythmic joy. Jolts of power burst from David's deep penetration, surging upward through her body, her heart, her soul, her very being.

"Sweet Savannah! I can't get enough of you," David cried. "Can't give enough!"

"Take more, David. Take it all."

He rolled until she was astride him. His muscles bulged as he lifted her, then brought her down. Sweat coated his chest and she reached to feel the moistness, discovering a rising crescendo of heartbeats beneath her fingers.

"You . . . belong to . . . me," he ground out.

"Yes," she whispered brokenly. "Yes."

He rolled again and the shuddering climax began. It went on and on until darkness flooded her mind and she couldn't see, could only feel her lover pour himself into her as her body convulsed again and again.

When he felt her surrender, he gave a strangled moan and all the strength left him. He began to move away from her, but she pulled him down and wrapped her arms around him. Their hearts beat as one, slowing. Their limbs tangled together, trembling. Their breathing stilled, mingling. And he knew a profound sadness, mixed with the ultimate joy.

He would not be completely a man until she was completely his woman.

"Marry me."

She ran her fingers through his damp hair and offered him the best she could—a way out. "Ask me again when all this is but a memory."

It wasn't the answer he wanted, but David grunted his assent. Then drowsiness overtook him and he sighed into the pillow of her breasts.

They slept, wrapped in the warmth of bodies replete.

David dreamed of a bonny girl-child, with her mother's soft black hair and her father's dark blue eyes. But something blasted his face from the comfort of sleep. A pounding. Hurried footsteps. Voices.

He fought to keep the dream but Savannah shook him roughly. Something . . . "What's wrong?"

"I don't know. Shouts below. Glass breaking."

A woman shrieked and a man bellowed.

David jumped off the bed and pulled on his breeches and shirt. He flung open the door to find two women hugging each other, tears running down their cheeks. A man thrust a tankard of ale at him and David automatically grasped it.

"To the Stalwarts," the man said.

"Stalwarts?"

The man's eyes traveled over David's shoulder and he winked. "Ye have no heard, sire? The Rebels 'ave taken the 'arbor! Dumped a cargo of tea and other stuff from Clough's ships. Didn't wait for dead o' night, neither. Took the bit 'atween their teeth and bullocked the King! The Stalwarts, God love 'em!"

David closed the door in the man's face and whirled to find Savannah sitting up in bed, blankets clutched to her chin and light dancing in her eyes. He looked down at the tankard of ale, cursed, and threw it across the room. Savannah jumped as if it had hit her.

"David?"

"Clough's ships! Did you hear that? Clough's ships."

He shook his fist in the air. "Damn this American spirit! Damn this insurrection!" He sat down heavily in the chair beside the deal table and ran his fingers through his hair. "Clough's ships. *My ships!* I signed for them this morning. And when I go to Williamsburg to finish the negotiations with Benjamin Clough, I will owe him for a full cargo which now lies at the bottom of New York harbor."

Oh, God! Even though she didn't know what that meant to David in terms of money, she did know what it would mean in his grandfather's eyes. He would be diminished. And her actions as The Shadow had caused it.

Chapter Nineteen

David left immediately to see to his ships in the harbor. When he returned well after the midnight hour, Savannah heard him cursing and slamming drawers in his own rooms. He did not approach her again that night, nor the next day. And she was too ashamed of her involvement in his trouble to approach him. They needed time to sort this out, time to find a common meeting ground.

Savannah immersed herself in her painting and in helping Olivia Butler get her exuberant brood to James Otis's house. Molly Worthington joined them for midday meal and extended an invitation for Savannah to move in with them when David left.

"You've seen him today?"

"Aye. He's a righ' bonny lad; but he's taking this tragedy very hard. Those Stalwarts! And that rascal The Shadow. Mister Morris and Warren Standish have my good husband convinced that the timing of the attack could only have been coordinated by the spy among us. I say every one of the lot should be found and hanged."

By the time Savannah returned to her rooms to have her things transferred to the Worthingtons, she was dirty, tired, and hungry. But she was also anxious to see David. She knocked on his door and called his name. The door opened and she smiled brightly. But her smile froze on her face when the man who looked out at her wasn't David.

"Be ye lookin' fer me, wench?"

"N . . . n . . . no," she stammered. She whirled and made for the stairs.

The man called after her, "If ye don' find 'im, hasten back. I'll show ye a good time."

Mistress Downs, the innkeeper's wife, informed Savannah that David had packed his things that afternoon. She produced a sealed letter and handed it to Savannah.

"Said for you to have this soon as you come in. An' he made arrangements for your things to be packed and taken to some Worth place. Said you'd know where. So I've already let out your room. But if you're hungry, I can lay a place for you in the keeping room."

"Yes, please. And then send for a carriage, to pick me up in an hour."

The keeping room was abuzz with the news of the New York Tea Party. Most were on the side of the Stalwarts, as they were now being called. Some, however, grumbled about cowards who stole up in the dead of night and took away an honest man's cup of tea. Steely glances gave way to shouted epithets. And Savannah was glad to flee the inn before the exchanges turned into brawls.

When she arrived at the Worthingtons, Molly apologized for not knowing that David had intended for her to join them that evening.

"You're to have the large study at the end of the hall. What used to be the nursery. There's a good bed and two fireplaces. Should be warm enough and roomy enough for you to do your painting. Will you join us in the drawing room for some hot mulled cider?"

"I do appreciate the offer, Molly. But I'm very tired and I'd like to go right to bed."

"Of course, dear. Clarissa, our Negro servant, will be at your call. If you need anything, ring the bell by the side of your bed." Molly patted her arm. "And I'll have a mug of cider brought to you, along with a warming pan for your bed. Have a good night, Savannah."

"Thank you, Molly." *I'll try.*

Savannah postponed reading David's letter—almost as a punishment for what she'd done to him—until she was tucked into bed.

The candle flickered, throwing light and shadow across the pale cream paper, and the words seemed to dance. But it wasn't the light that distorted the strokes. It was the tears that dammed up behind her lashes. She swiped at them and concentrated on the message David had left for her.

Savannah,

The devastation is complete. The Shadow has won this round. There does not seem any point to my staying in New York another day. With sadness, I am bound to do my grandfather's and the King's business. Ah, Savannah! I fell in love with you because you were not like other women. But now I wish you were, if only so I could keep you safe during this turbulent time. Promise me you will remain at the Worthingtons, so I may know you are out of harm's way. Promise me in your heart.

Oh, David! He asked too much. She could not promise him anything more than her love.

In the days that followed, Savannah was privy to information from all sides, as a guest in the Worthington home. Most of it she passed on through her publishers. And most of it helped the Rebel cause.

Secret locations of royal munitions stores were "discovered" and confiscated by the Americans. When attempting to land in the dead of night, revenue cutters were boarded, their crew off-hauled, and the ships set ablaze. Because so many tax stamps were found and burned, hidden presses were set up in barns and cellars by the King's magistrates. One by one, they were found and smashed. Shipments of foodstuffs, bound for military outposts, were stolen and distributed to the families of prisoned Rebel leaders. Dozens of secret jails, where Rebel prisoners were kept before trial, were "accidentally" located, stormed, broken into, and set ablaze by the very men they had prisoned. Farms and houses, which were about to be confiscated by Royal magistrates and revenue agents, were fired to keep them out of the hands of the Loyalists. And most important of all, Rebels in every colony were warned beforehand, enabling them to escape with their families before the King's militia could take them into custody for acts of rebellion against the Crown.

David's two weeks lengthened into four, then five, and Savannah heard naught from him. But because of the unrest the inhabitants of the city kept her busy, trying for some normality being the rule of the day. So Savannah had more commissions than she could finish in a half year. But with David gone, she worked into the night to fend off the loneliness and fears.

One night Clarissa awakened her, and she quickly came out of her restless slumber.

"Miz Worthington says if you wants to be at Miz Butler's birthing, you'd best to get dressed fast."

Savannah jumped out of bed, throwing on warm clothes and her sturdy leather boots. She hesitated over whether to wear her bearskin-lined cape or two woolen ones, but then decided warmth was more important. Besides, she wasn't going to wear the cape into the birthing room. It could hardly get dirty on a carriage ride.

The Otis house was ablaze with lights, and once Savannah and Molly were inside, they were escorted to the birthing room. There, Savannah found herself in the company of seven women who were her patrons, five of Olivia's kinsfolk, and the midwife who had been called—Abigail Drummond.

It was the first time Savannah had seen Abigail at work in her true profession. It was astounding how good she was at it. The birth was difficult, yet Abigail never lost her composure. She issued orders to maidservants and guests alike and kept a steady hand on Olivia's midsection to time the contractions. The hours stretched on and most of the guests repaired to the keeping room to help prepare meals for such a large gathering. But Abigail asked Molly and Savannah to stay with Mercy Otis and herself.

Abigail took the women aside. "Is this truly her

eighth delivery?" she asked Mercy, who nodded. Abigail frowned. "I don't understand it, then. It shouldn't be taking this long."

"Breech?"

"I thought that at first. But the head is in the right position. The baby just refuses to come out."

Savannah looked toward the bed, where a Negro servant sponged Olivia's head. "She's too tired to push."

"Yes," Abigail agreed. "So, you must do the pushing for her."

"How?"

"I want three brooms brought into the room. Each of you will take a broom and push down on Olivia's stomach with it as if you were rolling out piecrust. One behind the other, you must press and roll in a rhythmic motion, one behind the other."

"We'll hurt the baby!" Molly cried.

Abigail shook her head. "Trust me. I know what I'm doing."

It took another hour, but finally Olivia's eighth baby was delivered. A girl, its cord was wrapped around its neck and Abigail raced to unwrap it before the child died. She called for a large bowl of snow and smacked the baby's back again and again. When the snow arrived, she dropped the baby into it and rubbed the cold ice crystals over her skin. Suddenly, a tiny mewing sound escaped the baby's lips and Abigail grunted. She picked it out of the snow, stuck her finger into its mouth, and pulled out thick fluid. She smacked the baby again and got a feeble cry. Another whack and a screech rent the air. "Well, missy . . . you gave us all a bit of trouble." Abigail handed the baby to Mercy, who hurried to the fire to clean and dress it and keep it warm. Then Abigail turned back to Olivia. She picked up a broom and rolled it against her patient's stomach to expel the sack. "Tea and brandy or rum for Mistress Butler," she ordered. "Then a weak gruel." She turned back to check over the baby and seemed satisfied. "I will have my breakfast and be back. I want the bedding completely changed and fresh felt pads placed under Olivia. Change the pads every ten minutes. If they aren't kept clean, she may get a fever, sicken, and die. And I'll not have a death on my hands."

Savannah helped for the next half hour, until Olivia's sister spelled her and she could stumble down the stairs to the keeping room and a cup of hot chocolate. Abigail waved her over and offered her a platter of crisp fried corn cakes. Savannah bit into one quickly, then piled three on a plate, added butter and maple syrup, and began eating them more slowly.

"You did a good job up there," she said to Abigail.

"Almost as good a job as you're doing."

"They're nothing alike."

"No, they aren't. Yours is far more lucrative. And dangerous."

Savannah's skin felt clammy. What? Had Abigail found her out? Impossible. How could a woman who acted the whore discover the identity of The Shadow, when intelligent agents of the King had been unsuccessful? "Dangerous? Painting portraits?"

"And writing articles, Savannah."

Abigail gave her a sidelong glance, her eyes flashing with envy and cunning, and Savannah began to doubt her own deductions.

"In these days, being published only by Rebel-leaning publishers is not very safe, my dear."

Abigail slid off the settle bench and smiled coyly as she headed for the door, leaving Savannah breathless with astonishment. She was right, Savannah thought. Abigail had hit on the weakness of Savannah's position. And she had seen it easily! Had others?

Then and there Savannah decided her days in New York had come to a close. She had to strike out for other parts of the colonies, if only to protect herself in case Abigail let slip her deductions to the wrong ears. And, Savannah must get some Tory publishers to take her work, to get a more balanced, less political audience.

Luckily, she had been approached by an emissary of Mary Noyes Silliman, the wife of Connecticut's famous lawyer, Gold Selleck Silliman. Mary wanted a family portrait of all her children, those from her first husband and those from Gold Silliman. It was time to finish up what she had started in New York and head for Connecticut.

When Abigail left Savannah, she felt an elation such as she had not experienced since Williamsburg. She did not know for certain that Savannah was a spy. And she couldn't prove that she was The Shadow. But from the trepidation on Savannah's face when she mentioned the articles, Abigail was sure she had hit a mark. Why hadn't anyone else seen what she had—that the Rebel's best successes always occurred right after one of Savannah's columns appeared? Once or twice would have been coincidence. But it had happened over twelve times now. There must be some connection.

Although Abigail had to admit that Savannah was more cunning than she'd anticipated. Not every article was followed by a huge Rebel success. So Abigail surmised that there was some kind of pattern to Savannah's columns, times when she included information and times when she did not.

The only problem—if Abigail were right—was how did Savannah transmit the information? What did she use? Specific words? An alphabet code like the kind children used in word games? Or was it more complex?

She had already tried every alphabet combination she could imagine, poring over each article until her eyes blurred and her head ached. And she had come away with nothing but a pounding behind her temples and fury that this *scribbler* could get what Abigail wanted and couldn't grasp: a man like David Montgomery, with wealth and power and a title.

Abigail's mother had always told her that life wasn't fair. But her father, who was a drifter and a gambler, had told her to make her own luck, to grab for the prize, to wrest what she could from the pack.

The prize was the reward for The Shadow. As each Rebel success mounted, the reward had increased. It now stood at one thousand pounds sterling. A fortune. Enough to set her up in London, if she wished. Enough, mayhap, to attract a titled husband.

"Watch out, Savannah Stewart," Abigail whispered as she mounted the stairs. "I'm on your trail. And I won't give up until I've gotten everything I want."

* * *

That afternoon, Savannah penned a letter to Mary Noyes Silliman, accepting her commission and telling her she would arrive a week hence. Then she wrote to David, telling him what she had decided to do. She addressed David's letter to him through Lawrence Fenton and sent a messenger to deliver it. Then she walked to the post coach and paid the driver to take Mary's letter to New Haven. Before supper, she had notified everyone whose portrait she was painting that they would have their acquisition within two days and requested payment be ready at hand. For the next two days she worked every minute in her room to complete the paintings. They were still wet when she delivered them to their new homes and collected her bank notes.

Molly was sorry to see her go and had planned a fete to see her off. Everyone she had met was invited, including magistrates, military officers, merchants, publishers, and their wives and sweethearts. In short, everyone in society arrived to give Savannah Stewart a farewell party the likes of which no one had seen before.

Molly had cajoled Josiah into hiring two string players and a pianoforte player to accompany the dancing. Her servants and those from the Otis and Butler households had been cooking round the clock to stock the table with meats and pasties, vegetables and rice, macaroni pudding and egg tarts, and pies by the score.

"I wish Olivia could be here," Mercy Otis said as she lapped up her third eggnog with a dusting of nutmeg. "But I've left her in good hands. Abigail was wonderful at the birthing, wasn't she?"

"Absolutely," Savannah agreed. "She's an intelligent

woman."

Too intelligent, Savannah decided. She was very glad she had decided to leave New York.

"And it's too bad that her latest beau will have to move with the troops from the Brooklyn battery to the northern bank of Long Island. But His Majesty's forces will need him to help them get enough supplies to raid Rebel strongholds across the river into Fairfield."

Savannah felt the skin at the back of her neck contract with fear. "Fairfield? What in the world is important enough to raid in Fairfield? It's a sleepy little town."

"It looks sleepy on the outside. But Captain Richardson says it harbors the most important leaders of the rebellion in Connecticut. When they catch them, the captain says, they will turn out the American owners, and confiscate the lands and property for the use of British troops. What an exciting time we live in, Savannah!"

Exciting, yes. And dangerous. Though Mary Noyes Silliman was taking up residence in New Haven, where her family had ties to Yale College, her husband's headquarters and his property were in Fairfield. Gold Selleck Silliman was the leader Captain Richardson sought.

Abigail wiped Olivia Butler's brow and listened to her quiet breathing. The wet nurse was tending to the baby and there was a hot supper waiting for Abigail in the keeping room. But Abigail wasn't interested in the hot meal. She was still fuming about being here instead of attending the fete at the Worthington house, where she should have been holding court with the gentry.

The entire community would be feasting Savannah, dancing to wonderful music and gossiping about all manner of goings-on. And here she was, stuck in a Rebel's household, eating brown bread, ham, and rabbit stew, and listening to the plaintive cries of a baby who was constantly hungry.

Suddenly, Abigail's thoughts skipped backward. A Rebel's household! She was in the den of iniquity. In among a traitor's belongings. And where better to find information she could pass on to the right ears? Where better to find something . . . anything . . . that would help ingratiate herself with all the Tories?

She hurried to the only room she knew might disclose what she was looking for: James Otis's library and study. A great mahogany slant-top desk sat against the wall next to the fireplace. She hurried to it and pulled down the desktop. A rush-seated Windsor chair gave her a comfortable place to sit while she rummaged through the drawers.

Bills. It was amazing how many bills this Rebel owed. And letters. There must be hundreds!

She skimmed through them, discarding anything that was from Otis's family, concentrating on those from Rebels whose name she recognized. Patrick Henry, discussing rulings in the House of Burgesses. John Adams, writing about his delightful wife, Abigail. Pah! The woman was a martyr and a frump. Thomas Jefferson, extolling the virtues of a new grape strain he'd imported from Italy. George Washington, asking for an introduction to Mary Custis. George

Wythe, bemoaning the dearth of good carvers in Virginia.

What, did these men never discuss politics in their correspondence? Were they so mundane as to find only their household necessities of interest to their friends? She had read better letters from ordinary play actors!

When Abigail got to Benjamin Franklin's letter, which included a sketch of his latest interest, a round stove, she was ready to call it a night and go to bed. Obviously, James Otis kept his most important papers in his office at his place of business.

She refolded everything she had taken out of the cubbyholes in the desk and began to stuff them back, when her hand brushed against a nail sticking out of the wood. It scratched her and she hit it in anger. She heard a click and a panel popped open at the side of the desk.

Oh, clever! A secret compartment.

Inside she found three letters from Samuel Adams of Massachusetts. When she started to read them, she wondered why James Otis had bothered to secrete the things. The first contained nothing more than a rule for gingerbread cookies and a few words about people Samuel had met at a fete in Philadelphia. She was about to toss it aside, when she caught the phrase *"illustrious correspondent"* and *"her ingenious geometric embellishments which will bring us much happiness."*

Abigail's pulse raced. Illustrious correspondent could mean anything. But she'd bet her last ruby brooch that it referred to Savannah. And the rest of the sentence confirmed it.

So . . . she should have been looking for a geometric code, not an alphabetic one! But what kind?

Quickly, she unfolded another of the letters and gave a soft gasp of joy. Listed before her eyes were two columns. One contained simple geometric shapes. The other one contained words and letters that corresponded to the shapes.

She had Savannah roped and branded, but only if the code matched the artist's illustrations to her articles. There was only one way to find out. Within ten minutes, Abigail had the code copied as best she could. She tucked it into her pocket, refolded the letters and put them back in the desk, and closed the secret compartment.

Later that night, after she left the Otises with a few pence in her pocket for spending the evening with Olivia, Abigail bundled herself before the fire in her room at Gloucester Place and perused all the columns of Savannah's that she had saved. She had to work backward, because the code didn't match anything in the latest articles. It wasn't until she got to those articles which had first appeared when Savannah came to New York, that she found a correspondence. In one of them, by using the code, she spelled out a sentence that read: *"New military batteries forming in Brooklyn."* In another: *"Warning! Roger Morris not neutral. Has Tory leanings."* The rest were the same. Information but nothing up-to-date, nothing that would put a hangman's noose around Savannah's neck or bring Abigail the thousand pounds sterling reward. Obviously, the code had been changed, since she didn't for a minute believe that Savannah had stopped her spying. There was naught to do then except examine every last wiggle and bump in Savannah's illustrations. Now that she was on the right track, Abigail felt sure that by studying the dark shadows in Savannah's etchings, she could decipher ordinary pen strokes from obscure symbols.

And when she did . . . A cunning, calculating smile split her features. When she did, the good, handsome heir to a marquess's fortune would have to sit up and take notice of *her*, or be denounced along with his paramour.

Chapter Twenty

Savannah spent a sleepless two hours after the last guest left the party. She was worried about Mary Silliman and her family. The Silliman and Noyes families were prominent. Their ties to Yale College made Mary and Gold Selleck Connecticut's leaders. Mary was strong, stable, and compassionate. She had sustained excruciating troubles in her life and already lost one husband. To lose another . . . well, it was unthinkable.

Savannah's information about the British troop movements could save her friends. She must get it through. Her column would help, certainly. But it took more than a week to get it published. Mary and Gold would not have a week, never mind two. It was more important, therefore, Savannah decided, that she personally warn her friends.

Having made the only decision she could, Savannah spent the rest of the night getting her things together. She was already expected to leave in two days. She would simply push up her departure a day, leaving around noon. But to do what she had to do, she couldn't take the coach to New Haven. It would take too long. She would have to go by horse, over ground studded with British outposts. And she must muzzle the horse and muffle his hooves.

Thus, she needed several burlap sacks and strong pieces of thick leather. The only place she knew to get them was David's stores. Which meant appealing to Lawrence Fenton or buying them from one of the shop stewards.

If she bought them from Lawrence, she would have to give him a reasonable explanation, and she didn't have one. So, she had to wait until he left the stores, then slip inside and buy them unawares.

Damnation! This spying business was more complicated than making beggar's lace!

Once she was inside the Clough establishment, Savannah tried not to react to the morose faces that greeted her. No one here had recovered from the losses incurred during the New York Tea Party. And it was her fault.

Well, no. It was only partially her fault. The rest lay with the King and his Parliament and their damned import taxes. But tell that to the young man who took her order and came back with only half of what she wanted.

"We have to ration," he explained. "The Rebels, you know."

She nodded, then added something that she *could* get: several sets of men's clothing. Breeches were thick enough, if doubled, to take the place of leather, though they'd wear through faster. And she would make faster time astride a horse if she were wearing men's clothing instead of her own voluminous skirts. The only thing to do now was to try to find a horse.

She couldn't hire one and take it to Connecticut, because she probably would not be able to get it back. She wasn't of a mind to steal one, since that would put the militia after her . . . and she couldn't afford to have anyone speculate why she needed to *steal* a horse. Nor could she borrow one from a friend, since they all thought she was going to Connecticut by coach.

Was she to fail for want of a horse? For the first time in her life, Savannah could understand how Richard III must have felt.

She gathered her packages and left the stores. She took the alley next to Clough's warehouse, the shorter way back to the Worthingtons. And as she passed the courtyard where the stores were off-loaded from carriages and wagons, she spotted a familiar shape.

Sunshine. Bella's gelding. The favorite of all the students at Honesty Dunn's school.

Savannah had thought David had taken him back to Williamsburg. But mayhap he had taken an overland coach, since he would have to put up at several inns before reaching the Virginia capital.

She looked around to see if anyone were in the vicinity who knew her, then eased herself through the entrance of the courtyard. Keeping to the perimeter, she approached Sunshine and held out her hand. The horse whinnied, licked at her hand, then butted his head against her shoulder in recognition and welcome.

"Well, boy . . . how have you been?" The horse whinnied again and she laughed. "You could be the answer to my prayers, Sunshine. How would you like to take a trip to Connecticut?" Another whinny. "Good boy. I always knew you were intelligent." She patted his long nose and snuggled up to the warm, musky animal. "I'll be back, boy. You be ready."

Once she got back to Molly's, Savannah packed her purchases carefully atop her two Turkey bags, making sure there was equal weight in them. Then she hurried down to the kitchen and gathered as much food as she could beg from the cook for her journey. If the woman was surprised that Savannah wanted more than Molly had already made provision for, she didn't show it and did as Savannah bid, stocking two small sacks with dried fruit, cornmeal journey cakes, and dried, salted venison.

"Ye have enough there for a week, lass."

"I like to have something to share with the other passengers on the night coach. You know we don't make a stop until midday meal the next day. And every time I've been on a night coach someone has been hungry, especially the children."

"Oh, aye. That's sumpin' not many uh'd do. Yer a good girl, lass."

Not so good, Savannah thought. As she bid good-bye to Molly and Josiah, she felt very bad. She let them settle her in their carriage and let the hostler help her down with her purchases at the coach stop. But she only waited until the Worthingtons' carriage was round the corner, before she hailed a passing carriage for hire and had the driver take her to a corner a block away from Clough's stores. She paid him, waited for him to get a good distance away, then picked up her packages and half-dragged, half-carried them the length of the block to the warehouse alley. She set them in the shadows beside the courtyard and surveyed her surroundings before extracting a small bundle of clothing. There was lantern light coming from the stores; but she expected it was only for the night watchman.

Sunshine was in the same stall. He whickered when she eased open the gate and handed him a few slices of dried apple. "Shh, boy. I'll get you saddled and we'll be on our way."

It only took a few minutes to put bridle and bit on. The saddle took longer because she hadn't cinched a horse in a while. But with a few tries, Savannah managed to get it tight enough to keep the saddle from rubbing a sore on Sunshine's back. When the horse was saddled, she untied the bundle of clothing, stepped back behind Sunshine, and hurriedly changed from her skirts to men's clothing. By the time she finished, her teeth were chattering from the cold. She drew a letter from her skirt pocket and stuffed her own clothing into Sunshine's saddlebags. Before she led the horse from the stall, she jammed the letter onto a nail and prayed its contents would be enough to keep Lawrence Fenton from following her or calling out the militia to capture his horse thief.

She could swing from a rope for spying or swing from a rope for horse thieving. It was all the same.

Two hours later found her well away from the opulent neighborhood where the Worthingtons lived and near the outlying acres where tenant farmers worked off their indenture. There, she stopped to tie her precious leather pieces to Sunshine's hooves and bind his long brown nose with burlap.

"Connecticut, Sunshine. We're headed for Connecticut."

But heading for Connecticut wasn't as easy as it

sounded. Savannah couldn't keep to the roads for fear of being spotted by British patrols. She had to make for the woods, and once inside the dense growth of trees, she lost her sense of direction. From years spent wandering through southern countryside, she knew what the North Star was and its importance to navigation. But if the trees blocked out the stars, she couldn't tell north from nutmeg! Too often she had to stop Sunshine in a clearing and get a fix on the sky. Too often she found she had gone west when she should have been moving east. Still, this was better than a coach to New Haven. She was steadily getting closer to Fairfield.

At dawn, she stopped beside a small brook that was deep inside a dense growth of trees and bushes. She let sunshine drink his fill at the brook, then retied the burlap bags on his nose. She spread a blanket for him and made him lie down, tying his tether so he couldn't get back on his feet. She fed him dry fruit and some of her corn cakes, ate several herself, then curled up against the great beast to keep warm while she slept.

The sun was high overhead when she wakened. Sunshine winked his big brown eyes at her and she laughed. "Good morn to you, too, Sir Sunshine. Isn't this a beautiful day?"

Sunshine needed to be on his legs, and she loosened his tether to let him exercise for a bit while she scouted out the land and did her morning necessaries. Confound it! Getting into men's breeches was lots easier than getting out of them. How did David manage it every time he came to her bed?

David. Her heart ached with so much force, so quickly, she couldn't breathe. Her legs gave way and she plopped down to the ground.

302

"Oh, David," she whispered brokenly. "How can I live my life feeling like this? How can I go through each day wanting you, needing you? How will I make it?" She looked up through the trees to the heavens. "Why did You send him to me, Lord? Why did You let me love him when You knew it was not forever? How can it be good to love a man like this when he's never going to be able to acknowledge that love? Why, Lord? Why?"

Prayer or lament, she let it waft upward, waiting until the ache diminished and she could stand once more. She finally got the breeches off and then back on; then she scouted around for some shelter for the day, because she couldn't risk having British troops stumble on her and Sunshine. She found a small cave that smelled of rodent droppings but was free from bats and varmints. After eating some of her food, she led Sunshine to the cave and had the devil of a time getting him to go into the foul-smelling place. Once inside, however, he gave a baleful look, then quieted and settled himself in a corner. She took a book from one of the Turkey bags and read about some noodle brain named Penelope. She should have brought her Shakespeare!

Savannah napped. When she awoke, dusk was settling in and she led Sunshine back to the brook. Once again she shared her food with him, fought with the stupid breeches, and then checked Sunshine's hoof gear. Two had holes and she replaced them. She looped the other two with some of the wool squares she'd made from the men's breeches she'd bought, just to be sure Sunshine wouldn't cut through them while they were riding.

Once again she had to rely on the stars for guide, but they made good time and she got closer to Connecticut.

With all her precautions, however, Savannah nearly walked Sunshine straight into a British camp. If he hadn't reared at the smell of the smoke from the camp fire, she would have been caught for sure.

She patted his side and hugged him. "Good boy, Sunshine," she whispered as she tethered him to a tall oak. "Now stay quiet while I scout the patrol and find some way around them."

A small rise in the ground gave coverage and she peered down into the camp. Luckily, there was a small cloud cover, so she could see down into the British encampment but she wouldn't be silhouetted against the sky for them to see her.

Redcoats milled about. A watch was posted, but very close to the fire. The imbeciles! Did they think they were invincible . . . that no one would sneak up on them? No wonder the Rebels were having such success when they raided British patrols. Redcoats and camp fire pickets. Amazing King George's troops had ever won a war!

She watched the merriment of several officers as they played a round of cards and drank from tankards. Ale, probably, at this time of night. Her brows rose and she felt her stomach tighten when she saw three women come out of a tent and beckon in three men. Camp followers! Women who sold their bodies to anyone who would pay. She had heard of these women. She had heard, too, that most were widowed or orphaned and needed the coppers they'd collect that night. So, though it bothered her that they had been forced into that kind of existence, it bothered her more that no one did anything to help them so they wouldn't find it necessary to whore.

A Redcoat threw more logs on a fire and her eyes followed him as he moved to another. The wind picked up then, blowing up the hill toward her, and she clearly heard one man—not a Redcoat—say, "My winnings, gentlemen."

An officer grumbled, "That's forty pounds, my lord. I think I'll call for a new deck of cards."

"What? You think me a cheat?"

Someone moved out of the shadows and into the light of the fire, laughing. He put his hand on the gentleman's shoulder and said, "Roger, your reputation precedes you!"

Savannah's skin prickled. More than the cold of the wind chilled her body and set her hands atremble. *Oh, God! No, please! Let it be an illusion.*

She couldn't take her eyes off the imposing figure. She couldn't block out the words he said.

"Come, Roger, let us make plans to capture your Shadow. We shall bring the traitor to the rope for losing me the Clough shipments."

"But my lord, Montgomery, we know not who it is."

"I know enough, Mister Morris. And I will have my revenge." He picked up a tankard, drained the contents, and slapped Roger Morris on the back. "Come, let us enjoy the delights which await us inside the special tent Captain Richardson has set up for us. Your forty pounds if I can take them all on."

"My lord! There are seven of them."

"Seven? A frolic, Roger. A mere frolic."

She watched for a few more breathless minutes, then pushed herself to her feet. Tears wet the trail as she stumbled back to Sunshine and wrapped her arms around his neck. But even his warmth could not penetrate the chilling aspect of what she had seen and heard.

David . . . her David . . . laughing with British officers about hanging her . . . singing camp songs . . . bouncing a shapely camp follower on his knees . . . following her into the tent.

Quickly, Savannah swung into the saddle and urged Sunshine around the camp. She put him to the gallop immediately, giving heed only to icy patches of ground and fallen trees. She didn't care now whether she got caught or not. She only knew her heart had been shattered.

Ironically, because she didn't care, she arrived at Mary Noyes Silliman's Fairfield house within a few hours and delivered her warning to a stunned Gold Selleck Silliman. He thanked her, gathered his sons, and they rode quickly away to alert the other households along the river. Though Mary begged her to stay and rest — or at least accompany her to New Haven, where they would all be safe — Savannah refused.

"I have a mission, Mary."

"Your mission is unwise, my dear."

"He betrayed me. He lied to me. He seduced me. He used me just as my father warned me he would. But I can take the lies and the deceit. I cannot, however, allow him to destroy my country. Not when I can do something about it."

"And what can you do?"

"I can kill him."

Chapter Twenty-one

In the man's clothing she had on and with her hair tucked into a farmer's cap, Savannah rode one of Mary's horses, leaving Sunshine behind to be returned to Bella—somehow. She followed the trail of the British troops to the harbor, where she spotted David, three officers, and two camp followers boarding a frigate. As soon as no one was looking, Savannah hoisted a sack of flour and slipped aboard with other members of a docking crew. She searched the ship, planning to confront David and kill him as quickly and as quietly as possible with the dagger she had "borrowed" from Gold Selleck Silliman's study. . . . Oh, dear God! How could she do it? How could she think it? But she remembered the boastful way he'd swaggered into that tent, remembered that he was the King's *agent provocateur* and that if she didn't, she'd like as not put many necks in the noose.

She couldn't hear him on the officer's deck, so she headed down farther into the hold. But before she found him, the loud clang of a ship's anchor being hauled aboard, along with the flap of sails, alerted Savannah that the vessel was under way.

Damnation! Trapped in the forward hold, a reluctant stowaway on a voyage that could take as long as four months!

The frigate made two stops. At the first Savannah thought she had been seen, but she ducked down quickly and no one came for her. She dared not try again.

She had no food and no water and only some overly friendly rats for company, but she found some space behind several sacks, where she could pull down two of them to make a comfortable "bed." There she stayed for several hours, until her stomach growled and she had to search for food. Luckily, she was near many sacks of flour and meal. She slit a hole in one and greedily stuffed her mouth with dry millet. But there was no water and precious little air.

She spent a sleepless night, fighting off rats and trying to keep from choking on the fetid smells coming from the passageway to the aft hold. She must have dozed off, because she was awakened when something bit her leg.

"Ow! Damnation!"

" 'Ere, Jessup. Did ye 'ear that?"

Oh, no!

"Aye. Lucky we 'ad to use the 'ead. Keep yer cutlass to hand, lad."

She tried to blend into the shadows but there were no options. Within minutes the seamen had her in custody, dragging her down the hold and past the foul-smelling head—their comfort station. She ended up on the officer's desk, in the captain's quarters, staring across the room into the blue-grey eyes of Warren Standish, the descendant of Miles Standish and one of the company she'd met at Roger Morris's Christmas fete.

"Well, well . . ." Standish used the end of his saber to flick off Savannah's cap, letting her abundant growth of dark hair fall down on her shoulders.

"A woman!" the two said in unison.

"Yes, men. A woman. Miss Savannah Stewart, I believe? And to what do I owe this honor, Miss Stewart?"

Oh, Lord! Why couldn't it have been some fool nobody who didn't know her from the camp followers? But . . . Inspiration struck at almost the same moment as fear and anger. She had one chance. . . .

"Captain, you know the Viscount of Dwight and I are betrothed. I thought I'd surprise him by stealing aboard and hiding, but you got under sail before I could locate him. If you will show me to his cabin, all will be well."

Warren sighed and shook his head. "I wish I could do that, Miss Stewart. But your fiancé isn't aboard."

"But I followed him from the city. I saw him board this ship."

For a moment, Warren looked puzzled. His eyes drew into slits and he pursed his lips. A crafty smile split his face and he all but purred, "Yes, his lordship did board this ship. Unfortunately, he left at our last docking, to board a more comfortable—and faster—vessel. I'm sorry you missed him. But I offer you my hospitality, Miss Stewart. However, I have other females aboard, women who are, shall we say, servicing my crew? It would be dangerous for you to mingle with them. You do understand, don't you?"

"Absolutely."

"Then I will give you a small cabin where you can be relatively comfortable. A thunder jug will be provided you. And food and clean clothing, of course. But I must insist that you stay inside unless I accompany you on deck. It is the only way I may protect you from unwelcome advances."

"I understand, Captain. And am most grateful."

Grateful, hell! She wanted to get her hands on David to keep him from hurting other Rebels. But she didn't want to do it in England, where she knew no one and would probably be caught for her crime. Ah, but what mattered it? If she stayed in America, the authorities there would hang her. What was one rope compared to another?

Warren Standish took her arm and led her to a cabin so small it was little more than a storage hold. But there was a small cot, a chair, and a table.

"May I have paper, quill, and ink so I may draw?"

"Of course. And books. Whatever I have in my limited library."

"Very gracious, sir."

"Make yourself comfortable, Miss Stewart. We'll be at sea a long stretch."

When he shut the door, Savannah sank onto the cot and finally allowed her body to shake all it needed.

She hadn't realized her goal; but she was one step closer to it. She was on her way to England, David's home. And she had at least three weeks to plan what she'd do to him when she found him.

* * *

After he made another stop, Warren entertained a friend in his cabin and told her how and where his new guest had been found — and who she was.

"Your stowaway is *who?*"

"Abigail, shut your mouth. It's not that unusual for women to chase a fortune and title. You, yourself . . ."

"Captain Standish, I am with Captain Richardson. I am not chasing a fortune and title."

"No, of course not. You're merely accompanying one."

Abigail bristled. "You overstep your bounds, sir."

"Ah, Abby . . ." Warren chuckled. "If you had not come on with Captain Richardson, you would have come on with the other *women*. If not now, then someday soon. The captain is married, you know."

Abigail stood perfectly still, so Warren wouldn't realize that she hadn't known there was a Mistress Richardson. When she had been summoned to take this trip, she had assumed she had made a conquest . . . that she would acquire Captain Richardson's hand, a comfortable home, and a fortune to spend at the end of her journey. And here Warren was telling her that her role was the same as the camp followers who, even now, plied their trade in the forward cabins.

Well, a pox on the British and their sympathizers!

They were all so anxious to get their hands on The Shadow, and she was within arm's reach. But Abigail would be damned if she would tell Warren or her "traveling companion." The thousand-pound reward was so close, she could feel the weight of the sterling on her fingertips. And she would need it at the end of the journey. It would set her up in style and buy her entrance to society.

Let the damned curs chase their tails trying to find their elusive spy. She would keep her own counsel until the time was right.

Time dragged for Savannah, interrupted by the monotony of ship's bells, lapping waves against the hull, and creaking sails. The food was barely adequate. And though Captain Standish allowed her to bathe, it was in cold seawater because fresh water had to be rationed. Consequently, she always felt clammy, and her skin dried and itched. One day, however, Captain Standish stuck his head in her door and announced, "We dock tomorrow. Would you like to change out of those men's things and into a dress?"

"I would like that very much."

He left and came back presently with a soft woolen dress of bottle-green, with delicate lace round the neck and hem, and undergarments as well. "Some of the gifts for my cousin. They may be a trifle large."

"With needle and thread, I could make alterations.

"I'll have it brought to you."

She spent the rest of the day and into the evening drawing in the seams so each garment fit her body. It was a tedious job, not one of her most favorites; but it broke up the monotony of her confinement.

Warren strolled with her on deck the final night and the stars shone as brightly as any she'd ever seen. An omen? She hoped so.

When they went back to her cabin, she asked him inside and handed him a collection of the sketches she'd made on the voyage. "In repayment for the dress and your kindness."

For a moment Warren looked abashed and Savannah wondered what had occasioned it. Almost as soon as the thought flickered through her mind, however, he bowed and touched his hand to his tricorn. "My cousin will be pleased. You are already a well-known figure on the Continent. I'm sure once the populace find out who you are, they will make of you a great celebrity."

She wondered why his words held a mocking tone; but it fit so with what she was feeling, Savannah gave it little mind.

That night, she dreamt of the joys she'd had with David and the horror she'd felt at seeing him in that camp, besmirching all they'd shared, all she'd hoped. She woke with renewed thoughts of revenge.

The overseer's daughter and the marquess's heir. It had been impossible from the start. But it had been more than impossible. It had been perverted, polluted by the Montgomerys' penchant for thinking themselves better than ordinary people. For thinking they could do anything to anybody, take anything from anybody, and discard anything or anybody without once suffering the consequences.

David would suffer. As she had suffered. As her people would suffer because of men like him. She only hoped her nerve wouldn't fail her at the end.

Because she still loved him. God help her, after everything, she still loved him.

Captain Standish wanted to get her a hire coach, but Savannah thanked him and told him she preferred to see the city by foot before she found her way to the Montgomery London townhouse. Kentlands, that was its name. She would walk a little, get rooms at an inn, and find Kentlands. Once she found it, she could make her plans.

First, however, she had to provision herself with more than the one change of clothing she had. Boots, stockings, undergarments, dresses, nightclothes, brushes, combs, soap, toweling. And a Turkey bag to hold it all. How much would it all cost in England? And would she be able to use her American bank notes to pay for everything?

Not likely. She couldn't even pay for a room with what she had. Which meant that she had to find her London publisher, Randolph Wilson, and borrow money from him. All she knew was that his offices were on Fleet Street. Surely someone could give her directions.

It took most of the day to walk to Wilson's offices, and she was tired and hungry when she got there. Although Randolph allowed her inside, he wasn't convinced she was who she said she was until she sketched his portrait and presented it to him.

"My dear! I've waited almost seven years to meet you."

"Mister Wilson, I've come to petition you to advance me some funds."

"Advance you funds? Why, I can do better than that! I have your bankbook here. There is plenty in it for whatever you need."

"But I have no identification."

"A letter from me to the bank will be sufficient."

"You have been very kind to my family all these years. I can't tell you what is in my heart. . . ."

"Now, now, my dear . . . you and your family have helped me make my name and fortune. I owe you much."

The inn Randolph Wilson sent her to, The Silent Scot, was clean and comfortable. Savannah paid for a week's lodging with her first real British sterling.

Amazing! Parliament had outlawed any specie — silver or gold, sterling or sovereigns — from the Americas, insisting the colonials use bank or merchant notes as legal tender, thus keeping the real money base in England and allowing for rampant inflation in the colonies. Then they went ahead and taxed the stupid bank notes! The logic was beautiful. All power in the hands of the true British gentry. All supplication in the lives of colonials.

Savannah patted the pocket in her underskirt in which she'd hidden her dagger. No supplication from her, ever again. She stretched, sat in the curved-backed rocking chair before the fire, and consumed the simple meal she'd ordered: bread and cheese — a good, sharp green-veined Stilton — hot milk laced with rum, and a fresh apple pasty. Her eyelids grew heavy as she stared into the dancing flames and tried to remember why she was here, why it was so important to exact vengeance, why justice was out of her reach. But her head ached and her body lulled;

and soon she slept, warmed by the fire.

There was another fire in her dream, and David laughing as he moved into a tent. Her David. Her David . . .

She fought to waken, struggling against something that bit into her mouth and made her choke. She gagged and felt a rough hand yank her up and into a hard body.

"Get that hood on and bind her hands well, or it will be your head in the noose!"

She strained to hear. . . . David? . . . David! No! What was happening? What was he doing?

"Wrist irons, Miss Stewart," he growled. "Wrist irons for a traitor who cost us Montgomerys a rich cargo. Wrist irons, now." His hands roamed freely over her body, kneading her breasts painfully. "Later, a romp in a marquess's bed, then a rope for your pretty neck."

She kicked out, but he laughed.

"Bind her legs and watch your bullocks. She has grit and spirit for a thousand women."

Ah, God, David! She had almost decided to give it up as foolish . . . a stupid mission for an even more stupid reason. She had always known he was who he was; but she had not known he was far more, far worse. What they had shared had meant nothing. He had taken her with guile and glee; and now he would debase her as ruthlessly as his grandfather had once debased other Stewart women and the men who loved them. The pocket in her underskirts was still heavy, still a safe repository for her only weapon. And now . . . more than before . . . she had the true will to use it.

Chapter Twenty-two

The coach ride was agony. She had been thrown into the vehicle and allowed to stay crumbled on the floor, without a cloak to cover her, with her body absorbing every jolt, every wild turn. Her head had banged against the wooden sides of the seats. Her neck had snapped. And the bile that rose in her throat had to be swallowed or she might have chocked to death on it.

When the coach finally stopped, she was dragged out, slung over someone's shoulder, and finally thrown into a room. Only then was her hood removed and her gag untied. She looked up into dark blue eyes and spit at David's grinning, ferocious face.

He wiped the spittle off, grabbed her hair, and yanked her face up to his. "Scream, Miss Stewart. Scream with all your might. No one will help you. Your only hope in staying alive is to submit to my will . . . to do what I bid, when I bid it. You are the most comely of lasses. You warm my blood. You tease my desires." Once again he kneaded her breast, pulled it out of her bodice, and lowered his head to nip at her peak. "And you taste of warm peaches." He shoved her back, and her legs buckled because they were still tied. "Contemplate your fate, Savannah. The noose or my bed. Those are your only choices."

He turned on his heel and strode from the room, leaving behind two burly redheaded men whose eyes nearly popped at the sight of her. One blushed and lowered his head.

"Sorry, lass. The master orders us to attend ye." He untied the ropes round her legs and unlocked the wrist irons. "Chafe them good, to get the blood back into them." They both turned to go, but he turned back, his eyes on the floor. "A warning. You are in Kent, far from another soul, and there are guards at every landing and every door. He has given orders for us to kill you if you try to escape."

She nodded, numbed by the hatred that she had felt emanating from David, aching for the kindness she thought he'd had.

A key turning in the lock told her how alone she was. Cold sunlight streamed into a large room with a four-poster bed, several tables, two fireplaces, both roaring, yet unable to chase the chill from her bones, two chests of drawers, a three-sided standing mirror in the corner, a thunder jug, two pitchers and ewers, and four comfortably upholstered chairs.

Her reflection in the mirror showed a disheveled ghost of a woman long left behind. She picked at her hair, eased her bodice back over her swollen, hurt breast, and let the tears fall unchecked.

She slept. Food was brought in but she didn't eat it. She slept some more. She breathed. She still lived.

And the dagger still weighted her underskirt pocket.

The next time David came to her room, she tried to get to the dagger; but the guards were swift. Her hands were once more wrist-ironed and she was led from the room, down a long corridor, and into a large chamber. David shoved her forward and pushed her down into a hard wooden seat. Facing her was a long carved oaken table behind which were three similar high-backed chairs. Liveried men stood sentry on the perimeter of the room, all armed with pike, cutlass, or rifle.

A door behind the chairs opened and David hissed, "Rise for the magistrates!"

She stumbled to her feet, astonished to see three bewigged and robed gentlemen enter and seat themselves on the tall-backed chairs. One of the men, she noted, had eyes of midnight-blue, and they pierced into and through her with such cold hatred she knew immediately who he was.

"The Marquess of Lorton."

David leaned down and whispered in her ear, "Clever, Savannah. But then, you are known for your brains and wit. And for other more personal attributes. When the sentence you deserve is pronounced, remember the choice I've graciously given you, Savannah. My bed or the gallows."

"The rope sounds more inviting than your bed, my lord."

"After a week watching your gallows being built outside your dungeon window, I think you will change your mind."

"Never."

"We'll see."

Within moments, Savannah discovered she sat before a tribunal for the district of Kent, a tribunal that had been called to decide the fate of a traitor to the Crown. The only thing that astonished her was the introduction into evidence of numerous American newspapers, a copy of one of her codes, and a letter signed by Samuel Adams, which implicated her. When she was asked by Richard Montgomery, the sixth Marquess of Lorton, if she had anything to say for herself, she shook her head. What could she say? She was what they accused. She had known the consequences when she had agreed to help Patrick and Ben. Though they couldn't have foreseen this, they had not sugarcoated the difficulties she would have if she were caught. They had, of course, promised to try to rescue her. But they were a long way from Kent, and her fate was sealed.

Her sentence: death by hanging, three weeks hence.

The Marquess of Lorton stood imperially before her and commanded, "Contemplate your destiny, wench. And make your peace with God. It is all you have left of this world."

They did not take her back to her room. Instead, she was led down to the bowels of Lorton Manor and thrust into a barred cell that smelled of rodent droppings. A bare cot in the corner was her only comfort, a thunder jug, her only ornament. Three men stood sentry outside the cell. They could see everything she did.

She cried brokenly. David . . . the man she loved . . . would take her life. But that was not enough. He also had to rob her of her dignity.

Savannah lay on the cot, not knowing night from day, and tried to block out the images of David that intruded. The way he'd looked when he rescued Samuel. The way the moonlight had kissed him with silver that night in Georgia. The way he'd held her, so tenderly, so reverently, the night in George Wythe's garden maze. The unexpected "betrothal." The flash of fire that had burned in his gaze the first night he had made love to her. The rough pronouncement of love he'd cried into the night. The way his voice had broken when he'd said "Marry me."

How could it all have been an illusion, a mask that hid a demon? How had she, an artist who could see below the surface to the very heart of her subjects, have missed the horror that lay beneath David's outward appearance? How had she been so wrong about him?

How could love still burn in her heart for the David she had known . . . a David that didn't exist?

She curled up in a ball and hugged the ache to herself until she came to a decision. The dagger was still there. Though the carpenters banged together the gallows that the marquess planned to be her last mortal resting place, they could bang all they wanted. She was an American, a Rebel. She would not be subject to anyone, ever. If death were to come, it would come from her own hands, at a time she chose. And God would be her only judge.

It amazed her how sleep became a friend and foe at once. Amazed her that she could withstand scrutiny in her base and natural acts. Amazed her that she could put food in her mouth, chew and swallow it. Amazed her that she could chat with the portly maidservant, Miriam Hopgood, about the weather, Miriam's children, the goings and comings of Lorton Manor.

Miriam brought her water and towels, but no soap. "The master won't allow it. Unless . . ." Miriam avoided Savannah's eyes. " 'E says yer'll get soap when yer choose to follow me to 'is bedchamber. . . ."

"I'd sooner bed with the King."

"Oooh, don' let 'im 'ear that. 'E'd like as not sell yer to 'is Majesty."

One morning Miriam hustled down the corridor and announced in an awed voice, "Yer've got a visitor. An' 'is lordship says she ken see yer if yer agree."

"Who is it?"

"A colonial. A Mistress Drummond."

Abigail? Here? "Yes, I'll see her." Savannah plucked at her matted hair. "Oh, Miriam, you don't have a brush or comb, do you?"

"Yer wan' me ta be horsewhipped? 'E won' let yer 'ave 'em."

So it was that Savannah greeted Abigail looking like a half-dead rat the cat dragged in. Savannah shuddered at the thought; it was too close to the mark.

Abigail wore a red and blue striped satin gown, with a sable-lined cloak to keep out the cold Savannah had grown used to. Jewels flashed at Abigail's ears and throat, and she clutched the necklace every few minutes as if to make sure it was still there.

One of the guards brought in a gilded red upholstered chair for Abigail to sit in and a small Turkey carpet for her to put her feet on. Savannah had some satisfaction in knowing that the stones wept water, and it would soon saturate Abigail's prayer rug and the voluminous skirts she settled around her legs.

With a quick leap of intelligence, Savannah knew why the woman had come . . . and who had been the instrument of her capture. "You betrayed me to the magistrates?"

"No. Not the magistrates, Savannah. To the Marquess."

"Why?"

"One thousand pounds sterling, to start. And Drew Montgomery's promise to sponsor me at Court so I can attain the position I always knew was my destiny."

"Drew Montgomery? Ah, yes. David's younger brother. I haven't met him yet."

"Haven't met him?" Abigail's mouth dropped and her eyes widened. "Oh, no! You think the man who put you here is *David* Montgomery?" She laughed until tears bubbled over her lids. *"David?* The man you totally flummoxed? The man you were *betrothed* to? Hell, no! Drew put you here. Drew, David's younger *twin* brother! He's always hated David, of course. It's all the gossip at parties. He wants to be the heir but can't because he was born twenty-three minutes after David. But he gets what he wants because he's the image of his grandfather. . . ."

Savannah let Abigail chatter on as a roaring rage ripped through her. Drew Montgomery. Not David. *Oh, dear God, thank You. Thank You for letting me know before death claimed me.* She could withstand anything now. Her love for David and his for her could remain untarnished, untouched by the horror of what she was going through.

If David knew, she was sure he'd come to rescue her. But he did not know. He only had her note telling him she was going to Connecticut, leaving him in peace to carry out his position as a hereditary marquess. She had said her good-byes in that letter. She had asked him not to try to find her. David would honor her wishes. He was a loving, honorable man.

"Well," Abigail said gaily, "I must go now. Tonight, Drew is taking me to an entertainment at the house of his friend, Peregrine Martin, a rake and rogue, but a favorite at Court. It will be my introduction to the upper classes. Do you think this gown suits? No, I'd best get another with part of the reward money."

Savannah nodded. "I wish you well, Abigail."

"Do you? I couldn't care less."

Abigail swished her way down the corridor and round the corner. Miriam, who had been patiently standing outside the cell waiting for Abigail to leave, swept in in an exaggerated imitation of Abigail's hip-swinging motion. She set a tray of cheese and dark bread on the cot and thrust Savannah's last of two tankards of cider at her.

"So, the colonial wench thinks she's bein' interduced to the upper clahsses, does she?" Miriam cackled. "Upper bedchambers, more like it. We've all 'eard o' those intertaynments at Falcon's Nest. The women are fav'rits, awright. Fav'rits o' all the men invited fa the night. Yer friend will find 'erself passed from 'and to 'and an' bed to bed. She'll be used verr well by the best o' gentlemen, as long as she amuses. An' if she objects, she'll be roughly used, then tossed out without a care."

"Poor Abigail. She wanted nothing more than to belong."

"She'll belong, awright. To all o' 'em!"

Miriam's laughter was joined by that of the three guards. Savannah stared after her, unsettled for the first time in days. If what Abigail had said was true — and Savannah didn't doubt it for a minute — then she had a worse problem than the damn carpenters outside the cell.

Drew Montgomery.

Thus far he had done naught but threaten her. But the day for her hanging was getting close. She had no doubts he would make his move soon. If he made it here, the guards would stop any attack she might make. But . . . if she allowed him to take her up to his bedchamber, however, then she might be able to get to her dagger, press it against his throat, and use him as her shield as she made her escape.

325

That night, she sat on her cot, her chin on her drawn-up knees, and planned carefully.

David paced the deck of Robert Sears's pirate ship, watching the wind fill the sails, watching the horizon in case he caught a glimpse of land.

"Unless you can blow up a gale, you won't get us there any quicker, my lord," Robert said.

"Just so we get there in time, Robert. That's all that matters."

No, there was more that mattered; but he'd settle that once he had Savannah back in his arms where she belonged.

When he'd come back to New York and Lawrence had shown him the letter Savannah had left, David had nearly torn the countryside up riding posthaste to Connecticut. He'd had a devil of a time finding Mary Noyes Silliman. But when she discovered who he was and that he wanted to protect Savannah, she'd willingly told him about the British encampment. But he had missed her there, although he'd stumbled on the troops farther along on the trail.

He'd been welcomed as a friend, which had astounded him until he realized they thought he was supposed to be on a ship to London. So, his grandfather had sent an agent to America, had he? Drew, the agent. Drew, the provocateur. Drew, his dear brother, who wreaked havoc wherever he went.

A quick trip to the docks and a few pounds changing hands brought him the information he needed. Captain Warren Standish had found a stowaway on his ship . . . a woman.

Savannah? Had she seen Drew at the British camp and thought him David? Had she followed Drew aboard Standish's ship?

It fit. It fit too damned good.

David had no choice. He had to get to England as fast as he could. No ships were leaving that day, so he sought out James Otis, explained his predicament, and the good man had spirited him away to a rendezvous with Robert Sears, who had readily agreed to take David to England on his pirate ship.

Ironic!

Robert turned out to be what Savannah and Lawrence had said he was: an exceptional captain and a good man. He refused payment from David, asking only that the Viscount of Dwight pay him with a good game of chess each night.

"We're approaching the Orkneys, David," Robert said. "My pirate friends will meet us there, and you can get a good steed to take you overland to Kent."

"You will wait for us."

"Aye. As we discussed. But I can only wait three weeks. Then I must sail for France to drop off my cargo or forfeit my bond. And in these unsettling days, I cannot afford to lose so much money."

"We'll be there," David vowed.

The pirate settlement made little impression on David. All he knew was that he needed a good horse to get to London to find Savannah. One-eyed Jack

Saunders and two of his crewmen rowed David across to the mainland, then supplied a stout chestnut stallion, which Saunders promised ". . . Is the swiftest thing on four legs!" He helped David into the saddle and plopped a bag of food on the horn. "God speed, yer lordship! I'll ne'er fergit wha' ye did fer Samule. If ye canna make it back in time fer Rob, I'll leave orders fer enny other man to treat ye well."

It took a hard driving eight days for David to reach London. He called in on Randolph Wilson and was told that Savannah had not kept an appointment.

"She's been missing two weeks, my lord. I fear for her safety but can get nothing out of the landlords at the inn."

David did. His next stop was Kentlands, where he expected to see his brother. But he was met by strange servants who had their orders to give him food and a place to rest, but nothing more.

"This is my home, not my brother's!"

"But, my lord, we will feel the lash if we disobey him."

"You will feel the gaoler's whip if you do not!"

"He's at Lorton Manor, sir. There's to be a hanging."

David didn't bother to wash or change clothes. He stumbled to the carriageway to get a horse from the stables, when a coach pulled up and Abigail Drummond got out. She stopped to assess him and her lip curled up in distaste.

"The real David Montgomery, I suppose?"

"Miss Drummond."

"You're too late, you know."

"Not if God is on my side."

Abigail laughed and swished her skirts. "Sometimes, in this world, the devil has his way without interference from a higher power. Your Savannah is a particular treat for Drew. He has promised to usurp you. And he is a consummate lover, you know. Rough and demanding and very satisfying. I just came from seeing her. She's pathetic. Dirty. Smelly. Grey, with matted hair that droops lifeless. Her only companions are rats and vermin. So . . . there is nothing the little twit can do. Drew decided last night to take her today before she swings. Then he's going to take me to Falcon's Nest, introduce me to his friends, and . . . one day I intend to be your sister-in-law."

"You idiot! Drew has no intention of making you his wife. Grandfather would never permit it."

"Nor would your grandfather permit you to marry Savannah. But you did intend to do that, didn't you?"

"That's different because I'm different. I am the heir. Grandfather would do everything to protect the succession."

"Oh, yes. Just like he protected the succession by locking your father in a wing of the house and pretending that he was dead. What makes you think he won't do the same to you?"

"You need a lesson on the realities of life in England, Miss Drummond. God help me, I'm just beginning to realize what it means, myself." He took

329

her elbow and shoved her back into the coach. "Driver . . . to Burnham Castle!"

"Burnham Castle? Isn't that where the Duke of Morleigh resides? Are you to present me to one of the highest noblemen in England?"

"Oh, yes, Miss Drummond. The highest of the high. And a good friend of Drew's. Now, shut up and sit still."

Though he didn't want to take this side trip because it would take more time than he had to spare, David had a feeling this woman was partially responsible for Savannah's quandary. And she thought Drew would reward her for it? David would show her the kind of reward she could expect. He owed it to Savannah.

Burnham Castle loomed dark and gloomy on the road to Kent. The coach pulled up to the entrance and David tossed a sovereign at the driver, who bit it and tipped his hat. The door of the castle opened after David gave a series of loud raps with the heavy iron knocker shaped like a wolf.

"My lord," the butler said. "Lord Walter is in the library."

Dust sprang up in motes as David led Abigail down several twisting corridors to the door of the library. He pushed her inside and squinted through the gloom until he caught sight of the stout, tobacco-stained figure lounging on a ripped and faded settee in a corner, a tankard in his hand and several bottles on the floor.

The figure raised his head. "Drew, old friend!"

"David."

"Ah, the heir." Walter Attenborough rose with difficulty and stumbled to stand beside David. He tried to focus on the figures in front of him, but failing to do that, he giggled and waved them to seats by the fire.

"How long has it been since that suit has seen a washtub, Walter?"

"Ah, David . . . don't preach. I do what I like . . . and likes what I do!" He gave Abigail a long assessment. "Well, who's your lady friend?"

"Not a friend of mine, Walter. Drew's latest interest."

"The doxy from America? The one who brought him the evidence against the creature they call The Shadow?"

David's teeth ground together at the confirmation of his supposition. "Aye. The same."

"Here!" Abigail sniffed, got her first good scent of Walter, gagged, and put a hand in front of her mouth. "I'm no doxy, sir!"

David squeezed her wrist until she gasped. "No?" Though it made his stomach roil, he threw an arm around Walter's shoulder. "How much will you pay for her, Walter?"

"Pay for her? Are you mad? I'll have her for naught this evening at Falcon's Nest."

Abigail looked wildly from David to the duke. "What are you saying?"

David pushed her forward. "Explain it to her, Walter. I don't have time." He headed out the door, calling over his shoulder, "I'll be borrowing one of your horses."

"Take what you want. I'll get it back."

Walter picked up a curl that had broken loose from Abigail's wig. "Naughty Drew. He should have told you what would be expected of you tonight." Spittle ran from the corners of his lips and he brushed it away. "We have these nights once a month. There are twelve of us. All noblemen. All very rich. This is Drew's month. He supplies the treat. You, my dear, are tonight's treat." He ran a dirty long fingernail across Abigail's cheek, down her throat, and over the swell of her breasts. "And now I see you, I'll have to bid very high to have you first."

Abigail stood frozen. An icy calm controlled her revulsion. The devil would, indeed, have his day. And Drew Montgomery would pay dearly for deceiving her the way he had.

Abigail smiled at the pockmarked drunkard in front of her. "I look forward to it, my lord." She slipped her arm through Walter's. "Now, if you will be so kind, I would love to see your castle. Especially your gun room. You do have a gun room, don't you?"

"But of course. All gentlemen have a gun room."

Five minutes later, a loud retort echoed through the cavernous shell of Burnham Castle. The servants gave it no mind, ascribing it to the batty master who was always firing his pistols into the walls. And they gave less heed to the young lady who had come in with the Viscount of Dwight as she stumbled out the front door of the castle and around to the stables.

Chapter Twenty-three

Abigail's visit left Savannah surprisingly calm. Her plans were made. She could wait for Drew to initiate their encounter, or she could precipitate the confrontation herself.

When Miriam came in with her midday meal, she stood up and announced, "I'd like to be taken to Drew Montgomery, please."

"Ah, deary . . . do yer know wha' yer doin'?"

"Yes, Miriam."

"Well, I 'ave me orders. Iffen yer were ta ask, I'm ta take yer to the room yer was first in."

Savannah squared her shoulders and held her head high. "Then let's go."

"Yer a brave lass."

The guards saluted Savannah, and at a nod from Miriam, they went before and behind the women until they came to the cheery room Savannah remembered.

"There's a connectin' tub room . . . 'ere . . . fer yer bath, dear. I'll 'ave 'ot water brung up. An' there be dresses in the wardrobe. Though, it be bes' iffen yer don' bother. 'E ken get rough, dear. Bes' greet 'im the way 'e expects."

Savannah found several nightshifts in the drawer of one of the chests. All were sheer as cheesecloth. Embroidered and laced, but for what purpose? Even if she wore one, every hill and valley would be revealed.

Quickly, she stripped the filthy clothes from her body and put on a large woolen nightrobe she found in another drawer. She needed a good dousing with a concoction of ground tansy leaves, to kill the vermin in her hair and on her body. There was a medicine chest on one of the tables, and she found dozens of bottles of herbs and tinctures. Ground tansy! Wonderful.

When the large iron tub was half filled with water, Savannah ordered more be brought up and left outside the tub room door. She poured every bit of the ground tansy into the water and stepped in. How good it felt! The tansy bit into her skin, but she didn't care. The varmints floated in the water within minutes. And her hair came clean with liberal applications of strong lye soap. A fine-toothed comb finished the job. When she stepped out, she left her unwelcome companions behind.

"Jes' pull that there 'andle in the wall," Miriam said from behind her.

Savannah did and the water drained from the tub.

"Goin' to a cistern an' then out ta the river. All the bes' in this 'ouse." She scrubbed the iron tub with a stiff brush and more lye soap, then rinsed it with two buckets of water, which also drained down and out. Then Miriam reached under the tub and something clicked into place. "Plug," she said at Savannah's quizzical expression. "I'll bring in the res' o' the water."

Savannah felt no shame in front of Miriam, and no shame when the good woman poured a lavish amount of lilac-scented oil into the hot water. They both knew what Savannah was doing and were resigned, each in her own way. When Savannah once again eased herself into the tub, Miriam handed her a long-handled scrub brush with soft bristles and two large bars of French lilac soap.

"Thank you, Miriam."

"God be with yer, deary."

When she left the tub room, she had her apron to her eyes and Savannah heard the unmistakable beginning of sobs.

She could not let Miriam's sorrow and pity eat into her. She had to do something. . . .

She remembered a chorus of her favorite hymn. *Keep to the right,* it said, *and God will go before ye.*

In a clear, high pitch, which shook her because of its intensity, she raised her voice in song . . . and supplication, knowing only He could hear.

"Keep to the right, keep to the right and naught can Satan harm ye. Keep to the right. Close to the light. God's pure love will warm ye. Keep to the right. All through the night. God's sure strength love will bi . . ide ye!"

What was that? Was someone banging on the opposite door? She listened closely, but the noise came naught. Probably just her imagination.

Lathering the scrub brush, Savannah gave particular attention to her back, which had been aching for days from the hard straw mattress she'd endured. Over and over, as she washed her body and thick hair, she hummed and sang snatches of the hymn. It strengthened her, leaving a warm glow inside her body that matched the one on her skin from the scrub brush and the powerful French scent.

When she got out of the tub, she pulled the rope handle and let the water drain, then wrapped herself in a large towel and put another on her hair, twisting it until most of the water was gone. Taking another piece of toweling, she walked into the bedroom and shook out one of the abominable nightshifts, placing it carefully on the bed, ready to put on when she was completely dry.

Now, where to secrete the dagger?

She found that by working at the seam of the mattress she could open a good hole, big enough to slip the thin, deadly weapon inside. Nodding in satisfaction, she turned to retrieve it from her underskirt.

Oh, no! She whirled, thinking she might have thrown her soiled clothing on one of the chairs. No! Miriam . . . her good, kind friend . . . her protector . . . and a well-trained servant . . . Miriam must have picked up Savannah's offensive clothing and taken it to be burned.

She had no weapon to defend herself.

She sank in a heap on the floor. "No," she whispered. "No." She pushed her fingers through her hair, as the full realization of her predicament smashed through the play she had written in her mind. "No. Please, no! Please. No. No. Noooo!"

Drew smiled with delight as he opened the door and found his brother's lover half naked, raking her fingers through her hair and screaming in terror. "Oh, I like that. Make that sound when I take you, wench. It heats my blood."

Savannah jumped to her feet and the towel fell to the floor.

"Beelzebub! My brother has been enjoying a feast fit for the gods!"

She backed up and grabbed at anything at hand, throwing it at Drew. "Stay away from me! I'd rather hang!"

"Oh, you will, wench. I'll have the particular pleasure of springing the trap door myself. But first . . . I will sample the delights which kept my brother's bullocks puckered."

She threw the medicine chest at him and bottles broke, leaving shards of glass between him and her. Booted, he stepped over them easily. She heaved a chair at him and he ducked. Another chair went toward the window. The glass shattered but she saw the windows were barred. She could not jump. No one would save her.

"Dear God! Help me!"

Drew threw back his head, laughing as if he had conquered the world, and his hands went to the ties on his breeches. He had his breeches open, ready to pull down, when something stilled him. His voice trailed off. Another began. Higher and higher and higher the pitch went, and Drew stumbled to a halt and stared at the door to the tub room.

Savannah cowered behind the bed as wood splintered and a strangled cry filled the room, echoing out the door and through the cavernous manor. Something crashed. Footsteps, like a huge beast's, pounded on the floor, shaking the timbers with its fury.

She heard Drew's voice calling frantically in the distance, "Grandfather! Grandfather!"

She peeked over the bed to devise a possibility of escape and gasped in terror at the thing in her room.

A beast. A man?

Matted hair down to his waist. Beard white as snow. Eyes that pierced the room until they caught and held her own. Blue eyes. Midnight-blue eyes. Without knowing why she did it, she stood up as the creature walked toward her.

The first person to greet David as he burst into the manor was Miriam, who put out her hands and shouted, "Glory be! Yer've come ta save 'er!"

"Where is she?"

"West wing. Fourth door on the right."

"West wing?"

"Aye. Yer brother 'as a mean, mad streak in 'im."

"Guards?"

"In ta kitchen, belowstairs. I'll tell 'em yer 'ere. They won' bother yer."

"I may need their help."

She shook her head. Kindly but firmly, she pointed out, "Yer grandfather is master 'ere. They will do as 'e bids, first."

David rushed to the study, broke open a brace of pistols, and armed three of them. He grabbed up a cutlass from those on the wall and made for the stairs.

"David!" An old gentleman in full blue wool frock coat and tan suede breeches, with long black leather boots on his feet and a huge gold watch fob hanging from his embroidered waistcoat, stood at the top of the stairs glaring down at his grandson. "Where do you think you're going?"

"To get Savannah. And don't try to stop me."

"A traitor to the King? You would throw away your heritage for a woman who is at this minute selling herself to your brother to keep from going to the gallows?"

David began walking up the stairs, his heart aching with the knowledge that to protect Savannah, he might have to hurt his grandfather. "What gallows, sire? The King's? Or Drew's?"

"Ah, what difference does it make? Had a true trial been held, the verdict would have been the same."

"Let me pass, Grandfather. I love her. And I *will* take her out of here."

"You would force me to denounce you and send the militia for you? For a *Stewart* trollop, the granddaughter of the man who polished my boots?"

"For my *wife,* sire, if she'll have me after this!"

The old man stepped aside. "Go on. Take her from Drew, if you can. She won't be fit for much when he's finished with her, anyway."

"My God, Grandfather, how can you stand yourself? You besmirch the good name of our ancestors. You and Drew. Gods on Mount Olympus. Is that how you see yourself?"

"It's how we are, David. And you have to have the stomach for it if you wear the title. You never did, did you?"

"No, thank God."

As David searched the old man's eyes—eyes that matched his own in color but not in integrity—he was heartbroken to see no remorse, no waver of spirit . . . just pure self-righteousness. The man was a marquess. The title was power. And power was right, no matter how wrong or how inhuman it had become.

"I'm sorry, Grandfather."

"You should be."

"No, sire. You misunderstand. I'm sorry for you."

The old man cackled. "You'll envy me when you and the trollop are freezing to death in the highlands, without food or shelter. And you'll beg my pardon when you swing on the end of the rope as a traitor."

"The King's men will have to catch me first."

"They will."

David acknowledged the old man might be right. But he'd give it a good try. He was halfway down the hall to the west wing when he heard the first rumbling shout. It lifted in a crescendo that had his grandfather racing toward him. Drew's cries caught up where the other left off, and both David and Richard Montgomery knew what it meant.

"Grandfather!" Drew burst into the hall. "Grandfather! He's loose!"

"Where are the guards?"

"I sent them belowstairs."

David grabbed hold of his brother's shirt and

slammed him against the cold stone wall. "Where's Savannah?"

Drew struggled to keep his feet on the floor. He pointed in the direction from which he'd fled, as if all the demons of hell were chasing him. "With him!"

David dropped him and sped down the hall. His heart kept time with his pounding footsteps. "Don't kill her, Father. Please, don't kill her."

Drew stood trembling and quaking in front of his grandfather. "Aren't you going to do anything?"

"With any luck, your brother and father will kill each other, and we'll get out of this with our heads and reputations intact."

"What reputations? We haven't had any in years!" He pushed aside his grandfather and stumbled down the stairs. "I need a drink." The door knocker sounded and he grumbled, "Not now! Miriam! Open the damned door!"

He and his grandfather entered the library, ignoring the sounds of David's footfalls echoing in the distance and the great silence that fell. Drew picked up a jug of rum and shook it. "Can't anybody in this house keep the damned thing full? Miriam! More rum! And whiskey, too! Scotch whiskey!"

"Aye," Miriam said from the door. "Yer lady friend be back. Shall I send 'er in?"

Drew threw himself onto a lounging chair and hung his leg over the arm. "Send in the devil, for all I care. Just rustle up the spirits." Though his eyes took in the disheveled appearance of Abigail, his attention was directed to the west wing and the things he and his grandfather hadn't yet heard. "What are you doing here, looking as if you've been blown in by the wind? Didn't I tell you I'd fetch you from Kentlands?"

"Aye. And you told me you were taking me to a social entertainment at Falcon's Nest, too. But you neglected to tell me it was to debauch me."

"Debauch you? How could *I* debauch you? There have been scores of others who have beaten me to it. You should be grateful my friends would even be interested."

"Oh, I'm grateful. Grateful for your brother, who told me what you intended." She pulled out the loaded pistol she'd used to kill Walter and pointed it at Drew.

He sat up. "What? Are you crazy?"

"Nay, my lord. I'm saner now than I've been in my life."

She shot him, coldly and cleanly. He looked down at the gaping hole in his chest, put his hand up to it, and slumped to the floor.

"Trollop! You will hang!"

Turning, she took in the elderly man who spit fury at her. "Mayhap. But I will have the satisfaction of taking all the Montgomery vermin with me. Are you responsible for *that?*" She nodded toward Drew.

The old man stood tall and cold. "He's my grandson."

"He's dead. And so are you."

Far in the bowels of the manor, Miriam and the guard heard the two shots and came running. Miriam was first in the library door. She found the colonial woman sipping calmly the last of the rum. When she caught sight of Miriam, she held out her glass, saying, "Fill it, please. I wish to toast the dead."

The scene that awaited David was one he could not in a million years have expected: a very dirty middle-aged bestial man, covering Savannah with a wool cape, then cradling her in his arms and rocking her back and forth.

"Father?"

The man looked up and smiled. "David."

"Father . . . will you let Savannah go and come over here?"

"It's all right, David. He won't hurt me."

"Savannah . . . you don't know . . ."

"I know that under this filth and hair is the man who loves you and who would never hurt you nor I." She put her arms around Carlton Montgomery and laid her head on his shoulder. "Your grandfather locked his son away, David . . . told you he was insane when he knew he wasn't . . . treated him like an animal . . . wouldn't let him see you or Drew . . . when all he had to do to make your father whole was take away his son's liquor."

"But father hated me," Carlton said, his voice cracking from disuse. "I was weak. No true Montgomery, he said. No true heir to his kingdom. I've been all right for years. Ask Miriam. But you don't believe me, David, do you?"

"After this day, I'd believe anything." He shoved his pistols into his belt and crossed to the bed. "Let's get Savannah dressed, then we can figure out what to do with you. Grandfather is going to kick at the traces . . ."

"I'll go with you," Carlton offered. His head reared back. "What was that?"

"I didn't hear anything," Savannah said.

"My ears have become tuned to the slightest sound. That was a gunshot." He stiffened. "And another." He shuddered. "We'd best get belowstairs to find out what's happened."

"Father . . . mayhap you should wait here."

"I've waited almost twenty years, David. I'll not wait another minute." He picked Savannah off the bed and carried her over the broken glass. "I think she belongs to you," he said solemnly. He put her into David's outstretched arms. "Treat her well, son. She's as beautiful and brave as your mother was. And she loves you very much."

"I love her, too."

"Do you, now. Good." Carlton Montgomery checked himself in the mirror and snorted. "Think the guards will run in terror or shoot the beast?"

"If one of them goes for his gun, I'll cut him down."

"Ah, son. I want no killing. Killing tears the soul out of you. I know. I almost killed a very good man."

David followed the figure of his father through the winding corridors. As he went, he tucked Savannah's head against his shoulder and kissed her sweet-smelling hair. "What happened back there?"

"He heard me singing a hymn . . . one he said your mother used to sing. And then I screamed and

Drew laughed. And he knew what was going to happen, he said, because Drew has been bringing his women up there for years, to taunt him, he said. So he broke down the door to the tub room and scared Drew out of his wits. Scared me, too, for a minute. But as soon as I saw his eyes, I knew who he was. And his eyes were clear . . . not the eyes of a madman, as Bella had told me. But the eyes of someone who has been deeply wounded, has hurt someone, been hurt himself, healed, and is repentent. I was naked, and he and I thought naught about it. He talked to me. I listened. Then he found a cape and covered me. And that's when you walked in." She jerked her head up. "Late, you know! You should have been here three weeks ago, to rescue me from the dungeon."

"Drew had you down there?"

"Yes." She snuggled against him. "But you came for me. I prayed and you came." She put her arms around his neck and hugged him hard. "God, I love you, David."

"And I love you, sweetheart." He stopped and kissed her gently. "Drew has much to answer for."

But Drew and his grandfather could answer no more. And that was when Carlton Montgomery came into his own.

When he heard the provocation, he commiserated with Abigail. "But you cannot take a life and expect to get away with it, Miss Drummond. I wish I didn't have to do so, but I must have you bound over for the magistrates. You will be arrested and tried. I will give evidence. Perhaps we can mitigate the sentence, have you transported. . . ." He shook his head. "I don't know. Times have changed . . . but I will try." He turned to the woman who had served him all the years he'd been locked away. "Miriam, have a room prepared for Miss Drummond. Post guards. And send a footman for the magistrates."

"Aye, me lord." She shooed Abigail to her feet. "Up, goirl! Ye'll be treated well, 'ave no fear." She gave her into the charge of the guards and turned back to say, "All o' ye . . . get out o' this damned libry. Let Miriam 'andle it from 'ere."

While they waited for the magistrates to come and take over, Carlton Montgomery excused himself to go upstairs ". . . to make myself more presentable."

"You realize you are now the marquess," David pointed out.

"A weight removed from your shoulders, son?"

"Aye. A very great weight."

"Then you know how I feel."

David escorted Savannah into the drawing room and closed the door. He pulled her into his arms and held her, simply held her. "I thought I'd never see you alive again."

She sighed against him. "I thought I'd seen you betray me."

"Never."

"There is still a price on my head."

"I know. The Shadow, right?"

"Yes." She looked up at him. His expression was

unreadable. It frightened her. "Are you disappointed? You have no obligation to me, you know."

"I have every obligation. You are going to be my wife, the mother of my children. Future heirs to a fortune, unless you say naught. And if you say it, we will simply disappear. Your friend Robert Sears is waiting in the Orkneys for us as we speak."

"You've arranged for me to get out of the country? With *Robert?*" She started to giggle. "Oh, no! After all the chastising you gave me that day when I took Bella to his wedding, you sought out *Robert!*"

"Go ahead, laugh. I deserve it. I was a conceited, pompous ass. But you showed me the error of my ways, wench. I promise never to lord it over you or our children or our friends. Just you promise to marry me and keep me in line."

"Oh, I'll marry you, my lord. You deserve that much punishment. But David, if we go back to America, I cannot promise to mend my ways. I have to help my people."

"I know. All the way over the Atlantic I thought about what we'd have to do. . . ."

"We?"

"Do you expect me to allow you to put your neck on the line and not put mine there, too? Nay, love. If you go back to spying, then I will have to be part of it."

"You'll risk your inheritance."

"Not now. Not with my father as marquess. Besides, if there is war—and it looks as if there is no other course—the Rebels will need supplies. Who better to turn to than a respected member of the Tory community who can bring his goods through any blockade the British set up because he'd never be under suspicion."

"Can you act the part, David?"

"With your guidance, love, I can do anything."

The inhabitants of Kent—and all of England—were rocked by the reappearance of rejuvenated, handsome Carlton Montgomery and the deaths of his grandfather and youngest son. But the hereditary rules held, and Carlton was awarded the title and all that went with it.

Since no one in the village or in London knew that Savannah had been spirited to the manor house, Carlton requested his servants to keep the secret. They agreed with alacrity, especially since they had all been present at the hasty marriage of Savannah and David. Miriam served as attendant and gave the bride a wedding gift: every one of the outlandish gauzy nightshifts.

"They be put to better use wi' the right master," she said. "An' they be no taint to 'em, Savanny. I made 'em with me own 'ands atter ye were brought to the manor. No other women 'as e'er worn 'em. They be yours. Make yer 'usband 'appy. Wear one on yer first night at sea."

"I will, Miriam. I can see how they would be . . . uh . . . tantalizing in the right circumstances, with the right man. And David is the right man. Thank you."

Carlton clasped his son's shoulder. "Tell Fenton he has my respect and a position with Lorton Traders as long as he wants it." He kissed his daughter-in-law's cheek. "Take care, Savannah. And name my first grandchild after me."

"What if it's a girl?"

"Then Jean, please. For the most beautiful woman I've ever known. You would have liked David's mother, Savannah. You were very much alike."

"That's a compliment I'll cherish forever."

Savannah and David made the Orkneys with one day to spare, but Robert was damned glad to see them.

"Wind picking up. Gale may be coming. We best shove off now."

They were well out to sea when Savannah sought out David and found him on deck, looking back at the place where England had long been left behind. She wrapped her arms around him and snuggled against his back.

"Sorry you left?"

"No. Sorry my grandfather and Drew could not know the joys of this world."

"You haven't grieved, David."

"I have in my heart."

"I love you, David."

"I know. And I love you, wench."

"Then come to the cabin and prove it to me."

He did. And she did. And they proved it to each other again and again, every day of their lives.

Author's Afterword

All the historical figures in this novel are true, as is my attempt to portray them as they were, with all the blemishes of real human beings, using their own words when I could find them. Were they alive today, with the glare of media spotlights, their private lives would never withstand the scrutiny and expectations we now have for our political leaders.

Patrick Henry—for me, the ultimate patriotic revolutionary—was a kind and funny man, given to flirting outrageously. His first wife suffered from what would probably be declared today as postpartum depression. She was locked in a cellar room, where she died. He took another wife quickly and, apparently, was faithful to her.

Benjamin Franklin, though a great statesman, was no prude—regardless of the autobiographical diary he left. He had a mistress, an illegitimate son who inherited his estate, and a common-law wife who tolerated—and sometimes encouraged—his many love affairs. His attitude about ugly women, from which

I have paraphrased, was part of a letter he wrote to his nephew who contemplated marriage.

Lady Ann Skipwith has left her mark—if you can call it that—in Williamsburg. According to L.B. Taylor in his book *The Ghosts of Williamsburg*, she really did lose "a red high-heeled slipper with brilliants" after she fled a party at the governor's mansion because she saw her husband and her sister in a compromising situation. She died from complications of childbirth and her husband married her sister, Jean, only a few months later.

The account of the house party at Roger Morris's country estate is contained in the *Smithsonian Guide to Historic America: The Mid-Atlantic States*, and in the *Encyclopedia Britannica*, as is a discussion of the New York Tea Party.

Mary Noyes Silliman left a voluminous amount of written records of her life and time. Hers is a marvelous story of pride and courage, joy and despair, tragedy and triumph. She and her family can be found in the pages of Joy Day Buel and Richard Buel, Jr.'s book *The Way of Duty: A Woman and Her Family in Revolutionary America*.

The description of Savannah—the woman, not the city—is best seen in Anita Raskin's description of Savannah—the city, not the woman—in *Sojourn in Savannah: An Official Guidebook and Map of Historic Savannah and the Surrounding Countryside*.

There was, of course, no Shadow, but many shadows. The New York Tea Party was postponed because someone alerted the patriots that Roger Morris was not what he purported to be and told the militia about the planned imitation of the Boston event. And that same someone also discovered exactly when the British forces were to be pulled back, told the patriots, and they made their attack, thereby embarrassing Roger Morris so much the British never trusted him again.

It wasn't Savannah Stewart. But it might have been.